HAUNTED SUMMER

By: Timothy D. Wise

Printed in the United States of America

Published by:
WISEWIRX MEDIA
A Division of
Professor Theophilus' Emporium of Imagination, Inc.
Magnolia, Arkansas

Cover Design by:
Timothy D. Wise

Library of Congress Control Number:
201491869

First Edition
ISBN 0-978-0-9908690-3-0

Prelude

He was coming for her. How she knew it, she could not say, but she knew. He was coming for her, and she knew that he meant to kill her. Lightning burned into her retinas and thunder pounded the concrete walls. Darkness fell once more. It wouldn't be long now.

The girl squirmed on her mattress. The scarred metal band around her ankle was as tight as ever and the chain that bound her was practically indestructible. She had scraped one of the links against the rough concrete floor for hours, but the hard steel showed no signs of wearing away.

I'm going to die now, she thought. I'm finally going to pay for everything I've done. The thought was almost comforting.

Between claps of thunder, she heard a cry of rage. A pistol shot cut the air and echoed around her. She closed her eyes and tried to pray.

Chapter 1: Arrival

A moonless night had fallen over Oregon like a dark dream. Steam rose from the slick, black skin of the highway as a light rain fell from ebon skies. Headlight beams swept like brush strokes over the pale trunks and needled canopies of the Douglas Firs that swathed the highway in their collective darkness.

Lindsey Holland sat, strapped into the passenger seat of the minivan, while Neal Allen drove. His wife, Jolene and his friend, Tod Wilkes, sat in the back seat. Lindsey smiled with uneasy cheerfulness as Neal extolled the virtues of West Coast life.

"You should move out here," he said. "Just look at all this!"

"It is pretty here," Lindsey said. "But I don't think Pack would ever leave Texas."

"Staying close to Mama, huh?"

"Family is important to him," Lindsey said. That was true in a way. She fingered the ring on her finger.

"So, you're getting married this fall," Jolene Allen said from the back seat. "You must be excited."

"Yeah," Lindsey said. "Excited." She smiled what she hoped was a mysterious smile and looked out the minivan's passenger side window at the dark world beyond.

"She doesn't want to talk about it," Neal, Jolene's husband, said from the driver's seat. "I asked her about it twice at the airport, and all she did was change the subject. This guy must be a total loser."

"Neal!" Jolene gasped. "Don't pay any attention to him."

"Why should she?" Todd Wilkes chimed in from the seat beside Jolene. "Nobody else does."

"Lindsey knows how to take me," Neal said. "Just surprised she's not fighting back yet. It doesn't usually take this much to provoke her."

"I'm sorry I'm not better company," Lindsey said. "It was a long flight."

They rode for a while without speaking.

What's wrong with me tonight? Lindsey wondered. It wasn't just the rain and the darkness. There was something else—some pervasive air of melancholy—that seemed to creep into everything.

Neal turned onto a paved side road, a narrow trail sliced into the side of a mountain. Trees crowded close to the path, their limbs blocking out the rainy sky.

"Are you sure you know where this place is?" Todd asked.

"Do you doubt me?"

"Yes," Todd and Jolene chorused. Neal shook his head and waved them off. He stopped when his headlights fell across a tall iron gate that blocked the way ahead. The hinges of the gate were impaled into pillars of moss-encrusted stone. Neal lowered the van's power window, reached out, and punched a sequence of numbers into a lighted keypad on a panel beside the road. The modern security system seemed out of place. The gate creaked open, and Neal coaxed the minivan into the dark, narrow path that lay beyond. As Neal drove, a tall bluff rose on the right side of the vehicle. It was covered with gnarled roots and clumps of wet, weathered rock. Barely a foot from the left side of the road, the ground tumbled away into a mossy, tree-lined abyss. Lindsey peered down through the tops of trees into the deepening gloom. She never found the bottom.

"This looks like the beginning of a Scooby Doo episode," Todd said from the back seat. "Four people in a van on a long, scary road. All we need is a great dane."

"Scooby Doo's not a great dane," Neal said.

"Sure, he is," Todd said. "Trust me. I'm a film student."

"So, who do you think you are?" Neal asked. "Shaggy?"

"Sure," he said. "I've got the longest hair."

"But Shaggy is funny," Neal said. "I'm the comedian. You're the straight man."

"Freddie is the leader," Todd said. "That's why you're Freddie. Pastor Freddie. I like the sound of that."

"No way," Neal said. "I'd never wear an ascot."

"Who are Freddie and Shaggy?" Jolene asked.

"Characters from a cartoon," Lindsey said. "We all watched it when we were kids."

"You didn't have Scooby Doo in Vietnam, honey?" Neal asked.

"Not where I lived," Jolene said. "My childhood wasn't a lot of fun."

"Do you think Jolene's Velma or Daphne?" Todd asked.

"That's a dangerous question," Neal said.

"Why?" Jolene asked.

"Daphne's pretty," Lindsey said. "Velma's smart."

"Lindsey's definitely Daphne, then," Jolene said.

"Pretty and dumb," Lindsey said. "That's me, all right."

"And that makes me Velma?" Jolene said.

"I always liked Velma," Neal said. "Especially in the live action versions."

The road twisted sharply to the right. Lindsey bit down on her knuckles. Why did Neal have to wait until the very last instant to turn? This was a twenty-year-old minivan, not an SUV. At any second, it could lose its purchase and tumble backward into the ravine below.

"Who's this lady Lindsey's staying with?" Todd asked.

"Her name's Cutler," Neal said. "She's a rich old widow lady. Kind of a recluse. I was kind of surprised when she volunteered to keep Lindsey."

"How do you know her?" Todd asked.

"Her housekeeper goes to one of my churches," Neal said. "She told me a little bit about her. Seems her late husband was a world traveler, kind of a Hemingway. Climbed Mount Kilimanjaro, hunted exotic animals, that sort of thing. Traveled the world looking for rare treasures. Their house is practically a museum."

"How did he meet Mrs. Cutler?" Lindsey asked.

"He met her in China," Neal said. "She was a missionary's daughter. He was a lot older than she was. About twenty years, I think."

"So, he made off with the missionary's daughter," Todd said from the back seat. "Rare treasures come in many forms."

Neal kept right on talking, laughing and gesturing wildly with both hands and then grabbing the wheel again. Lindsey smiled sweetly and tried not to look nervous. The van clung to the road as the incline grew steeper. Neal dropped it down into low gear and coaxed it uphill. The headlight beams cut through a blanket of fog over damp pavement and glided across tree trunks and a thick blanket of ferns.

"My phone just lost its signal," Todd said. "Just how secluded is this place?"

"It's not far now," Neal said cheerfully.

"I don't like this," Jolene said. "We should let Lindsey stay with us."

"In that tiny apartment?" Neal said. "Not unless we get rid of half the furniture."

"Or your drum set," Jolene said.

A dark shape stood at the edge of the road. Was it a dark rock or a clump of bushes? It looked as if it was moving. *What is that?* Lindsey thought of their earlier conversation about Scooby Doo. There was no way....

"That drum set is sacred, woman."

The ragged shape rose to full height and stepped into the road. It spread its arms like dark wings and leaped into the air. A dead white face hurtled toward the glass.

Lindsey screamed. She seized the steering wheel.

"Whoa! Whoa! Whoa!"

The van shot toward the edge of the road. The brakes squealed as the tires blistered the road. Neal tore the wheel from her grasp. They skidded to a stop. The bumper brushed a wooden guardrail. The headlights glared out into space.

"Why did you do that?" Neal cried.

"A man," Lindsey gasped. "A man in the road." Her heart was pounding.

"What man?"

"Didn't you see?"

There was no one there. As Neal backed up and straightened the wheels, the lights raked the path ahead of them. The road was empty.

"You saw a guy in the road?"

"He was right there. Didn't anybody else see him?"

No answer. Lindsey stared at them in disbelief.

"Well, where is he now?"

"I don't know."

"I shouldn't have talked about Scooby Doo," Todd said.

"It doesn't usually scare anybody older than six," Neal said. He looked at Lindsey, looked back through the windshield, and sighed. "I'd better go check." Neal jerked the gearshift into park and threw open the door.

"No," Lindsey said. "Don't...." *Don't go out there*, she had started to say just as the door slammed. She thought of the face she had seen. It had been pale, ghostly. It had not been the face of a living person. *This is a Scooby Doo episode,* she thought, and I just *saw the monster.*

Neal walked through the headlight beams and past the passenger window. Lindsey watched him in the rearview mirror as he walked around the back of the van and disappeared. A moment passed.

"What's he doing back there?" Todd squinted into the gloom. "Do you think he found something?"

"What did you see, Lindsey?" Jolene asked.

"It looked like a man," Lindsey said. "A man in a black coat. He had a...."

A hand slapped the glass. Lindsey screamed. Writhing fingers squeaked down the glass, leaving twisted paths in the condensation.

"Neal!" Lindsey cried. "Nea...."

Neither Jolene nor Todd reacted. A moment later the door opened, and Neal dropped, laughing, into the driver's seat.

"Will you stop acting like a teenager?" Jolene sighed. "You nearly scared Lindsey to death."

"Get some new material, man," Todd said. "He did that to me last week. I nearly wet my pants."

"You guys just don't appreciate good comedy," Neal said.

"Did you see anything?" Lindsey asked.

"Not a thing." Neal snapped his safety belt into place. "What did you think you saw?"

"Nothing," Lindsey said.

"You nearly killed us for nothing?"

"I'm sorry."

Neal restarted the van, and they resumed their trek down the dark road. The trees sank into darkness on either side of them as the road skirted the top of a grassy ridge. Directly in front of the van was a high hill covered with hemlock trees and, in the midst of them, a huge saltbox mansion. Lindsey swallowed hard.

"Is that it?"

"That's it."

Lights from tall, pointed windows glowed through the drizzle that was still falling. The hill on which the house stood was, Lindsey soon realized, a narrow ledge of rock and soil extending out into the Pacific Ocean. Looking down the hill to her right, she could see a rocky cove. Ocean waves slammed into the rocks with a wild ferocity she had not seen during her sunny trips to the beaches at Corpus Christi, Texas. These were both stunningly beautiful and deadly. A short distance from the shore, a small slab of rock thrust itself above the pounding waves. A dark cone jutted up through the haze.

"Is that a lighthouse?" Jolene asked.

"I don't see the light," Todd said. "It must be deserted."

"It is," Neal said. "It's been abandoned since the forties."

Neal navigated the last turn. His headlight beams slid across a wooden fence that encircled the hilltop. There were gaps where sections of it had fallen away as the edges of the hill had eroded. A cluster of tall trees surrounded the house. Beneath them were statues, rosebushes, and flowerbeds. Behind the house, overlooking the ocean, was a gazebo.

Neal stopped in front of the house and shut off the engine. As Lindsey climbed out of the minivan into the cool evening, she got her first clear view of the mansion. It was three stories tall and built in the shape of a rectangular box. In some ways it resembled a ship, something that might have sailed a wild and ancient sea filled with pirate ships, hostile natives, and the wonder of undiscovered lands. The sight of it filled her with apprehension.

"That's a big place for one person," Jolene observed.

"She used to have servants," Neal said. "She still has one or two, but she's mostly got the place to herself."

Todd and Neal carried Lindsey's luggage to the front door for her. Jolene rang the bell. No one answered for a moment. A moment later, the door creaked open. In the portal stood a slim, dark woman who wore her hair in a bun.

"Miss Cornelia," Neal said. "How are you?"

"Good evening, Pastor," the woman said without a trace of a smile.

"This is Lindsey, the art teacher who will be staying with Mrs. Katherine this summer."

"It is a pleasure to meet you." She had a thick German accent. "Come with me, please." She turned around and led them through a dark living room to a lighted hallway beyond.

"Enter freely and of your own will," Todd muttered.

"Dracula," Lindsey said. She kept her voice down. "I just saw that."

"You like monster movies?"

"Sometimes."

"Honey," Jolene whispered, "are you sure about this?"

"It will be fine," Neal said.

The house was beautiful in a gothic way. The walls were lined with paintings, statues, and dark wood display cases filled with relics from around the world. Lindsey thought she saw a sarcophagus in one of the alcoves and wondered if there was still a mummy inside.

"Look at this place," Todd said in wonder. "It *is* like a museum. I wonder if Mrs. Cutler would let me shoot some video of this."

"Todd makes documentary films," Jolene explained.

"No pictures," Cornelia said without turning around.

"There's so much history here," Todd said. "Every one of these artifacts is a story in itself."

"No pictures."

Lindsey hoped Mrs. Cutler would be a bit more inviting than Cornelia was.

The housekeeper led the group to an elegantly furnished sitting room in the back of the house. An elderly woman sat in a high-backed chair. In front of her was a large round table. A china tea pitcher, cups, and ladyfinger cookies were carefully arranged on silver trays. Behind her stood a huge bay window and a set of French doors that opened onto a balcony. Beyond it lay a narrow strip of grass, a board fence, and a fifty-foot plunge into the dark waters of the Pacific. The lighthouse they had seen earlier lay to the right. The sun still clung to the edge of the horizon, even though it was nearly ten o'clock. A few bright stars glowed like haloed angels through a brooding swirl of clouds.

"The young lady is here, Mrs. Cutler," Cornelia said.

"Come in," the old woman said. "Come in. All of you, sit, please."

"We can't stay long, Mrs. Cutler," Neal said.

"Nonsense," Mrs. Cutler said. "We've prepared tea and cookies for all of you, and I do not intend to eat all of it myself. Now come in here and let me look at you." She had a slight accent. Scottish, perhaps.

"Yes, ma'am."

"Now," Mrs. Cutler said. "Which of you is to be staying with me?"

"I am," Lindsey heard herself say. It almost sounded like a question.

"And your name is?"

"Lindsey Holland, ma'am."

"A Southern girl, I see."

"I'm from Texas, ma'am."

"Courtly Southern manners," Mrs. Cutler said. "I appreciate that. Indeed, I do. Now what about the rest of you?"

"We don't have any manners," Neal said. "Southern or otherwise."

"Neal!"

"Sorry. I don't think you've met my wife. This is Jolene."

"Oh, dear," Mrs. Cutler said. "You're not Japanese, are you?"

Lindsey cringed inwardly. Jolene didn't react. Not outwardly, at least.

"I'm from Vietnam," Jolene said, "but I grew up in America."

"Please forgive me," Mrs. Cutler said. "World War II was a lifetime ago. My family lived in China then. The things the Japanese did there...." Her voice trailed off as she saw it in her mind. Her lips trembled. "It doesn't matter now. I'm sorry, Jolene. You're a lovely young lady. I shouldn't have mentioned it. And who is this young man?"

"Todd Wilkes," Todd introduced himself.

"What's your connection to this entourage?"

"I'm a member of Neal's church."

"Are you a college student?"

"A graduate student," he said. "In film."

"Really? Mr. DeMille would be pleased."

"Cecile B. DeMille?"

"Yes. I met him once."

"You met Cecile B. DeMille?"

"Yes. My husband knew quite a few influential people, and he enjoyed introducing me to them. Mr. DeMille was a fine gentleman."

"I'm impressed," Todd said. "He was a pioneer in the industry."

"*The Ten Commandments*," Neal whispered to Jolene. "With Charlton Heston."

"Who?"

"You're kidding. Right?"

"Well, you all seem like lovely people to be keeping company with this ruffian. A pastor with an earring. Have you ever seen the like?"

"I'm a musician," Neal said. "We're a pretty motley bunch."

She laughed. "My father would not have approved," she said. "There was very little he did approve of. He was a very stern man. Brave, though. Very brave and very dedicated to his work. Well, sit down, everyone. Sit down."

They sat.

"Am I to understand that Miss Holland will be working with you at the center this summer?"

"She'll be coordinating our children's programs," Neal said. "Summer school, English as a second language classes, that sort of thing."

"And this is just for the summer?"

There was a pause. Lindsey and Neal looked at each other.

"I'm trying to talk her into coming out here long-term," Neal said. "But she's marrying a guy who can't cut the apron strings."

"Neal!" Jolene said. "Just because you moved across the country from your family…."

"When God leads," Neal said, "I follow. You can't let yourself cling to what's familiar. Get out of your comfort zone. Take some risks."

"You'll have to pardon us," Todd told Mrs. Cutler, who had been watching the exchange with amused curiosity.

"It's all right," Mrs. Cutler said. "You're interesting people, all of you. But you're not eating enough. Get more. Get more."

"Yes, ma'am."

They sat, ate, and conversed for while longer. Finally Neal stood.

"I really hate to cut this short," he said, "but I've got to get Todd and Jolene back home."

"I'm sorry," Todd said. "I've still got a project I need to finish. It's due tomorrow."

"If you'll show us where Lindsey's staying," Neal said, "We'll drop her luggage off."

"Very well," Mrs. Cutler said. "It has been a pleasure meeting all of you. Cornelia, show them where Miss Holland will be staying, please."

"Yes, Mrs. Cutler."

"Thanks, Mrs. Cutler," Todd said.

"It was very nice meeting you," Jolene said.

"Nonsense," Mrs. Cutler said. "The pleasure was mine, believe me."

"We'll see you later," Neal said.

"Good night, Pastor Ruffian."

Cornelia led them down the hall, up a long flight of stairs, and down a dimly lit hallway. At the end of the hall was a tall door with a transom on top. Cornelia pulled out a key and unlocked the door. Inside was a lavishly furnished room with a four-poster bed, a mahogany dresser with a round mirror, a roll-top writing desk, and a steamer trunk. Gauze curtains hung over French doors that opened onto a balcony.

"Looks like she set you up in the luxury suite," Neal said. "My whole apartment would fit in here."

"And when are you planning to do something about that?" Jolene asked.

"I'm not getting rid of my drum set, if that's what you mean."

Lindsey followed her friends back out to the front porch as they prepared to leave.

"It's been good to see you again," Jolene said. "We've really been looking forward to having you out here."

"Thanks."

"Are you sure you'll be all right here?"

"I'll be fine."

"It was good to meet you," Todd said.

Lindsey hugged everyone and stood on the porch watching as the minivan pulled away. She fought the urge to run after it.

Chapter 2: In the Dark

Lindsey stood on the porch and watched as the minivan's taillights vanished through a gap in the trees. The engine noise faded a moment later.

On my own, Lindsey thought, *maybe for the last time* She fingered her engagement ring and wondered what was wrong with her. She had dreamed of marrying Pack since junior high, but now the very thought of her upcoming wedding tied her stomach in knots. She guessed most people felt the same way in the weeks before a wedding. If she could just ride out the emotional storm, she told herself, everything would be great. By Christmas she would be living the life she had dreamed of since childhood. She tried to be excited about that but found herself on the verge of tears instead.

Lindsey closed her eyes and felt the cool ocean breeze. The air in Texas was already blazing hot by this time of year. She could hear the waves crashing in the distance and the seagulls crying overhead. Suddenly, she detected a movement in the shadows leading up the driveway. She thought of the man in the road, saw the dead face and the white-filmed eyes. The touch of icy fingers traveled up and down her spine.

Lindsey went back into the house, locking and bolting the door behind her. It was presumptuous, she knew. This was not her house. Still, the thought of the bearded spectre filled her with dread. If the figure turned out to be as ghostly as it looked, no locked door would prevent it from entering, but leaving the door unlocked still felt like the wrong thing to do. *This is silly,* Lindsey thought. *There's no way I really saw a ghost.*

Cornelia, the German housekeeper, had disappeared. Lindsey shrank from every shadow as she made her way back down the ornate, dimly lit hallway to the sun room on the back of the house, where they had met Mrs. Cutler earlier. The elderly woman was still there. She was drinking tea and gazing out at the waves. She didn't see Lindsey at first. Suddenly, she spun around and stifled a scream. Her cup and saucer tumbled from her hands and exploded against the marble floor. She covered her mouth with both hands.

"I'm so sorry!" Lindsey said with a gasp.

"It's all right, dear," Mrs. Cutler said. "I thought you were someone else. Forgive me." Her hands trembled as she pulled them from her face.

"Who were you expecting?"

"Expecting?" Mrs. Cutler said. "Oh, no one. No one at all, certainly. How silly of me. How completely silly."

"Let me get something to clean this," Lindsey said. "I'm so sorry."

"Not at all," Mrs. Cutler said, regaining her composure. "Could you pour me another cup of tea? Two sugars, please." There was still an empty cup on the service tray beside an ornate silver-plated pitcher. Even the bowl that held the sugar cubes and tongs looked expensive. Lindsey poured the tea carefully, dropped in the sugar cubes, and took the steaming mixture to Mrs. Cutler.

"Thank you, darling," the older woman said. "Pour yourself another cup."

"But I need to clean...."

"Nonsense," Mrs. Cutler said. "I'll summon Cornelia." She picked up a bell and rang it.

The German woman appeared almost instantly. It was as though she had materialized from the ether or come through a secret passage.

"Yes, ma'am."

"I've broken another cup," Mrs. Cutler said with a sigh. "Soon we'll be drinking our tea from Styrofoam."

"I'll clean it at once."

"Thank you, darling."

Cornelia left to find a dishrag, broom, and dustpan. Lindsey was still standing.

"Sit, dear," Mrs. Cutler said. "Pour yourself some tea and sit."

Lindsey did as she was instructed.

"Well," Mrs. Cutler said. "You certainly are a lovely girl—even with the things you young people wear these days." She leaned forward. "You don't have any tattoos, do you?"

Lindsey blushed. "Just one, ma'am."

"Dreadful," she said. "May I see it?"

Embarrassed, Lindsey stood, turned around, and raised the back of her shirt. Even without seeing it, she sometimes thought she could feel the butterfly fluttering its wings against the bare skin of her lower back.

"Dreadful," Mrs. Cutler said again as she ran her thumb across it. "Christian young ladies getting tattoos like sailors. I suppose your father was quite put out with you." Something in her tone said she somewhat relished the idea.

"A little," Lindsey said as she sat back down.

"My father would have…." Mrs. Cutler began. "I don't know what he would have done. Just playing cards was enough to merit two whole days of Bible-reading."

"Using the Bible as punishment seems wrong somehow," Lindsey said.

"He was a stern man," Mrs. Cutler said. "In many ways a great man, but he had little patience with children. I don't think he quite knew what to do with us."

"What about your mother?"

"I never knew her. My sister and I were twins, you see, and there were… complications surrounding our arrival. My mother didn't survive."

"I'm sorry."

"It's all right, my dear. At least my sister and I had each other. If it hadn't been for Katie, I don't know what I would have done."

"Weren't there other children?"

"My father didn't want us playing with the local children. They were heathen, you see, and he didn't want us to learn their ways."

Cornelia came back with a dishrag, a broom, and a dustpan. She wiped up the spilled tea and cleaned up the broken cup and saucer without a word. Mrs. Cutler kept right on talking. She seemed delighted to have a captive audience, and Lindsey was fascinated by the stories of her childhood. The clock chimed midnight.

"Oh, no," Lindsey said suddenly. "I forgot to call home. I promised my mom and my fiancé I would call them as soon as I got here."

"Then you must call them," Mrs. Cutler said. "We don't get cellular service here, but there is a telephone on the kitchen cabinet." She pointed, indicating a swinging door that led to the sunroom. "The kitchen is just through that door."

"Thank you."

Lindsey hurried through the door. She had half-expected to see Cornelia standing there glaring at her as soon as she opened it, but the housekeeper was nowhere to be seen. The telephone was mounted on the wall. It was a black, rotary dial telephone. She dialed Pack's number and waited, twirling the ring around her finger as the phone rang.

"Hey!" It was Pack's voice.

"Hey," Lindsey answered. "I'm…."

"I'm not here right now. Leave a message."

The tone sounded.

"Pack," Lindsey said. "This is Lindsey. I'm in Oregon, and everything's fine. I love you. Good night." She hung up.

Her heart, she realized, was pounding. She didn't know whether she was disappointed or relieved. She took a deep breath and dialed her parents' number. The phone rang twice.

"Hello."

"Mom?"

"Lindsey! How are you? We were starting to get worried. Do you know what time it is?"

"Yes, ma'am. I'm sorry. Neal and Jolene took me out to eat after they met me at the airport. Then I started talking to Mrs. Cutler and lost track of the time."

"It's all right. I couldn't sleep anyway, knowing you were so far away. Does this Mrs. Cutler seem like a nice person?"

"Very nice," Lindsey said. "And…interesting."

"And the house?"

"It's beautiful. It's on a hilltop overlooking the ocean. You can see the waves crashing in, and a lighthouse."

"That's fine, honey. Is that Neal still trying to talk you into moving out there?"

"He's mentioned it. I told him Pack would never leave Texas."

"Of course not. He would be crazy to. He has everything he needs right here. I wish you could see that."

"What do you mean?"

"I've heard you talk about being a missionary and traveling around the world. And here you are, the summer before your wedding, hopping around the country and leaving all the planning to me."

"What planning? We've got everything scheduled and reserved. There's nothing else to do. You saw to that. Every last detail!"

"What in the world are you talking about?"

You overrode every decision I tried to make, Lindsey wanted to say. The color of the dresses. The kinds of flowers. The music. But that's not enough for you, is it? You've got to sit around and worry about everything for three months, even after it's all taken care of. You want me to sit around and worry with you, but I'm not going to.

"Nothing," was all she said.

"I just don't know what's gotten into you, Lindsey. You just don't appreciate anything I do for you anymore."

"Let's just drop it. Okay?"

"Okay. Whatever."

Lindsey sighed. "I'm sorry, Mom. It's just that…."

"Just what?"

"It's a big step. I just need some time to think about it, pray about it."

"What's there to think about? You're marrying Pack. That's it."

"Maybe I just need to get used to the idea of not being single anymore."

"Most girls your age want to get married."

"I do. You know I want to. It's just...I don't know."

"Just don't let that Neal fill your head with ideas. Look at him. He's nearly forty years old, and he's still floating around the country from one place to another."

"He's a church planter. He's following God."

"That's his excuse for not wanting to grow up. Is he still married to that foreign girl?"

"Her name's Jolene. They're still married, and they have a great relationship."

"That's good. I'd hoped he wasn't getting any ideas about you."

"Mom! That's crazy!"

"It's not as crazy as you think it is."

"Whatever."

"I just hope you don't get out there and do something stupid. You've got a good life waiting for you here."

"I know. And I'll be back in three months. I just needed to get away for a while. That's all."

"If you say so. I still think...."

"Good night, Mom."

"Good night, Lindsey."

Lindsey hung up. She clenched her fists, growled, and shook her head. She had meant to talk to her father, too, but all she could think of was getting her mother off the phone. How was it that she instinctively knew every emotional button to push, everything that made her want to scream with frustration? Lindsey fought to shove her emotions back into their genie's bottle and twist the cork firmly into place before she stepped through the swinging door back into the kitchen.

"Is everything all right?" Mrs. Cutler asked.

"Everything's fine," Lindsey said. She sighed again. "Just the way it always is."

"Ah."

"My mother makes me so frustrated sometimes. She wants to micromanage every detail of my life and doesn't understand why I don't just fall to my knees and thank her for everything she does."

"Oh, yes," Mrs. Cutler said. "Some parents are like that. Not all of them are female. Do be careful of the choices you make, darling. Some of them are not so easy to reverse." She stared out at the ocean as though she could see all the way to China, all the way to the distant land that had once been her home.

"Is it okay if I turn in?"

"Certainly. You must be tired after all of your travel, and there is a two-hour time difference."

Lindsey walked back upstairs to the room where her friends had dropped off her luggage. The hall was long and gloomy. Her footsteps echoed off the walls, giving her a weird sense that someone was following her. She looked back more than once, expecting to see some shambling horror creeping after her. She thought she heard whispers coming from around the corners and wasted no time getting to her room. She closed the door behind her and breathed a sigh of relief.

This is ridiculous, she told herself. It's just a house. You're such a chicken.

She laughed at herself, but the strange sense of creeping horror she had felt in the corridor did not vanish entirely. She was not exactly afraid, but there was an air of melancholy about the chamber, as beautiful as it was, that she found unsettling.

A gilded cage. The old cliché popped into her head suddenly, and she wondered where the thought had come from.

Lindsey went into the bathroom to brush her teeth and undress for bed. As she was changing into the long T-shirt she usually slept in, she felt, more than once, as if someone was watching from just outside the field of her vision. Her eyes kept darting back to the mirror, but there was nothing reflected in the glass but her own image.

I'm really acting like a coward tonight, she thought as she slipped between the sheets of a four-poster bed. *It must be this house and the rain. What else could it be?* The figure she had seen in the road must have been some kind of reflection, or maybe a trick of the shadows. It had to have been.

Sitting up in bed, Lindsey twisted the engagement ring from her finger and placed it back in the velvet case from which it had come. She stared at it for a long time. She had turned out the lights in the room but left a light on in the bathroom. Even if the sense of dread she felt was only her imagination, the idea of being alone in the dark in the big old mansion was just too much. The yellow rays angled through the imperfections in the stone, forming tiny images in the glass. Lindsey could imagine holographic images from her future taking shape in the crystalline lattices: a big house, children, a happy home in a close-knit community. Those thoughts should have made her happy, but they didn't.

God, she silently prayed. What are You trying to show me? This is what I prayed for all of these years, but it feels so wrong. As irritating as she can be, Mom is right. How could I be so ungrateful?

Lindsey's troubled prayers did little to relieve the maelstrom of emotions that raged inside of her. She wanted God to lift her above the storm to some peaceful refuge, someplace where she could see clearly and think clearly, someplace where she wouldn't be worried or afraid. It didn't happen. Lindsey could imagine God shaking His head in exasperation.

"You silly girl! Look at everything I've given you, and here you are worrying and fretting because you don't appreciate what you have. I don't know why I even waste my blessings on spoiled little girls like you."

God wouldn't say that, she told herself. *Would He?* She lay beneath the covers with her eyes closed and her stomach churning. The weight of exhaustion smothered all conscious thought, but the anxiety remained.

***

Lindsey heard waves rolling around her and felt sharp rocks digging into the soles of her bare feet. She was holding a lantern. The orange flame danced weirdly, almost hypnotically inside the glass. She could almost envision the tiny figure of a ballerina dancing inside the fire. Lindsey placed her hand against a wall to steady herself and looked up. The concrete wall rose until it brushed the swirling clouds overhead. It was a lighthouse. There was no beacon at the top. The place looked dark, brooding, and haunted. The word *cursed* sprang into Lindsey's mind, but she didn't know where it had come from.

"This place is cursed," Lindsey said to herself. "This place is cursed, and something is coming."

Lindsey woke up suddenly. It took her an instant to recognize the room. The bathroom light, she realized, had gone out. A dim gray light from one of the mercury vapor lamps on the lawn below filtered up through the curtains. Lindsey could see the contours of the old-fashioned dresser and the mirror, the chair in the corner.

There was someone in the room with her.

Not daring to move anything but her eyes, Lindsey looked around the room but could see no sign of anyone.

The feeling was strong, pervasive. Lindsey felt the hair on the back of her neck stand up. Then slowly, gently, she felt a weight settle on the edge of her bed. The sheets tightened around her and the springs compressed beneath her as though the weight of a body was pressing against the bed beside her. Lindsey could still see the gray light from the window. There was no shadow, no silhouette of anyone in the room, but the weight remained.

Lindsey clamped her eyes shut and silently began to pray. She prayed for what seemed like twenty or thirty minutes. The feeling of weight slowly subsided, and the sense of a presence faded. Lindsey began to tell herself she had imagined it, that it was some trick her relaxing muscles had played on her. It was the result of the anxiety she was feeling. That had to be it. Stress played all kinds of tricks on the mind, she told herself.

She was not convinced—not fully, anyway.

Chapter 3: Space and Shadow

The alarm penetrated the jumble of dreams that swathed Lindsey's sleeping mind. She opened her eyes and fumbled for the travel alarm on the nightstand beside her bed. Her clumsy fingers found the switch and silenced the piercing ring. Sun was streaming in through gauze curtains onto a beautiful, old-fashioned room. Lindsey did not remember falling asleep that second time, yet she obviously had. Yawning, she pushed back the covers and stretched her arms high.

She climbed out of bed and walked across a throw rug to the French doors. She opened the doors and stepped out onto the balcony, into the cool morning air. Stone tiles were rough and damp with dew against the soles of her bare feet. She looked out onto a finely manicured lawn with tall trees, flower gardens, and an old-fashioned gazebo with a slate roof. Directly behind the house was a long, wooden stairway leading down the side of a cliff to a dock that extended out into the ocean. To the right, across a cove, were steep cliffs, a rocky shore, and the glistening waves of the Pacific Ocean. The old lighthouse guarded the cover from its rocky base. It looked like something from a painting. She could almost imagine sailing ships from another age tossing about on the waves. The terror of the previous night faded in the light of the morning sun. A narrow spit of land, Lindsey noticed, connected the lighthouse to the shore. She had not seen it the night before and wondered if it had been shrouded in darkness or buried beneath the churning waters at high tide.

Lindsey had left herself enough time for prayer, devotional reading, and journaling before breakfast. That was how she started her days. It was a discipline she had adopted after returning from a very special week at a church youth camp in the mountains. It had been a time when she had felt closer to

God than ever before, and there had not been many experiences since then that matched its joy and intensity. Lindsey had taken her reading, writing, and praying habits with her into college and out into the work world. She supposed she would take them with her into married life and motherhood as well.

Last night I dreamed someone or something invisible came into my room and sat down on my bed, Lindsey wrote in her journal. *I don't know if this is a symptom of pre-wedding jitters or what. The place I'm staying is big, old, and a long way from town. They don't even have cellular service here. I can't even text my friends. I never realized how dependent I was on that connection. I think I let my imagination run away from me.*

After taking a hot bath in a claw-foot tub, Lindsey dressed, fixed her hair, and hurried down to breakfast. Cornelia was in the dining room setting out plates. Mrs. Cutler was nowhere to be seen.

"Good morning," Lindsey said.

"Good morning," Cornelia said. "The orange juice is on the table. There's coffee in the kitchen."

"Thank you."

A young woman appeared in the doorway. She was tall and thin with wavy, strawberry blonde hair.

"Good morning, Cornelia," she said brightly.

The German woman left the room without speaking.

"I can't believe she just ignored you," Lindsey said.

"Cornelia?" The girl, like Ms. Cutler, had a slight accent. "She's a dear. She's just a bit taciturn. Always has been."

"We haven't met," Lindsey said. "I'm Lindsey Holland."

"The teacher from Texas? Yes. Katherine told me about you. I'm Caitlyn, Mrs. Cutler's niece."

"Oh," Lindsey said. "It's nice to meet you. I didn't realize there was anyone my age staying here. At least, you look about my age."

"I'm twenty-four," she said. "I'm sorry I wasn't here to meet you last night. I was at the hospital."

"Do you work there?" Lindsey saw Caitlyn was wearing scrubs under her sweater.

"I'm a nursing student. I'm just finishing up my rotations. And, yes, I also work there. My hours are pretty odd."

Caitlyn poured herself a glass of juice and picked up a piece of toast.

"Aren't you going to sit down?" Lindsey asked.

"I wish I could," Caitlyn said, "but I've got to go. I'm glad I got to meet you, Lindsey. I've looked forward to having you here this summer."

Caitlyn vanished into the hallway. Lindsey looked around at the breakfast Cornelia had prepared. Scrambled eggs. Freshly sliced apples. Crepes. Lindsey served herself and ate alone. Cornelia stepped back into the room. Lindsey noticed the woman was eyeing her strangely.

"Is something wrong?" she asked.

Cornelia just shook her head.

***

When Neal and Jolene arrived in the minivan, Neal's eyes looked puffy.

"Are you all right?" Lindsey asked him as she climbed into the back seat beside him.

"I'm fine," Neal said. He sounded like he had just woken up.

"He sat up playing videogames until four in the morning," Jolene said. "No wonder we don't have any children. Not that I need any more with him around, anyway."

"You see what a submissive pastor's wife she is," Neal said. "Poor little thing hardly says a word."

Jolene smiled. "How did you sleep last night?"

"Fine," Lindsey said. "Well, okay. I guess."

"Were you afraid?"

"A little."

"Neal, I told you we shouldn't have made her stay there."

"It's okay," Lindsey said. "I just had a lot on my mind. The room is great. You saw it. It's beautiful, and the view is unbelievable."

"Are you sure?" Jolene asked. "You're not just saying that?"

"It's fine," Lindsey said. "Really."

"You're sure?"

"I'm sure."

"Okay."

"What are we doing today?"

"I've got some calls to make," Neal said. "You're helping Jolene out in the coffee shop. I thought maybe you could draw portraits."

"For whom?"

"Anybody who wants one."

"Neal tells me you're quite an artist," Jolene interjected.

"Neal exaggerates," Lindsey said.

"Surely not," Jolene said.

"So, I'm going to sit in a coffee shop and draw portraits of customers?"

"Yep."

"And how does this coffee shop relate to your mission work?"

"It's where we meet most of the people who go there. It helps if you've got a personal connection. It helps with funding too, though not as much as I'd hoped it would."

They rolled down a hill and around a corner. Cannon Beach was a lovely tourist town, with rows of quaint shops selling clothing, stained glass, freshly made candy, and wind chimes. There were art galleries, vacation homes, and seaside resorts. One restaurant was shaped like a log cabin. Neal pulled the van into the parking lot beside a row of shops. The first, a coffee shop, had a sign that said *Dawn Treader Café* with a hand-carved image of a sailing ship.

Jolene was unlocking the front door when a thin, red-haired man in odd, mismatched clothing approached. He stepped about six feet from them and stared.

"Morning, Space," Neal said.

The man didn't answer. He just kept on staring.

"Space," Neal said, "this is Lindsey. She's going to be working here with us this summer. Lindsey, this is Space."

"It's nice to meet you, Space," Lindsey said, extending a hand.

Space stared at her as if she'd just come from Mars.

"Is Space your first name or your last?"

No answer.

"It takes him a while to get used to people," Neal said. "What's on your mind, Space?"

"I need some money, Preacher," Space told him.

"You know I'm not going to give you money, man. What do you need? Food? Clothes?"

"Cigarettes, man. I'm having a nicotine fit."

"Maybe it's time to kick the habit," Neal said.

"Are you going to give me any money or not?"

"Not for cigarettes," Neal said, "but I'll buy you some food or clothes if that's what you want."

"How 'bout a donut?"

"All right. We'll get you a donut."

"Okay, then."

"Ladies," Neal told the women, "Space and I have some business to attend to. I'll be back in a minute."

Lindsey watched the minister and the scarecrow figure disappear into a bakery down the street.

"Space had a little too much fun in the sixties," Jolene said. "Permanent brain damage. He's been in and out of treatment centers for years."

"That's sad."

"Come on in," Jolene said. "I'll start the coffee, and we'll find you some art supplies."

Lindsey followed her inside. The walls were varnished wood and covered with paintings and photographs. One wall was lined with books.

"Why don't you look around the shop while I open up?" Jolene suggested. "Familiarize yourself with what we have here."

Lindsey scanned the books on the shelves. They were mostly Christian books, she noticed, but they were geared more to a coffeehouse crowd than the middle class mother of three most Christian bookstores seem to target. There was a big section of C.S. Lewis books and a science fiction and fantasy shelf featuring books like Madeleine L'Engle's *A Wrinkle in Time* series. One section contained the work of non-Anglo authors like Japanese novelist Shusaku Endo. There were old classics like *Pilgrim's Progress, In His Steps*, and *Ben Hur,* and the books of John Donne, George MacDonald, and G.K. Chesterton.

"Quite a collection, huh?" Jolene said.

"Some of these are pretty deep," Lindsey said.

"We get a lot of college students, artists, and intellectuals in here," Jolene said. "Neal believes in challenging them. I finally talked him into adding some chick lit and historical romances. He kept saying it was against his religion. Most Christian bookstores cater mainly to women. I think he was rebelling against that, but I told him the selection needed a little bit of femininity."

Jolene unlocked a closet and pulled out an easel and a tackle box filled with oil pastels.

"These are our art supplies," she said. "I think the paper's on the top shelf. Your arms are longer than mine."

Lindsey ended up pulling a chair up to the closet and standing on it. She found the paper and, beneath it, a sign that said, "Portraits Free With Purchase." She pulled both down and set them on the nearest table.

"Is that everything?"

"I think so."

Lindsey pulled away the chair, and Jolene locked the closet. Lindsey set up the easel near the front window and pulled up a chair.

"Why don't you just draw whatever you want until people start to arrive?" Jolene said. "I'll hang up the sign."

Moments later, the bell above the door rang. Lindsey looked up to see a young woman. She was about fourteen years old and dressed all in black clothes and silver jewelry. Black lipstick and nail polish and some piercings rounded out her Goth wardrobe.

"Are you the artist?" she asked.

"I guess so," Lindsey said.

The bell rang again as Neal returned.

"Do I have to buy something to have my portrait made?" the girl asked.

"You're the first customer of the day," Neal said. "It's on the house. Just don't tell anybody."

"Okay."

"Do you want a portrait or a caricature?" Lindsey asked.

"Can you just draw me in a graveyard?"

"Okay." Lindsey was a little bit taken aback by the request. She saw Neal smile.

"And don't put any religious symbols in it," the girl continued. "I'm a witch."

"No crosses in a graveyard?" Neal asked. "What about your necklace?"

"Oh," she said. There were a variety of religious symbols attached to the beads she wore around her neck. One of them was a crucifix. "Never mind."

"Sit down," Lindsey said. "What's your name?"

"Shadow," the girl replied as she took a seat.

"That's pretty," Lindsey said as she sharpened a pencil. "It fits you."

"I think so."

"So, what kind of witch are you?" Neal asked. "A good witch or a bad one?"

"Mostly good," she said. "I guess. Dark spirits can be unpredictable."

"I've heard that," Neal said.

"It's not a joke," she snapped. "They're all around us. I've seen them." She turned to Lindsey. "So have you."

Lindsey opened her mouth to speak, but words failed her.

"They're hungry and angry. They don't have any faces except the ones they steal from our thoughts. They hunger for sensation but only feel it through us. They feed on lust and rage."

"That's…interesting."

"I know you don't believe me. Even though you know its true, you're too afraid to accept it, so you just deny it. I understand."

"Shadow. Honey…."

"It's okay. I understand."

"Are you coming to our party?" Neal asked. The question seemed odd after the talk of dark spirits.

"When is it?"

"Tonight."

"What kind of party is it?"

"A beach party."

"Why didn't you tell me?" Lindsey interjected. "I didn't even bring my swimsuit."

"You don't need a swimsuit."

"Excuse me?"

"This isn't Panama City. The beaches here are cold. If you went out into this water without a wetsuit, you'd turn blue."

"So, I need a wetsuit?"

"Not for a party. We're just going to eat and put on a show."

"What kind of show?" Lindsey asked.

"Music. Comedy sketches. That sort of thing."

"Is it a church party?" Shadow asked.

"Something like that."

"I don't do church parties," Shadow said, "but thanks for asking. I'd better go." She stood.

"Don't you want your picture?" Lindsey asked. "It's almost finished."

"Okay." She sighed and sat back down.

Lindsey added a few more strokes. "There." She unclipped the paper from the easel and passed the picture to Shadow.

"You're good," she said. "It really does look like me. Do I really look that sad?"

"Enough to make my heart ache."

"Thanks for the picture. I'll see you later."

"Goodbye, Shadow," Lindsey said. "It was nice meeting you."

"Goodbye, Lindsey."

The bell on the door rang as she left.

How did she know my name? Cold fingers danced up and down Lindsey's spine.

"New Age spirituality is pretty big around here," Neal said.

"Did you hear what she said?"

"I hear things like that every day. Don't let it get to you."

"Let it get to me?"

"Do you still think you saw something in the road last night?"

"I don't know what I saw."

"There wasn't anything there, Lindsey."

Lindsey started to argue with him, but she knew there was no point in it. Neal would go right on making his jokes and being skeptical, and she would just keep getting angrier.

"Whatever. Tell me more about this party. You didn't say anything about it earlier."

"I wanted to surprise you," he said. "It's straight from the pages of the Blue House Blowout."

"What's a Blue House Blowout?"

"Back when I was in college, my friends and I rented this blue, rundown house. We used to have parties there, and we would invite everybody from all the campus ministries: the Baptist Student Union, Wesley, Campus Crusade, Navigators, Catholic Student Center, Chi Alpha. Everybody came and brought friends. Some Buddhist monks even came one time. I don't think they agreed with the theology, but they were pretty cool guys."

"What did you do?"

"We'd grill hamburgers, and then we would do a show from the roof of the garage. It was multimedia. We had bands playing, and we projected a slideshow onto a bed sheet. The neighbors called the police on us for making too much noise the first time we did it."

"It sounds great. Other than the police."

"We talked to the neighbors before we did it again. Once they realized we weren't having a drunken orgy out there, they were pretty cool with it. One of them even paid for the food."

"That's great."

"One of the guys had a python. We used to take turns getting our pictures made with the snake."

"That's not so great. We're not going to have a snake tonight, are we?"

"Nah. I forgot to rent one. Jolene's people would probably try to eat it, anyway."

"He's full of laughs this morning," Jolene said.

The bell rang as another customer, a man in a business suit, walked in.

"What can I get for you?" Jolene asked.

***

Lindsey spent most of the day at the coffee house drawing portraits of customers and managing the coffee bar and cash register while Jolene ran errands for Neal. When there were no customers in the shop, she thumbed through the books on the shelves in an attempt to familiarize herself with the authors and stories represented there. At around three o'clock, she decided to call Pack. She felt nervous as she opened her cellphone, punched up the directory, and entered the number. Why should she be nervous? It wasn't as though they had just started dating.

The phone rang six times.

"Hey! I'm not here right now. Leave a message."

"This is Lindsey. Call me when you can. Bye."

It seemed odd, she thought, that Pack had not already tried to call her. Maybe he'd tried to reach her before she left Mrs. Cutler's house, and the call had not gone through. She punched through the directory for "missed calls," but Pack's name and number were nowhere to be found. The phone vibrated in her hand. She looked down and saw Pack's name on the screen.

"Hello."

"Hey, what's up?"

"I just tried to call you. Where are you?"

"I'm in Dallas. I've been visiting one of my friends from law school. Her name's Jessie."

"Her?"

There was an awkward pause.

"Well, yeah. Jessie's a girl, but she's just a friend."

"I'm sorry," Lindsey said. "I didn't mean to sound like the jealous girlfriend. I mean, it's okay. We have to trust each other."

"Right. Yeah. Where are you?"

"I'm at a coffee shop. Neal and Jolene run it."

"I thought they were some kind of missionaries."

"They are. This is just part of what they do. They sell Christian books here, and they have Christian art. Are you still studying for the bar exam?"

"Yeah," he said. "That's all I ever do anymore."

"You'll do fine," she said.

"Wish you were here to help me study."

"You don't need me for that, Pack. I'll pray for you, though."

"Sure. Great. I'd better go. I'll see you later."

"Bye." She started to say *I love you*, but the words caught in her throat. The line went dead.

Lindsey sighed. So, Pack was spending the day with a female friend named Jessie—probably short for Jessica. She wondered if that was where he had been last night, if that was why he had never returned her call. Was it paranoid to worry, she wondered, or would it be naïve not to?

She turned around and almost screamed. Space was standing on the sidewalk, staring through the front window at her. This was the third time. She had smiled and waved to him the first couple of times, but he had never responded. Like before, he just stood and stared, his expression vacant. She saw his lips moving slightly and wondered whom he thought he was talking to.

She forced a smile, picked up her cell phone, and called Jolene. She turned her back to the window but kept her eyes on Space's reflection in the polished glass panel on the front of the checkout counter.

"Jolene," she said. "Space is here."

"Is he just standing out on the sidewalk, staring at you and talking to himself?"

"Yeah."

"Don't worry about it. He just does that."

"He's creeping me out."

"Space has a way of doing that. I'll tell Neal."

"Thanks."

Space's image had vanished from the glass. Lindsey spun around. The rumpled vagrant was nowhere to be seen. She looked around the store to make sure he wasn't hiding behind any of the displays. There was no sign of him.

Chapter 4: The Sacrifice

"Do I have time to go home and change?" Lindsey asked as she and Jolene were cleaning up the shop at the end of the day.

"Sure," Jolene said. "Do you want to borrow the minivan?"

"Well, I never really drove one."

"It's not hard."

***

The burnished light of the evening sun clothed the forest in a bronze tint. Lindsey was relieved when she finally saw the mansion ahead of her. She drove slowly along the path that led to the rocky, tree-covered outcropping on which the mansion sat, carefully made her way along the winding driveway, and parked the van in the courtyard. When she reached the front door she found a note taped there. It was folded and had her name written on the outside.

I am buying groceries. Let yourself in.
~Cornelia

Lindsey unlocked the door with the key. She heard voices as she was walking down the hall. She recognized Mrs. Cutler's voice and her boisterous laughter. The other voice sounded like that of a young woman. She wondered if Caitlyn was home, but the voice didn't really sound like Caitlyn. She couldn't make out many words, but Lindsey could tell the other woman had an accent.

"Hi, Mrs. Cutler."

Mrs. Cutler turned with a start.

"Oh, Lindsey," she said. "I didn't hear you come in. You startled me."

There was no one else there.

"I'm sorry," Lindsey said. "I didn't mean to disturb you. Was there someone else here?"

"Oh, no, dear. Cornelia is in town. She won't be back for quite some time."

"But, I thought I heard...." she stopped. "Never mind. It's...Neal's having a beach party for the youth, and I needed to change."

"Oh, yes. By all means."

"I didn't mean to interrupt anything."

"It's quite all right."

Lindsey went upstairs. After working around the shop all day, she wanted to take a hot shower but had to settle for a bath instead. She pulled on some casual clothes—long sleeves for warmth, tennis shoes because she didn't want to ruin her leather shoes walking on wet sand—and looked at herself in the mirror. She pulled up her shirttail, turned sideways, and tried to tell if she was gaining weight or losing it. Working at the coffee shop every day wasn't going to be any help in that department. She would have to start jogging again.

Lindsey went back downstairs to say goodbye to Mrs. Cutler. She found the older woman still sitting alone and gazing out at the ocean. She knocked lightly on the side of the arch as she entered.

"Mrs. Cutler," she said softly, trying not to startle her hostess again.

"Come in, dear. Come in."

"I was just wondering. Were you talking on the phone when I came in earlier?"

"No, dear."

"Was there someone else here?"

"No. Just me."

"That's so strange. I really thought I heard voices."

"The acoustics in this house are strange," Mrs. Cutler said. "It's as if the walls themselves have voices. I suppose I've gotten used to it."

"I'd better get back to town," Lindsey said.

"You needn't rush off."

"I've got to be at the party," she said. "It's already started. We can talk when I get back, if you're still up."

"Certainly. Have a wonderful time, darling."

"Good night, Mrs. Cutler."

"Oh, and do be careful. There's a storm coming."

Lindsey looked out the window behind her. There was no sign of a storm.

***

The sun's orange disk hovered just above the horizon. Waves whispered along the shoreline like a distant conversation. Lindsey could hear the music in the distance as she walked down the road to the beach. A line of solar-powered tiki torches marked the path to a makeshift stage that had been set up on a boat dock behind a beach house. Neal was onstage, giving instructions to the band. The only one of them Lindsey recognized was Todd, the long-haired film student she had met the night before. A bonfire burned on the beach below, and a crowd of teenagers had gathered around it.

"Welcome to the Beach House Blowout!" Neal roared into the microphone. His teenage audience applauded. "I'm the plain white rapper, and these are my gangstas for God."

He threw a cap on sideways, and a group of guys in baggy pants and "bling bling" stepped up beside him. Lindsey put her hand over her mouth and tried not to laugh as he started rapping: "J.B. was preachin' in the land. He said, 'Turn or burn, the kingdom's at hand.'"

"When did he come up with that?" Lindsey whispered to Jolene, who was standing at the edge of the crowd.

"College," Jolene said. "The Jesus Rap is a Blue House tradition."

"Who's J.B.?"

"John the Baptist."

The guys behind Neal had choreographed dance moves to go with the rap, and some of the teenagers in the audience joined in as if they had seen it before.

The audience applauded as Neal reached the end of the rap. He spoke a few words, and the band began its next high-octane performance.

Lindsey saw a brooding figure standing at the edge of the crowd.

"Shadow!" she called as she moved over to where the girl was standing. "I really didn't think you were coming."

"I wasn't going to come," the girl said, "but the spirits insisted. I'm tonight's sacrifice."

"I don't understand."

"You will." She stared at Lindsey. Her eyes were intense, penetrating. "You will."

There was an uneasy pause.

"Well, I'm glad you came, whatever the reason. Do you want something to eat or drink?"

"I'm not hungry. Thanks, though."

Lindsey smiled uneasily and walked away. What was it about that girl that made her so uneasy? Lindsey looked back and saw Shadow standing as stiff as a statue. Instead of watching the band onstage, she was staring at the ocean.

The band played for about twenty minutes. As the driving beat subsided, Neal took the microphone.

"For everything there is a season," he said. "That's what it says in the book of Ecclesiastes. 'For everything there is a season, and a time for every purpose under heaven: a time to laugh, a time to cry, a time to mourn and a time to dance.' The guys have put together a slide show for you. As the music plays, I want you to pause and reflect. John 3:16 says, 'For God so loved the world that He sent His only begotten Son that whoever believes in Him should not perish but have everlasting life.' At their last meal together before His death, Jesus took the bread and said, and I paraphrase, 'This is my body that's about to be broken for you,' and He took the wine and said, 'This is my blood that's about to be shed for you, and it's going to form the basis of a new covenant, a new relationship between God and people.' I leave you with that thought." Neal left the stage to stand beside Jolene.

As the rest of the band left the stage, Todd sat at the keyboard and continued to play a melody, sweet and sad, hopeful and mysterious, as a collage, still pictures and film clips, poured from a hidden projector onto a wind-rippled bed sheet that hung behind the stage. Images from classical and modern paintings, clips from movies—old and new, full-color and black-and-white—melded together across time to create a portrait of an amazing life that would create ripples across the face of history.

"Go home, you crazies!" someone yelled.

"What the heck?" Neal wondered aloud.

Three college-age guys with paint guns stormed the stage and started firing paint pellets at the screen and into the audience. Todd jumped to his feet as one of the hecklers fired into his chest.

"There is no God!" one of the men yelled into the microphone. "These people are lying to you!"

Lindsey watched in fascinated horror and wondered if Neal had staged the assault to teach a lesson about religious persecution, tolerance, loving one's enemies....

"Call the police," she heard Neal tell Jolene as he ran toward the stage.

"You guys get out of here!" one of the band members yelled.

"Sell your poison somewhere else!" the man on the stage cried out.

Two of the band members, both college guys, leaped onto the stage.

"Oppress me, you religious fascists! You bigots! Do what you always...!" Someone pulled the plug on the sound system.

Deprived of his voice, the spokesman picked up a chair and slammed it into the drum set. One of the band members grabbed him by the arm and threw him off the stage. The stage exploded into violence. Someone tore down the sheet that was serving as a screen. One of the guys fired red paint pellets at the band members and at the teenagers in the audience. They looked as if they were covered in blood.

"Hold it!" Neal yelled. "Break it up!"

Dear God, Lindsey prayed. *Help us.* Horror collided with anger and a struggle to meet hate with forgiveness, to want to forgive. How could you love your enemies when they were pounding your friends' faces in the dirt?

Todd held one of the hecklers in a Nelson. He was trying to reason with him. Both of them were covered in red paint. The one who had been flung from the dock leaped back onto the platform, seized an electric guitar, and hurled it into the audience.

Lindsey heard screams from the teenagers in the crowd and fought her way through.

"Somebody got hit."

"The guitar hit somebody."

"She's knocked out."

"She's bleeding."

Lindsey felt strangely detached, as though her mind was pulling free of her body and climbing to a high place above the chaos. People ran past her, but she couldn't hear what they were saying. She saw running feet digging into the sand. Firelight and shadow transformed their faces into weird tribal masks. She saw a body lying crumpled on the beach. Teenagers were gathered around their fallen friend. Their backs blocked Lindsey's view as she moved around them. Finally, she could see the face. The eyes were open but blank, and the features were masked in blood. With raven hair and black lips, she looked like a teenage vampire.

"Shadow!" Her cry twisted into a sob.

Lindsey fell to her knees in the sand. The other students turned and looked at her. Fighting for control, she reached for Shadow's throat and felt for a pulse. The heartbeat throbbed, steady and strong, beneath her fingers.

"She's alive," she gasped. "Thank God. Shadow! Shadow!"

She didn't respond.

"The police are here," someone said.

Lindsey heard running feet and saw two policemen rushing through the crowd toward the stage.

"Help!" Lindsey cried. "Help us! We need an ambulance!"

They didn't hear.

"I understand we have an injury here."

A third policeman had appeared, seemingly by magic.

"She was hit by a guitar," Lindsey said. "One of them threw it off the stage."

The man knelt down beside Shadow. He checked her pulse and shined a light into her eyes to check her pupils for signs of a concussion.

"Her pupils are reacting to the light," he said. "That's a good sign. I just don't understand why she won't wake up." He pulled a radio from his belt, called the dispatcher, and requested an ambulance.

Lindsey held Shadow's hand and spoke to her while they waited for the ambulance to arrive. She watched the other two policemen haul the paint-spattered hecklers, screaming and cursing, to a patrol car with its lights flashing.

Don't let her die, Lord, Lindsey silently prayed. Not now, and not like this.

"I wasn't going to come. But the spirits insisted. I'm tonight's sacrifice."

"I don't understand."

"You will."

The memory of Shadow's words gripped Lindsey's heart like an icy hand from a nightmare. She thought about the dark forces Shadow had feared so much. She pictured them waiting and hungry, just beyond the physical realm, for Shadow to cross over. The thought was too terrible to consider. *Hold on, baby. Hold on.*

Lightning flashed, and a roll of thunder split the sky. A storm was coming.

***

"I used to be a lot like those guys," Todd said as they sat in the waiting room. "I understand where they're coming from—up to a point. I used to get so frustrated at Christians acting like they had all the answers and looking down their noses at the rest of us. I never tried to hurt anybody, though. I don't think they meant to hurt anybody, either. They were just stupid and reckless. Guys like that give atheists a bad name."

Rain drummed against the windowpane. Distorted by the rain, the gray world through the glass looked like a doorway into the phantom reality where Shadow's spirit-beings dwelled. Lindsey trembled at the thought.

The outside door swung open. Neal came in holding a cell phone.

"Were you able to get through to her mother?" Jolene asked.

"I talked to her," he said. "I'm not sure how much of it she understood."

"She doesn't speak English?"

"It was English. Pretty disjointed, though. I think she was high on something. I had a hard time making her understand anything I said. I'm still not sure if she understood me. I told her about three times that Shadow was in the emergency room. She finally said okay and hung up."

"Great," Todd said. "She'll probably wake up in two days and wonder where her daughter is."

"How'd you get her number?" Lindsey asked.

"It's in her cell phone." He held out a black cell phone with a skull emblazoned on the skin.

"That's really sad," Jolene said.

The door swung open, and a tall, thin man walked in.

"Hey," he said. "Are you Shadow's friends?"

"How is she?" Lindsey asked. "Did she ever wake up?"

"She's conscious," he said. "Still pretty groggy, though."

"Can we see her?"

"Just for a minute," he said. "She doesn't really need to be disturbed, but I think she'd rest easier if she knew somebody was out here."

"Thanks."

"Did you say that happened at a *church* party?"

"We had a few party crashers," Neal said.

"I hope they're in jail."

"They are. I may have to stop in on them and see if they need Jesus. Prepare a nice, long sermon just for the occasion."

"With lepers and *begats*," Jolene said.

"Especially *begats*."

"Here she is," the doctor said as he led them into a patient room. Shadow was lying on an examination bed with a bandage on her forehead.

"How are ya, princess?" Neal asked. "Or do you prefer 'princess of darkness'?"

She smiled. "I'm okay. It doesn't hurt much."

"Just another piercing."

"I'm glad you're okay," Lindsey told her. "When I first saw you…well, I thought they had killed you. You were knocked out, but your eyes were open."

"Really? I looked dead, huh? That's kind of cool. Is my mom coming up here?"

"She's coming up later," Neal said.

"Later, huh? Couldn't tear herself away from sex and drugs, I guess."

"We'll stay with you," Lindsey said. "You won't have to be alone."

"It's okay," she said softly. She closed her eyes. "I'm used to being alone." Her breathing grew steady as she faded off to sleep.

***

Lindsey was walking barefoot on sharp rocks with a lantern swinging in her grip. A lighthouse clung to the island beside her, its stony mass rising to the heavens like the neck of a great beast. Wind tore through her hair and threatened to rip her long nightgown from her body. She held it in place with one hand and held the lantern with the other. Lightning danced, and thunder cracked the dark sky. Lindsey saw a dark ship, a sailing vessel, anchored offshore and a boat full of men rowing toward the dock. Panic surged within her as she searched for the path to shore and found it buried beneath the waves. She could have hidden behind the lighthouse, but they had surely seen her lantern. Terrified of what they might do to her, she ran to the lighthouse, pulled open the heavy wooden door, and ducked inside. She was trapped now, but there was no other place to go.

Lindsey slid the bolt into place but knew it would not hold the marauders out for long. She would have to barricade the door. Holding the lantern, she searched wildly for heavy objects to stack against the door. She saw two crates, a wooden bench, a barrel, and an anchor. She set the lantern on the stone steps and started with the heavy bench. If she could brace one end against the door and the other against the stairs....

"Help me." A voice echoed, thin and hollow, from the dark tower above. "Somebody, please, help me." It was the voice of a young woman. She sounded familiar, but the voice was so choked with sadness that she couldn't place it.

Lindsey, now wearing jeans and a sweater, stood frozen in darkness. She heard the wind whistling around the tower. The cries from above melted into heartrending sobs. The flame in the lantern had burned down to almost nothing.

"Who's there?"

The voice continued to sob.

"Hold on! I'm coming."

The threat outside the door forgotten, Lindsey raced up the stairs. The hard soles of her shoes sent echoes rolling into darkness. She climbed for what seemed like hours, but the tower continued to grow taller. Finally, when it seemed she would never reach the top, the light of her lantern brushed across a wooden door with a chain and padlock. Spider webs covered the surface.

"Help me!" the voice inside whimpered. "Please, help me."

"I'm here," Lindsey told her. "I'm here. Don't be afraid."

"Get out!"

A cold hand seized Lindsey's ankle.

She woke up with a cry and lay, gasping, on a couch a strange room. The muscles in her legs ached. Lindsey realized as she was sitting up that she was in a hospital room. Street lamps burned over the parking lot outside. Their pale light glowed feebly through plastic blinds. The rain had stopped. Shadow lay sleeping in a hospital bed, her heartbeat registering on instruments joined by wires to electrodes taped to her thin chest.

Even though the dream had ended, Lindsey was still angry over her inability to save the woman in the tower. If she had only had a lug wrench, a crowbar, or even an ordinary hammer.... As Lindsey stood over Shadow's sleeping body, her concern for the unseen dream-woman was replaced by her more immediate concern for the girl in the hospital bed. Without the vampire makeup, she looked young and even innocent. Freckles, so light they might have been airbrushed, gently spotted her cheeks and the bridge of her nose. Lindsey went to the bathroom and then took a walk down the hall. Neal, Jolene, and Todd were asleep in the waiting room. Lindsey passed them and walked down to the maternity ward. She hoped to catch a glimpse of the newborns, but the blinds to the nursery were closed. She bought a soda at one of the vending machines and returned to Shadow's room. A nurse was checking her temperature and blood pressure.

"I'm thirsty," Shadow said. Lindsey poured a glass of ice water from the pitcher on her nightstand and gave it to her.

"How do you feel?" Lindsey asked after the nurse left.

"Okay, I guess."

"It looks like you're going to live after all," Lindsey said with uneasy brightness.

"Maybe," Shadow said, "but don't be too sure."

Lindsey lowered the rail, took Shadow's hand, and sat on the bed beside her.

"Why do you say that?"

"Just something I feel."

"You said spirits had spoken to you. What did you mean?"

"Just something I feel." Her voice was fainter this time. Lindsey held her hand as she drifted off to sleep. Her heart continued to beat.

Chapter 5: Dinner With Bigfoot

Breathing threats of lawsuits, Shadow's mother arrived at the hospital early the next morning. Finally convinced that Neal's church was neither responsible for Shadow's injuries nor wealthy enough to be worth a lawsuit, she gathered information about her daughter's attackers, collected Shadow, and left.

Lindsey and Jolene spent most of the morning at the coffee shop drinking cappuccinos to stay awake. Just before lunch, the bell rang and the door swung open. Neal and Todd walked in.

"How did it go?" Jolene asked.

"They weren't so tough without their paint guns," Neal said. "Especially when they were afraid we might press charges. I told them Shadow's mom was the one they should worry about."

"They don't know anything about Christianity," Todd said. "They've mostly been conditioned by media stereotypes."

"And their parents," Neal said. "Anti-establishment types. 'Organized religion is of the devil. Oh, I forgot. There is no devil.' Listen, I've got to visit some people at the hospital. Some of our stuff is still on Leo's patio. Lindsey, could you go with Todd and help him pack it up?"

"I can handle the heavy lifting," Todd said.

"I'm stronger than I look," Lindsey said.

"Body odor isn't everything," Neal quipped

"You...!"

"Sorry. We used to say that when I was in junior high. Sometimes I regress."

"Space was in here earlier," Jolene said. "He asked if you were coming back anytime soon."

"Probably out of cigarettes," Neal said. "If he comes back, just give him a couple of bucks. No more than a couple, though. I'd better get going."

* * *

Leo had packed the party supplies into three plastic storage containers and stacked them against the back wall of his porch. It didn't take Lindsey and Todd but five minutes to load them into the backseat of Todd's Honda.

"What are you doing tonight?" Todd asked as they were riding back to the coffee shop.

Lindsey was speechless for a moment.

"It's not like that," he said. "I know you're engaged. I just need a favor. I'm shooting a documentary film. I set up an appointment to interview a guy in Seaside tonight, and my cameraman bailed on me this morning. I'll do most of the shooting myself, but I need somebody to handle the shots I'm in."

"I'd like to help you," she said, "but I've never done anything like that before."

"That's okay," he said. "You're an artist. I figure you at least understand about framing shots and all."

"I'm not sure. I really don't want to mess this up for you."

"There's really nothing to it," he said. "The camera will be mounted on a tripod. The main thing we'll need to do is make sure the lighting is right and the camera is turned on. I'll do a sound test before the shoot."

"I don't know," she said. "Are you sure you wouldn't rather have somebody more experienced?"

"I've called everybody I know," he said. "If you can't do it, I'm going to have to postpone the shoot."

"No pressure."

"I didn't mean it like that. If you can't do it, I'll just call the guy and reschedule the shoot. I can probably move it to sometime later in the week. I really do think you can do this, though."

"Okay," she said. "Why not? It sounds fun."

"All right. Great. I'll be there around six."

***

Lindsey was sitting in the sunroom with Mrs. Cutler when the doorbell rang. Lindsey leaped to her feet.

"That's Todd," she said. "I've got to go."

"Sit down, dear," Mrs. Cutler said. "You mustn't look too eager."

Lindsey started to protest.

"Cornelia will bring him," Mrs. Cutler said. "Sit."

Lindsey sighed. "Yes, ma'am."

"Now," Mrs. Cutler said, "sit back. Relax. They really don't teach young ladies anything these days, do they?"

"I'm not into games," Lindsey said.

"Sincerity is an admirable trait," Mrs. Cutler said. "So is patience. When a young lady is dancing, she must let the gentleman lead."

"But, it's not even a date," Lindsey said. "I'm engaged. He just needed a favor, and I'm helping him out."

Mrs. Cutler didn't respond. Lindsey gazed out at the ocean, trying to wait patiently. A moment later she heard footsteps in the hall. She turned and saw Todd following Cornelia with a look of sheepish amusement on his face.

"Come in, young man," Mrs. Cutler said. "Take a seat."

"Yes, Mrs. Cutler "

Todd started to take a seat beside Lindsey.

"Over here," Mrs. Cutler said. "Beside me."

"Sorry."

Properly chastised, Todd sat down beside Mrs. Cutler.

"Now, young man," Mrs. Cutler said, "before I release Miss Holland to your care, there are some things you should know. Since Miss Holland is staying with me, I consider it my responsibility to look after her wellbeing. If you want to be her escort, you'll do it according to my rules. Is that clearly understood?"

Todd nodded. Lindsey started to protest but thought better of it.

"When you come to pick her up," Mrs. Cutler said, "you will come inside the house and present yourself like a young gentleman. Sitting in the driveway and honking your horn is not acceptable. I assume you know about opening doors and that sort of thing, so I won't lecture you about that. You will bring Miss Holland back home by eleven o'clock or, if delayed, you will call and explain the circumstances. You will return her home in the same condition she was in when you picked her up. You will escort her to the door. If the nature of your relationship changes, and she allows you to kiss her goodnight, you will do it in a chaste and respectful manner."

Lindsey felt the heat rising in her face. She wanted to bury her face in her hands but fought the urge.

Todd waited to see if there were any further instructions.

"That's all," Mrs. Cutler said dismissively. "Have a good time."

"Yes, ma'am," Todd said gravely.

Cornelia followed as Todd led Lindsey down the hall and out to his Honda. She stood on the porch and watched as they pulled away. As soon as the house was out of sight, they both burst into laughter.

"I'm sorry about that," Lindsey said. "I'm so embarrassed. I had no idea she was going to do that."

"It's okay," Todd said. "She must really like you, to be that protective of you."

Gravel cracked beneath the tires as the vehicle wound its way down the curving road.

"I don't know if it's that so much as the way she was brought up," Lindsey said.

"I'm sure that's part of it," Todd said, "but I think it's more than just that. I think you're really special to her."

"Maybe."

The narrow road ahead was swathed in the shadows of Douglas firs.

"I really do appreciate you going with me," Todd said. "I've already had to reschedule twice."

"You said you're making a documentary film?"

"Yes."

"What's the subject?" Lindsey said.

"Marriage, dating, and sexuality."

Lindsey's eyes widened.

"Just kidding. Actually, it's about people's belief in the paranormal. You know, ghosts, monsters, and aliens. The Pacific Northwest is full of stories like that."

"I knew about the Bigfoot stories, but I didn't know about the rest."

"Mount Rainier was the site of the first flying saucer sighting," he said. "The whole modern UFO craze started out there."

"I didn't realize that."

"There are also a number of allegedly haunted houses."

"What's your angle? Do you really believe in Bigfoot, aliens, and ghosts?"

"I'm really not sure," he said, "but that's not the point."

"What is the point?"

"The point is that people will pay money to see films about the paranormal."

She wasn't sure whether he was serious or not.

"Okay," he said. "I admit the possibility of producing a movie people are actually interested in does have its appeal. I spent a lot of time on a documentary about glassblowing, but the theater was mostly empty."

"Glassblowing? Are you serious."

"Totally serious," he raised his right hand. "I even got a grant to go to Venice and interview some of the glassblowers there."

"That's cool."

"Oh, it was amazing. I got some of the best pictures. The production won first place in three different film festivals."

"But the theater was empty?"

"Mostly empty. My parents, some friends, and a few other film students and teachers showed up. That was about it."

"I bet you were disappointed. I'd like to see it, if you've got a copy."

"I'll give you a copy," he said. "I have three boxes full of DVDs in my closet."

They had reached the gate at the bottom of the mountain. It creaked open, and then they drove through. Todd waited for a moment before pulling out into the highway.

"So, you're doing a story on ghosts and monsters?"

"And aliens."

"And aliens. What's your angle? Those stories are on TV all the time."

"You mean why do another one? Glad you asked. I believe those stories serve a purpose in our lives, and they teach us something about ourselves."

"What do they teach us?"

"They show us we still have a hunger for the awesome. We used to think magic was everywhere. Magic made the sun come up. Fertility gods made the plants grow. Comets and eclipses were signs in the heavens. Now all of that has been explained. It's just nature doing what nature does. With Darwin's theory of evolution in place, not even creation itself is magic anymore."

"Do you believe Darwin's theory?"

"Parts of it, sure. I don't know about the rest. I mean, I think God was involved, but I'm not sure about the mechanics. But, you see what I'm saying, though?"

"I think so."

"Answer me this: what's the difference between seeing Bigfoot and just seeing an ordinary animal like a gorilla or a humpback whale? I mean, those used to be legends, but now we know they're real animals. They're still impressive to see, but not like before. Once we proved that they were just flesh-and-blood creatures, some of the awesomeness just went away. Why do you think that is?"

"I never really thought about it."

"And, what about this: some behavioral scientists think emotions like love are just the result of chemicals in our brains. They drive us to reproduce and protect our young. Basically, they're just evolution's way of keeping the species from coming to a dead end."

"That's cold."

"Isn't it?" he said. "Cold and clinical. It's called Reductionism. All of life, everything that makes life meaningful, dissected and laid out on an autopsy table. It makes a certain amount of sense, I admit, but it's not a world you could really live in."

"No," she said. "It isn't. And this is what your movie is about?"

"Partly. The thirst for the awesome, the desire to see something wonderful, even if it's scary, is a powerful drive. Part of the appeal of a good ghost story is gathering around a fire with friends on a dark night and speculating about what might lie beyond the reach of that little circle of light. In a strange sort of way, it's kind of cozy."

"So, you think it's good that people are interested in ghosts and aliens?"

"I think everybody's curious about the unknown, and I don't really think that's a bad thing. Sometimes it can be downright destructive, though. You should see some of the cults we have around here. Even with God out of the picture, our thirst for the awesome remains. We try to live in a world of logic, but we still know something is missing."

"I heard you tell Jolene you used to be an atheist. Is that what changed your mind? Your thirst for the awesome?"

"I'm not sure. I used to take part in discussions in Neal's coffee house. I enjoyed taking their arguments apart and all that."

"You don't seem like someone who would like to argue."

"I like to ask questions. That's what good interviewers do. I asked a lot of questions. Some of the answers were pretty weak, but some of them made me think."

"And that's why you're a Christian?"

"Partly," he said, "but I'm not sure how much of it was the answers and how much of it was the people themselves. There was something about them that made me *want* to believe, even if I couldn't be sure whether it was true or not. Finally, there was a kind of tipping point where faith was stronger than doubt."

Moments later, they pulled into the parking lot of a rustic building with a big, hand-lettered sign: *Sasquatch Steak and Ale*. A wooden statue of a huge, apelike creature guarded the parking lot like a tribal totem.

"Sasquatch Steak and Ale?" Lindsey stared at the sign. "This is the place you picked to do the interview?"

"Good visuals," Todd said. "That's important in a visual medium. And, believe it or not, they've got the best steaks in town." A look of concern crossed his face. "Are you a vegetarian?"

"No. I'm too much of a Texan for that, I'm afraid."

"The trail behind the building leads to the site of an alleged Bigfoot sighting," Todd explained. "That's why the owner bought this building, remodeled it, and located his restaurant here." He opened the door. "I'll get the lights. You can carry the camera."

They got out of the car and went around to the trunk. Todd opened it with a key, pulled out two nylon shoulder bags, and passed them to Lindsey. Then he wrestled a big, black, plastic case out of the trunk and set it on the ground.

"That looks heavy," Lindsey said.

"Mostly just bulky," he said, then slammed the trunk. "Let's get some pictures of the outside while we've still got the sun. It will give you practice using the camera."

"Okay."

He took the longer of the shoulder bags from Lindsey, unzipped it, and pulled out a tripod. Lindsey waited as he extended the legs and locked them into place. Then he took the second bag, unpacked the camera, attached it to the tripod, and flipped open the viewfinder. He guided Lindsey as she shot images of the Bigfoot statue and the sign.

A bell rang as they stepped into the restaurant's lobby. On the wall beside them hung a laminated map peppered with pushpins. Strands of yarn connected each pin to a newspaper article. The headlines all mentioned "Bigfoot," "Sasquatch," or some other kind of apelike creature. Directly in front of them a furry, life-sized manikin pushed its way through a clump of artificial bushes. Beneath its gaze sat a rough-hewn lectern and a rustic sign with the words "Please Wait to Be Seated" seared into the wood. A pretty teenage girl in a hot pink "Sasquatch Steak and Ale" shirt and denim shorts stepped up to the counter.

"Hi," she said. "Table for two?"

"Actually," Todd said, "we've got an appointment with Mr. Monroe. Tell him Todd Wilkes is here."

"I'll be right back."

"Let's get some shots of the lobby," Todd said. "We'd better unpack the lights. It's pretty dark in here." There were no other guests waiting to be seated. Todd unpacked a lamp and quickly assembled it. He plugged an extension cord into a socket on the wall and took shots of the Sasquatch manikin and the map. He was still shooting when the girl returned. She waited until he lowered the camera.

"Come on back. He's waiting for you."

Todd passed the camera to Lindsey.

"I'll get the light," he said. He turned to the waitress. "I'll come back for the case."

"Okay. Just put it beside the bench so it won't be in the way."

Todd and Lindsey followed the girl into a dimly lit room with artificial trees and murals of dark forests along the walls. The tables were covered with checkered tablecloths. Lanterns hung above each one. In one corner sat a burly, middle-aged man in a flannel shirt. His salt-and-pepper hair was pulled back into a ponytail.

"Thanks for meeting with us, Mr. Monroe," Todd said. "I'm Todd, and this is Lindsey."

Mr. Monroe stood and shook their hands. His fingers were thick and rough to the touch.

"Mr. Monroe owns this restaurant," Todd explained.

"Kind of a retirement job," the man explained. "I spent my career on logging crews. I broke my back falling out of a tree and decided it was time for safer work." He laughed. "You two sit down. What can I get for you? How about a steak with a baked potato and salad?"

"You don't want to do the interview first?"

"Let's talk first."

"Okay."

"Go take care of that order, McKenzie," he told the girl who had escorted them. "And bring out a pitcher of beer, too, while you're at it." He gestured to Todd and Lindsey. "Sit down, you two. Let's talk."

They sat.

"So," Mr. Monroe said, "you're doing a film. Is this like one of those reality TV shows?"

"Not exactly," Todd said. "I like to think of myself as an artist who's really into helping people tell their stories. Story is one of the most powerful ways we communicate our culture and beliefs."

"And the weirder the story is, the better?"

"You could say that."

"Well, I've certainly told enough tall tales in my time, but the craziest one of all just happened to be true. Not that anybody believes me. A logger doesn't have the credibility of a PhD, and maybe I should count my blessings he doesn't have to. If a college professor had come back to work with a story like mine, he might not have kept his job for too long, if you know what I mean. But loggers—most people probably expect us to have been hit in the head a few times. Don't have any effect on the quality of your logs."

McKenzie came back with a pitcher of beer and a tray full of chilled mugs. She filled them and passed them around.

"But, you had an experience?"

"Oh, I've had a lot of experiences. You can believe that. You'd be amazed at what you can see and hear out in the woods at night when you're miles from civilization. I've heard plenty of stories around the campfire. You can chalk most of them up to imagination. A dark night and a little beer after a hard day's work can make you imagine all kinds of things. Most of them vanish when the sun comes up. That one experience, though—it wasn't like that."

"Let me set up the camera," Todd said, rising to his feet. "It sounds like you're warming up to this story, and I don't want to miss any of it."

"Okay. Suit yourself."

With Lindsey's help, he unpacked the camera and mounted it on a tripod. He placed a flat screen video monitor beside it, and set a light up in a corner.

"This is going to be bright," he warned Mr. Monroe. "Get ready." He switched it on.

"That *is* bright," Mr. Monroe said.

"Don't look directly into it. Give your eyes a little time to adjust."

"Got it."

Todd focused the camera on him, placed a microphone on the table, and let Lindsey take over as he sat down beside Mr. Monroe.

"Okay," he said. "You don't have to worry about this being perfect. Just relax and try to pretend the camera isn't here."

Mr. Monroe squinted into the light, started to talk, and forgot what he was saying.

"It's okay," Todd said. "Start again. You were telling us about something that had happened to you, an experience you'd had."

Mr. Monroe took a swallow of beer from one of the mugs on the table before him.

"I've seen a lot of things," he said. "Nothing quite like this, though."

He stared out into the dimly lit restaurant around him, but his eyes were focusing on another time and place.

"It was back in the seventies. My crew and I had spent the day cutting a logging road back into a section of forest that I swear no white man had ever seen. The trees were ancient and so tall it seemed almost unholy to kill them. I've cut down a lot of forests, but there was something different about that one. It almost seemed to have a life to it, and I kept getting the strangest feeling that we were being watched."

Lindsey watched his face on the monitor. His expression was serious, reflective.

"That night, we were lying around the fire in sleeping bags, and I kept thinking I heard something moving around out there in the dark. I started to wonder if somebody else had followed us out there, or if a grizzly was circling the camp to see if we had any food. The men started to get nervous. One of them snatched up a flashlight and shined it out into the darkness. It brushed across something big and hairy with eyes that glowed red when the lights hit it. Whatever it was vanished before we could get a good look at it. Some of the men said it was a bear, but the proportions were all wrong."

"How do you mean?" Todd asked.

"The legs were too long, for one thing. Bears have a long body and short legs, but that's not the impression I got. This thing was proportioned more like a man, but a whole lot bigger."

"How much bigger?"

"Eight or nine feet, maybe. It was big."

"But, it vanished before you could get a good look at it?"

"Right. All I got was a glance, and then it was gone. After that, we heard more movement out there in the dark. McMasters picked up a shotgun, fired out into the dark, and I heard something scream. I told him to stop shooting, that it might be a man. Then another scream answered back, and the woods filled up with the strangest howling I've ever heard. Then we heard glass breaking. McMasters started to take another shot, but Echohawk took the gun away from him. He said we had angered the spirits of the forest by violating their holy ground."

"Echohawk was Native American?"

"Right. Salish. He's from Canada. As I sat there and listened to the sounds around us, it was easy enough to believe. My heart was pounding in my chest. I spent the rest of the night sitting up with my back to the fire. I was never so glad to see the sun come up."

He raised his mug and took a swallow.

"When we got to where we'd parked the truck, the windows were all broken out, and there were footprints in the mud around the truck. They had five toes like a man, but they weren't human footprints. They were about twice the size of an ordinary man's foot, and the heel was large and out of proportion. We didn't have anything to make a casting, but I found a newspaper in the truck and traced it."

He spread a yellowed sheet of newsprint out on the table before him. Etched into it was the print of a huge humanoid foot.

"How about that?" he said. "Is that crazy enough for you?"

"Hold it up so I can get a picture of it."

He held it.

"Lindsey, are you getting this?"

Lindsey zoomed in closer. The outline was clearly visible.

"I've got it."

"Did you get any samples of hair or blood?" Todd asked.

"I didn't," Monroe said, "but one of the other men did. He was going to take it to a professor he knew at a university and get him to run tests on it. I never heard anything else about it."

"Who was this man?" Todd asked. "Do you think we could talk to him?"

"Not unless you're studying ghosts, too," Monroe said. "He's been dead for years. Shot to death by his old lady."

"That's too bad."

"Knowing him, he probably had it coming. It's still a shame, though."

"Is there anything else you remember about that night?"

"Yeah," he said. "Those things smelled really bad. I could smell that stink in the truck every time it rained."

"Do you still have the truck?"

"No. Sold it years ago."

"Mr. Monroe, I'd like to thank you for talking to us. Since we're here at the Sasquatch Steak and Ale, why don't you show us around?"

Moving the tripod and the lights, they shot footage throughout the restaurant. McKenzie, the waitress, told them about the Bigfoot Burger, the Bigfoot Bean Roll, and other delicacies. Mr. Monroe and Lindsey posed with the Bigfoot statue in the lobby. Mr. Monroe stood in front of the bulletin board and explained the map of Bigfoot sightings and newspaper articles.

As they neared the conclusion of the interview, Mr. Monroe led them back to the table where they had filmed him earlier.

"Is that everything you wanted?"

"Almost," Todd said. "We'll set back up. I want to ask you one more question."

They moved the lights and tripod again. Mr. Monroe and Todd sat back down.

"Okay," Todd said. "One last question."

"Is that a promise?"

"No. You might say something that makes me ask more questions."

"Hah. Fair enough."

"Are you ready?"

"Sure. Let's go."

Todd nodded to Lindsey. She switched from the pause setting to record. Todd watched the red light on the front of the camera. It stopped flashing.

"Thanks for talking to us, Mr. Monroe."

"My pleasure."

"There's one last question I'd like to ask you."

"Okay."

"Overall," Todd said, "would you say you're glad the experience happened or that you wish it had never taken place?"

"Well, I have gotten a lot of ribbing for the story. Some people just accuse me of lying to get attention. I suppose I can understand that. Before it happened to me, I'd probably have thought the same thing." He stopped and took a sip from his mug. "Am I glad it happened? Mostly I'd have to say 'Yes.'"

"Why?"

"Because I got a glimpse of something most people never get to. Maybe it's just some kind of ape we've never seen before, or maybe Echohawk's people are right. Maybe it's something more than flesh and blood, something from a reality we can't usually see. Maybe there's a door that only opens at certain times when everything is lined up just right, and we just happened to be there at one of those times. Who knows?" He stopped and waited. "Is that pretty much what you wanted?"

"That was perfect," Todd said.

"Great." Mr. Monroe stood. "I want to see this when you get it edited."

"I'll bring it by," Todd promised, also standing.

"Sit down, you two. I've got McKenzie bringing you a pair of steaks."

"Thanks. You didn't have to do that."

"It's my pleasure."

***

"Thanks," Lindsey said as they stopped in front of Mrs. Cutler's house. The porch light was on. "That was the most unusual evening I've had in a while."

"Unusual, huh?" Todd said. "In a good way, I hope."

"It was… different."

"Different. Right."

Lindsey got out of the car. Todd sighed and shook his head. He started to leave then remembered Mrs. Cutler's instructions.

"Wait," he said as he got out of the car. "Bigfoot could be lurking around out here."

Lindsey laughed and waited for Todd to catch up.

"Listen," Todd said. "I really do appreciate this. I owe you one."

"I think the steak was payment enough. Or maybe I owe you. When is the next shoot?"

"Friday. There's supposed to be a haunted castle across the bay from Seattle. You have to take a ferry to get there."

"Sounds interesting."

"A group of guys from a ghost hunters' society is holding a séance there. They're going to let me film it. You're welcome to come."

"Let me think about it."

"Oh," he said. "You're engaged. Hey, don't worry about that. My friend Drew is coming too. And there will be other people around once we get there, so it's not like we'll be spending the whole time alone."

"Let me think about it," she said again.

"I'll give you my cell number," he said.

"Okay."

She unlocked the door with a key. He stood there watching her. She smiled back at him, opened the door, and started inside.

"Good night," she said.

"Good night," he said as Lindsey pulled the door shut. Todd stood on the porch for a moment and then wandered back to his waiting car. Night insects sang in the darkness around him. Far below, he could hear the crashing of the waves.

"It's like they say," he mumbled to himself as he got in the car. "All of the best ones are taken."

***

Lindsey pulled the door closed behind her, sighed, and leaned against the door facing. A moment later she could hear him driving away.

"How was your evening?" Mrs. Cutler asked as Lindsey stepped into the sunrcom.

"Fine," she said. "Unusual."

"He seems like a fine young man."

"Yes, he does. I think I'd better get to bed," Lindsey said. "Good night, Mrs. Cutler."

"Good night, dear."

Chapter 6: Girls and Guys

"So, you and Todd went out last night," Jolene said. She scooped coffee grounds into a filter while Lindsey wiped down tables.

"It wasn't a date!" Lindsey snapped, her face coloring.

"I didn't say you went on a date," Jolene said, smiling at Lindsey's reaction. "I said you went *out*."

"It's the same thing."

"Forgive me! No speak English!"

"Your English is better than mine." Lindsey went back to wiping the table as Jolene closed the top of the coffee maker and filled a carafe with water. She poured it into the spout and flipped the power switch.

"How did it go?"

"Fine."

"What did you do?"

"We went to the Sasquatch Bar and Grill. He was doing an interview for one of his documentary films. His cameraman backed out on him at the last minute."

"He let you shoot the video?"

"Some of it."

The coffee maker began to hiss and rumble, and the shop filled with aroma. A dark stream of coffee trickled down into the carafe. Lindsey finished wiping down the tables and dropped the rag into the sink.

"I'm sorry I embarrassed you," Jolene said. "I think Todd is a very nice person. I don't know why he hasn't found anybody yet. It just takes some people longer, I guess, but I keep telling him God has somebody very special for him."

"People always tell single people that."

"You're right. He's probably tired of hearing it."

"I was just helping him with his video," Lindsey said. "That's all."

"That's fine."

"He's going to Seattle Friday for the next shoot. He said I could go if I wanted to see Seattle. There are other people going, so it wouldn't just be us alone together."

"What would your fiancé think?"

"He can be pretty possessive. That was one of our problems."

"What would you tell him about it?"

"Exactly what I told you. The truth. If he asked."

"How would you feel if it was the other way around? If you called him and he was helping one of his friends with a project, and she happened to be a girl?"

"Actually," she said, "he was visiting a girl in Dallas yesterday."

"Do you know her?"

"No. Her name's Jessie. He said he met her in law school."

"But, you don't know anything else about her?"

"No."

Jolene walked around the counter and started dusting off a bookcase. "What's your gut feeling about this? Do you trust him?"

"I want to trust him, but I keep thinking maybe I'm too trusting."

"Has he ever given you reason not to trust him?"

"I don't know."

"And you're about to *marry* him?"

Lindsey felt her face growing hot.

"I'm sorry," Jolene said. "You don't have to answer that. Just think about it. If you're going to spend the rest of your life with somebody.... Just think about it."

"I will."

"What about this project Todd's working on? Can I ask about that?"

"Sure. He's interviewing people who claim to have had unusual experiences."

"What kinds of experiences?"

"Paranormal. You know, ghosts, aliens, and Bigfoot."

"The occult?"

"Not that so much. I guess it could get into that, but if you're thinking about witches and exorcisms, that's not really his focus."

"Who did he interview at the Sasquatch Bar and Grill?"

"Mr. Monroe, the owner. He says he had an encounter with Bigfoot once. Actually, it was a whole group of Bigfoots—I mean Bigfeet. Sasquatches. That's what inspired him to open the restaurant."

"What did you think about him?" Jolene asked. "Did he seem credible?"

"I thought so," Lindsey responded. "He didn't see it clearly. He just said he saw a glimpse of something. And he said he heard noises in the dark and found footprints in the mud. He said one of his friends was going to take hair and blood samples to a university somewhere, but nothing ever came of it. I guess that was the most suspicious part of it. If I had evidence like that, I don't think I would let anything happen to it."

Jolene sat on a stool. "Have you ever had an experience like that?" she asked. "Something you can't explain?"

Lindsey thought about the man in the road and the pressure she had felt on the bed the first night she had spent in the Cutler house. A chill ran up her spine.

"I'm not sure. What about you?"

"I think I may have seen an angel once."

Lindsey scanned Jolene's face to see if she was joking. "Really? You saw an angel?"

"I don't know for sure," Jolene said. "I'm sure Todd's teachers at the university could come up with plenty of natural explanations for what I saw. I've thought of them myself. Somehow, though, they just don't ring true to me."

"What happened?"

"Have you heard of the Vietnamese boat people?"

Lindsey shook her head.

"It happened in the mid-eighties," Jolene told her. "You probably weren't even born then."

"Not until eighty-eight."

"Wow!" Jolene said. "I really feel old now. Thanks."

"You look wonderful," Lindsey said. "I hope I look half as great as you when I'm as old as... when I'm your age."

"Stop," Jolene said. "You're not helping."

"I thought Asians valued age."

"I've been in America too long."

"What happened to you?"

Just then, the bell rang and a man in a business suit walked in.

"Good morning," Jolene said as she rose to her feet. "What can I get for you?"

"Coffee," he said. "Kona blend. And an espresso bean brownie."

"Got it. Anything else?"

"Does it cost anything to use your computers?"

"Dollar an hour."

"I won't need it for that long," he said. "I just want to look something up."

"No charge then," Jolene whispered. "Just don't tell my husband. He's a tyrant."

"Not a word," the stranger said. Moments later, he was sitting at the computer and sipping coffee.

"All right," Lindsey said. "What were you about to tell me? It was about the boat people."

Jolene nodded. "I was eight years old when my older brothers decided we would climb into a fishing boat and sail to America."

"Are you serious?"

"Life was hard there. The Americans had pulled out, and the Communists had taken over. A lot of people were leaving the country in boats. Whole families of people just packed into fishing boats. The Americans called us 'boat people.'"

"And your brothers thought they could sail to America?"

She nodded. "They packed all the food they could find—or steal. It wasn't enough. The Pacific is a lot bigger than you might think. By the time we ran out of food, we were completely lost. My brothers managed to catch fish, and that helped for a while. Then we ran out of fresh water. You can't imagine what it's like to be that thirsty, to float for days with the sun beating down on you and nothing to drink."

"What about the sea water?"

"We were told it would make you go mad. Since then, I've heard that if you drink a little of it every day before you get dehydrated, you can survive that way. I didn't know it then. Actually, I tried to drink the water, but my brothers wouldn't let me. They would slap my hands, and I would cry. I finally got so dehydrated that I couldn't even form tears. The moisture in my eyes was pasty. So was the spit in my mouth. My lips were dry and cracked. Those were the longest, most miserable days I've ever had to live through. Sometimes I still have nightmares of being in that boat, lost at sea."

"There weren't any islands?"

"No land at all. Just bottomless ocean from one horizon to the other for days on end. I remember lying under a tarp in the bottom of the boat, too weak to talk or move. One day, I woke up and saw a man standing in the boat, adjusting the sail. He was a white man with blond hair, and I thought he must be an American. He could just as easily have been German or Norwegian, but we were sailing to America, and I thought we had finally gotten there. I tried to talk, but I couldn't say anything. Finally, I just drifted off to sleep.

"A few hours later, we were spotted by a Navy ship heading for Guam. Later, after I learned to speak English, I talked to one of the men who had rescued my brothers and me. He said that if we hadn't been at that exact spot at that moment, they would have missed us, and we would have kept right on drifting into empty ocean. I asked him about the man I saw on the boat, but he said there was no one in his crew who had looked like that. I don't remember seeing a boat, either. It was as if the man had just stepped out of nowhere. Then again, I was pretty sick. My memories might have gotten confused."

"But, you don't believe that's what happened?"

"No," she said. "I believe that man was there, and that God sent him to save us."

The bell on the door rang as someone walked in.

"'Every time a bell rings, an angel gets his wings,'" Lindsey recited. "Sorry. It just reminded me."

"I love that movie," Jolene remarked.

"Where's the preacher?" Space had returned.

"Hi, Space," Jolene said. "He's not here right now. Is there anything I can do for you?"

"No," he said as he turned around and left.

***

"So, you and Lindsey went out last night?" Neal said. He and Todd were sitting in a seafood restaurant overlooking the Columbia River.

"No," Todd said. He moved his pasta around with a fork. "Not exactly. She's engaged."

"Then what did happen, exactly?" Neal tore open a packet of sweetener and poured it into his tea.

"She was helping me with a project. I needed someone to operate the camera."

"Why didn't you call me?"

"She's an artist, for one thing, and I thought she might just want to see the town."

"Right."

Todd took a long swallow of soda.

"What do you think of her?"

"She's great. Easy to talk to. Easy to get along with." He peeled one of his shrimp.

"Easy on the eyes."

"That, too."

He dipped the shrimp in cocktail sauce and stuck it into his mouth.

"What else? Honestly."

Todd chewed for a moment and then swallowed.

"Well," he said. "She takes her faith seriously, but she's not a legalist. And she's kind of hard to read."

"How do you mean?"

"She's so polite, you can't tell if she really likes you or agrees with you or if she's just being nice."

"That's my Lindsey. She's a Southern belle in the best possible sense. What else? A little bland, maybe? A tad conventional?" Neal picked up a shrimp and started peeling.

"I wouldn't really say that." Todd frowned. "Well, maybe a little. I wouldn't use the word 'bland,' though. It has a negative connotation. She seems like the kind of girl you don't meet much anymore. You know, the classic nice girl you see in the old black-and-white movies. Is she really as innocent as she seems?"

"Yeah. Pretty much."

"Pretty much?"

"Well, nobody's perfect, but Lindsey's about as close as they come—other than Jolene, of course. What does she think about all this stuff you study?"

"She was a good sport about the Bigfoot study," he said. "She did say the experience was unusual." He lifted his glass. The ice clinked against the side. It was empty. He set it back down with a thump.

"What if she wasn't engaged?" Neal asked. "What would you do then?"

"Same thing I'm doing now. Get to know her as a friend and just see where it went."

"You wouldn't man up and ask her for a real date?"

"I kissed dating goodbye. Remember?"

"That's a spiritual excuse for not having any stones."

"Are you sure you're a preacher?"

A waitress came by and brought Todd another soda. "Do you need anything else?" she asked.

"I think we're fine," Neal said. "Do you need anything, Todd?"

"No, I'm okay."

"Well, call me if you need anything."

"Thanks."

Todd took another swallow of soda.

"How did you and Jolene meet?"

"We were college students on a summer missions project in Hawaii."

"You did summer missions work in Hawaii?"

"Yeah," Neal said. "It was great. It was hard work, though. Christians are a minority there."

"And you started dating on the mission field?"

"We weren't allowed to date each other. It was against the rules, so we had to keep it on the 'down low' until the summer was over. There's nothing that makes people want to date each other like telling them they're not allowed to."

"In Hawaii and not allowed to date. That's almost sadistic." Todd joked as he filled his mouth with pasta.

"And necessary when you're dealing with a bunch of hormonal college students. Imagine sending your daughter to Hawaii with a bunch of other students."

"Yeah." Todd swallowed. "I guess there is that side of it "

"It really wasn't that bad. We had a lot of fun. That was a great group of people."

"So, you met in a community and got to know each other without the pressures of being on a date."

"Well, yeah. By the time we started dating, we knew we were pretty serious about it." Neal peeled another shrimp, dipped it, and popped it into his mouth.

"That actually sounds like a better way to start out," Todd remarked.

"I think it is."

"That's what I was trying to say earlier about just being friends and getting to know somebody."

"I think you're just being a wimp. Be a tiger, man. Step up to the plate."

"Whatever."

"Do you and Lindsey have any more of these homework assignments planned?"

"I asked her to go to Seattle Friday."

"Okay."

"Other people are going. It's not a date."

"Sure. Of course not. What did she say?"

"She said she'd think about it. I don't think she was really comfortable with the idea. And she'd have to ask you for the day off."

Neal didn't say anything for a moment.

"You're right," Todd said. "I probably shouldn't have even asked her."

"I didn't say that."

"She's trying to be faithful to her fiancé, and I'm just making it hard for her."

"Maybe."

"Do you know this guy she's engaged to?"

"I met him when he was in high school."

"What's he like?"

"Football player. Big man on campus."

"He was in your youth group?"

"He came some, mostly with Lindsey. I'm not sure how committed he was."

"Did he seem like a nice guy?"

"He was okay."

"And now he's going to be a lawyer."

"His dad's a district judge. The family's pretty well off."

"A rich lawyer. Thanks for warning me."

"Intimidated by the competition?"

"I'm not competing. She's engaged. She's made up her mind."

"Right. Now, what are you investigating in Seattle? UFOs? Zombies?"

"A séance."

Chapter 7: A Day at the Mansion

Thursday morning, Lindsey had a few hours to herself. After two days of working with the youth, she desperately needed some time to read, pray, listen to music, and recharge. She called home and talked to her father for a while. Then, when she saw her pasty complexion in the mirror, she decided to get some sun. Oregon was experiencing a heat wave, but the air was still cool by Texas standards. Lindsey changed into the swimsuit she had thought she would need before she'd found out how cold the Oregon beaches were. She pulled on an oversized T-shirt and tossed a book, some sunscreen, a towel, shades, and an MP3 player into a woven tote bag. She saw no sign of Mrs. Cutler, Caitlyn, or Cornelia as she made her way through the house and out to the back patio. There was a lounge chair on the patio, but, judging from the mildew, it hadn't been used in a while. She rinsed it off at a faucet, but the black specks remained. It would have to do.

She dragged the lounge chair and bag to an isolated strip of lawn in the rose garden behind the gazebo. The spot was perfect. She was about fifty feet from a steep bluff that dropped down into the ocean, and the view was exquisite. She could see the waves crashing over the rocks, the lighthouse, the ocean's shifting shades of aquamarine and blue as it receded into the distance. She could hear the waves and the cries of seagulls. The spot was also secluded. She would be invisible from the house, and she doubted anyone could see her from the ocean. Satisfied with her privacy, Lindsey stripped away the T-shirt, stuffed it into the bag, and pulled out a tube of suntan lotion. She wiped it onto her face and ears, her pale midriff and back, onto her long legs, and under her arms. Satisfied with the coverage and smelling like coconut oil, she put on her sunshades and the earphones to her MP3 player, then stretched out beneath the sun's gentle rays.

She prayed silently for a while and then let her thoughts drift.

***

Lindsey woke up suddenly. Something was wrong. She had no idea how long she had been sleeping in the sun or what had jolted her awake.

She sat up and swung around. A cry escaped from her throat before she could clamp down on it. There was a man standing in the shadows of the gazebo, glaring down at her. He was a big man with a long, dark beard and a fearsome glare. It was the man she had seen standing in the road the first night they had arrived. Or was it? The spectre she had seen that night had been deathly pale and had the blind eyes of a corpse. This was a living man.

"I'm sorry," she said, not really sure what she was apologizing for. There was no reason for him to glare at her unless her lack of modesty had offended him. "I didn't know there was anyone else around."

The man said nothing. He just stood and stared at her. Lindsey looked down at her sweat-soaked body and felt uneasy. She turned away from the stranger and fumbled through her bag for her T-shirt. Her hands, she realized, were shaking. Fumbling, she pulled the shirt down over her head and cried out as her sunglasses and earphones were wrenched away. She had forgotten to remove them.

Lindsey's fear suddenly turned to burning anger. Who was this man, and what right did he have to glare at her that way? She had done nothing wrong. If she had offended him, it had been an accident, and surely he knew that. With knitted brows and clenched fists she swung around.

The gazebo was empty.

The stranger had vanished as suddenly as he had appeared. Lindsey exhaled and dropped her face to her hands. When she looked up again, she realized the golden sun had vanished. The sky was shrouded in clouds, and she was starting to feel cold. *So much for the perfect morning.* Lindsey packed away her towel, sunglasses, and MP3 player, dragged the chaise lounge back to the patio, and went inside.

"Well, good morning." Caitlyn was standing there dressed in the same brightly-colored scrubs she had been wearing the last time Lindsey had seen her.

"Hi," Lindsey said.

"Are you all right?"

"I'm okay. There was a man outside. I don't think he expected to find a sunbather on the lawn."

"What did he look like?"

"He had a beard."

"A long, black beard?"

"Yes."

"Probably Teach, the caretaker," Caitlyn said. "You mustn't worry about him. He's a bit odd."

"But I think I offended him. I spoke to him, but he just stood and glared at me. I wanted to sink into the ground."

"Don't pay any attention to him. He's like that with everyone. We don't have many guests here, and he's used to having the place to himself."

"I'll try not to bother him."

"Don't worry about him," Caitlyn insisted. "You're a guest here. His bad manners are nobody's fault but his own."

"Are you on your way to work?"

"Not for a few hours yet. What about you? Are you working at the center?"

"Neal gave me the morning off."

"I was about to go for a stroll," Caitlyn said. "Would you like to come along?"

"Sure," Lindsey said. "If—well, it looked like it was about to rain."

"It rains a lot in Oregon, I think we'll be fine, though."

"Let me change," Lindsey said.

"I'll wait on the patio."

Moments later, Lindsey emerged from the house in jeans and a sweatshirt. Caitlyn led her down a steep hill covered with tall grass and wildflowers. The path at their feet was rocky

"Watch your step," Caitlyn warned. "It's easy to turn an ankle here."

"I'll be careful. Where are we going?"

"There's a path down here. It leads to the water's edge."

A path opened in the wall of trees before them. Through the trees to the left, Lindsey could see that it wound along the edge of a high bluff that overlooked the ocean. Sometimes she could feel the spray of the ocean as it slammed into the rocks below. They walked for nearly twenty minutes, until they reached an opening in the trees. The trail before them split, with one rocky fork tracing a jagged path down the side of a cliff and the other continuing along the ridge. The ocean's rugged shore lay about fifty feet beneath them. A wall of water collided with a slab of rock and sprayed the hillside. Droplets blew across Lindsey's face like pellets of ice.

"Follow me," Caitlyn said, "but be careful."

Placing her hands on the side of the hill to steady herself, Caitlyn made her way down the first few meters of the steep path. Crouching, Lindsey followed her. Grasping rocks and tree roots, they made their way to the rocky shore below. The battered remains of a wooden dock and a weathered fishing boat awaited them there. The lighthouse Lindsey had seen from Mrs. Cutler's sunroom loomed close now. Scarcely a thousand feet of raging water and jagged rocks separated it from the rocky beach. A winding spit of land, like the spine of a dragon, connected the island beneath the lighthouse to the shore. Waves crashed against it, and Lindsey could feel the cold droplets from where she stood. Any thoughts she'd had about venturing out to the old lighthouse quickly vanished. Lindsey realized, as she stood at ocean level, that viewing the lighthouse from the mansion had not given her a true sense of its scale. The old structure had looked small from the house, but now Lindsey could see that it was much taller than she had believed—taller and more dilapidated. A metal door hung loose on its hinges, and the spray of the ocean was starting to scour away the paint.

"Have you ever been to the lighthouse?" Lindsey asked.

Caitlyn nodded.

"Could we go sometime?"

"It's dangerous," Caitlyn said. "Haunted, you might say."

"What do you mean?"

Caitlyn smiled enigmatically. "I'll tell you sometime, but not today. Not here."

A cold droplet of water tumbled from the sky, rolled down Lindsey's collar, and slithered down her spine. She shivered involuntarily.

"Is that rain? I think I just felt a drop."

Caitlyn closed her eyes, spread her arms, and stood with her head back. She was beautiful with her long, slender neck, light complexion, and strawberry blonde hair.

"I think it was rain," she said after a moment.

Lindsey felt another cold drop, then another, then another. Bullets of cold crystal riddled the rocks around them. Caitlyn stood for a moment, luxuriating in the icy shower. Then she turned, smiling, to Lindsey.

"Come with me," she said. She sprinted along the shore, her feet splashing through puddles between the rocks. Lindsey followed. She tried, at first, not to get her feet wet but soon tired of the effort. Caitlyn edged her way around a large rock that hung out into the ocean and vanished from sight as the face of the cliff turned sharply. Lindsey followed. As she rounded the corner, she could see a deep indentation in the side of the cliff, a deep indentation and a cave. Caitlyn stood, smiling, in the shadows.

"Come on in," she said.

Lindsey trudged carefully along the rocky ledge. Her back was to the wall. A circular pool of water reflected Lindsey's own face. Then a blast of ocean water washed through it.

Lindsey edged on into the shadows of the cave. Caitlyn had seated herself on a large rock just inside the entrance.

"Have a seat," she said. "We'll be fine. The water doesn't come up this high, not even at high tide."

Lindsey seated herself on the smooth stone. A burst of ocean water tumbled through the channel below her and lost itself in the subterranean darkness behind her. The echoes of the waves whispered from the shadows like voices from the distant past. When Lindsey's eyes adjusted to the darkness, she could see names and initials spray-painted crudely across the cave's walls. Charred embers from a campfire lay a few feet away. A crushed beer can lay between a large rock and the cave's wall.

"This place has become something of a hangout for the local college students, I'm afraid," Caitlyn said. "I don't mind them coming here, but I wish they would clean up after themselves."

"I know," Lindsey said, her finger brushing across one of the spray-paint inscriptions.

JOSH N TINA 4-EVER

"I wonder if Josh and Tina found true happiness," Caitlyn mused. "Sometimes I wonder if anybody does."

"I think so," Lindsey said. "My parents still love each other. I think they're happy most of the time. As much as anybody."

Caitlyn nodded. "My parents aren't around anymore. They were good people, though, and I think they must've loved each other. It's so easy for people to talk about forever when they're in love with each other, but life is so temporary."

"How did you lose them?" Lindsey asked.

Caitlyn sighed. "Another story for another time and place."

"I'm sorry. I shouldn't have asked. It's not any of my business."

"Don't be silly," Caitlyn said. "There's nothing wrong with asking questions. I've been known to be a bit nosy myself. I suppose I should tend to my own business, but other people's business is much more interesting."

Lindsey laughed.

"So, tell me about yourself. I notice you're wearing an engagement ring."

"There's not much to tell," Lindsey said. "I'm getting married this fall."

"Tell me about him."

"Well, we've been dating since junior high."

"Your parents let you date in junior high?"

"Not much," Lindsey said. "We did go to a church Valentine's banquet together in seventh grade, though. And a hayride. We didn't get to go on our first non-chaperoned date until we were high-school juniors."

"You still haven't told me about the man himself."

"His name is Pack."

"Pack?"

"Jason Packard. Everybody calls him Pack. He's studying to be a lawyer. His father is a district judge."

"That's wonderful. You must be excited."

"I am. Well, some of the time."

"What's wrong?"

"I'm not sure. Lately, it seems like I'm having doubts about our relationship. It's probably just pre-wedding nerves."

"Maybe. Maybe not. Is there anything specific that worries you?"

"Not really. It's mostly just a feeling I have."

"Is he good to you?"

"Oh, yes. Yes, he's always been good to me. Well, almost always. But nobody's perfect all the time, are they?"

"No, I suppose not."

"He drank some when he started college. I guess that's normal for guys. We broke up for a while, and there were other girls. Sexual relationships. I never asked for details. As long as it's in the past, it doesn't really matter."

Caitlyn didn't comment.

"I guess that's normal. A lot of guys are like that when they go to college."

"It is common," Caitlyn said.

"We're not supposed to judge. We all sin, and we're all in need of forgiveness."

"Does it bother you? The things he did?"

Lindsey didn't answer. Another jet of water washed through the cave. Lindsey listened again to the ghostly rumblings in the blackness behind them.

"How far back does this cave go?"

"The Indians said it went all the way to the center of the earth," Caitlyn said. "That's why they stayed away from it."

"Really?"

"That was the legend." Caitlyn walked to the entrance and peered out into the pale light beyond. "It looks as though the rain has stopped. If we hurry, we might even make it back to the house without getting ourselves soaked."

Lindsey stood and followed Caitlyn as she edged along the rocks. They picked their way carefully around the pools of water that lined the shore. Caitlyn knelt down, scooped something up, and tossed it out into the waves.

"What was that?"

"A crab," Caitlyn said. "They get trapped in the pools when the tide rushes in. If they're not carried back out, they die."

"Unless someone helps them."

"That's right," Caitlyn said. "Unless someone helps them." The expression on her face looked strange and haunted as she said it. Then she turned away and started up the steep path that led them away from the sea. Lindsey hadn't noticed the ruined dock and the boat that marked the spot. She followed Caitlyn up the side of the hill and stopped to catch her breath when she reached the top. The trail leading back to the house was mudcy now. Lindsey placed her feet on roots and clumps of grass and tried to avoid the puddles. Caitlyn made her way effortlessly along the path without even looking down. She seemed to find the dry places by instinct. They hardly spoke as they made their way back up the hill to the waiting mansion. Caitlyn pulled off her shoes when they reached the door.

"Well," she said, "I'm glad we had a chance to talk."

"Yeah," Lindsey agreed, as she untied her shoes

"I'm sorry if I was too nosy," Caitlyn said.

"It's okay. It was a beautiful walk. I may have ruined these shoes."

"Just give them to Cornelia. You wouldn't believe the stains I've seen her get out of things."

"What do you want to do now?" Lindsey asked.

"What do most friends do on a rainy day?" Caitlyn replied. "I suppose we could play Monopoly or put a jigsaw puzzle together."

"Really? Is that what you want to do?"

"Unless you'd rather smoke cigars and play poker."

"Monopoly will be fine."

"What about the cigars?"

"Maybe later."

Caitlyn laughed. Lindsey followed her up two flights of stairs to a long attic room.

"Don't look at my room," Caitlyn said. "I'm a terribly messy housekeeper." There were clothes piled on an unmade bed and stacks of schoolbooks in the corners.

"You work so much, you don't really have time to clean," Lindsey said.

"Yes, but that's not really a good excuse. Thanks for trying to make me feel better though." She went to the closet. "What do you think? Jigsaw or Monopoly?"

"I don't really care."

"Don't start that," Caitlyn said. "Make a decision, girl."

"Jigsaw."

"Jigsaw it is, then." She pulled down a tattered box and set it on the floor. On the lid was a faded picture of an English castle sitting on an island in a pond filled with lily pads. Caitlyn emptied the box onto the polished wood floor. Rain pattered on the windowpanes as the two of them spent the better part of three hours putting it together. Finally, when Lindsey dropped the last piece into position and smoothed it with her finger, Caitlyn stood, stretched, and rubbed her long, slender torso.

"I'm so hungry," she said. "Let's go raid the pantry."

Lindsey followed her down the stairs, down the hall, and into the kitchen. She expected to see Mrs. Cutler and Cornelia there, but neither of them was anywhere to be seen.

"I wonder where Ms. Cutler and Cornelia are Today," she said.

"Who knows with those two?" Caitlyn said. "They're such scamps."

"Scamps." Lindsey repeated the word. "I haven't heard that one in a while."

"Are you making fun of the way I talk, Miss Texas?"

"No, ma'am."

Caitlyn rummaged around the refrigerator. She pulled out a jar of pickles, a bottle of ketchup, a jar of olives, and part of a ham and piled them on the cabinet. Lindsey expected her to stop, but she opened the door a second time and filled her arms with a second load of jars and covered dishes. She set them down on the cabinet, went back to the refrigerator, and started gathering a third armload.

"What are you doing?" Lindsey asked. "Are you getting us lunch or getting ready to defrost the refrigerator?"

Caitlyn laughed. "We haven't even started on the pantry yet."

Moments later, they were seated around a table piled with food.

"How do you eat like that and stay so skinny?" Lindsey asked as Caitlyn filled her dessert plate for the third time and started to eat.

"The women in my family were blessed with a high metabolism," Caitlyn said. "I can eat most men under the table."

"I'm so jealous," Lindsey said.

"Well, I'm jealous of your perfect skin," Caitlyn said as she delicately sliced her cake with a dessert fork. "This pale hide just can't handle the sun. I either burn or turn into one big freckle. Do you want anything else?"

"I'm full as a tick," Lindsey said.

"Did you say 'full as a tick'?" Caitlyn said.

"It's an expression," Lindsey said, her face coloring.

"Well," Caitlyn said severely, "I was taught that proper young ladies say, 'I've had a sufficiency.'"

"I've definitely had a sufficiency," Lindsey said. "I ruined my diet for a week."

"Full as a tick," Caitlyn mused. "I love it. I wish my father were around to hear me say it."

"Why?" Lindsey asked. "Would he have had a cow?"

"Had a cow?" Caitlyn cackled. "Oh, my goodness!" She laughed uproariously while Lindsey grinned sheepishly. Caitlyn laughed for what seemed like a solid minute. Lindsey looked at her glass to make sure they were drinking from the same tea pitcher. She began to wonder if Caitlyn was laughing at her for sounding like a stereotypical Texan.

"That's not an expression I use ordinarily," she said defensively.

"I know." Caitlyn held up a hand. "You're so proper, it's almost painful sometimes. That's why it was so funny. Oh, well. I'd better start cleaning up. We don't want Cornelia to have a cow." She started laughing again as she gathered dishes. Lindsey stood and opened the refrigerator door as Caitlyn shoved the first load inside. They had everything put away in less than two minutes.

"Katherine tells me you're something of an artist."

"I do okay."

"I bet you're being modest. I want to see some of your work."

Lindsey went to her room and got her sketchpad. Caitlyn thumbed through the pages.

"These are wonderful. You really have a gift for catching the nuances of expression, the look in the eyes, everything. How long would it take you to draw me?"

"About twenty minutes," Lindsey said.

"Twenty minutes? That's all?"

"I've gotten pretty fast."

"I'll say you have. Where do you want me to sit?"

"By the window is fine."

Caitlyn seated herself. "How do you want me to pose?"

"Just try something."

Caitlyn tried on several different poses.

"There," Lindsey said. "That one."

"I don't think I can hold a smile for that long," Caitlyn said between her teeth.

"You don't have to. Let me get your overall face shape down, and I'll tell you when to smile. I'll rough out your mouth and eyes, and then you can relax, and I'll add the detail."

"You are experienced at this. All right, then."

The tip of Lindsey's pencil flew across the page. She established the shape of Caitlyn's face and placed the eye sockets, the bottom of the nose, the position of the mouth and chin.

"All right," she said. "Smile."

"Cheese," Caitlyn said.

"Hold it." She roughed out the shape of the lips, the corners of the mouth, and the curve of the eyes. "It's okay to relax now. Just give me a few minutes to clean it up and put in the details."

"Will do."

Lindsey added the detail in the irises and pupils, put in eyelashes, the fine detail of the lips. She even added the hint of freckles without leaving blotches all over the face. She crafted the sweep of the hair, suggesting every strand without actually drawing each one. She shaped the nostrils, used shading to round out the neck, added detail to the ears. Finally, she stopped sketching and held the picture upside down.

"What are you doing?"

"It's an artist's trick. Sometimes you can see your mistakes better when you hold the picture upside-down. I think it's ready."

"Let me see," Caitlyn said. "I can't wait."

Lindsey handed her the sketchpad.

"Will you look at this! That is truly amazing. You even gave me freckles. I'm glad I don't have dandruff."

"I can erase the freckles if you want."

"Don't change a thing," Caitlyn told her. "It's wonderful just like this."

Lindsey started to tear it out of the pad.

"Keep it for me," Caitlyn said. "I have to decide what to do with it, and I'd rather you keep it until then."

"Sure, if that's what you want."

"Let me see it again."

Lindsey handed the pad back to her.

"It's perfect. I thank you so much, and not just for the portrait. Thank you for spending the time. Playing. Laughing. Sometimes it seems like all I ever do is work. It's like being a robot sometimes. You forget how to smile and have fun."

"I can't imagine you ever forgetting how to smile," Lindsey said.

"Well, thank ya kindly, Texas," Caitlyn said with an affected drawl. "I'd better get ready for work."

Chapter 8: Haunted Mansion

Lindsey sighed as she watched the rain blowing against the windows of her room. This was the day Todd had planned their trip to Seattle, and even though the odds of rain had been high, Lindsey had still hoped, even prayed, for sun. The storm had blown in during the night, and rain had been falling all day. She'd spent the afternoon hoping that the rain would subside, but the gentle spatter of water on glass just kept right on.

It was almost time for Todd to arrive. Lindsey went downstairs and found Mrs. Cutler sitting in the sunroom, as inappropriate as the name was on that day, and staring out at the pale sky and the storm-tossed ocean. Rain spattered against the glass, and Lindsey felt as though she were on the inside of an aquarium.

"Isn't it beautiful?" Mrs. Cutler said as Lindsey came to stand beside her.

"Not when you have a trip planned," Lindsey said sadly.

"Oh, my," Mrs. Cutler said as she took Lindsey's hand, "I hope you hadn't planned on going sailing."

"Nothing like that. Just driving to Seattle."

"A lovely city," Ms. Cutler said. "Even in the rain. Especially then, perhaps. Some people are dark, brooding, and mysterious by nature, and some cities are the same way. Visit London on a foggy night, and you'd almost swear you'd stepped through time. Seattle is very much the same."

Cornelia rolled a cart into the room and started unloading plates of food onto the table.

"I can't stay for dinner," Lindsey said.

"This is just a snack," Ms. Cutler said. "It's almost five hours to Seattle."

The doorbell rang.

"That's Todd," Lindsey said. She started for the door, but Mrs. Cutler gripped her hand and pulled her back.

"Patience," Mrs. Cutler said. "Let him anticipate."

But, it's not a date. We're just friends. Lindsey fought the urge to argue as Cornelia went to answer the door. She took a deep breath and stared out at the ocean. The water had taken on the silvery color of the sky. The lighthouse and the slab of stone it clung to were almost completely hidden by the blanket of fog that swirled above the ocean's churning surface. The dark shapes of hemlock trees framed the scene with their needled branches. She had to admit, Mrs. Cutler was right. It was beautiful.

"Well, good afternoon, young man," Mrs. Cutler said as Todd appeared in the doorway. "Who is this with you?"

Standing behind Todd was a stocky young man with three days of beard growth. He was wearing a black *Star Wars* T-shirt.

"This is Drew. Drew, meet Ms. Cutler and Lindsey."

Drew nodded to them.

"Cornelia has prepared a snack for you."

"We're kind of...on a tight schedule."

"Speak for yourself," Drew said. "I haven't eaten anything but a slice of cold pizza since last night."

Todd started to protest but thought better of it. "It looks great. Don't mind if I do." He started to sit beside Lindsey, then stopped and looked at Mrs. Cutler.

"Well, go on," she said. "Have a seat."

"Thank you."

Lindsey started to laugh, then coughed to hide it.

The table before them was adorned with white cloth. Slices of cake were served on china plates and silver trays.

"Would you like some coffee?" Cornelia asked.

"Sure."

"Lindsey tells me you're taking her on another excursion."

"Yes, ma'am. In Seattle."

"I haven't been there in some time," she said. "I'm sure it has changed tremendously."

"The Pike Place Market is still there," he said. "It's supposed to be about a century old."

"As old as me?"

"No! That's not what I meant."

She laughed. "It's all right. I'm sure I am quite the antique by your standards. What do you plan to see there?"

"We're going to Pike Place," he told her, "and we're going to take the ferry across to Bainbridge Island and traveling up to Port Townsend."

"Wonderful, and when should I expect you back?"

"Late," he said. "My appointment is at midnight."

"Oh, dear. And Lindsey has church tomorrow."

"We'll get her back in plenty of time," Todd said.

"Do you young people ever sleep anymore?"

"Not much," Drew said.

When they had finished their cake and Cornelia was clearing away the dishes, Mrs. Cutler looked out the window and then back at Todd, Drew, and Lindsey.

"I guess you'd better be on your way," she said.

Todd, Drew, and Lindsey rose to their feet.

"Help me up, young man," Mrs. Cutler said. Drew took her arm and helped her to her feet. They started down the hall.

"You'll need a jacket," Todd told Lindsey as they were nearing the front door. "It gets cold on the ferry. We may want to go up on deck for the view."

"I'll be right back," Lindsey said. She ran upstairs.

Drew nudged Todd. He turned around. Drew was focused on something in an alcove.

"Is that a sarcophagus?"

"Why, yes," Mrs. Cutler said.

"Is it real?"

"Oh, yes. Quite real."

"Sweet!"

Todd and Drew walked over to the box and examined it. It wasn't gold-plated like King Tut's famous caskets, but it was ornate. There was a face carved into the front. It looked like the face of a woman.

"What country is this from?"

"It's Egyptian, of course."

"Sweet!"

Drew lightly traced the edge of the box with his finger.

"This is awesome. Where did you get this?"

"My husband brought it back from one of his buying trips," she said. "You must realize that owning an authentic Egyptian mummy was quite the rage in the earlier part of the twentieth century. Some people treated them rather shabbily, I'm afraid. No respect whatever for the dignity of the deceased. My husband bought this one to sell as a novelty, but I pleaded with him to let her stay here, where I could look after her."

"Her?"

"The mummy."

"The mummy's still in here?"

"Why, yes. She's a young lady. She's far from home, with no family to look after her. I didn't want her traded around like some lifeless thing, though I suppose she is lifeless now. She wasn't always that way, though. Sometimes I can picture her walking along the Nile, standing beneath the palm trees, and dreaming of some dark and handsome Egyptian prince."

Lindsey came down the stairs with her coat folded across her arm.

"Who are you talking about?" Lindsey asked.

"The mummy," Todd said.

"What mummy?"

"The one in this sarcophagus."

Lindsey's jaw dropped.

"You've got a dead body in here?"

"Well, yes," Mrs. Cutler said. "She certainly is that. I suppose I should give her a proper burial, but burying an Egyptian girl in American soil just seems wrong somehow. So, until I can think of a more appropriate place for her, she's staying here with me."

"You've adopted her," Todd said.

"I suppose, in a way, I have. I've always had a special place in my heart for young people, especially young women, who have no one to look after them. I remember a young German girl who had lost her family in a concentration camp. She wasn't but seventeen when an American soldier married her and brought her back here. He treated her horribly, and his family never accepted her. She ran away, and Niles and I took her in. She insisted on earning her place here. Did you know the Germans wash their windows every day? The poor dear nearly worked herself to death washing all of these windows. I finally convinced her that once a week was enough."

"What ever happened to her?" Todd asked.

"She's still here."

"Cornelia?"

"The very same."

"That's actually quite a story," Todd said.

"I wish she could have had a happier life," Mrs. Cutler said. "She was young. She could have had her own family, but here we are—two old spinsters."

"I think she's lucky to have you," Todd said.

"That's very kind of you," Mrs. Cutler said. "Well, I suppose you'd better be on your way."

"I'd like to talk to you about your husband sometime," Todd said. "From what you've said, it sounds like the two of you had quite a life. I don't know how you feel about preserving that story."

"Preserving it?"

"As a documentary film," Todd said.

"Yeah!" Drew said. "This place is a gold mine. Imagine the visuals."

"Oh, no. I couldn't do that."

"At least let me show you some of my work," Todd said. "If you let me do the story, I promise it would be a work of dignity and beauty."

"I'm certain that it would be. It's just that…well, my husband became a rather private man in his later years. He would never have approved of such an undertaking. Even though he's gone, I still feel I should honor his wishes."

"I understand," Todd said. "If you ever change your mind, be sure to let me know."

"I certainly will."

Todd opened the door and held it as Lindsey and Drew stepped out into the cool, damp air. Rain dripped off the roof and spattered against the pavestones on the courtyard. Todd stepped out and pulled the door shut behind them. The three passed through a light rain on the way to the car. Todd opened the door for Lindsey and closed it when she was comfortably seated. Lindsey strapped herself in and looked back at the house to see Mrs. Cutler watching through the window. Drew climbed into the back and stretched out on the seat. Todd climbed into the driver's seat, snapped his seatbelt into place, and started the car.

"Mrs. Cutler's an interesting woman," he said.

"She sure keeps you on your toes," Lindsey agreed.

"I guess she does," Todd said. "I really wish she would let me do that story. This house is like a treasure trove of stories."

"I get the feeling they're not all happy stories," Lindsey said.

"The place is like a museum," Drew said.

"I kind of wish you hadn't asked her about that mummy," Lindsey said.

"How do you like staying there with her? Ms. Cutler, I mean." Todd made his way carefully along the curving drive that led down the side of the hill. If he had taken the first hard turn too fast, they'd have crashed through a fence and rolled down a hill until they'd landed on the rocks at the water's edge.

"It's nice," Lindsey said after thinking for a moment. "She doesn't have a television set, and I miss that a little bit in the evenings. Caitlyn keeps things from getting too gloomy there."

"Who is Caitlyn?"

"Mrs. Cutler's niece. She's a nurse."

"And she lives there?"

"Yeah. She works odd hours and goes to school so I don't see her much, but I like her."

Water dripped from tree canopies as Todd navigated the winding road through the rainforest. In the gray light and fog, it looked like a realm from another time. One might have expected to find hunting parties of Native Americans, prehistoric beasts, or elves from a Tolkien novel running beneath the branches. A Celtic instrumental with dancing violins and thundering bass played on Todd's radio. It conjured up images of storm-tossed sailing ships and waves crashing onto Scottish shores.

***

Storms lashed the sky over Puget Sound. Rain pounded the ferry's gently rocking deck. The lights of Seattle receded into the haze as the dark shore across the sound grew closer.

"I've never seen it like this," Todd said. "It rains all the time here, but I've never seen it this violent." He, Lindsey, and Drew sat in the sheltering warmth of the ferry's lounge as the storm raged outside.

"It's perfect," Drew said. "Perfect haunted house weather. The spirits should be rocking tonight."

"And we're going to a séance?" Lindsey said.

"In one of the most haunted houses in the country," Drew added.

"It also has one of the few remaining psychomantiums—or is it psychomantia?—in the country," Todd said.

"What's a psychomantium?" Lindsey asked.

"It's a chamber lined with mirrors," Todd said. "People used to think mirrors were windows to another world. The idea is ancient, but the rooms were popular during the Victorian era."

"And we're going to a séance in one of those rooms?"

"We're not participating," Todd said. "Just filming."

"Speak for yourself," Drew said. "I'm here for the whole experience. What are you afraid of?"

"I'm not afraid of anything," Todd said. "It's superstition."

"Then what's the deal?"

Todd hesitated.

"It's a religious thing, isn't it? Now that you're born again, sex, drugs, and séances are off limits."

"Something like that."

"That's cool. I respect that. Just don't judge me if I don't choose to live by your standards."

"Are you sure it's all superstition?" Lindsey said. "What if there's really something there? What if we're playing around with something that's really dangerous?"

"Then we'll get it on film," Drew said, "and make a lot of money."

"I'm serious. What if you call something up, and you can't get rid of it? What if it follows you home?"

"Whoa!" Drew said. "That's pretty scary." He turned to Todd. "She needs to say that again. You've got to have that in the film, man."

***

The road across the sound led through miles of dark forest. Even on their highest setting, Todd's windshield wipers could barely push the torrent of water aside long enough to afford fleeting glimpses of the road ahead. Wind tore through the trees, coating the windshield and roadway with leaves and needles. The car threatened to hydroplane more than once. Drew filmed from the backseat, supplying colorful and profanity-laced narration.

Finally, just after eleven o'clock, they came to a stone arch with an iron gate. The gate was open. Beyond lay a dark path so shrouded by trees that it looked like a cave. Wet leaves and broken limbs blanketed the surface of the road.

"Look at this!" Drew said, laughing with delight. "I mean, look...at...*this*! Do you want me to get out and get a couple of shots? I don't mind."

"Are you sure?" Todd stopped the car and looked back.

"I'm serious. I don't mind. This will look fantastic, man."

"Okay. Let me back up so we can get the gate."

Todd backed up, and Drew mounted the camera to the tripod.

"I'll try to get the arch in the headlights."

Drew bailed out into the rain, screaming as the cold water instantly soaked him. He ran around to the driver's side of the car and set up the tripod. Lindsey and Todd could hear him laughing and cursing outside the car.

"Now, that's a true friend," Lindsey said.

Satisfied with his footage, Drew pulled open the door and rolled into the backseat.

"Thanks, Drew."

"Gonna look great, man! That's gonna look so great!"

Todd drove back under the arch and into the dark corridor beyond. He drove slowly, not knowing when he might encounter a fallen tree or a large branch in the road ahead of him. Finally, the lights brushed across the shape of an enormous stone fountain. Beneath the falling water sat the crouched figure of a young woman in a flowing gown. Droplets clung like tears to her stone cheeks. Her eyes were blank and empty. Thunder rumbled overhead. Todd turned into a circular drive and parked at the end of a row of cars that lined the curb in front of the mansion.

Denholm Castle looked out of place in Washington. With its jutting towers and limestone walls, it would have been more at home in England or Germany. It even had a moat.

Donning rain slickers and fumbling with umbrellas, Todd, Lindsey, and Drew wrestled their equipment from the trunk of the car. The cobblestones beneath their feet were wet but still rough enough to provide traction. A stone bridge spanned the moat and led to the arched front entrance. The moat was filled with lily pads. Rain pounded against its dark surface. Breathless and damp, the three reached the overhang that guarded the castle's two massive front doors. Gas lamps flickered on either side of them.

Todd pulled at the door handle. The giant door opened easily with no sound of creaking, rusty hinges. A group of people stood in a spacious lobby with couches, staircases, and a fireplace large enough to drive a carriage through.

"Are you the filmmaker?" a middle-aged woman in a black dress asked them.

"Yes, I'm Todd Wilkes. This is my crew. Drew Alexander and Lindsey Holland."

"Excellent," she said. "I'm Elena Berkshire. We spoke earlier." Her accent was not exactly British, but something about her manner gave her an old-world air. "Our guest list is complete, then. Welcome to Denholm Castle. Some of you know about the history of our castle, but others do not. Suffice it to say that Denholm Castle has a colorful and haunted history."

Todd, Lindsey, and Drew unpacked the camera and the lighting equipment. Todd began to film as Ms. Berkshire recounted the castle's history:

"Wilfred Denholm was a world renowned stage magician. He had the mansion built in the 1800s as a home for his young wife and the family they planned to have. His wife died during the birth of their first child, and he spent the rest of his life looking for a way to pierce the veil between the world of the living and the unseen realm of the dead. Using mirrors imported from around the world, he constructed a psychomanteum, a chamber for contacting the dead.

"Some guests have claimed they could actually make out the forms of spirits in the distortions in the glass. Others dismiss them as illusions. The room is closed to tourists now. I will warn you that the effect can be a bit...disturbing. Come with me, please."

They followed her to a polished wood door surrounded by Egyptian symbols. Ms. Berkshire pulled a tarnished key from her purse, pushed it into the lock, and twisted. The door creaked on its hinges.

"I apologize for that," she said. "As I said, this room is closed to tourists, and few employees ever go in here."

A set of carpeted stairs led upward into the gloom.

"Place your hands on the rail," she instructed. "Don't let go. No matter what happens, don't let go."

Their footsteps were muffled as they ascended into darkness. Lindsey felt something brush against the back of her neck.

"There's something here," one of the psychics said. "A presence."

"We're nearing the top," Ms. Berkshire said. "As you reach the end of the rail, follow the sound of my voice. Do not turn to the left or the right."

A padded floor absorbed the sound of their footfalls. A cool draft blew past them. Somewhere far away the thunder rumbled.

"Stop here," Ms. Berkshire said. "Give your eyes a moment to adjust to the darkness."

The lights came up. The change was barely perceptible at first. There were brief flashes of light. Lindsey wasn't sure whether the flashes were really there or if they were merely tricks of perception. As the lights came up, Lindsey could see that they were standing in a round room with a domed ceiling. A crystal chandelier dangled from a chain in the center of the room. Beneath it sat a round table surrounded by high-backed chairs. The walls were lined with mirrors.

"These mirrors were imported from houses around the world," Ms. Berkshire explained. "As a stage magician, Mr. Denholm often used mirrors for his illusions, but he came to believe mirrors were more than merely silver and glass. He believed everything seen by those mirrors, even consciousness itself, was somehow contained in them. Because of this, he believed they had the power to open doorways to other times and places."

"Sounds like he bought into his own illusions," Todd whispered.

"This is going to be tricky," Lindsey said. "Staying out of the shot, I mean."

"I'm going to set up some stationary cameras," Drew said.

Something was wrong. The moment they had entered the room, Lindsey had felt a sense of unease creeping over her. She tried to tell herself it was just the storm and the disorienting effect of the mirrors, but the sensation remained. As she set up the lights, she had the strangest sensation of being watched, of someone standing behind her. The sensation was so strong at one point that she had turned around, only to see her own face in the mirror behind her. She began to wonder if the mirrors might, in fact, be one-way windows. Maybe someone really was watching them invisibly from behind the glass.

"Now," Ms. Berkshire said, "those who are participating in the séance may seat themselves in the inner ring of chairs surrounding the table. The rest will seat themselves in the outer ring along the wall."

They did as they were instructed. After sitting silently for a moment, Ms. Berkshire began to chant then, finally, to call upon the dead.

"Wilfred Denholm, we summon you from beyond. If you are here, if you want to speak to us, make your presence known. By sight, sound, or touch, reach out to us and let us know you're here. Come to us, and let us know that death is not the end but only the beginning."

As the older woman spoke, Lindsey felt sweat breaking out on her forehead. She began to feel lightheaded. The room spun around her.

***

"Lindsey."

"Lindsey, can you hear us."

The voice spoke softly from far away. Was it real or was it a voice from a dream?

"Lindsey. Lindsey, can you hear me?" Someone was stroking her forehead. She opened her eyes and saw Todd and the others standing over her. The camera's cyclops eye was focused on her, all but concealing Drew's face.

"Are you okay?"

"What happened?" Lindsey asked. She cleared her throat.

"You passed out," Todd told her.

The other guests began to ask questions:

"Did you see anything?"

"Did you sense anything?"

Fanning herself, she sat up.

"Did you see anything?" one anxious woman asked.

"I don't remember. I was watching Ms. Berkshire. A strange feeling came over me. That's all I remember."

"Did you sense anything?" the woman demanded. "A presence?"

"I don't...maybe. Maybe something."

"Can you describe it?"

"What did you experience?"

"Tell us what you remember."

"Please," a tall, gaunt man said, "don't push. Don't push."

"Let's try this again," Ms. Berkshire said. "This time we'll gather around Ms. Holland. We'll...."

"No."

"But the spirits have chosen you. Don't worry. We'll...."

"No. I won't do it."

"Now, really, Ms. Holland...."

"That's enough," Todd said. "If she doesn't want to do it, that's her decision. I'm taking her downstairs."

"But, there's no danger."

"Can you guarantee that?" Todd turned and stared them down. "Based on what you believe, can any of you guarantee that?"

No one answered.

"That's what I thought. I'm taking Lindsey downstairs. I'll be back in a minute or so."

"Hey, man," Drew said. "If you want to stay with her, I can film the rest of this."

"Are you sure?"

"Yeah. No problem." He sneaked a look at Lindsey. Lindsey thought she heard him murmer, "She's hot. Work your magic," but she wasn't sure.

Todd led Lindsey back down the winding staircase into the large room below. They never could find a kitchen, but Lindsey found a bathroom and rinsed her face with cold water. Something about her reflection in the glass made her uneasy. Lindsey and Todd sat downstairs and made small talk for about forty minutes. Then they heard labored breathing and grunting and looked up to see Drew carrying all of the equipment downstairs by himself.

"Easy, man," Todd said, jumping to his feet. "Let me help you with that." Todd and Lindsey went to the stairs and relieved Drew of some of his burden. Breathing hard, he set down the last pieces and sat down on one of the couches.

"How was it?" Todd asked. "Did you get anything?"

"Just a few interviews with the people. I guess Lindsey was the most exciting part of the night."

"Thanks for taking over," Todd said. "You didn't have to do that."

"Not a problem, man. No problem at all." He smiled. "Now you owe me one."

***

Thunder reverberated weirdly through the walls of the lighthouse. Lindsey saw lightning flashing through the tiny window below her.

"Don't worry," she said. "I'll get you out." She had been pounding on the padlock with a rock for what seemed like hours. The muscles in her right arm ached with exhaustion, but the lock wasn't even scratched. Lindsey listened for the quivering voice of the woman on the other side of the tower's trap door entrance, but she was no longer crying and pleading for help. She was singing.

Lindsey stirred beneath the sheets, and sighed with relief, knowing she wasn't really in a lighthouse. She was at home in bed. She could hear the rain drumming on the roof of the house. She was afraid of the thunder, so her mommy would sit on the bed and sing to her until she fell asleep. That's what she was doing tonight. Dressed in her Winnie the Pooh pajamas and holding her stuffed Winnie the Pooh in her arms, she felt safe and warm as her mother gently stroked her hair.

Lindsey woke up suddenly and knew she was not five years old and that she was not at home in her parents' house, sleeping in her bed. The drumming of the rain outside the window continued, and someone really was singing. Lindsey felt the weight of another person sitting on her bed. *No,* she thought. *It couldn't be.*

She opened her eyes a crack and saw no one. Even when she opened them all the way, there was no sign of anyone else in the gray light of the room, but the singing still kept on. Soft and sweet, the voice was that of a woman, and she was somewhere close. Could it be a trick of the acoustics, maybe? Maybe Cornelia was singing in the next room as she finished up some late night chore. Maybe her voice carried through a vent in the wall and sounded as if it was right in the room. Todd's project and the trip to Seattle had her imagining things. She had heard so much about ghosts that she was dreaming about them.

Lindsey realized her heart was pounding. As much as she didn't want to believe it, she knew there was someone—or something—in the room with her. The presence was feminine, and it was invisible.

I'm dreaming, she thought. I'm dreaming, and I just think I'm awake.

The phantom song had no discernable lyrics. The invisible presence was humming and singing notes rather than words. The melody she sang was both beautiful and sad.

Dear God, Lindsey thought, please protect me from anything dangerous. Protect me from anything that is not of this world.

The singing continued. The singer had to be somewhere in the room. There was just no getting around it. Lindsey closed her eyes tight and pretended to be asleep. She silently prayed for God's protection against the unseen forces of darkness. She would have no memory, the next morning, of ever having fallen asleep.

Chapter 9: Churches

Lindsey stumbled groggily onto the porch, the chilly air biting into her bare arms. She hoped her cheery sundress made her look more energetic than she really felt after getting home at 2 a.m. and waking up at 6:30. And the nightmare she'd had about an invisible person sitting on her bed and singing to her... Surely that had been a nightmare. Splinters of light poured through the high branches of century-old hemlock trees. They clothed the shady courtyard in a kind of holy serenity. They also hurt her eyes.

Jolene pulled into the paved courtyard, a big smile on her face. Lindsey slipped into the passenger seat beside her, pulled the door shut, and buckled up.

"Well," Jolene asked. "How did it go yesterday?"

"Fine," Lindsey said. "It went fine."

"That's all I get? Fine? What did you do? What did you see?"

She turned the SUV around and started down the drive. Lindsey looked through the fence at the hillside and the ocean below them.

"Go easy on me this morning," Lindsey said. "I didn't get but four hours of sleep."

"That's all Neal ever gets," Jolene said. "I keep telling him it's going to catch up to him someday, but older people I know tell me they don't need as much sleep as they used to, either. I guess he's just getting a head start. So, you're not going to tell me about yesterday?"

"It was strange. I'll tell you about it later."

"Okay. I won't push."

They drove for five minutes without talking. Jolene turned off the highway, and they passed through an arched gate into a smartly landscaped complex of condominiums. Neatly trimmed shrubs, beds of colorful flowers, shaded walking paths, and a canal with an ornate footbridge all accented the grounds. Jolene pulled into the parking lot of a two-story structure with tall windows. A wide wooden bridge at the entrance led past a waterfall.

"Wow," Lindsey said, "Neal didn't tell me the early service was so upscale."

Lindsey and Jolene walked through the main entrance. A crowd of men and women, mostly gray-haired seniors, stood around a table covered with refreshments. Neal was standing in the midst of them, telling one of his stories. He looked up as Lindsey and Jolene entered. He was wearing a suit and tie, and his trademark ear stud was nowhere to be seen.

"Hey," he said, "come on over."

Lindsey pasted on a smile.

"He told me this was a youth service," she whispered to Jolene. The other woman, she suddenly noticed, had thrown a choir robe over her casual clothes.

"Most of you know my wife, Jolene," he said. "This girl beside her is Lindsey. She was one of my youth back in Texas. She's an art teacher now."

The men and women around Neal greeted them warmly.

"We're from Texas," one of the women told Lindsey. "We moved out here to be closer to our son."

"I'd better get ready for the service," Neal told the group. Lindsey followed him as he and Jolene stepped out into the hall.

"What are you trying to do to me?" Lindsey said. "You told me this was a youth service."

"That's what it is," Neal said. "It's for these guys."

He gestured toward a collage on the wall. Black and white photographs showed young men and women eating picnic lunches from checkered tablecloths, dancing together at sock hops in the school gym, and cheering at football games. The women wore knee-length skirts and tight rolled jeans. Young men wore plaid shirts and baggy jeans. They had transistor radios instead of iPods. Some of the men wore military uniforms.

"The youth of the 1950s," she said.

"With a few from the forties and sixties sprinkled in." he said.

"What are you wearing?" Lindsey asked. "I didn't know you even owned a suit."

"The youth of the fifties like their worship services a little more formal than we do," he said. "They're pretty patriotic, too. A lot of them had family members who fought in World War II. A couple of my older guys were in it themselves. Some were in the Korean War. One of the women lost her husband in Korea when she was barely out of high school. Memorial Day is a big thing here."

"Why didn't you tell me?" Lindsey asked.

"About Memorial Day?"

"You said this was a youth service."

"You don't like old people?"

"I love old people, but that's not the point. Look how I'm dressed."

"You look adorable," Jolene said.

"Adorable?" Lindsey said. "Is that like 'precious'?"

"What's wrong with precious?" Jolene said. "I like precious. Why doesn't anybody ever call *me* precious anymore?"

Neal pretended not to hear as he picked up a big, leather-bound family Bible.

"I can understand the suit," Lindsey said, "but that big Bible is too much. If you get up in that pulpit and start rolling your *r*'s and talking about *Gaw-ud*, I'm going to crack up."

"Repent of your wickedness, child," Neal told her as he touched his Bible to her head.

"I've got to play the organ," Jolene said. "You can help Mildred hand out programs. Then we'll seat you in the front."

Neal left to finish with preparations. Jolene took Lindsey into a multipurpose area. Padded chairs faced a platform at the front of the room. Wooden light boxes with stained glass patterns in them hung on either side of a mahogany lectern. Jolene introduced Lindsey to Mildred, a short, lively woman who knew each one of the residents and visitors by name.

"Are you training your replacement?" one of the men asked Mildred when he saw Lindsey.

"She's just visiting," Mildred told him. "I'm afraid you're stuck with me."

"Too bad."

"Sit down, you old goat."

"You see how she treats me," the man said to Lindsey. "Week after week, I put up with her abuse. It's penance. That's what it is. Penance for the sins of my youth." He smiled and went to sit down.

"He's cute," Lindsey said.

"Don't tell him that," Mildred said. "He's enough of a ham as it is."

Lindsey heard organ music and saw Jolene sitting at a keyboard in the front of the room.

"I don't know why they always start the service with that funeral music," Mildred said. "I guess he thinks that's what old people like. We'd better go sit down."

Mildred led Lindsey to a seat in the front row. There was a row of empty chairs in front of the platform. Lindsey was about to ask Mildred why they were there when Neal entered. He reverently took the stage, set his Bible on the lectern in the front of the room, and opened the service with announcements and prayer. He was a little more subdued than usual, but Lindsey still saw a glimmer of mischief in his eyes from time to time. Starting from a passage about King David's mighty men, Neal preached a message about courage and bravery, and ended by calling the veterans to the front of the room.

After the service, Neal led everyone outside to a patio that overlooked a golf course. The tables were filled with dishes of food. The ocean sparkled on the horizon. Neal led the group in a prayer of thanks and started passing out plates.

"What did you think of the service?" Jolene asked Lindsey.

"It was moving. I didn't think I would like it, but I did."

Lindsey's cellphone vibrated. She fumbled through her purse, found it, and flipped it open.

"Hello."

"Hey, Lindsey."

"Hi, Pack. What are you doing?"

"Skipping church to study for the bar exam. I guess you're working at the Church of the Holy Cappuccinos again. I tried to call you yesterday. The old lady said you were in Seattle with another guy."

"Two other guys, actually. They're film majors, and...."

"You're engaged to me, and you're out with another guy?"

"You went to see Jessie in Dallas."

"And this is your way of getting even? I should have known you'd find a way to make me pay for that."

"No," she said, "it's not like that. If we're going to trust each other...."

"You never have trusted me."

"That's not true."

"You always act like you're little miss Goody Two-Shoes, but you always find a way to twist the knife. You're passive-aggressive, Lindsey. You've always been passive- aggressive."

"I just wanted to see Seattle, and Todd invited me to go. He knows I'm engaged."

"Then he shouldn't have asked you."

"What about you and Jessie? Did she ask you to come to Dallas, or did you just volunteer?"

"She's just a friend. That's all."

"Well, Todd's just a friend, too."

"Probably another one of those artistic people you like so much. If that's what you want, why don't you just dump me and hook up with one of those limp-wristed little geeks?"

"He may be a geek, but I'd rather spend the day with him than you when you're acting like this."

She snapped the phone shut, turned around, and saw Jolene staring at her.

"Did you just say Todd was a geek?"

"No," Lindsey said. "I mean, that's not what I meant. You were right." She shook her head. "I never should have gone to Seattle. No matter what Pack did, I'm engaged to him, and I shouldn't have gone."

"I never told you not to go."

"But, you didn't think it was a good idea."

"There were two guys," she said. "That's innocent enough in itself...unless you're actually attracted to Todd and are starting to have second thoughts. You're not, are you?"

"No," she said. "Of course not. I do like Todd. A lot. But, no."

"Are you sure?"

"Positive."

***

New Hope Fellowship's contemporary service was held in the historic Orpheum Theater in downtown Astoria. According to the bronze plaque between the entrance and the box office, the Orpheum had been built during the final years of the silent film era. The walls of the lobby were paneled in dark wood. The door handles and the rails of the stairs that led to the balcony were polished brass. Potted palm trees stood in the corners. The lobby was already filling up with people when Lindsey and Jolene arrived. Two young women were serving cappuccinos and lattes from a concession table. Stacks of paperback Bibles sat on the table outside the theater's entrance.

"Did Shadow come to the youth study this morning?" Jolene asked one of the teenage girls.

"I didn't see her."

"That's disappointing. She said she would be here. I'll have to call her later."

Lindsey could hear the praise band warming up inside. Todd would be with them. She prayed God would give her the right words to say as she pushed through the swinging doors and stepped into the cavernous auditorium.

In spite of her concerns, Lindsey couldn't help but be captivated by the ornamentation that covered the theater's walls and ceiling. Brass-hued relief sculptures of godlike figures in flowing robes and theatrical masks flowed around fluted columns and beneath archways. The casually dressed praise band on the stage looked out of place in such baroque surroundings. Lindsey could easily picture men in tuxedos and top hats and women in bustling floor-length dresses making their way down the aisles and seating themselves on seats padded in red velvet. Lindsey scanned the room for Todd. Someone else was playing the keyboard. Finally, she turned and saw him standing in a control booth beneath the balcony. She followed Jolene down the aisle as she greeted the friends she saw sitting there. When they reached the front of the room, Lindsey seated herself on the front row while Jolene sat down on a bench behind a keyboard.

Moments later, the house lights went dark while the lights on the stage brightened. Neal, no longer dressed in a suit and tie, took the stage and led the group in a prayer. Then he stepped down and let the praise band play for a while. The casually dressed audience stood and swayed, many of them raising hands.

As the music played, Lindsey tried to sneak a look at the control booth. She was surprised when she saw Cornelia standing in the back of the room, singing along with the others. She watched in disbelief and wondered, for a moment, if this was another woman who just happened to have a strong resemblance to Mrs. Cutler's housekeeper. If this truly was Cornelia, she was probably the only person over fifty in the whole crowd, and the expression of bliss this woman was wearing was completely unlike any expression Lindsey had ever seen the German woman wear. Come to think of it, she had never seen any emotion on Cornelia's face other than what might have been slight irritation. Lindsey glanced back at the woman repeatedly throughout the worship choruses.

After the music ended, Neal reappeared onstage, a Bible in his hand, and seated himself on a stool. He was wearing a wireless microphone. He read the passage from the Old Testament about David's mighty men of valor. Then he told the story of a young man named Tony who had just become a Christian who went to the Army recruiter's office after getting a draft notice in the mail. Then he wrestled with the question of Christians in combat with the sharpness of a philosopher and with more gentle sensitivity than Lindsey sometimes thought he possessed.

At the end of the message, Jolene returned to her place on the bench in front of the keyboard.

* * *

"I thought I saw Cornelia in the audience," Lindsey said.

"Oh, yeah," Neal said. "She never misses."

"Here's your copy of the service."

Lindsey turned and saw Todd standing behind Neal with a CD.

"Thanks, man," Neal said as he took the disc.

"Hi," Lindsey said. "Thanks for taking me to Seattle."

"That was weird," Todd said. "I hope it didn't scare you too much."

"It's okay. It was fine. I enjoyed it—most of it. Where's your next interview going to be?"

"It's at Mount Rainier," he said, "but you don't have to go if you're getting tired of all the *X-Files* stuff."

"No," she said, "I want to go."

"I was thinking you might like it better if I showed you some of the art galleries around here."

"That would be okay, too. We could do both. If that's okay."

"Sure," he said. "If you're sure that's what you want."

"I'm sure."

"Well, all right, then. I—uh—had better pack the microphones. I'll call you."

"Okay, thanks."

"Sure."

She breathed a sigh of relief as he walked away.

"What was that all about?" Neal asked.

"Nothing," she said. "Just planning our next adventure."

"What did you think about the services today?" Jolene asked.

"They were both good," Lindsey said. "It's just that...."

"What?"

"I wish the people in the later service could have seen the service at the retirement center. All those people and their stories. It doesn't seem right for the church to be split up the way it is. Everybody gets what they want, and nobody has to share or compromise."

"That's just the way it is," Neal said. "For now, anyway. Where do you want to go for lunch?"

"I don't know," Lindsey said. "I'm not from here. You pick something."

They left the auditorium together.

***

Todd was packing away the microphones when his cellphone vibrated in its holster. Drew's name appeared on the screen.

"Hey. What's up, Drew?"

"Hey, Todd. What are you doing?"

"Just finished lunch. What's going on?"

"I think you'd better come by the studio."

"Why? What is it?"

"You need to see this for yourself."

Five minutes later, Todd burst into the studio. Drew was sitting at the controls eating Doritos, a bank of screens in front of him.

"All right," Todd said. "I almost got a speeding ticket getting over here. This had better be good."

"It's good."

"Well, what is it?"

"You remember what Lindsey said about the challenges of filming with all the mirrors?"

"Keeping yourself out of the shot. Sure."

"Well, she mostly did a pretty good job of it," Drew said, "but there were a couple of times she filmed herself in the mirror."

"And you called me over here to tell me that?"

"No," he said. "I called you over here to show you this."

He tapped a button. An image appeared on one of the screens. Lindsey was there in the image, holding the camera. Behind her was a hazy, yellow-white blur.

"Keep watching."

He advanced the clip, going frame by frame. The image shimmered, resolved itself into the shape of a person then blurred out again.

"Did you see that?" Drew asked. He rolled it back and played it again. "What does that look like?"

Todd swallowed hard. "Like a woman in an old-fashioned dress."

"Yeah," Drew said. "Exactly. Do you see this blur here?" He pointed to a spot on Lindsey's shoulder. "Watch this." He enlarged the image.

"Are those fingers?"

"Yeah, see the nails. And that looks like a ring."

"Is this some kind of joke?"

"No, man. I swear. This is exactly what the camera saw."

"Run it back."

He replayed the image.

"This is weird."

"What are you going to tell Lindsey?"

"I'm not sure."

Chapter 10: Rage

"Get out!"

Lindsey woke suddenly. She peered into the darkness around her bed but saw nothing. She had heard a voice, a male voice. But, had she really heard it, or was it part of a dream? She closed her eyes and listened.

"I SAID GET OUT!"

SLAM! Something struck her hard across the face, and the bed collapsed. Lindsey screamed, tried to get out of bed, and got tangled in the sheets. She fell hard into the floor and landed on her elbow. Pain lanced through her arm. She lay on the floor, gasping. Her face was wet. She tried to remember if she had left a glass of water on the bedside table. She touched her face. The liquid running down her cheek was warm. It was blood. She was bleeding.

Gasping, she scrambled to her feet and lunged toward the place beside the door where the light switch should be. Her fingers groped along the wall until she found the switch and flipped it. The switch clicked, and there was a momentary flash as the bulb exploded, then the room went dark again.

Lindsey found the doorknob and twisted, but the door refused to open. She pulled frantically and pounded on the door, but it refused to budge. She was locked in.

"Let me out!" she cried. "Let me out!"

Crying and hysterical, she pounded on the door with both fists. After a moment, sanity descended.

What's wrong with me? Lindsey thought. Surely, she was panicking over nothing. This was nothing more than a dark room. The voice had probably been a nightmare. Something must have fallen off the ceiling and hit her. Lindsey turned around and pressed her back against the door. Taking a deep breath, she focused on the gray light that was flowing through the curtains. There was something there, something big. What was it? She tried to remember if there had been a piece of furniture there—something huge and shaped vaguely like a man. Then she saw the face. It was a man's face, with heavy brows and a thick, tangled beard. The eyes were pale and glazed, and the skin was deathly pale and starting to decompose. The body was dripping wet and tangled with seaweed.

Lindsey tried to scream, but all that came out of her mouth was a frightened gasp. She felt a vibration, and heard a clicking noise. The door behind her shivered and opened.

Lindsey nearly knocked Cornelia off her feet as she stumbled into the hall.

"There's a man in my room!" She choked out the words.

Cornelia peered into the shadows.

"There's no one there," she said.

Lindsey looked back at the place beside the window where she had seen the burly stranger standing. The area was empty.

"He was there." Lindsey gasped.

Cornelia sighed. She checked the French doors leading to the balcony. They were locked. She walked through to the bathroom and flipped the bathroom light on.

"There's no one here," Cornelia said without a change of inflection. She turned around. "What happened to your face?"

"I...," She followed Cornelia into the bathroom and peered into the mirror. There was a gash beneath her right eye, and blood was flowing down her cheek. The skin around her eye was already starting to turn black and swell.

"And what happened to your bed?"

One of the bed's tall wooden posts had broken off. The rounded top was lying on Lindsey's pillow. The post had apparently broken off and struck her across the face like a club. That was what she had felt. But the face? The voice?

"Why did you lock me in this room?" Lindsey suddenly asked, her voice shaking. "What were you trying to do to me?"

"I didn't lock you in," Cornelia said. "The tumblers in the lock are old. Sometimes they shift around."

"But, why does it lock from the *outside*?"

"What's going on here?" Mrs. Cutler demanded as she stumbled into the room. She saw Lindsey's face and covered her mouth with both hands. "Oh, my. Oh, darling, what happened?"

"There was a man in here," Lindsey gasped. "A dead man. He attacked me."

"The bed broke," Cornelia said. "The post hit her. She must have imagined the rest."

"I didn't imagine…," Lindsey began.

"Oh, my," Mrs. Cutler said again. "This is terrible, just terrible." She seemed to be on the verge of tears as she held Lindsey's face between trembling hands. "Oh, my dear, I'm so sorry. Call Neal. We have to get her to the hospital, to the emergency room. I'm so sorry."

"It's all right," Lindsey said. "I think it looks worse than it is."

"It's such a beautiful old room," Mrs. Cutler said. "I never thought you would be in any danger here. I didn't realize. I'm so sorry."

"There's no sign of anyone in the room," Cornelia said.

Lindsey went to the bathroom window. With shaking, blood stained hands, she tried to push it open, but the window was locked from the inside.

"Wash your hands, darling," Mrs. Cutler said. "There's blood all over them." She turned on the water and let it run for a while. Lindsey went back to the lavatory and held her hands beneath the warm water. She looked at her own haunted face in the mirror and was horrified by her appearance. Her face was pale, and her eyes were bloodshot and swollen. Blood was running down her cheek. The front of her shirt was covered with it. Cornelia pressed a damp washrag to her cheek. Lindsey held it in place. Her hand trembled. She realized, to her embarrassment, that her teeth were chattering and her knees were shaking.

Mrs. Cutler apologized several more times. She took Lindsey by the arm, led her down to the sunroom, and urged her to sit. Cornelia packed a sandwich bag with ice and brought it to her.

"You wait right here," Mrs. Cutler told her. "I need to freshen up before Neal sees me."

"Please," Lindsey said. "I don't want to be alone."

"Then I won't leave you," Mrs. Cutler said. She took Lindsey's hand and held it. "If I frighten Neal half out of his wits, he'll just have to be frightened."

"You look fine," Lindsey told her. Her voice was weak.

"On the contrary," Mrs. Cutler said, "I look like a thousand-year-old witch who has just flown her broomstick through a typhoon."

Lindsey laughed in spite of everything.

"I'm sorry," she said. "The way you said it…."

"That's all right, darling."

Lindsey looked down at her bare thighs and realized the blood-soaked T-shirt she was wearing didn't completely cover the panties underneath.

"I'd better get a fresh shirt and some jeans," she said. "Can you go back to the room with me?"

"Cornelia will fetch them for you," Mrs. Cutler said. "Don't worry about anything."

Cornelia reappeared a moment later, her hair and clothing arranged so perfectly that she almost looked like a department-store manikin.

"Cornelia," Mrs. Cutler said. "Could you please bring Miss Lindsey a fresh shirt and some pants to wear? The sight of her underwear might be more than Neal can handle."

"I'll get them."

"Where in the world did you get those bloomers, dear? They hardly cover your bottom at all. In my day, they came nearly to our knees. We left more to the imagination then. Sometimes we got a bit carried away with it."

Cornelia returned a moment later with Lindsey's clothes. Lindsey stood, her knees still weak, took the clothes into the hall bathroom, and changed without closing the door. She avoided looking into the mirror for fear that some face other than her own might be staring back.

This is crazy. There couldn't have been anybody there. It must have been a dream, or maybe the blow to my head jarred my brain. She was afraid just the same.

"This is terrible," Lindsey heard Mrs. Cutler telling Cornelia in a low voice. "Just terrible. That poor child. I never thought he would hurt her."

Cold, invisible needles prickled Lindsey's skin. *I never thought he would hurt her.* Had she really heard what she thought she had heard?

"It's all right, Mrs. Cutler," the German woman told her. "She's going to be okay."

After she dressed herself, Lindsey went back to the sunroom. Mrs. Cutler sat beside her and talked to her until Neal and Jolene arrived.

"You poor thing," Jolene said as she knelt beside Lindsey. "Let me see your face."

Lindsey pulled back the bag of ice.

"That's going to need stitches," Neal said. "What did you say happened?"

"A bedpost broke off and hit her," Mrs. Cutler said. "It was solid oak."

"What were you doing in there?" Neal asked. "Jumping on the bed?"

"Just sleeping. I dreamed there was somebody in the room. At least, I think I dreamed it."

"The windows were locked from the inside," Cornelia said.

"Let's get you down to the emergency room." Neal took her by the arm and led her down the hall. Jolene, Mrs. Cutler, and Cornelia walked with them.

Lindsey stepped out into the cool night air with only flip-flops on her bare feet. Neal and Jolene helped her gently into the passenger seat and even buckled her seatbelt for her. Mrs. Cutler and Cornelia stood on the porch and watched.

"You're going to be okay," Jolene told Lindsey as she squeezed her hand. Then she closed the passenger side door, opened the rear door, and climbed into the seat behind Lindsey. Neal started the engine. The van's headlight beams brushed across the trunks of trees as he drove down the hill. Lindsey halfway expected to see the spectral intruder standing in the road as they passed the spot where she'd seen him that first night, but he failed to make an appearance. As her fear faded, weariness set in. She faded in and out of sleep as Neal drove.

"Wake up," she heard Neal say. "We're here."

She opened her eyes and saw the haloed lights of the hospital glaring through the windshield. An ambulance was parked beneath the awning outside the emergency room door. She recognized the hospital as the same one they had taken Shadow to on the night of the beach party.

Neal opened the passenger door and helped Lindsey out of her seat.

"Are you okay?" he asked.

"I'm drowsy," she said. "I can hardly stay awake."

"Are you dizzy?" Jolene asked. "Do you think you've got a concussion?"

"I don't think so."

Neal and Jolene hovered around Lindsey as she stepped out into the parking lot. They held onto her arms, patted her, and kept telling her she would be all right.

They're being so sweet, she thought, but I'm okay.

"What have we got here?" a nurse asked as they brought Lindsey in.

"Her bed broke," Neal said.

"She got *this* from falling out of bed?"

"I didn't see it," Neal said, "but that's what she tells me."

The nurse looked at Lindsey suspiciously.

"Name, please."

"Lindsey Holland."

"Have you ever been admitted here before?"

Lindsey stumbled.

"I think you'd better sit down," Jolene told her. Lindsey sank into a plastic chair and sat there as the nurse asked about insurance and other personal factors. The nurse left for a moment, and the doctor came out. It was the same doctor who had tended to Shadow's injuries a week earlier.

"Neal," he said, "what are you doing back here?"

"Another injury," Neal said.

"What kind of parties is your church throwing?"

"I didn't have anything to do with this one."

The doctor sat beside Lindsey. "I'm Doctor Lee," he said. "And your name's Lindsey?"

"Yes, sir."

"You don't have to call me 'sir.' Is that a Southern accent I hear? Where are you from?"

"Texas."

"A cowgirl, eh? Let me see your face, Lindsey."

She moved the ice pack aside. The doctor placed his hand under her chin and moved her head around as he studied the injury.

"What did you say happened?"

"I was in bed. It was a big, wooden bed. One of the posts broke off, and the knob hit me."

"Where did this happen?"

"At Mrs. Cutler's house. She's the lady I'm staying with."

"This is going to have to have a stitch or two. Come on back."

"Is this where Caitlyn works?" Lindsey asked as she walked toward a room.

"What's her last name?"

"I don't know."

The doctor led Lindsey into a room with a medical bed, cabinets, and posters on the wall. She sat down on the bed. Paper sheets rattled beneath her.

"Just lie still," the doctor said. He patted her shoulder and helped her lie back.

A doctor returned with a nurse a few minutes later. They cleaned Lindsey's wound, gave her a shot to dull the pain, and stitched the wound shut. Neal and Jolene stood in the room and waited.

"It shouldn't leave much of a scar," the doctor told Lindsey, "but the area around your eye is going to be black and swollen for several days." He turned to Neal and Jolene. "I'm going to need the two of you to step out for a few minutes."

"Okay," Neal said. "What's going on?"

"Routine procedure," the doctor said. He opened the door, and a police officer came in. Neal's mouth opened, but he didn't say anything for a moment.

"We'll be outside," he told Lindsey.

The policeman came in and stood by the bed. He had salt-and-pepper hair and Hispanic features.

"I'm Detective Montoya," he said, "from the sheriff's office. Ordinarily, a deputy would be doing this interview, but I just happened to be here already. I need to ask you a few questions."

"Okay," Lindsey said.

"I need you to tell me exactly what happened to you tonight. Don't leave anything out."

What's going on here? she wondered.

"I was asleep in my bed at Mrs. Cutler's house."

"Was there anyone else sleeping in the bed with you?"

"No," Lindsey said. The question offended her, but she tried not to show it.

"Was anyone else in the room?"

"No," she said. "At least...."

"At least what?"

"There wasn't *supposed* to be anyone else there. I dreamed I heard a voice."

"What did it say?"

"I thought it said, 'Get out.'"

"Get out?"

"That's what it sounded like."

"Did you recognize the voice?"

"No," she said. "It sounded like a man's voice."

"And who else was staying in the house?"

"Just Mrs. Cutler and her housekeeper. Caitlyn might have been there. She works unusual hours."

"And these are all women?"

"Yes."

"Then what happened?"

She considered editing her account for fear of sounding insane, but she told the investigating officer everything— everything but the half-heard conversation between Mrs. Cutler and Cornelia. *I didn't think he would hurt her.* Had she really heard it? Montoya listened and made notes as Lindsey talked. His eyebrows shot up when she mentioned the locked bedroom door. He was frowning deeply by the time Lindsey reached the end of her story. She wondered what he was thinking.

"Has anything like this ever happened to you before?" he asked.

"No," she said.

"How much of this story can your friends confirm?" he asked. "Did they see the room or check the house for intruders?"

"No."

"Are you afraid to go back to that house?"

She paused for a moment. "I…don't guess so."

"One more thing," he said. "Can you describe the shape of the knob on the end of the bedpost? Was it a simple ball, or did it have ridges?"

"Just a ball, I think. Why?"

"Because the bruises on your face look a lot like knuckle marks."

Chapter 11: Hauntings of One Sort or Another

The sun was just starting to rise when Neal and Jolene brought Lindsey back to the Cutler house.

"I think we'd better give you the morning off," Neal said as they walked up to the door. "We'll let you get some sleep and check up on you around eleven."

"Okay, thanks. How does my face look?"

"Like you've been in a fight," Neal said as he knocked on the door. "You still look cute, though. Nobody will be disgusted or anything."

"He has a way with words," Jolene said.

Cornelia opened the door. "Come in," she said. "Mrs. Cutler is expecting you."

They followed her back to the sunroom. Mrs. Cutler had arranged a big breakfast for them with Belgian waffles, pineapple slices, homemade whipped cream and cherries, coffee, hot chocolate, orange juice, grape juice, and biscuits.

"What's all of this?" Neal asked.

"It's for Lindsey," she said, "and both of you. Please, sit."

"Well, thanks," Neal said.

"How are you, darling?" she asked Lindsey. "Come here and let me look at you."

Lindsey smiled awkwardly and did as Mrs. Cutler requested. A bandage covered her stitches, but the skin beneath her left eye was black and swollen.

"Oh, you poor thing," Mrs. Cutler said. "I have a new bedroom for you. You'll never have to go back to that terrible room again."

"I'm afraid the problem isn't the room," Lindsey said, "or even the house."

"What do you mean, dear?"

"Never mind. It's okay."

"Would you mind showing me the room where it happened?" Neal asked.

"Not at all," Mrs. Cutler said. "Cornelia will take you."

"Thanks."

Lindsey was relieved not to be going back to the same bedroom but wondered what it was about that particular room that would make any difference. Though she had told Mrs. Cutler and Cornelia about seeing –or thinking she had seen—a man in her room the previous night, she had never told either of them about the phantom presence that sat on her bed and sang to her or about the strange dreams she sometimes had. For some reason, however, Mrs. Cutler blamed the room itself for Lindsey's experience. Lindsey thought of asking more questions, but she was too drowsy. As much as she appreciated the breakfast Mrs. Cutler had prepared for them, her desire for sleep was stronger than her hunger. She was afraid she would nod off and fall face-first into her plate.

Neal and Cornelia returned a moment later. Mrs. Cutler asked Neal to lead them in a prayer of thanks, and they ate together. Lindsey gazed out the window at the sunny skies and the rolling ocean, and the terrors of the previous night seemed as far away as a half-forgotten dream.

After breakfast, Mrs. Cutler and Cornelia led Lindsey to her new quarters. This bedroom was located in the corridor between the front door and the sunroom. The new room was smaller than the first room, and it didn't have the ocean view or the adjoining bathroom, but, under the circumstances, Lindsey had no problem with any of the new room's shortcomings. The only real drawback was her nearness to Mrs. Cutler's mummy. The alcove in which the Egyptian maiden slept was only about twenty feet from the bedroom door. Lindsey didn't want to sound like a total coward by complaining about the little corpse. As least the sarcophagus was too small to contain anything as intimidating as the hulk from her nightmare.

"I'll call you later, precious," Jolene told Lindsey as she got ready to leave. Jolene and Neal both hugged her like a daughter before they departed.

"I'll let you rest now," Mrs. Cutler said as she pulled the door shut behind her. Lindsey pulled off her jeans, climbed into bed, and fell asleep.

***

"It was so strange," Lindsey told Todd as they walked down the sidewalk between shops. "I was sure I was awake, but there's no way there could have been anybody else in the room."

"That's not that uncommon," Todd told her. "There's a twilight state between sleep and consciousness where you're aware of your surroundings but you can still dream."

"The Twilight Zone?"

"That's what it is."

The sidewalks of Cannon Beach were packed with people, both locals and tourists, exploring the shops and galleries. Lindsey and Todd had been walking for about an hour. Walking in the sun with crowds of cheerful shoppers lifted Lindsey's spirits and made it easier to talk to Todd about her experience. They had just enjoyed a Tex-Mex lunch at one of the restaurants and were busy exploring galleries. They stepped into a wooden building with glass sculptures of dolphins in the window. Recordings of waves and soft Hawaiian music gently transported them to a place of warm beaches and gently swaying palm trees. The paintings on the walls were mostly of whales, dolphins, and sailing ships.

"These are beautiful," Lindsey said. "That last gallery was just weird."

"Abstract art just doesn't do it for you?"

"I like some of it," she said, "but those pictures were creepy. You should take a picture of my face. It would fit right in."

"Your face doesn't look that bad," he said. He squeezed her arm to reassure her. Everyone was treating her with such tenderness. It was sweet…up to a point, anyway.

"You should have seen me without makeup. My cheek is the color of an eggplant. What were you saying about the twilight state?"

"People have hallucinations when they're half-awake," he said. "Hypnagogic hallucinations are the ones that happen when you're falling asleep, and hypnopompic hallucinations happen when you're waking up."

"And they're common?"

"Pretty common, yeah. Especially when you're sleep-deprived or narcoleptic."

"Narcoleptic? That's when you fall asleep all the time?"

"Right."

"I hope I'm not narcoleptic. I don't think I sleep that much."

"I don't think you're narcoleptic."

"How do you know about all of this?"

"Research," he said. "For my film."

"I wonder how much this picture costs," Lindsey whispered. It was a painting of a tropical shoreline at sunset with a wooden church, palm trees, and brightly colored flowers. Dolphins, sea turtles, and bright yellow, orange, and blue fish swam beneath the surface. Coral covered the rocks.

"Twelve hundred," Todd said, checking the tag beside it.

"That's a little too much to put on my credit card," she said.

The picture beside it showed a sunken ship surrounded by exotic fish and coral. Smokey rays of sun brushed across rough wood and broken timbers.

"I like this one," Todd said. "Look at the detail."

"So, what about these hallucinations?"

"They're pretty common," he said. "That's all I'm saying. There's also sleep paralysis. That's a related phenomenon."

"Paralysis?"

"There's something in our brains that causes our muscles to relax so we won't hurt ourselves while we're asleep. The effect can linger into the early stages of consciousness. You're partly awake but completely unable to move. Then some scary nightmare creature comes into the room with you, and you can't get away from it."

"This happens a lot?"

"So often that some cultures have traditions built around it. One culture calls it the 'Old Hag' dream because it's like having an evil spirit sitting on your chest, crushing your lungs. It's one of the explanations for UFO abduction experiences."

"And it's not a sign of anything serious?"

"Not usually, no. It could mean you're under a lot of stress or behind on your sleep."

"That makes me feel a little better, anyway."

"Have you had any more of these experiences?"

"A few," she said.

"Before or after the séance?"

"Both. I had the first one the night I came into town."

"And the figure you saw was of a man?"

"Yeah."

"And you've never seen a woman?"

"No. Why are you asking this?"

"No reason. Just wondering."

They left the gallery and stepped back into the sun.

I didn't think he would hurt her. Even after Todd's words of reassurance, the half-heard comment still clawed at the corner of Lindsey's mind.

Lindsey and Todd were laughing when they walked into the Dawn Treader Café, but something in Jolene's expression stopped Lindsey cold. There was a man sitting at the bar, a dark-haired man with the build of a linebacker. He turned and rose to his feet as they entered. It was Pack.

***

"Hello, Lindsey."

"Pack," Lindsey said. "It's…good to see you." She turned to Todd. "Todd, this is Pack. He's my fiancé."

"It's nice to meet you," Todd said. He extended his hand. "Lindsey talks about you all the time. I know that sounds cliché, but…."

Pack stared at him. He was a big man, about six-four with shoulders a yard wide and a face like a male model.

"Look," Todd said, "when I invited Lindsey to Seattle, it was just...."

"I need to talk to my fiancé," Pack said. He didn't bother to shake the extended hand. "Please."

"I'll see you later, Lindsey."

"Thanks, Todd."

Pack stood there like a statue. The bell above the door rang as Todd walked out.

There were no customers in the café. "I'll be in the back, Lindsey," Jolene said. Jolene walked back into the kitchen. *Don't go,* Lindsey wanted to say.

"What happened to your face?"

Lindsey stammered.

"Answer me. What happened to your face?"

"A bedpost," Lindsey said. "It broke off and hit me."

"A bedpost? Are you kidding me? It looks like somebody hit you."

"It was just a bedpost."

"And that's all?"

"I had a nightmare about a ghost in my room, but there wasn't really anybody there."

He stared at her for a moment. "Well, as long as you're okay. I'm sorry about the things I said to you over the phone, and I was probably pretty rude to your friend just now."

"Yeah. You were."

"I'm sorry about that. You can tell him for me. I came out here to try to smooth things over, and it seems like I just keep making them worse. After all of these years, we're finally about to get married. It's finally within reach, and I don't want anything—or anybody—to spoil that. You can understand that, can't you?"

"It's just that it's happening so fast."

"Fast? Lindsey, you're twenty-four, and we've been dating since junior high. What's fast about any of this?"

He was right, of course. They had known each other for over eleven years. Why had she said that? Lindsey took a breath.

"I just keep wondering if we're making a mistake, but we can't admit it to ourselves because we've been together so long."

"No," he said. "Don't say that. Don't ever say that. This is what we've wanted. It's what we've dreamed about." He took her by the hands. "I know you're having some doubts. That's natural. But, everything is going to be all right."

"I don't know."

"What do I have to do to prove it to you?"

"I don't know if you can. I don't have a peace about this, Pack."

"A peace?"

"You know. The peace of God."

"God hasn't given you permission to marry me? What are you expecting, Lindsey? Engraved tablets? Good luck waiting for that. You might as well be a nun."

"Haven't I heard you talk about your 'little voice' that tells you when you're about to do the wrong thing? How is that so different?"

"Because my little voice is telling me you're the best thing that ever happened to me, and if I let you go, my life won't be worth crap."

"Pack."

"What's it going to take, Lindsey? What do I have to do?"

"I don't...."

"What's it going to take?"

What could she tell him?

"Stay here for a few days," she said. "Go to church with me, and be nice to my friends. I'll pray about it, and I'll try to give you an answer. If I still don't feel a peace about it, it will be up to you to decide whether you want to keep waiting or let me go."

"Okay," he finally said. "Can we go somewhere more private?"

"I have to go to work now," she said. "I get off at six."

"Can I pick you up at six, then?"

"Yes. I'll need to go home and change, but you can meet me here and follow me out to Mrs. Cutler's house."

"All right, I'll see you at six."

"I don't want to stay out too late," she said. "I was awake most of last night, and I'll probably start nodding off around ten."

"Just a couple of hours, then. I just want to see you."

He kissed her. It was not a lingering, passionate kiss. She didn't really feel like kissing him at that moment but didn't want to reject him, either.

"I'll see you at six," he said again. The bell rang as he walked out. Lindsey exhaled and sank into a chair.

"I could have given you the afternoon off," Jolene said as she emerged from the back room.

"No. It's okay. I need time to think about this."

"He's a hulk," Jolene said. "Or is the word 'hunk'? I never could keep those straight."

"It's okay," Lindsey said. "They both describe him pretty well. What do you think?"

"What do I think? About what?"

"Pack. What's your impression of him?"

"Very good-looking, of course," Jolene said. "I see what you mean about him being possessive. Did you see the look he gave Todd?"

"Oh, yeah. I guess he had a right to be upset. He came out here and caught me running around with another guy. It's my fault. I need to apologize to Todd."

"*You* need to apologize?"

"For putting him in such an awkward situation. Did anything like that ever happen when you were dating Neal?"

"A few times. I used to get mad at him for ogling the Victoria's Secret window displays. One time he told me I was too insecure about my body. That really made me mad. I used to wonder if he regretted marrying me, if he'd have rather have married a tall, blonde Caucasian girl with big boobs. That's what I thought every time we passed Victoria's Secret."

"Did you ever tell him that?"

"Yeah. He laughed, and I started crying. He was really sweet after that. He told me he married exactly who he had wanted to marry, and I finally believed him."

"That's nice."

"It's not really my business, but if you and Pack have trust issues, you'll save yourself a lot of heartache if you resolve them before you get married."

"I know. I know." She shook her head. "This is really strange."

"What's strange?"

"This whole day. Everything since I went to bed last night. It's like I woke up in some strange alternate life."

"Just try to take it easy."

***

"What happened to you?" Neal asked as he passed Todd on the sidewalk in front of a hair salon.

Todd stopped walking, and shook his head. "Nothing much. I just met Lindsey's fiancé."

"He's here?"

"Yeah. I took Lindsey around to some of the art galleries here. We were really having a good time. Then we walked into the café, and her boyfriend was in there waiting. It was pretty awkward."

"What happened?"

"I introduced myself, and he said he needed to talk to his fiancé. I held my hand out to him, but he just looked at it."

"That's pretty awkward, all right. What did Lindsey do?"

"Looked like she was about to sink into the floor. I didn't stay around long after that."

"He was rude? He acted like a jerk?"

"I don't know. A little bit, maybe, but I guess I can understand that under the circumstances. We probably looked pretty guilty."

"Hmm. How guilty are you?"

"I'm guilty of being attracted to her, but that's all. I don't think she's attracted to me at all. Girls like her don't go for geeks."

"Don't underestimate yourself. Or her. It's a frustrating situation, but don't make it out to be worse than it is."

"I'll try to keep that in mind."

"I'd better get back to the café," Neal said. "I don't want to miss the drama."

A car zipped by. The big man inside locked eyes with Todd as it passed.

"Was that him?"

"Oh, yeah."

"Man, he's bulked up since high school. You're lucky he didn't pound you."

"Thanks. That really helps my ego."

"Hey," Neal said. "You're tough, as cocker spaniels go, but that guy's a rottweiler."

"A cocker spaniel? At least let me be a scrappy little mutt."

"I'm sorry. That's what I meant. You're a junkyard dog if I ever saw one."

"That really makes it better. I'll see you later. I've got some video clips to edit."

"Hang in there, Scrappy."

Chapter 12: A Matter of Trust

Mrs. Cutler was staring out at the ocean when Lindsey and Pack entered the sunroom.

"Mrs. Cutler, this is Pack, my fiancé."

"Oh, my," Mrs. Cutler said. "I didn't realize we were having company. I look a fright."

"You look fine," Lindsey assured her.

"Oh, bosh."

"We won't be here long," Lindsey said. "We're going out, and I wanted to change first."

"So, you're the young man who is marrying my Lindsey?"

"Yes, ma'am."

"Well, you're a healthy-looking fellow, aren't you? Lindsey said you were quite the athlete, and I certainly believe it. And your name is Pack?"

"Jacob Packard, really. People just call me Pack."

"I see. Well, sit down, won't you? Let's talk for a while."

"We really can't stay long," Lindsey said. "We've got dinner reservations at seven-thirty. I need to run to my room and change."

"Well, if you must. I suppose Pack will have to make do with my company while you're getting ready."

"I'll be right back," Lindsey said. She rushed down the hall to her room. She threw off her work clothes, refreshed her deodorant, went to the closet, selected fresh clothes, and quickly pulled them on. She had tied her hair back in a ponytail that morning. Now she untied it, shook her hair out, brushed it, and sprayed it. She usually washed it before a date, but they'd miss the movie if she spent as much time on it as she ordinarily did. She wished, at that moment, that she was back in the upstairs bedroom with its adjoining bath. Instead, she had to cross the hall to the downstairs bathroom where she washed her face and put on fresh makeup. Her eye was still swollen, but it didn't look as bad as it had that morning. Makeup hid most of the bruising, but one eye was still puffier than the other.

A chill crawled up Lindsey's spine as she turned away from the mirror. She spun back around, expecting to find someone watching her from the mirror, but the glass showed only an empty room. Her heart, she realized, was pounding. What was wrong with her these days?

Lindsey bounded back down the hall to the sunroom where Pack and Mrs. Cutler were waiting for her. Pack rose to his feet as she entered the room.

"Are you ready, Lindsey?"

"I think so."

"We'd better get going."

"Enjoy yourselves," Mrs. Cutler said. "I'll expect her home by eleven o'clock. You have my telephone number, and I do expect to hear from you if there are any delays."

"Yes, ma'am," Pack said.

"Good night, Mrs. Cutler," Lindsey said.

"Good night, dear."

Pack lost no time getting Lindsey down the hall and out of the mansion.

"That is one nosy old biddy," Pack said as they stepped out the front door. "You wouldn't believe what all she asked me." He pulled the door closed behind them.

"She can be a little protective," Lindsey said as they were walking toward the car.

"Did you hear her telling me when to bring you home? I had half a mind to tell her you're twenty-four years old, she's not your grandmother, and that I'd bring you home anytime I wanted."

Pack opened the door for her and held it until she got in. Lindsey pulled on her seatbelt. Pack dropped into the driver's seat, and started the car.

"How much time have you been spending with this Todd guy?"

"Pack…."

"I'm serious, Lindsey. You act like you're getting cold feet, talk about wondering if our relationship is a mistake, and I come out here and find you with another guy. What's really going on?"

"Watch it!" Lindsey cried as the car rushed toward a hairpin turn. Pack braked, slowed the car down, and rounded the curve.

"What's going on?" he asked again.

"Nothing is going on. I helped him with a film he's making, and this morning he showed me some art galleries. That's all."

He stared at her for a moment. She met his gaze until it became uncomfortable, then looked away.

"And you're not attracted to him? Not even a little bit?"

"Well, I…I mean, he's nice, and he's interesting, but he's not really my type."

"And you're not attracted to him? Not at all?"

"I don't know. If I weren't already engaged so someone I've loved for most of my life…."

"You're not answering the question."

"You tell me about Jessie. Are you attracted to her?"

"She's a friend. That's all. And you're still avoiding the question."

"No," she said. "I'm not attracted to him."

"You haven't been dating him?"

"No."

"You haven't been kissing him?"

"No."

"You've never slept with him?"

"No! That's ridiculous. You know I would never do that."

"And meeting him has nothing to do with these doubts you keep talking about?"

"I had doubts before I even met him. I came out here to try to think them through. I told you that. You kept saying you were sure about our relationship, even if I wasn't."

He didn't reply. He just stared at the winding road ahead.

"Have you been faithful to *me*?" she asked. Pack turned and glared at her, his eyes flashing with rage. Lindsey met his stare for a moment, then looked away. "It's good to see you, too," she said, her voice cracking.

Neither of them said a word as Pack drove down the mountain, down the highway, and into Astoria.

"Look," he said as they pulled into the parking lot of the restaurant. "Forget what I said, all right? Let's just try to enjoy the evening."

"Okay." Lindsey wondered if he really thought she could turn her feelings on and off so easily.

"I'm sorry about the way I act sometimes," he said. "It's just that we've come so far together, and I don't want to lose you when we're so close to having the life we always wanted. You can understand that, can't you?"

"I guess."

"You guess? She guesses. I guess I deserve that."

Farrell's Landing was a good choice. Lindsey had to admit that. Located in a refurbished warehouse that overlooked the Columbia River, the restaurant was surrounded by wooden docks that extended out into the river's dark waters. Boats were tethered into their slips at a nearby marina. They gently rose and fell with the movement of the tide. A cool wind rippled through Lindsey's hair as she stepped out into the fading light. Pack held his hand out to her, and she dutifully took it. They crossed a bridge, their feet echoing on the weathered planking. Pack pushed open the door, and they stepped into a large, dimly lit room with heavy ceiling beams and nautical décor. The pale light of a large saltwater aquarium illuminated the guest waiting area. A hostess in a white shirt and black pants stood behind a counter that looked as if it had been made from a wooden shipping crate. A hand-lettered sign said, "Please wait to be seated."

"I've got a reservation," Pack said as they approached. She took his name and scanned a chart.

"Follow me, please," she said as she picked up a pair of menus.

Pack and Lindsey followed her to the back of the restaurant. It was a nice view. A large window overlooked the river. The hostess took out a book of matches and lit the lamp that sat in the middle of the table.

"Your waitress will be with you shortly," she said as she turned to go.

"Thanks."

Pack held Lindsey's chair out for her as she seated herself, then sat down across from her.

"Is this okay?" he asked her. "We can go somewhere else if you want to."

"No," she said. "It's fine. It's nice."

"Nice?"

"Really nice. It was a good choice."

"I'm glad you approve."

Lindsey scanned the menu. None of the entrees was priced below $30.

"The food's pretty expensive here," she said.

"Don't worry about it. Order anything you want."

"Are you sure?"

"Yeah. Don't worry about it."

"Okay."

The waitress came by and took drink and appetizer orders.

"Lighten up a little bit," Pack said. "We used to have fun."

"I am having fun," Lindsey said, forcing a smile.

"You're a bad liar. You always were."

And you could always lie straight-faced, Lindsey thought. She said nothing. Pack really was doing his best.

"What's *really* wrong, Lindsey? Why are you acting so strange? Is it because we're about to get married?"

"I think so."

"Why? Can you at least tell me that?"

"I don't know. I think maybe I didn't want to admit there were any problems between us. Not even to myself. For years,

I've just pushed everything to the back of my mind and hoped it would go away. Avoid conflict at any cost. Now, we're about to get married, and I can't ignore it anymore. It's all right there, and there's so much of it, I don't know where to begin to deal with it. I don't know if I can deal with it."

"Why didn't you say something sooner?"

"I tried. Over and over. You always managed to talk your way around the problems. Like a good lawyer, you always found a way to shoot holes through every argument I had. You won every time, but not really. All you proved was that you're better at arguing that I am. Nothing ever changed, because, in your mind, you were always right. I finally just stopped trying to talk about it."

"I don't know what to say to that," he said. "If I try to defend myself, you'll just say I'm doing it again."

"Why do you have to defend yourself?" she asked. "Why does it always have to be a competition between us to show who's right? Why can't we work together to improve our relationship, because it's something we both want?"

"I don't know what you want," Pack said.

"How about honesty?" she said. "And just to hear you admit you're wrong sometimes?"

The waitress came with the drink orders. They stopped talking about their problems and placed their orders. The tension vanished momentarily or at least, it was hidden from view. Finally, as she disappeared into the bar, they faced each other, and the tension returned.

"You asked me if I'd been faithful to you," he said. "The truth is, I haven't always been. I think you know that."

She stiffened. She hadn't expected such a direct revelation. He had always denied it before. Was she finally going to hear the truth?

"The first year of college, I partied pretty hard. With the football team and the fraternity guys…yeah, I got pretty crazy. I lost myself for a while, and there were plenty of drunk sorority girls there to help me do it. There wasn't any love there. I became friends with one or two of them, but there was no real love there. Then you showed up on campus, and you were Miss Perfect. College life didn't faze you at all."

"It fazed me," she said. She was sure the tattoo on her back had started itching as soon as she'd thought about it.

"Not that I ever saw."

"You used to call me Miss Goody Two-Shoes and accuse me of never having any fun."

"Yeah, I did. It was like dating my mom. Look, I admired you and resented you both. I wanted somebody in my life I could look up to. You've always been that. But, I'd gotten used to partying on a pretty regular basis. You crashed my party and shut it down."

"I didn't shut it down," she said. "You kept on doing it behind my back."

"Only for the first few months," he said. "After a year of total freedom, it was hard to go cold turkey, but you got me back into church, and made me straighten out. I owe you for that. If you hadn't shown up when you did, I'd have partied my way out of any chance I ever had of getting into law school."

"And you haven't cheated on me since we were sophomores?"

"I swear I haven't."

"And you're not still drinking?"

"Never touch it."

"For how long?"

"Come on, Lindsey."

"How long? A week? Six months?"

He sighed.

"A little over a year."

"Are you getting any help? Counseling? Alcoholics Anonymous?"

"I don't need any of that. I'm okay."

"Pack, I wish I could believe you. I wish I could trust you, but down deep, I really don't."

"What will it take to make you trust me?"

"I don't know."

"Do you want me to take a polygraph test?"

"You'd really do that?"

"You'd really want me to? You distrust me that much?"

"I've always wanted to believe you, but you've taken advantage of that. You've told me what you thought I wanted to hear for so long that I never know what to believe anymore."

"So, you think I'm a liar?"

"You just admitted you lied to me about being faithful."

"I should have just kept on lying instead of telling you the truth now?"

"You never should have lied in the first place."

"You think I'm a liar. What else?"

"I saw what you did to that boy at the party that night. I'll never forget that."

"That was an isolated incident. I was drunk, and he mouthed off."

"You outweighed him by over a hundred pounds."

"Little jerk needed to be taught a lesson."

"Taught a lesson? You put him in the hospital."

"I shouldn't have done that. I know. I should have just walked away."

"Did you ever apologize to him?"

"Of course, I apologized to him. I apologized to him and to his family. My dad had to pay the family $10,000, and he made me work for him all summer to pay it off. I paid my dues, Lindsey. I learned my lesson."

"What are you going to do when we have children? What if they're assertive like you? Are you going to put them in the hospital?"

"No. Of course not! I'd never do that. You make me sound like some kind of monster."

"You became a monster that night," she said. "I don't ever want to see that monster again."

"You won't," he said. "I swear you won't."

"I wish I could believe that."

"Believe it, Lindsey. You've got to believe it. I don't know how long it will take to convince you, but if we have to put off the wedding until you're sure, then that's the way it has to be. If I've waited this long, I can wait a little longer."

"Are you sure about that?"

"I don't want to, I admit, but if it's what we have to do to put your mind at ease, I'm willing to wait a little while longer. Your mom will go crazy, but if you're willing to put up with that, I am."

"Will you help me tell her?"

"I'll tell her myself, if you want me to. Just think about it first and make sure it's what you want to do."

Lindsey nodded. As she was about to respond, the waitress returned with their food. The conversation was lighter after that. It moved away from the subject of marriage and trust, and they talked about what they'd been doing during their time apart, about things they had seen. The tension that had hung like a shadow over the earlier part of the evening lifted, and Lindsey actually found herself having fun. Maybe a little extra time was all it would take for them to work through their problems, and she'd be able to marry Pack without doubts. That was her hope.

Pack took Lindsey home early, just as he had said he would. They kissed goodnight at Mrs. Cutler's front door. After he drove away, Lindsey unlocked the door and crept to the back of the house. Mrs. Cutler was still awake. She was sitting in the sunroom rocking and gazing out the window as the last rays of a late sunset clung to the horizon.

"How was your evening?" she asked.

"Fine," Lindsey said. "We talked about things we'd been needing to talk about."

"I see," Mrs. Cutler said. "He's a very intense young man, isn't he?"

"That's one way to describe him."

"He's a powerful presence. I'm sure he'll make a good lawyer."

"I think he will."

"It's strictly your decision," Mrs. Cutler said, "but I really liked the other young man better."

Lindsey smiled slightly but said nothing. "I'd better get to bed. I'm pretty tired."

"Good night, darling."

Lindsey walked back to the downstairs bedroom. She wondered if this change in location would make any difference. It was possible that her experiences had less to do with the room and everything to do with the doubts she had been struggling with. It was possible that seeing Pack in person and discussing the doubts with him had relieved the pressure on some level. Perhaps without that inner conflict to fuel her nightmares, there wouldn't be any more of them. As she changed into the T-shirt and panties she usually wore to bed, she hoped the spectral visitors of previous nights would leave her alone.

Chapter 13: Zombies

It was nearly ten o'clock when Todd climbed into his car and started for Portland. It would be a late night, and he'd probably regret it in the morning, but that was all right. Earlier that evening, Todd had been locked in a dark apartment, plodding through the edits of his documentary and eating cold pizza. He wasn't really in the mood to work on anything, but he had made himself do it anyway. If he kept himself busy enough, he reasoned, he wouldn't think about Lindsey and about what had happened earlier that day. He wanted to punch the flat-headed jock Lindsey was dating but knew his attitude wasn't Christian.

He should have known better than to allow himself to think there was any chance he and Lindsey might get together. He cursed himself for his stupidity. Lindsey had been engaged when he'd met her, and she had made it clear to him that she had every intention of marrying her high-school sweetheart in October. What part of that had he not understood?

If Todd had thought, even for a moment, that working on his project would take his mind off Lindsey, he was quickly disappointed. When he saw the shots she had taken at the Sasquatch Steak and Ale and on the trip to Seattle, all he could do was think about her and wallow in self-pity. It was disgusting and pathetic, he told himself, but he kept right on wallowing. Then his cell phone rang. He flipped it open and pressed it to his ear.

"Hello."

"Hey, Todd, this is Drew."

"Hi, Drew. What's going on?"

"You owe me one. Remember?"

"I remember. What do you want me to do?"

"I'm making a movie, man. I need some help."

The last thing Todd needed was another project. He had plenty of his own work to finish. Still, he had to ask: "What kind of movie?"

"Horror."

Todd had grown up on the Universal horror classics. As a child, his room had been filled with posters and glued-together models of Frankenstein, Dracula, Wolf-Man, and the rest. The thought of working on a monster movie was more than he could resist.

"When?"

"Tonight. I've got the place reserved. We're going to film all night."

"Where?"

"Outside Portland."

"I don't know. I've got classes tomorrow, and I'm not going to be able to stay awake if I'm up all night filming."

"I'm in a pinch, man, and I need somebody with some technical skills. I wouldn't ask if I wasn't desperate."

"Fine," Todd said. "I'll do it. It sounds like fun." He got driving directions before he hung up.

Todd wondered if he'd lost his mind, but the closer he got to Portland, the more his spirits lifted. Before the phone call, he'd been moping about Lindsey. Now he was actually starting to feel good.

It took him a while to find the house. It was on a winding back road in a dark forest. If Drew had been looking for a place with atmosphere, he had chosen well. Todd crossed a narrow, wooden bridge and pulled his car in beside the others he found there.

The house was a dilapidated two-story with a long porch across the front. Todd could hear screaming inside as he climbed the stairs onto the porch. He stopped outside the door and listened. He didn't want to ruin a take by bursting in at the wrong time. Finally he heard someone yell, "Cut!" and he stepped inside.

Drew was drinking a beer and giving directions to a blood-soaked girl wearing nothing but a bra and panties and smoking a cigarette. A zombie stood behind her and gnawed on a severed arm. The rest of the room was filled with zombies, victims, demons from hell, and members of the technical crew.

"Todd!" Drew yelled. "Glad you could make it. Everybody take five. Get a beer. Have a smoke. Save the weed for later. That's dessert."

"What's going on?" Todd asked as he and Drew shook hands.

"Attack of the zombies," Drew said. "You know zombies. They're hungry. They're horny."

"Do you have a script?"

"Yeah. It says, 'Hungry, horny zombies attack.'"

"So, basically, you're making it up as you go along? Framing the shots as you go?"

"Exactly."

"And what do you need me to do?"

"Operate the camera. I have to direct and operate the camera at the same time. I need to direct, but I want somebody behind the camera who won't cut the heads off the actors."

"Not until they're supposed to be cut off, anyway."

"Right, man." He laughed. "Get yourself a beer. Mellow out a little bit, if you can still do that."

"I'd better not, but thanks for the offer."

"Suit yourself, man. We're having a party after the shoot. Stay around if you want to."

"I've got class tomorrow."

"So do the rest of us. We're skipping."

"I try not to do that anymore."

"Me, too. Just not very hard. So, what's going on with your friend? Did you show her that video?"

"No. Not yet."

"Afraid she'll freak out?"

"Something like that."

"You should have brought her with you. I could always use a real spectral appearance in my film."

"I don't think she'll be making any more movies with us. Her boyfriend's in town."

"Oh, man. He didn't beat you up or anything, did he?"

"No, but he looked like he wanted to."

"Call me if you get into any trouble."

"I don't think you'd be much help. This guy is pretty big."

"I don't want to fight. I just want to film it."

"Thanks, Drew. You're a real friend."

"I was just kidding. You know that. I've got your back all the way."

"I know you do."

"Listen. I've got to take care of some things. Just look around. Get anything you want to eat or drink, and try not to think about Lindsey's boyfriend."

As Drew walked away, Todd looked around the room at the walking dead as they laughed and drank. The lighting was dim and dismal, and Todd could almost believe he was in the outer corridors of hell, that these college students really were walking around dead and didn't even realize it. He almost expected them to turn on him and attack.

Todd managed to make it through four hours of filming, four hours of screaming, cursing, artificial bloodshed, and simulated cannibalism. When he had heard Drew was making a horror film, he'd hoped for something with gothic, Old World charm, some kind of haunting mystery, or a battle between the forces of good an evil. This film, Todd had to admit, was about as entertaining as watching a guy with a bad case of the stomach flu throw up his guts. *I've got to get out of here,* he kept thinking, but he didn't want to abandon Drew after agreeing to help him. He really hated to be responsible for helping inflict such an atrocity on the audiences who would watch it, but doubted it would make it far enough down the distribution channels for that to be much of a problem.

Finally, at about four in the morning, Drew called an end to the shoot. Todd started for the door.

"Wait," Drew said. "Are you sure you don't want to stay around for the party?"

"I told you," Todd said. "I've got class tomorrow."

"These girls are hot, bro."

"I don't do that anymore, Drew."

"I know. You found Jesus. Your partying days are over."

"You got it."

"Suit yourself. Say a few 'Hail Mary's' for my movie."

"I'll see you, Drew. You take care of yourself."

"Thanks for helping me out."

"No problem. God bless you." Todd wondered after he said it if he'd meant it more as a blessing or as an attempt to aggravate Drew.

"Yeah. I'll see you."

A bra went flying past Todd's head as he opened the door. He didn't look back. Todd thought about Lindsey and about his humiliation at the hands of her jock boyfriend. He remembered his early years as a college student and the parties he had gone to then. He could smell the beer and the cigarette smoke and hear the laughter and swearing. His memory of the zombie makeup sent a shudder through him. *They're all dead, and they don't even know it.* He could still hear the noises of the party in the distance as he walked to his car. The night around him was still and somber, and he could imagine hordes of flesh-eating zombies stumbling out of the darkness to attack him. He made sure the backseat of his car was empty before he climbed in and locked the doors. He had to laugh at himself just a little bit as he turned the key.

Driving through the forest, even in the dark hours or early morning, was a welcome relief from Drew's house of zombies. The trees and mountain streams hinted at a world of family camping trips and river rafting that seemed a world away from the living death he had left behind. The lights of Portland, when he finally saw them, welcomed him back to the world of the living, but he kept thinking about Drew and the young zombies he had left back at the rundown house in the forest. The very atmosphere of the place was hellish to him, but none of them even seemed to notice. let alone to be bothered by it. It took him over an hour to get back home, and he only got an hour of sleep before it was time to get up for school.

Chapter 14: Sasquatch on Film

"What are we doing?"

"It's a reinactment," Lindsey said, "of a Bigfoot sighting."

"So, this is like a monster movie?"

"Kind of. It's a documentary about real-life monster stories." She told him about the earlier interview.

"That's kind of cool," Pack said.

"One more thing," she said. "We need somebody to wear the Bigfoot costume. It has to be somebody over six feet tall."

"Great," he said. "I bet you already volunteered me."

"I told Todd I would ask. Think about it. Bigfoot is the star."

"All right. I'll do it. But tell Todd he owes me one."

"He'll be delighted."

**

The borrowed Bronco had been a faithful friend. Muddy and scratched, it had climbed steep and rutted mountain roads, forded rocky streams, and bounced over fallen trees that threatened to block the path ahead. Todd drove with unerring precision. The vehicle smelled of hunting dogs, and shotgun shells rolled along the floorboards, out from under the weathered seats and back again.

"You didn't know what you were signing up for, did you, Lindsey?" Neal spoke from the backseat after riding in silence for over half an hour. Jolene was squeezed between the two of them.

"I love it," Lindsey said. "It's great."

"And here I took you for a mall rat."

"I'm a mall rat, too."

"Just try sitting on this hump," Jolene said.

Pack was squeezed into the passenger seat beside Todd. His long legs didn't allow him to sit anywhere else. The vehicle didn't allow him much headroom, either.

"Are you sure you know where you're going?" Pack asked.

"Yep," Todd said.

"Just checking."

"I'm starting to hear the banjo music from Deliverance," Neal said.

"We're almost there."

They could hear the whine of chainsaws. A towering fir tree came crashing to the ground as they pulled into the clearing.

"That just doesn't seem right," Lindsey said. "Those trees look ancient."

"Some of them are," Todd said as he climbed out of the truck.

***

The area around the campfire formed a bright island in a world of primeval darkness. Power flowed through coiling black snakes of extension cords from gasoline-powered generators to work five-hundred-watt lamps that lit the scene. The logging crew, their days' work done, filled the forest with the echoes of their boisterous laughter and their raw, good-natured humor. They flirted with the girls and ribbed the guys as they filled their paper plates with top-quality grilled steaks Todd had purchased as payment for their participation in his project.

"We ain't used to eating like this," one of them told Todd as he grabbed a second steak. "You got any more movies you need to make?"

"I'll keep it in mind," Todd said.

"She's married," Neal told one of the men who had just told Jolene how great she looked. "To me."

"Well," the man said, "just keep me in mind if you ever get tired of him."

"I'll add you to the list," Jolene told him with an enigmatic smile. "Be sure to include your yearly income and how much you can bench press."

The man laughed as he walked away.

"Where did you get that?" Neal asked.

"It's an old waitress joke," Jolene said. "I used to use it to fend off customers who got a little too friendly."

The sun had stayed up long enough for Todd to get footage of the trucks, the chainsaws, and the stacks of fallen logs The trees stood tall at the edge of the clearing. Their tops, high overhead, faded into darkness. In the brief intervals when the voices of the men grew quiet, they could hear the chirping of insects and the hooting of owls.

"Okay," Todd said as most of the men finished eating. "Jake and Leo have read the script, but we're mostly going to improvise. I'll play the tape of the sound. Everybody will react to it. Leo's going to talk about the Indian legends. Got it?"

"Got it."

"Okay."

"Is this going to be on YouTube?"

"What about America's Funniest Home Videos?"

"Everybody, get ready. Start talking like you would around the campfire." He turned to Lindsey. "Start filming. Get some shots of the whole group and then zero in on the faces." He leaned close and whispered in her ear. "They don't know Pack's out there in a gorilla suit. When I tell them to shine the flashlight, get ready."

Lindsey filmed the group. She zeroed in on their faces as they laughed and talked around the fire. The hot orange glare of the work lamps blended with the flickering glow of the fire. It was artificially bright, but Todd assured her he could tint it to look like real fire. Unnatural brightness, he said, was an illusion movie viewers accepted readily enough. In films, caves and secret tunnels are usually lit up by off-camera light sources.

"I'm about to play the sound," Todd said. "So get ready."

A long, throaty scream rolled out of the darkness.

"What's that?" one of the men said.

"I don't know, man."

"That was pretty close."

"We better hope that's not a Sasquatch mating call. Nothing worse than a sexually frustrated gorilla."

They all laughed.

"Cut! Do it again."

"Sorry, man. I couldn't resist."

"It's okay. We need more than one take anyway. Everybody get ready. You talk in low tones, then you hear the roar. Action."

The men started talking. Their campfire banter sounded realistic enough as they talked about how much lumber they had cut, football scores, and racecars. The roar came from the forest.

"What was that?"

"I don't know, man. It sounded pretty close."

"Could have been a coyote."

"That wasn't any coyote. They don't sound like that."

"Then what was it?"

"It was the spirit of the forest," Leo said. "The Sasquatch."

"Don't start that Bigfoot crap," one of the others said. "That's hokum, man."

"Can we cuss in this movie?"

"Cut."

"Sorry."

They went through about five more takes. Lindsey was starting to get the giggles. Finally the group executed a perfect take. Leo delivered his lines about the Native American legends, the spirits of the forest, and the logging crew intruding in their world. One of the men shined a flashlight into darkness. It brushed across a hairy shape ambling through the trees. A torrent of swearing erupted from around the campfire, followed by gales of howling laugher.

"He's got a guy out there in a suit."

"Oh, man, you got us."

"I didn't know he had a suit."

"Who says it's a suit?" Todd said. "Maybe the mating call attracted a real Sasquatch."

"Maybe it's a female," one of them said. "We'll send McCabe out there to her. He likes the big women. Did you ever see his ex-wife? Looked like an orangutan with rollers."

This triggered a colorful response from McCabe.

"Did you get their reaction to the suit?" Todd asked Lindsey.

"Oh, yeah. But, if this is for a family audience, you may have to edit it."

"Just as long as you got the facial expressions."

"All you could want."

"Great." He turned to the logging crew. "Let's get it one more time. Then I'll get a shot of the guy in the suit, and we'll have some dessert."

"We get dessert?"

"Homemade ice cream."

"Son, you'll make somebody a good wife one day."

More laughter.

"Is that all you wanted from us?"

"You don't have a truck with a cracked windshield, do you?"

"Yeah. Thanks to Harris."

"Wasn't my fault."

Pack came out of the forest, holding the Bigfoot mask. There was black makeup around his eyes, and sweat had plastered his hair to his head.

"You okay, Pack?" Neal asked.

"Yeah," he said. "That was kind of fun. I scared the crap out of those guys."

"Where did you get that roar?" Neal asked.

"Those are howler monkeys from the zoo," Todd said. "They're not that big, but they sound terrible."

"I'd run if I heard that behind me," Neal said.

It was after midnight when Todd finished up the shoot. His friends on the logging crew helped Todd, Neal, and Pack load the lights, generator, camera equipment, and tables back into the Bronco. Lindsey and Jolene packed up the food.

"We've got extra tents and sleeping bags if you want to stay over," Jake told them.

"That actually sounds like fun," Todd said. "But I think we'd better be getting back."

"Thanks for the steaks. Let me see the movie when you get it finished."

"I'll burn you a copy."

"Is this going to have an outtakes section?"

"As long as it has McCabe wetting himself when he saw that gorilla suit."

"Shut up, man."

"You'll get your outtakes," Todd said. "Just don't let McCabe's ex-wife hear what you said about her."

The men laughed.

"Your friend knows what he's doing," Pack told Lindsey as he watched Todd interact with the loggers. They were as blue-collar as he was artistic, but there was a sense of mutual respect there.

"He's pretty organized," Lindsey said. "And good at getting along with people."

From the look on his face, Lindsey could tell Pack was wondering if her remark had been intended as a personal jab. She had not meant it that way. He really had been on his best behavior throughout the shoot; he had even seemed to enjoy it. That day, she realized, he seemed more like the Pack she had known in high school than he had in years. It wasn't until then that she realized how much his time in college had changed him and how much she had missed the old Pack. That was the Pack she had first fallen in love with.

Chapter 15: A Night at the Mansion

"It's lonely out there," Lindsey said as she wiped down the counter, "and she never goes anywhere. I don't see how she stands it." She yawned. She'd had a hard time getting up that morning, and the Dawn Treader opened for business at seven.

"Does she ever have guests?" Jolene asked as she poured water into one of the coffee makers.

"Not that I've ever seen. Just us."

"I wonder if she'd let us have a party out there. Something for the students. Do you think she'd go for it?"

"I don't know," Lindsey said. "Do you think she's ready for that? What if they broke something? She has some pretty expensive things."

"Hmm," Jolene said. "You're right. It was a bad idea."

"No. I'll ask her. We'll see what she says."

***

"A party? For the children?"

"For the teenagers," Lindsey said. "They're pretty well-behaved most of the time, and we'll make sure they're on their best behavior."

Mrs. Cutler set down her cup. "I don't know," she said. "It's been so long since we had a party here. I wonder sometimes if the sound of laughter would crack the very plaster off the walls."

"Maybe it's not a good idea," Lindsey said. "You have so many nice things here."

"Yes," she said, "like treasures buried in the tomb of an Egyptian mummy. No one sees them or enjoys them, not even the mummy. I should probably have sold it all a long time ago, but I couldn't bring myself to part with Niles' treasures. His collection was his life's work. He had his business, yes, but his passion was exploration. He was such a remarkable man."

"The party was a bad idea," Lindsey said. "I shouldn't have asked."

"Nonsense," Mrs. Cutler said. "I think we should do it. Throw caution to the wind and do it. I think I can afford to repair anything those young ruffians break, and I do enjoy young people."

"Are you sure about this?"

"Oh, yes, dear. I'll have Cornelia order the invitations. We'll begin planning the menu at once."

"I wasn't thinking about anything that formal," Lindsey said. "Just chips and cheese dip."

"There hasn't been a party in this house for decades," Mrs. Cutler said. "If I'm going to have a party, I want it to be memorable."

"I'm sure it will be."

***

A light rain drummed on the car's metal roof and spattered against the pavestones in the mansion's courtyard. Pack pulled his car in behind the minivan. Lindsey rode in the passenger seat beside him. Shadow and Jolene were sitting in the back. Neal had driven the ministry association's fifteen-passenger minivan. Lindsey watched as the doors slid open and the teenagers emerged, luggage and sleeping bags in hand, and looked warily around. Empty dormer windows stared down at them like hollow eyes from the slate-shingled roof.

"I like this place," Shadow said as she stepped out into the misting rain. "It has character."

"That little girl is strange," Pack whispered to Lindsey. "I don't think she likes me much."

"Give her time," Lindsey said. She followed Shadow to the porch and introduced her to the other teens.

Stormie was the "perfect" Christian teenager who reminded Lindsey of herself. Her father was an associational missionary. Nefertiti was a tall, stately African-American girl with a sharp mind and strong opinions. Karma was a peace-loving flower child. Kim was a tomboy. Jennifer, a tiny Korean girl, drove the others crazy with her cheerleader's pep and her doggedly sunny disposition. Nefertiti called her "Tinkerbell."

The guys, Cody, Casey, and Ryan, were fewer in number. They all loved music and computers and played Halo to the point of exhaustion. Cody, the oldest of the three, operated the church's soundboard. Lindsey recognized Casey and Ryan from the praise band. They, along with some college guys, had been onstage on the night of the Beach House Blowout and in the contemporary worship service.

Todd was there with the guys. Lindsey hadn't seen much of him since the encounter in the Dawn Treader. She felt a stab of guilt for not keeping in touch with him, but she didn't want to set Pack off. Todd passed her as they entered the house.

"How are you?" she asked.

"I'm okay, Lindsey."

She saw Pack glaring at the back of Todd's head and made a silent slashing motion with her hand.

Mrs. Cutler sat in her fan-backed chair in the sunroom like a queen on a throne and graciously welcomed her young guests. Though Neal had insisted on bringing pizzas to save the ladies from having to work, Cornelia had prepared a veritable feast of finger foods and desserts. The pizzas looked out of place alongside the ornate serving trays and goblets.

Just to the left of the sunroom, the great room awaited the young guests' arrival.

A low fire burned in an enormous stone fireplace. Even though it was only a few degrees below sixty outside, the rain drumming against the tall windows and the churning, fog-shrouded ocean beyond made the fire somehow appropriate. With soft drinks and plates in hand, the teenagers found places on the overstuffed couches, the hearth, and the carpeted floor. Lindsey nervously repeated her warnings to them about not spilling anything, but Mrs. Cutler did not seem bothered at all by the possibility.

"This is delightful," she told Neal.

***

Todd mostly avoided Lindsey and Pack while the teens chatted and ate their snacks. Earlier that day he had helped Neal and Cody set up a big-screen television set. He double-checked connections and made sure the DVDs they had brought were in place. They had a big enough stack for a DVD marathon, though they didn't really want to spend the whole night just showing movies. They had *The Blind Side*, *Amazing Grace*, two of the *Narnia* movies, and *The Passion*. They had also brought *The Book of Eli* but thought it might be better suited to the guys.

They'd discussed bringing in a sound system for the music but had decided to "go acoustic" instead. Todd was relieved when the program finally started. He and Casey played guitar while the others sang and led in choruses. Neal led the group in a devotional message. Pack had offered to give a word of testimony as well, and Neal and Lindsey had given him a place in the program's loosely organized schedule. Lindsey introduced Pack, and he took his place before the fireplace.

"Back when I was in college," Pack told them, "I was on the football team with a guy named Andre. He was the biggest guy on the team. He weighed about three hundred fifty pounds. I remember one Halloween when he painted himself green and dressed up as *The Incredible Hulk*. He looked just like him, except for the dreadlocks. One night, we were out in a parking lot, and this gang of guys jumped on us. One of them had me down on the ground and was threatening me with a knife. Suddenly, he just lifted up into the air. Andre had grabbed him by the collar with one hand. This was a big guy, but Andre picked him and threw him like it was nothing. That's how tough he was."

Todd saw Neal look at Lindsey and could tell he was wondering where this story might be leading.

"One thing about Andre though: he was more afraid of ghosts than anybody I've ever seen. He wouldn't drive by a cemetery in the daytime if there was any way around it, and you couldn't get him to go near one at night. Forget about getting him into a funeral home. One time, somebody brought a coffin up to the fraternity house for a Halloween party, and Andre slept in his car to keep from having to spend the night in the same house as a coffin.

"Another time, we were down in New Orleans for a playoff game, and we saw a haunted house set up in one of those houses in the French Quarter. I don't know how we talked Andre into going in there in the first place, but we finally got him to go in. We hadn't gone very far when this little scrawny guy in zombie makeup jumped out in front of us, and Andre went crazy and started running. He knocked me into the girl who was taking us through and tore a hole right through one of their cardboard walls. They ended up kicking all of us out and threatening to call the police.

"Not long after that, Andre went to a campus revival and ended up becoming a Christian. After that, death just didn't seem to bother him as much. He didn't like it, but he just didn't seem to have that same kind of fear. He had been pretty wild before he became a Christian, but after that he settled down. He started speaking at Christian Athletes' rallies, and he talked about becoming a preacher.

"When the Iraq War started, he enlisted in the Army, and they sent him overseas. He made it through his first tour of duty, came home, and got engaged. Then he got called back to Iraq a second time. He was walking through the street with his buddies when a guy stepped out with a bomb strapped to his chest. Andre tackled him without a second thought, and the bomb exploded. Andre died saving his friends. The whole time I was sitting at his funeral, I thought about how afraid of coffins and funeral homes he used to be. It was as if he'd known what was going to happen even then.

"I think about that every day, and wonder if I would have had that kind of courage. And I think about how the same guy who ran away from a man in a zombie suit came face-to-face with death in the streets of Baghdad and tackled it head-on, and I ask myself what made the difference. And I keep coming back to the same thing. It was the power of God in him. He was ready, and when the time came, he faced it head-on.

"Andre didn't like cemeteries much, and I don't like to think about him being in one. But I know God's not going to leave him there, because His Son did the same thing for us that Andre did for his friends. I believe that."

The group was silent as Pack finished his story. Neal led them in a prayer and the group broke apart for snack time.

Todd watched as Shadow drifted up to Pack and handed him a slip of paper. He smiled as he unfolded Shadow's note, looked down at the words she had written, and froze. Terror flashed across his features for a split-instant before he buried his reaction. That, at least, was what Todd thought he saw. Her message delivered, Shadow turned away and slipped into the crowd. Pack was still looking down at the note when Todd approached him.

"That was quite a story you told."

"Huh?"

"You know. About your friend, Andre."

"Oh, yeah. Thanks."

They shook hands. Pack looked shaken, distracted. After they had spoken, Todd sneaked a look back and saw Pack toss Shadow's folded note into the fireplace.

***

The group sang, snacked, shared testimonies, and watched movies until after midnight. The rain continued to fall outside. It blew against the windows and distorted the world beyond. When it came time to turn in for the night, the girls spread out their sleeping bags on the couches and floor of the great room, and Neal led the guys downstairs to a spacious den where Niles Cutler had entertained his male guests. The mahogany walls were lined with trophies from hunting expeditions. The severed heads of deer, elk, moose, a bison, and a water buffalo were mounted on the walls. A Kodiak bear reared itself menacingly upright in one corner, and a shark and marlin swam along the walls. A zebra-skin rug and the mounted skin of a Burmese python rounded out the silent zoo.

"This place is kind of scary," Ryan said. He started to unroll his sleeping bag at the feet of the bear but then moved away from it. Todd couldn't really blame him. Once the lights were out, the rain-distorted flashes of lightning lent an eerie illusion of life to the long-dead beasts.

Todd tried to sleep, but the padding of his sleeping bag did little to soften the hard floor beneath him, and thoughts of Lindsey and Pack kept intruding into his fading consciousness. He also kept thinking about Shadow, about the note she had written and the way Pack had reacted to it. Todd wondered if he had read Pack's expression correctly. What could Shadow have written that would have caused him to react that way?

***

Shadow couldn't sleep. She pushed back her covers, rolled off the air mattress, and stood. The rain was still falling outside. Pale light from a streetlamp in the backyard, filtered through sheets of rain on the glass, cast ghostly ripple-dances on the great room's mahogany walls. Halloween orange amidst powdery gray, the embers of the fire spoke in crackling whispers. Somewhere in the distance, Shadow could hear someone sobbing. She thought—at first—that it must be her imagination, but as she crept out into the hall and toward the stairs, the sound grew louder.

The boys were asleep downstairs in a room full of animal trophies. She wondered if one of them was suffering from some secret tragedy, but the sobs sounded female. She descended, her bare feet quiet on the stairs. When she reached the base of the stairs, she could see a young woman standing at the window. She was looking out into the stormy night and softly weeping. Her hair was straight and dark. It was not one of the girls from the group.

"Are you all right?" Shadow whispered.

The woman turned to her. Heavy lines of black paint surrounded her eyes. Her tears had smeared them. The joints of her metal necklace clinked against each other as she moved. Her face, Shadow thought, was oddly familiar. Then it struck her: It was the face on the sarcophagus upstairs.

Chapter 16: Missing Shadow

Todd woke to the sound of distant screams. He sat up in his sleeping bag. The room was dark around him, but he could make out the contours of Niles' trophies on the walls. Rain was still blowing against the windowpanes. Todd heard movement in the darkness around him.

"The electricity's out." He recognized Neal's voice. He was over by the door, testing the light switch.

"What's wrong with the girls?" Cody asked.

"They're scared of the dark," Casey groaned. "It's part of being a girl."

"Everybody stay cool," Neal said. "I've got a flashlight out in the van. I think I can find my way out there without tripping over anything."

"Need any help?"

"No, I've got it. I'll be right back."

"I'm gonna go upstairs and check on the girls," Todd said.

"I'll go with you," Cody said.

"There was a girl in a bloody nightshirt over by the fire," Jennifer wailed. "Her eyes were white."

"Girl," Nefertiti said, "you did not see a ghost. You are talking like a fool."

"What's going on?" Todd asked.

Jennifer screamed.

"Is everybody okay?"

Todd and Cody stepped through the arch. The great room was still illuminated by a faint orange glow from the embers in the fireplace. Todd could see the girls huddled in their sleeping bags or sitting up on the couches.

"Hi, Todd," Lindsey said, her voice rough from sleep. "Where's Neal?"

"He's going after a flashlight."

"I don't know what difference it makes," one of the girls groaned. "We were asleep anyway."

"This house is haunted," Jennifer said. "It is so haunted."

"Will you stop saying that? It's just a house."

"Everybody calm down," Jolene ordered.

A light flashed on in the doorway. Neal's head floated in the darkness. It laughed maniacally. Screams ripped through the darkness.

"They were already scared," Jolene said with a sigh. "Did you have to make it worse?"

Neal walked through the room, stepping over girls in sleeping bags, and seated himself beside Jolene.

"Hello, my Asian princess. I missed you."

"That's sweet," she said. "Now go back to bed."

"Where's Shadow?" one of the girls asked.

"Shadow?" Lindsey called out. "Shadow, are you in here?"

There was no response.

"She was right over here," Stormie said. Neal shined the light onto an air mattress with a blanket and pillow.

"Where could she have gone?"

"Maybe she's in the bathroom."

"In the dark?"

"Girls don't go to the bathroom by themselves," Cody said. "It's against the code."

"Shadow!"

"Shadow, can you hear us?"

"Shadow!"

"Everybody calm down," Neal said. "I'll go check."

"Knock first."

"What did you think I would do? Try to scare her off the toilet seat? Give me a little bit of credit." Neal and the cone of light vanished into the hall. Only the faint orange glow remained.

"Hey," Neal called back, "I think the mummy went out for a stroll."

Jennifer wailed.

"Honey," Jolene moaned, "will you stop teasing them?"

"The bathroom door was open," Neal said as he reappeared "There's nobody in there."

"Where could she have gone?"

"Maybe she was in another part of the house when the lights went off."

"What would she be doing in another part of the house?"

"Maybe she couldn't sleep and went for a walk."

"What's going on?" Pack asked as he stumbled into the room.

"One of the girls is missing," Neal said. "Probably nothing to worry about."

"You don't think she went outside?" Jolene suddenly asked. "The cliffs behind this house are steep, Neal. If she fell off one of them…."

"There are fences back there," Neal said. "She'd have to have crawled under them."

"I know, but…."

"You're going to make me go outside in the rain and look for her, aren't you?"

"Don't you think we should?"

"We? Are you coming?"

"If you want me to."

"Never mind." He sighed. "I'll go."

"I'll go with you," Todd said. "She probably went out through the front. Did you look for her on the porch?"

"I didn't look for her, but I think I'd have noticed if she was sitting out there."

As they were heading out, they passed a bamboo cylinder filled with umbrellas. Each of them took one. The wind was blowing hard as they stepped out onto the porch. It threatened to rip the umbrellas from their hands.

"Shadow!" Neal called into the rain. There was no answer.

"Her mother was looking for a chance to sue somebody the last time she got hurt," Todd said.

"I know," Neal said. "If she wants to sue me for my drum set and the little bit I've got in the bank, she can be my guest. Being almost broke has its advantages."

With Neal shining the flashlight ahead of them, they made their way slowly around the house. Because the mansion had been built on the side of a hill, the front entrance was actually on the second floor. The first floor, the basement level, opened into the backyard. Stone stairs—steep, weathered, and slick with rain—ran along the side of the house to the back.

Tree limbs shivered and groaned in the darkness above them as the wind ripped through them. Leaves and water pelted their umbrellas and showered the sidewalk around them.

"Shadow!"

They scanned the ground for any sign of muddy footprints but found none. Todd glimpsed something in his peripheral vision. He glanced at the gazebo and thought he saw a shape.

"Neal," he said. "Shine a light on the gazebo."

The beam cut through a wall of falling water and feebly probed the wooden structure. There was no sign of anyone. Beyond the gazebo was a steep set of stairs that descended into darkness. Juggling their umbrellas and lights while trying to hold onto the handrails, they carefully made their way down the rain-slick steps. They could hear the crashing of the waves below them and felt the spray of the ocean before they were close enough to see it. They'd gone down about eighty feet when they came to a sturdy wooden dock and realized they had reached bottom. Waves roared through the pilings beneath them. Their flashlights probed along the dock, but there was no sign of Shadow.

"Let's get back to the house," Neal said.

"Do you think we should check the fuse panel?" Todd asked as they returned to the porch.

"It wouldn't hurt," Neal said. "I wonder if Lindsey knows where it is."

"Let's see where the cable connects to the house," Todd said. "That might give us a clue."

They saw no sign of the cable and decided it must be underground. Neal finally spotted a piece of conduit running along the wall and connecting to the basement level.

***

Lindsey and Pack had decided to search inside the house while Neal and Todd searched outside. The two guys had taken the only flashlight, but Lindsey remembered seeing a collection of scented candles on the sunroom table. She and Pack lit them using fireplace matches they found on the mantle, then set out to search the house. Cody, Ryan, and Kim lit candles and set out to conduct their own search while Jolene stayed in the great room with the rest of the group.

The mansion's layout, even in daylight, was sprawling and complicated with rooms interconnecting and passages turning back upon themselves. In the dark, it was a veritable maze.

"I don't think we've been down this hallway yet," Lindsey said at one point.

"Yeah, we have," Pack told her. "It's the same one that branches off the dining room."

"I don't think so."

"Sure it is. It circles around."

"I don't think it does. I don't remember passing these pictures."

"Fine," Pack said. "I tell you what. You wait right here. I'll go down there and circle around behind you."

"I don't think I want to be in the dark by myself."

"It won't take but a minute," he insisted. "Stay right here."

"All right," she said. She watched as he stepped into the corridor and vanished around the corner. She waited for a moment, and began to feel nervous.

"Pack?"

A cold chill tickled Lindsey's spine. There was something moving in the darkness behind her. All of her friends had been carrying flashlights and candles. Whoever or whatever was standing behind her had come out of the darkness. Maybe it was at home there. The floor creaked directly behind her.

"Pack?"

Lindsey spun around. A scream caught in her throat.

"Caitlyn?"

The girl smiled. "Sorry if I scared you."

"What are you doing here? I didn't know you were home."

"I got off early. Well, early for the late shift. We didn't have many patients."

"Why are you walking around in the dark?"

"I couldn't find a flashlight. Your eyes adjust to it after a while. What's going on?"

"Some of the teenagers from the church are staying here tonight."

"I heard. That's great. Auntie always did love a party."

"It's not so great now," Lindsey said. "One of the girls is missing. We're trying to find her. We've been all over the house."

"What about the hidden room in the wine cellar?"

"There's a wine cellar?"

"Didn't I show it to you?"

"No, I don't think so. I think I would have remembered that. And there's a hidden room?"

"Yes. It's behind a shelf. Uncle Niles rigged it with a switch. There's a statue of a lion sitting on the top. You have to pull down on it. But be careful. The door can't be opened from the inside."

"Why would he design something like that?"

"An oversight, I suppose." Caitlyn's tone said otherwise, but Lindsey didn't press the issue.

"Do you really think she could be in there?"

"I don't know, but if you've looked everywhere else, there's nothing to lose by looking there, too."

"I'm waiting for my boyfriend," Lindsey said. "We were searching together, and he wanted to prove something to me. He must have gotten lost."

"I'll wait with you if you like," Caitlyn said, "but it shouldn't take long to check the room."

"Okay," Lindsey said. "As long as we come right back."

The orange tongue of flame in Lindsey's candle danced as Caitlyn led her down the hall, to a set of back stairs Lindsey had never seen, and down to the mansion's ground level. In one of the front corners was a doorway that opened onto a narrow set of stairs, which led deeper to a hidden sub-basement. Lindsey followed Caitlyn down creaking wooden stairs into the echoing darkness. They emerged into a long, low room. The rays of Lindsey's candle brushed across heavy wooden timbers and limestone walls. Dusty, fabric-insulated wiring linked a network of bare light bulbs mounted in white, ceramic fixtures. The room was lined with shelves. Lindsey passed her candle across them and saw that they were loaded with bottles and encrusted with cobwebs. Barrels were stacked along the walls. The room had a musty, underground scent like the inside of a cave.

"Listen," Caitlyn whispered.

In the darkness at the far end of the room, someone was crying and pounding on the wall. The sound was muffled and had a ghostly echo to it. Lindsey shined her light along the concrete floor and saw footprints in the dust.

"Shadow?"

Holding the candle ahead of her, she followed the sound. She reached a shelf in the back of the room. Sitting on the top corner was a bronze statue of a lion. The style was Chinese. It looked, to Lindsey, like a cross between a lion and a dragon, with the huge eyes and snout of a Chinese pug. A red gleam reflected from the eyes. *Rubies*, Lindsey suspected. The dust was disturbed at the base of the shelf. The sobbing seemed to be coming from behind it.

"Shadow!" Lindsey called. "Is that you?"

"Help me!" the disembodied voice cried. The impact of pounding fists shook dust from the shelf.

"Pull down on the head," Caitlyn instructed.

Lindsey reached up, took hold of the head, and pulled. The lion rocked forward on a hinge, a latch clicked, and the shelf creaked open.

Shadow leaped out of darkness and nearly knocked the candle from Lindsey's hand. Sobbing, she fell into Lindsey's arms.

"Shadow!" Lindsey gasped. "Honey, what are you doing down here?"

"I had to come," she said. She took a breath and struggled to regain control. "They drew me down here."

"Who drew you down here?"

"The beings. The ones who dwell here. I was wrong about them, Lindsey. They're not what I thought they were. They're...," She screamed.

Lindsey spun around. Pack was right behind them, holding a candle.

"Pack! Oh, thank God."

"You found her?" Pack said. He started to move closer to them.

"No!" Shadow cried. She ducked behind Lindsey. "Stay away from me. He didn't come here to help us, Lindsey. He's after me because I know what he is."

"Are you crazy?" Pack said. "I've been looking all over for you." He took a step closer.

"Stay away!" Shadow cried. "Stay away! Stay away! Stay away!" She put her hands to her head and howled. Pack recoiled.

"All right! All right!" Pack took a step backward. "I'm getting away. See, I'm backing up."

"Shadow, honey, that doesn't make sense. Why would Pack want to hurt either of us?"

"Because he's a monster," she whispered.

"I'll wait for you at the top of the stairs," Pack said.

"No," Shadow yelled. "He'll shut the door and trap us down here."

"Fine," Pack said. "You can go first." He stepped aside and motioned toward the open door at the end of the room.

"I'm sorry, Pack," Lindsey whispered. "She's been through a lot."

"It's okay," Pack said. "Go ahead."

Lindsey led Shadow up the stairs and to the mansion's ground level. Shadow continued to cling to her arm. Lindsey pushed open the door and stepped into light. The electricity was back on.

"The main breaker had been flipped," she heard Neal say. He was just around the corner from them.

"Neal," she called. "Neal, I found her. She's okay."

Neal and Todd appeared at the end of the corridor. Pack emerged from the door behind her.

"What's down there?" Neal asked when he saw the stairwell.

"A wine cellar," Lindsey said. "There's a secret room behind one of the shelves."

"A secret room?" Neal said. "You're kidding. I've got to see that."

"I'm not going back there," Shadow said.

"It's okay," Lindsey said. "We'll take you back upstairs. You can stay with Jolene and the others."

"I'm not going back down there," she said, more to herself than anyone else.

Lindsey took Shadow upstairs to the rest of the group. They surrounded her and asked her where she had been. She told them about the secret room but made no mention of spirits.

By the time Lindsey rejoined the guys, they were already in the wine cellar exploring the secret room. Inside was a small bed with a table beside it, a table with a kerosene lamp on it, and a stack of old books. Everything was shrouded in dust and spider webs.

"It could have been some kind of escape tunnel leading outside," Todd told her, "but the end is boarded up."

"How did Shadow ever find this place?" Neal asked.

"That's a good question," Lindsey said. "She said spirits led her down here."

"Spirits?"

"'The beings that dwell in this house.'"

"Ghosts?"

"I don't know. She said something else. She said they weren't what she had thought they were."

"Then what are they?"

"I don't know."

"She's crazy," Pack said. "That little girl needs to be in a mental hospital."

"How did you ever find her?" Todd asked.

"Caitlyn knew about the room," Lindsey said. "She led me down here."

"Who's Caitlyn?"

"Mrs. Cutler's niece. Didn't you see her?"

Neal, Todd, and Pack looked at each other.

"Pack must have seen her."

"I didn't see anybody. Just you and Spooky."

"That's strange," Lindsey said. "She must have gone back upstairs before the lights came on."

***

The group spent the rest of the night watching movies in the great room. Some of the teens huddled in their sleeping bags and napped. Shortly after sunrise, Neal heard the sound of squeaking wheels coming from the kitchen. He sat up in his sleeping bag and looked around the corner. The kitchen door swung open, and Cornelia, who had somehow slipped into the kitchen unobserved, emerged with a serving cart. It was stacked high with steaming metal trays, pitchers of juice, and jars of syrup and marmalade. She unloaded it without fanfare and vanished back into the kitchen. Neal climbed out of his sleeping bag, tiptoed into the sunroom, crept over to the table, and lifted the lid from one of the trays.

"Belgian waffles?" he said. "I wonder what else she has here." He lifted the lid of a second tray. It was stacked with bagels.

"Breakfast has not been served yet," Cornelia said from the kitchen. Lindsey laughed silently.

"Sorry," Neal said as he dropped the lid back in place. He lifted it again, snatched a bagel, and stepped away from the table.

Cornelia appeared a moment later with another cartload of dishes. Mrs. Cutler, spry and well-rested, joined the group for breakfast. She had apparently slept through the night's events.

"I always sleep well when it's raining," she told them. The teenagers, who had spent much of the night without sleep, were groggy and sullen until they saw Cornelia's feast.

"It looks like a German bakery in here," Neal said when he saw the crepes and strudels. He reached for a second bagel, but Cornelia slapped his hand.

"We pray first," she said.

"Yes, ma'am." Neal led the group in a prayer, and breakfast began. Todd led the group in a brief devotional after breakfast. Then the group loaded up the luggage and boarded the minivan.

"That was wonderful," Mrs. Cutler said as she waved to the teenagers in the van. "We simply have to do this again."

Chapter 17: A Fine Date

"You're going out tonight?" Mrs. Cutler inquired as she and Lindsey were sitting in the sunroom together.

"Yes, ma'am."

"With the fiancé from home?"

"Yes." Lindsey thought about asking whom else she would be going out with, but she already knew.

"So, your long-haired filmmaker really was just a friend after all. Too bad. He's a fine young man."

"Yes, he is," Lindsey agreed. She was not sure what to say. She looked out at the crashing waves. The sun was low but still well over the horizon. In the summer, the sun didn't set until ten o'clock in Oregon. Lindsey was still getting used to that.

The doorbell rang. Lindsey knew by now not to stand up and race to the door. She heard Cornelia's footsteps in the hall. A moment later, Pack appeared in the door, looking a little bit awkward.

"Come in," Mrs. Cutler said. "Have a seat."

"We really don't have much time," he said. "Our reservations are in fifteen minutes."

"Oh, dear," Mrs. Cutler said. "Well, I guess you'd better be going."

Lindsey stood. "Good night, Mrs. Cutler."

"Good night, dear. Do have a good time."

"I'm sure we will."

"That old lady's something else," Pack said as they walked across the courtyard to his waiting car. "Right out of the eighteenth century."

"I think she's sweet."

"To you, maybe. She looks at me like she expects me to steal something." He opened the passenger side door for Lindsey.

"Thank you." She sat down and strapped herself in. Pack walked around the car and climbed into the driver's seat.

"Are our reservations really in fifteen minutes?" Lindsey asked.

"No," Pack admitted, "but I didn't want to spend the next ten minutes being cross- examined." He started the car.

"I thought lawyers were used to that."

"I'm not a lawyer yet."

They made it to Seaside nearly an hour before their dinner reservations and spent the time walking around town and going into shops. Pack was patient with Lindsey's shopping habits, but she tried not to take advantage of it. The restaurant Pack had chosen for them was a converted house sitting on a hilltop. The walls were covered with dark paneling, and the décor was nautical. An enclosed back porch looked out over the ocean.

The hostess led Pack and Lindsey back to their table. Pack stood behind Lindsey's chair as she seated herself and pushed it up to the table.

"Thanks," Lindsey said as Pack seated himself. "This is perfect."

"Do you really like it out here?" Pack said. "In Oregon, I mean."

"I do. It's great."

"Do you want to stay here? Raise children here?"

"I don't know. It's a long way from family. I love coming out here, though."

"Where would you live if you could live anywhere you wanted to?" Pack asked. "No obligations. No expectations. No worries about the cost."

"I don't know," Lindsey said. "Maybe a beach in Florida or somewhere with mountains."

"What about a city like New York?"

"I love shopping there, but I think I'd get tired of the crowds."

"Why don't we run away?" Pack said. "Just pick a place on the map and go there?"

"Just like that?"

"Why not?"

"Wedding plans, for one thing. The invitations are already paid for. And you've got law school. I've got my job."

"Is a big wedding what you really want, or is it something your mother pushed you into?"

"I haven't made a single decision for myself since the whole thing started," Lindsey admitted. "Every time I tried to, she talked me out of it. 'Don't you think we should do this? Wouldn't you rather do that?' Every time, she kept on until wore me down."

"Same way with my dad and law school," Pack said. "I told him I was going to change my major once, and he threatened to stop paying for school and cut me out of his will. Things were pretty frosty around our house for a while after that."

"When did that happen?"

"When I was a freshman. I thought about being an architect and designing skyscrapers, but it was law or nothing."

"You don't really want to be a lawyer?"

"I don't know what I want, and I'm pretty sick of other people telling me what I *should* want."

"I can understand that."

The server came by and took their drink orders.

"I guess we'd better look at the menu," Pack said.

"Only if we want to." Lindsey smiled.

"Right."

Lindsey studied the food items listed and scanned the prices. Pack seemed to like picking places with expensive entrees.

"Were you serious about running away?" Lindsey asked.

"Would you go with me if I was?"

"Pack, it's just…It sounds great, it really does, but it's crazy. Our parents would throw a fit."

"They'd get over it."

"What would we do for money?"

"Get jobs. I've got enough in savings to tide us over for a while."

"But, it's totally irresponsible."

"Exactly! That's the beauty of it."

The server returned with their drink orders. They ordered their entrees, and the server disappeared into the kitchen.

"We've got our whole lives ahead of us, and it's time we started living them the way *we* want to live them."

"But, we don't know what we want," Lindsey said. "I don't know where I want to live. You don't know what kind of work you want to do. We'd be making it all up as we went along."

"Totally," he said. "A blank canvas. An empty field. Paint anything you want. Build anything you want."

"Just pack our bags and go."

"To Florida, Hawaii, Paris."

"Do you speak French?"

"No."

"I don't, either."

"Okay. Not Paris. London maybe. Or what about Australia? Mountains, beaches, and coral reefs."

"You're crazy."

"Completely. But you know you're tempted."

"It's fun to talk about."

"We could be married and on our way by this time tomorrow."

"We'd have to get marriage licenses."

"You can get them quick in Las Vegas."

"But Neal's performing the ceremony."

"He'll understand."

"Could we get married here? In Oregon?"

"Is that what you want?"

"I'm not sure."

Lindsey thought about the church back home, the church in which she had grown up. She thought about her high school and college friends serving as bridesmaids and her brother being a groomsman. Yes, her mother had controlled everything from start to finish, but the thought of the church wedding with the family and friends was dear to her.

"What's wrong?"

"It's just that I always pictured getting married in Texas with all of our families and friends gathered around. It's hard to imagine anything else."

"Well, you don't have to decide all at once. But we don't have to wait, either. We can do anything we want to do."

"I have to go to the bathroom."

"Sure. Go ahead."

Lindsey practically ran through the restaurant. She found her way to the ladies' room and ducked inside. She pushed open the door to a stall, sat down on the toilet seat without pulling down her pants, and held her face in her hands.

This is insane, she thought. A few days ago, she hadn't even been sure she wanted to marry Pack at all, and now she was actually considering running away with him. Or maybe she was just tempted by the offer. She couldn't run away with Pack after all the money her parents had already spent, the planning they had done. Still she was tempted.

Lord Jesus, help me, she thought. *Calm my mind and help me to hear Your still, small voice. Take away this spirit of confusion, and give me a spirit of peace.* Her heart, she realized, was pounding in her chest. She sat in the stall for several minutes and tried to pray, but her thoughts were all awhirl, and she could hardly put two sentences together. She went to the sink and splashed her face with water. Finally, she took a deep breath and went back to the table where Pack was waiting. The food had come while she had been in the bathroom. She wondered how long she had sat in that stall, trying to compose herself.

"Are you all right?" Pack asked. "I didn't mean to upset you."

"I'm okay," she said. "It's a lot to think about."

"You don't have to think about anything," Pack said. "I was just saying that we've got a choice. We're grown-ups, and we've got a choice how we want to live our lives. That's all I'm saying."

"How's your food?"

"Great."

Lindsey took a long swallow of her soda and tasted her food. It was a kind of seafood lasagna, and it was delicious. As she ate, she quickly felt her body relaxing. The burst of anxiety she had felt earlier melted into a calm bordering on euphoria.

"Looks like you're feeling better," Pack said.

"I'm fine," she said. "I'm sorry I panicked earlier. I overreacted, but I'm okay now." She laughed. It came out a little louder than she had meant for it to. She covered her mouth and looked around at the other guests.

"And what about running away together?"

"I don't know."

"What about just for one night? Just drive and see where we end up? You know, a road trip?"

"What about Mrs. Cutler?"

"It's not her business, Lindsey. She's not your mother, and you're not fifteen years old. What's she going to do?"

"It wouldn't be right, Pack. I'm working for a church, working with teenagers. I have to think about the kind of example I set for them."

"We could get separate rooms," Pack said, "if that's what you want."

"The Bible says to flee the appearance of evil. Even if we didn't do anything wrong, people would still wonder."

"You worry too much about what other people think."

"And you don't worry enough."

They finished eating, Pack paid for the meal, and they left the restaurant. Lindsey stumbled as they started down the steps. Pack caught her by the arm.

"Are you okay?"

"Fine," she said. "I feel great."

And she did. Lindsey was practically floating. She felt more relaxed, more at peace than she had felt in months. She and Pack laughed and talked as she lay back on the seat and fell asleep.

Chapter 18: The Taking

Automatic weapons fire pounded Neal's eardrums. He pulled back, reloaded his weapon, and studied the readouts on his view screen. Music, strangely familiar, sounded in the distance. It almost sounded like the ringtone on his cellphone. The ringtone? Neal paused the game and pulled off his headset. His phone was singing away on the coffee table.

"Neal," Jolene called from the bedroom.

"Got it," he said. He snatched up the phone and opened it. "Neal's Body Shop. What can I do for you?"

"Is this Neal Allen?"

"Yes, it is. Who is this?"

"Katherine Cutler. I'm sorry to call you at this hour."

What time was it, anyway? He looked over at the clock and saw that it was 2 a.m.

"It's okay," he said. "Believe it or not, I wasn't even asleep. What's going on?"

"I don't know. Lindsey isn't home yet. Have you heard from her?"

"No, ma'am. Not a word. Do you know where she went?"

"She had a date with that fiancé from Texas." She said the word *fiancé* as though it were something distasteful. "They were going somewhere to eat. He said he had made reservations."

"What time was this?"

"Hours ago. Around seven o'clock. They should have been back by now."

"Have you tried calling her?"

"I didn't know if I should. She thinks I'm a bossy old biddy as it is."

"You are a bossy old biddy. That's what we like about you."

"I'm serious, Neal. I'm worried about her."

"I'll call her," Neal said. "If she decided to get married in Vegas, she should have told her friends about it. Don't worry about it. I'll track her down."

"I'm sorry to bother you."

"It's not a problem."

Neal hung up the cellphone.

"Who was that?" Jolene asked from the bedroom.

"Ms. Cutler. Lindsey isn't back yet."

"Back from where?"

"A date with Pack." He scrolled to Lindsey's number on his cellphone. "I'm going to call her."

"Do you think you should?"

"If she was going out for a wild night of passion, she could at least have lied and said she was going to a late movie or something."

"What part of the Bible did you get that from?"

"Song of Solomon. It's right after the sock on the door part. I'll have to put it in my next sermon."

"Text her."

"Okay. How do you spell 'wanton immorality?'"

"Neal!"

"I'm texting."

He punched through the menus, typed "Where R U?" and pressed *send*. He climbed up onto the couch, turned off his game console, and waited. Five minutes passed. He turned on the TV set and channel-hopped for about thirty minutes.

"Enough of this," he said. "I'm calling her." He scrolled to Lindsey's name, punched "call," and waited.

"The Visiontel customer you are trying to reach is unavailable at this time. Please leave a message at the sound of the tone."

"Lindsey, this is Neal. Call me and tell me you're okay." He punched *end*. Then he stood, went to the kitchen, and pulled the phonebook out of the drawer where Jolene kept it. He flipped through until he found the number of the hotel Pack had been checked into. He punched the number.

"Westside Inn. How may I help you?"

"I'm looking for Pack—uh—Jason Packard. Is he still checked in there?"

"If you'll give me just a moment."

"Sure."

Neal waited.

"Mr. Packard checked out this afternoon. Is there anything else I can do for you?"

"No. Thanks." He hung up. "Okay. Now I'm starting to worry."

***

Lindsey was cold when she woke up. The surface beneath her body was hard and rough. It felt like concrete. Suddenly, she realized she wasn't wearing anything but a dirty nightgown and panties. Gasping in horror, she forced herself into a sitting position. The room around her was dark, round, and full of machinery. The last feeble rays of dusk glowed through the overhead windows and reflected on a parabolic mirror. A mirror. She was in the lantern room of a lighthouse. She had to be.

What am I doing here? she wondered. *How did I get here?* She put her hands to her head and tried to remember, but she had no recollection of this place.

There was a metal band locked around her ankle, a metal band attached to a chain. With a cry, she folded her arms defensively across her chest and rose to her feet. Her teeth were chattering, and her knees were trembling. She didn't know if it was the cold or the terror that made her shake. She looked down at the gown she was wearing. Dark blotches stained the front. Was that blood? She realized her face felt numb on one side. The area under her nose was caked with clotted blood.

She pulled against the band on her ankle. The adjoining chain was about ten feet long and bolted to the wall. It rattled against the floor as she made her way around the base of the lantern to the trapdoor. The chain pulled tight. Lindsey dropped to the floor and stretched her arm as far as it would reach. The tips of her fingers barely reached the edge of the metal door.

"Help me!" she cried. "Somebody help me!"

"Lindsey," someone whispered.

"Who's there?" she whimpered. "Why are you doing this?"

"Lindsey."

"What do you want? What do you want?"

Lindsey woke up gasping. The room around her was dark. The ceiling was vaulted and supported by heavy timbers.

Where am I? she thought. *How did I get here?*

Lindsey turned on the light beside her bed. The room around her was completely unfamiliar. The décor was rustic but probably expensive—like a rich person's vacation cabin. A bison's head stared at her from the mantle of a stone fireplace. Groggy, Lindsey pushed back the covers and saw that someone had dressed her in a new nightgown. It was a short, sexy, black nightgown, the kind a woman would buy for her honeymoon. She swallowed hard as she sat up and swung her feet out of bed. The room spun as she rose to her feet. She started toward the door and realized she was having trouble walking. Her vision was blurry.

What's wrong with me?

Just as she reached the door, she heard a knock. She squinted through the peephole. Pack was standing out in the hall. The door opened, and Lindsey nearly fell into his arms.

"Easy," he said. He put his hands on her shoulders to steady her. "You've been out for a while."

"Where are we?" Lindsey demanded. "What did you do to me?"

"Now, don't jump to any conclusions," Pack said. "I just thought we needed to get away and talk."

"Get away and talk?" she said. "Did you drug me?"

"Now, calm down, Lindsey."

"You drugged me! And you abducted me! You undressed me!"

"Lindsey, you really need to calm down."

"You're not even going to deny it?"

"Look," he said, "I didn't want to have to do this, but I didn't really have any choice. Your friends practically had you brainwashed. I had to get you out of there."

She pushed away from him, stumbled back to the bed, and sat down on it.

"I don't believe this," she said. "I can't believe you did this. Where are we?"

"It doesn't matter."

"Of course it matters! Where are we?"

"The road to this place washed out back in the spring," he said. "The electricity still works, but you can't get here by car, and there's no cell service. It's just you and me, Lindsey. It's like we're the only people in the whole world."

***

Todd was just finishing breakfast when he heard his smartphone vibrating on the counter. He snatched it up and saw Neal's name on the screen.

"What's up, Neal?"

"Have you heard anything from Lindsey since last night?"

"No. Why?"

"She went out with Pack and never came back. Pack checked out of his hotel before the date."

Todd's mouth went dry.

"Do you think they decided to elope?"

"Lindsey didn't take any luggage with her."

"Maybe they had an accident."

"I called the police. Nobody's reported anything. I called the hospitals, and nobody's seen them there, either. A couple lost control and skidded into a tree outside of Astoria, but they were older. Did Lindsey say anything to you about going anywhere?"

"We haven't talked much since Pack came to town."

"I gathered that, but thought I'd ask. I'm going to call a few other people. If you think of anything, let me know."

"I will."

Todd hung up. He thought about Lindsey and Pack in Las Vegas, shook his head, and sighed.

***

Lindsey woke up to the sound of a knock on her door. She opened her eyes and recognized the room. Dread knotted her stomach. The knock sounded again. She sat up in bed. She was still wearing the nightgown Pack had dressed her in. She pulled the covers up to her armpits.

"Come in."

The door opened, and Pack walked in, smiling and carrying a tray full of food.

"I brought you breakfast in bed." He set the tray down across Lindsey's lower body. The folding legs closed her in like restraints. Under other conditions, the breakfast would have looked delicious. Pack had even put a freshly cut rose on the tray.

"Thank you," Lindsey said with as much enthusiasm as she could fake. Maybe if she humored him, he would lower his guard.

Pack walked over to the outer wall and opened the curtains. There was a sliding glass door and a balcony that gave them a breathtaking view of the mountains. The house had obviously been built on a hilltop, maybe the edge of a ravine. There was a hot tub on the balcony.

"Look at that view, Lindsey."

"It's beautiful."

"And you can wake up to it every morning, for as long as you like. This is ours, Lindsey, for as long as we want it."

Lindsey's head was still aching from the drug Pack had used on her the night before. She tried to eat a bite of the Belgian waffle he had prepared for her, but she almost gagged when she tried to swallow it. She put down her fork. Tears formed in her eyes. Pack ran to her and sat down on the bed.

"Don't cry, Lindsey," he said as he stroked her face. "Everything's going to be all right."

"You didn't have to kidnap me to show me all of this. You could have just invited me."

"You've got it all wrong, Lindsey. Nobody's making you stay anywhere. This is just a preview of what our life together would be like. Just stay a day or two, and I'll take you back to town, no questions asked."

"No questions asked? Just like that?"

"Cross my heart." He crossed his heart with his finger and raised his right hand as though he were swearing an oath.

"And you won't drug me again? Or try to force yourself on me?"

"Oh, no. I wouldn't do that. I never would have drugged you in the first place, but I knew, even before I asked, that you'd never agree to an overnight trip because of your church friends." He kissed her on the cheek, went to the closet, and pulled out a robe.

"I'll let you finish your breakfast," he said. "Then come on down, and I'll show you the rest of the house. You're going to love it, Lindsey. It's what we've always dreamed of."

Chapter 19: Investigation

"This is Deputy Parker," the administrative assistant said as a man entered the room with a clipboard.

"Neal Allen." Neal rose from his chair and shook hands with the deputy.

"What can I do for you, Mr. Allen?"

"I'm concerned about a friend. She went out on a date with her fiancé last night and never came back. She's not answering her phone."

"I can think of plenty of reasons for that," the deputy said. "Can't you?"

"Yeah," Neal said, "I can. But this girl's pretty level-headed. It's not like her to just disappear. Her fiancé checked out of the hotel he was staying in, but she didn't pack any luggage."

"Well," the deputy said, "there's not much going on right now. It wouldn't hurt to do a little bit of checking around. Why don't you start by giving me your friend's name and the name of the fiancé?"

"Her name's Lindsey Holland."

"Address?"

"She's from Texas, but she's staying at the Cutler Mansion."

"What's the address?"

"Did you say the *Cutler* Mansion?" asked a voice behind Neal. He turned, and started to rise. "Keep your seat." A distinguished-looking Hispanic man walked up to the desk. He was probably in his late forties or early fifties. His dark hair was feathered with gray. Neal recognized him.

"This is Detective Montoya," the deputy said.

"We've met," Neal said. "At the emergency room."

"Right," the detective said. "Your friend had quite a bruise on her face. Said her bed had broken?"

"You've met this girl?" the deputy asked. "The one who's missing?"

"Missing?" Montoya echoed. "How long?"

"Since last night," Neal said. "She went out on a date and never made it back."

"And you think something might have happened to her?"

"I'm concerned."

"Has she had any other unusual injuries?"

"Do you two mind?" the deputy said. "I'm trying to fill out a report here."

"Sorry," Montoya said. "Go ahead. I'll wait."

"I think I've got this under control, detective."

"If it involves the Cutler House, I'm interested," he said. "I'll wait around."

"Suit yourself."

***

Neal was leaving the sheriff's station when his cell phone vibrated. He saw Todd's name on the screen.

"Hey, what's up?"

"I thought of something."

"What is it?" Neal braked for a stoplight.

"Does the name Zoe or Chloe Davis mean anything to you?"

"No. Should it?"

"I don't know."

"Todd, you need to start making sense."

"Right," Todd said. "Do you remember the night we had that lock-in at Ms. Cutler's house? Pack was there. Shadow didn't like him much."

"Shadow doesn't like a lot of people."

"I get that, but there's something else. After he'd gotten through telling his story, everybody broke up. Shadow walked up to him and handed him a note. The expression on is face when he read it...."

"Yeah, go on."

"He looked like a trapped animal, like he'd been caught at something. He turned poker-faced almost immediately, but just for a fraction of a second, he looked scared and guilty. After Shadow walked away, he wadded up the note and threw it into the fire."

"Did you see what it said?"

"Not before he threw it into the fire. I dug it out as soon as he turned his back, but it was burned around the edges. I could make out part of a name. Chloe or Zoe Davis."

The light turned green. Neal pulled ahead.

"Wait right there. I'll pick you up, and we'll pay Shadow a visit. Maybe our dark princess can shed some light on things."

***

Montoya was sitting at his desk when Parker walked in.

"Can I help you?"

"What is it about you and that Cutler House? Why are you so interested?"

"Have you ever been out there, deputy?"

"No. Why? Have you?"

"Only once," Montoya said. "Right after I came to work here. Did you ever meet Detective Danforth?"

"No," Parker said. "I think he died before I even joined the force. I've heard a lot about him, though."

"I took over for him in 1980," Montoya said. "I was new to the area. He trained me, showed me around. He went through his files and told me about all the cases he'd worked. He spent a lot of time going over the unsolved ones with me, in case I ever got a lead that might help close one of them. And he told me about the Cutler Mansion."

"There was an unsolved case out there?"

"Not exactly unsolved," Montoya said, "but it haunted him for some reason. The whole place haunted him. Once I saw it, I could see why." His eyes took on a faraway expression. "It's built on a hill overlooking the ocean. There's a winding road leading up to it. There's nobody living there but an old lady and her housekeeper, but the place has a presence to it: something dark, lonely, and mysterious. It's like it doesn't quite belong in this world."

"You think it's haunted?"

"I've tried to avoid using that word, but there's no other word for it."

"What happened out there?"

"A death," Montoya said. "He ruled it a suicide but never really felt he had the full story. He was sure he'd missed something, that whatever had happened in that house was just the beginning, and that it was just a matter of time before something else happened."

"And you think this girl's disappearance could be related?"

"I don't know, but like I told that man, I'm always interested when the Cutler Mansion is involved."

***

Neal and Todd rode out to the aging condo Shadow shared with her mother. Neal rang the doorbell, but nobody answered. They were driving away when they saw Shadow walking down the sidewalk. Neal braked.

"What are you guys doing here?"

"Looking for you."

"Should I be flattered?"

"Always. But, seriously, we need to ask you something."

"What is it? I hope you're not here to pressure me about God."

"She doesn't want us to pressure her, Todd. What do we do now?"

"I really wanted to ask you about something else," Todd said. "It's about Pack. You know, Lindsey's fiancé."

"Why would I know anything about him?"

"That's just it," Todd said. "There's no reason you should know anything about him, but I think maybe you do. The night we had the lock-in at the mansion, I saw you pass him a note. I also saw the look on his face when he read it. He looked like a trapped animal."

"Chloe Davis."

"Chloe," Todd said. "I knew it was Chloe or Zoe."

"You saw my note?"

"He threw it into the fireplace, but I got it out before it completely burned through. Who is Chloe Davis?"

"I don't know, but he does. Ask him."

"We would if we could find him. Where did you get the name?"

"It just came to me," she said. "I know you don't believe I'm really psychic, but I know what I know. That guy is evil, and Lindsey needs to break up with him before something really bad happens to her."

"It may be too late for that." Todd sighed.

"Don't jump to any conclusions," Neal said.

"Conclusions about what? What's going on?"

"Lindsey's missing, Shadow."

"Missing?"

"She went out with Pack last night, and no one has seen them since."

"Well, what are you doing about it? You should be trying to find her."

"We are."

"And you came to me? You guys must really be hard up for answers."

"Pretty much. Is that all you know? A girl's name and an overall bad impression."

"A very bad impression. That guy is scary. If he's got Lindsey, she's in trouble. I don't think she's dead, though. I think I would have sensed that."

"Well, thanks for talking to us."

"Thanks for listening. Not many people do, you know. Just you and Lindsey. I really hope she's all right."

"So do we."

***

"What are you doing?" Jolene asked as she came out of the Dawn Treader Cafe's kitchen.

Todd didn't look up. "Research." He just kept staring at the screen of his laptop.

"Research about what?"

"Chloe Davis," he said. "Do you know how many Chloe Davises there are in the U.S. alone?"

"No," she said. "But I'm sure there are more Chloe Davises than there are Jai Linh Nguyens."

"Yeah," he said. "I bet there are."

"Who's Chloe Davis?"

"That's just it. I don't know."

"Where did you get her name?"

He paused. "I'm embarrassed to tell you."

The bells over the door rang as Neal walked in.

"Any news?" Jolene asked.

"'Fraid not," Neal said. "I called the sheriff's office and Lindsey's parents, but nobody's heard anything. I think Lindsey's mom is more afraid of being out the cost of a wedding than she is worried about Lindsey. She said she'd kill Lindsey herself if she eloped without telling her."

"Wonderful," Todd said.

"Any luck?" Neal asked.

"I'm not sure."

"What have you got?"

Todd typed, scrolled, and clicked. "This."

Neal pulled up a chair and sat down beside his friend. A headline was splashed across the screen.

"No Leads in Teen's Disappearance."

Beneath the headline was a picture of a pretty girl with long, dark hair.

"Is that Chloe Davis?"

"It's *a* Chloe Davis," Todd said, "but I'm not sure if it's the one we're looking for. This one disappeared from Chevy Chase, Maryland, about five years ago."

"Disappeared, huh?"

"Yeah," Todd said. "She was a college student from Michigan. She was working as a lifeguard at an expensive country club in Maryland when she vanished without a trace. Nobody ever found out what happened to her."

"Is that the only Chloe Davis you found?"

"No," Todd said. "The world is full of girls named Chloe Davis, but this one stood out for some reason."

"I see what you mean," Neal said. "The story's dark and mysterious, and she's about the same age as Pack and Lindsey. But, there's nothing to connect Pack to this."

"Connect Pack to what?" Jolene said. "Where did you get this girl's name, anyway?"

"Shadow," Neal said. "She says the name just came to her."

"I see why Todd didn't want to tell me," Jolene said.

"Have you called Pack's parents yet?" Todd asked Neal. "To see if they've heard from Pack?"

"Not yet," Neal said. "But I think I see what you're getting at."

Chapter 20: Gilded Cage

The sun was starting to set. Lindsey sat in a hot tub, looking out at the mountains. A river wound beneath them. The roar of rushing water was relaxing, almost hypnotic.

"Are you hungry yet?" Pack asked her.

"A little."

"Stay right here," he said. "I'll bring you something."

"You don't have to...."

"No, I insist." He climbed out of the hot tub. Water splashed from his muscular body. He grabbed a towel and began to dry himself. Lindsey felt sure he was posing for her.

"Do you need any help?"

"Not at all. Just stay right here. Pretend you're at a resort."

"Okay."

Lindsey sighed as Pack vanished into the house. *What a strange situation.* Pack had drugged her and abducted her, but he had spent the entire day going out of his way to please her. He had bought her new clothes, books he knew she would enjoy reading, and art supplies. Was this just his clumsy way of taking her on a surprise vacation? Had he really felt so threatened by her friends that he'd felt all of this was necessary?

Lindsey looked down at the swimsuit she was wearing. He'd actually bought her a selection of swimsuits. This one was the most modest, but she still didn't feel entirely comfortable wearing it in front of Pack. Not under the circumstances. She tried to forget that he'd changed her clothes after drugging her. He had to have seen her when he was changing her. She had been completely helpless before him. Lindsey swallowed hard. She stood and grabbed a towel from the back of a lounge chair. The air felt cold on her wet skin. She dried herself and went back into the bedroom to change.

She found dry clothes in the chest of drawers beside her bed, gathered some together, went into the bathroom, and locked the door. She took a quick shower and dressed herself more quickly than she usually did. She halfway expected Pack to come bursting in. He'd probably play innocent, maybe tell her he was making sure she had a towel to dry off on.

What am I going to do? she asked herself as she looked in the mirror to comb her hair. Pack had told her he'd let her go once they had spent some time together. Did she really believe he'd let her go so easily? Lindsey had to admit, she had her doubts. She had known Pack for years, and the familiarity of that comfortable relationship pulled at her heart, told her to trust him. The sight of his tan, muscled body drew her as well, chipping away at her self-control. She'd promised, along with many of her friends in the church youth group, to save herself for the marriage bed. How many, she wondered, had made it this far?

Lindsey combed out her hair, touched up her makeup, and went downstairs to the kitchen.

***

"Mrs. Packard, this is Neal Allen. I live in Oregon now, but I used to live in Texas. I was the youth director at First Baptist Church. That's right."

Jolene and Todd sat at the table and listened.

"Yes, he has been out here. I was wondering if you'd heard from him in the last day or so. He's checked out of his hotel room, and nobody seems to know where he went. Lindsey's gone, too."

Todd and Jolene looked at each other.

"I'm sure it's nothing to worry about, but if you hear from them, could you have them call me? I'd really appreciate it."

"Ask her," Todd whispered.

"I had something else I was going to ask you. Has Pack ever lived in Chevy Chase, Maryland?"

He waited. "Did he ever mention a Chloe Davis? I think she worked there during the summers."

Neal frowned.

"I'm not sure. The name just came up." He listened. "Well, thanks. Be sure to have them call me. Thanks. Good night."

Neal punched the "end" button.

"Well?"

"Well, she hasn't head from Pack since he got out here, and she said she'd never heard of Chloe Davis."

"We struck out?"

"Maybe not. It was strange. She said she'd never heard of Chloe Davis, but when I mentioned the name, her whole tone changed. She asked what *that* had to do with anything."

"So, you think she *does* know who Chloe Davis is?"

"Maybe. And Pack used to coach tennis at Chevy Chase during the summers...at a country club."

***

Pack was pulling a pan of lasagna out of the oven.

"Hey," he said. "I told you to relax. I've got this."

"I know," she said. "I was starting to wrinkle up."

"There's nothing else for you to do," he said. "It's all ready."

He had plates sitting on the table. He'd already prepared bread and salad. The lasagna was the finishing touch...almost. He pulled out a bottle and set it on the table.

"What is this?"

"Champaigne."

"Pack, you know I don't drink."

"It won't hurt you, Lindsey. You know Jesus drank wine."

"I know," she said. "If you want to drink it, I won't judge you, but it's just not something I do."

"You're an adult, Lindsey, and none of your church friends are around to see you."

"It's not about that."

"Well, what is it about?"

She looked at him.

"It's because I drugged you, isn't it? You don't trust me because of what happened last night." He picked up the bottle and popped the cork. "It's never been opened, Lindsey. Not until now. What if I drink it myself? Will that convince you it isn't poisoned?"

"Maybe."

"You really don't trust me, do you? I guess I deserve it."

"You could say that."

"You're still mad at me, aren't you? For the way I brought you here?"

Lindsey paused and gave her answer some thought. "It's not so much a matter of being mad, Pack. It's a matter of trust, and treating people with respect."

"What about forgiving people? Isn't that what Christians are supposed to do?"

"It's not about forgiving," she said. "It's about trusting, and treating people with respect."

"I've treated you with respect the whole time we've been here."

Lindsey didn't respond.

"Haven't I?"

"Other than the way you brought me here in the first place."

"But you've enjoyed it, haven't you? Some of it, at least?"

She paused, considering it. "Some of it."

"That's something, at least. Maybe if we stay here long enough, you'll even begin to trust me."

"You said you'd let me go if I gave you two days. 'No questions asked.' Those were your exact words."

"It hasn't been two days yet," he said.

"But nobody knows where I am. They've got to be worried about me."

"Let them worry. This is our time."

"Pack. We can't just think about ourselves. What about our parents and our friends?"

The look in his eyes changed to something distant, haunted.

"Never mind," she said. "We'll talk about it later."

***

Detective Montoya set down his coffee mug and put on a pair of reading glasses. He frowned as he studied the printout. Finally, he looked up. Neal and Todd were sitting across from him.

"And you think this is connected how?"

"We think he was working there that summer," Neal said. "Maybe even at the same country club."

"Yeah? And?"

Todd sighed.

"I heard Lindsey mention the name Chloe Davis to him once," Todd said. "And I saw how he reacted."

"How did he react?"

"Guilty. Like he'd been caught."

"And you think Lindsey suspected something?"

"I don't know. Maybe."

He looked down at the printout, cleared his throat, and looked back up. "And you think this might have something to do with her disappearance?"

Todd and Neal looked at each other.

"It's just a hunch," Neal said. "But, if there's anything you can do to find them—trace credit cards, cellphones, anything like that...."

The detective nodded. "That can be arranged. And I can put a BOLO out on his vehicle."

"And if you could contact the people in Chevy Chase," Neal said. "Find out if there is a connection, if Pack was ever under suspicion."

"I can do that. I'll contact the sheriff's office in Texas first. If it's a small community, and Packard's lived there most of his life, they might know something."

"You should probably tread carefully," Neal said. "His father's a judge."

"I always tread carefully," Montoya said. "Anything else?"

"No, that's pretty much it."

"I'll get to work on it. Call you if I find anything."

"I'd appreciate that," Neal said.

Neal and Todd crossed the hall, rode down the elevator, and stepped out into the parking lot.

"Not exactly the truth," Neal said. "But close."

"I didn't want to tell him I'd gotten a tip from Shadow. Can you blame me?"

"Nope."

"You think God will forgive me for lying?"

"Maybe."

"Where are we going now?"

"Back to the cafe," Neal said. "I've got work to do."

***

Lindsey pushed back the sheets and climbed out of bed. She crept across the dark bedroom to the door. She thought Pack might have locked her in the bedroom, but when she tested the knob, the door opened. Maybe he was trying to gain her trust by showing that he trusted her.

I have to get out of here, she thought. *I'm sorry, Pack.* He had bought her gifts, cooked for her, done everything he could to win her over and Lindsey realized, to her surprise, that it was starting to work. She had read about women bonding with their captors; Stockholm Syndrome was the technical term for it. Pack had drugged her and abducted her, and she actually felt *guilty* for wanting to get out and call home. Was she really so weak? But, Pack wasn't just a stranger, she told herself as she pulled on jeans and a sweater. They had known each other for years. They were engaged.

We're still engaged, Lindsey thought, *but there's no way we could ever have a normal marriage after this. Is there?* She put on her shoes and a jacket. She had seen a flashlight on the mantle downstairs. She would need it once she got outside, but she wondered if she could get it without alerting Pack. Lindsey opened the door of the bedroom. She stood in the dark and listened. The house was quiet. *Silent as the grave*, she thought, finding the old cliché oddly chilling. She was not in mortal danger, she told herself. Pack would never actually hurt her.

Navigating the house in the dark would be tricky. She didn't know if Pack was downstairs in the den or in one of the bedrooms. What would he do if he caught her sneaking out? She didn't want to think about that. She tried not to think about it, tried to convince herself that Pack would understand, and that he wouldn't even be angry.

She crept down the hall, the carpet absorbing most of the sound of her footsteps. She made it to the stairs and began her descent. One of the stairs squeaked beneath her foot. She cringed, froze, and listened. The house was silent. She had just reached the first floor when the heating unit kicked on. Startled, she nearly fell backward but managed to keep her balance. Her pulse was pounding now, but she pushed herself forward. The noise from the heating unit would help to cover the sound of her own footsteps, but it could conceal the sounds of Pack's approach as well.

Lindsey reached the den. The big room and the adjoining kitchen, so far as she could see, were both empty. Gray light filtered through the tall windows and the sliding double doors that opened onto the porch. Lindsey could make out the shape of the flashlight on the mantle. She started toward it and heard something: an indrawn breath. Lindsey froze. *Pack was sleeping on the couch.* She could hear his soft snoring above the white noise of the heating unit. Lindsey was afraid to move for a few long seconds, but then she remembered Pack had always told her he was a deep sleeper, that nothing could disturb him once he was asleep. She hoped that was true.

Lindsey managed to keep her hand steady as she lifted the flashlight from the mantle. She considered leaving through the patio's sliding doors but thought it would make too much noise, and that Pack might feel the draft. She decided instead to leave through the door in the back of the kitchen, so she crept as quickly and as quietly as she could through the dark room. In the pale light, she could see the dishes from the meal she had shared with Pack still lying in the sink, and once again, she felt a pang of guilt. He really had tried to please her.

I'm sorry.

Gathering her courage she made her way to the door. In the gloom she could make out a deadbolt lock. Holding her breath, she turned the knob.

Snick!

The lock disengaged. The sound was deafening in the dark house. Lindsey listened for the sound of Pack's breathing. She couldn't make it out over the hiss and hum of the radiator, but she also didn't hear any sounds of movement. Quickly she turned the knob, stepped out onto the porch, and, as quietly as she could, pulled the door shut behind her.

The air was cold and clean, and she could smell the tang of the forest around her. Insects sang their nocturnal songs. A full moon peered through the clouds overhead, and an owl hooted somewhere in the forest.

Lindsey started down the steps into the yard. She looked back at the beautiful, rustic cabin with its huge front porch. Part of her wanted to stay with Pack, to try to understand what was happening, to try to "talk him down" from whatever mania had seized him. He had said he would let her go after two days. Perhaps she should just wait and be patient.

No. She had to let Neal and Jolene and her family know where she was. She didn't want to get Pack into any trouble. Perhaps she wouldn't even tell them that he'd drugged and abducted her. She could just say he was upset and needed to talk. That wasn't even a lie. Not really.

Which way should she go? The river ran along one side of the house. The water was clear, but it looked deep, and mountain streams were usually very cold. Lindsey looked back at the house and noticed a garage. The door was open and there were two vehicles inside: a car and an SUV. That was strange. Pack had said the road was washed out. Maybe the owners had been in the house when the road had washed out and had been forced to leave their vehicles. Maybe. Neither of the cars looked like Pack's rental, but it was possible that he had changed vehicles.

Lindsey wondered if she should take a closer look. What if one of the vehicles still had keys in the ignition….

Lindsey crept into the garage and peered into the window of the SUV. She couldn't see anything and decided to risk turning on her flashlight. The key wasn't in the ignition. She walked around and checked the truck, but there was no key there either. Lindsey was walking around the truck when she accidentally kicked something in the dark. The sound echoed through garage. Lindsey gasped and bit down on her lips. She listened for a long time for any indication that Pack had heard her and was coming after her, but heard nothing. Satisfied, she left the garage and edged around the corner toward the forest. As she was passing one of the garage's windows, she thought she saw something move inside.

Pack? No. It couldn't have been. If he had come from the house, he would be outside with her. She decided to risk using the flashlight. She snapped it on and shined it through the window. A half-scream escaped her throat before she could clamp down on it. She turned off the light, covered her mouth, and pressed her back against the wall. There was a body in the garage. It was the body of a young girl. She was gagged and tied to a chair.

Lindsey had to chance another look. She gathered her courage, aimed the flashlight at the window, and turned it back on. The face was still there. It was a young blonde girl in a coat and cap. Her pale blue eyes stared out at Lindsey…and blinked. She was alive. Lindsey scanned the area around the window and saw that there was a man in the room too. He was gagged too, and tied to a chair. Lindsey thought she saw cuffs around his wrists. She turned off the flashlight.

Heart pounding, Lindsey turned away from the garage and ran for the woods as fast as she could go. She ran on the tips of her toes and tried to be quiet, but she still heard the crunch of leaves beneath her feet from time to time. Lindsey didn't risk using the flashlight until she was well away from the house. There was enough moonlight to navigate by, but the inky shadows beneath the trees were thick. Finally, when she was well away from the house, she sunk down beside a tree and caught her breath. Her mouth was dry and her pulse was still hammering. The image of the man and girl—probably the owner of the house and his daughter—was frozen on the theater screen of her mind. Pack wasn't just trespassing. This was a full-fledged home invasion, and she had been an unwilling accomplice.

Her mind whirled with conflicting emotions. Earlier that day, she'd almost convinced herself that Pack's controlling behavior was nothing more than his clumsy way of showing love. He'd been given so much growing up that he just couldn't cope with losing someone close to him. The thought of losing her had driven him a little bit crazy, she supposed, but that was understandable wasn't it? But this…? Pack wasn't just a little bit crazy. He had completely snapped. Well, maybe not completely. At least the people were alive. Maybe they had come home unexpectedly and surprised Pack, and he'd had to improvise. Maybe they had threatened to call the police, and he'd panicked.

Am I trying to make excuses for him? On some level, Lindsey realized, maybe she was. If the man she had almost married was full-on crazy, and she had never even seen it, what did that say about her?

Dodging branches, she walked to the main road. Pack had told her the bridge was washed out, but she knew she should no longer afford to take anything he had told her at face value. The road was littered with treelimbs in spots, and Lindsey had to find her way carefully. She looked back more than once to see if Pack was following her, but she saw no sign of him.

Lindsey switched on the flashlight. She focused its pale, elongated disk directly onto the damp pavement in front of her.

She began to run. She had been on her high school's track team at one time, and still jogged when her schedule allowed it. Not knowing how far she had to go, she adjusted her pace and breathing. Lindsey thought once that she heard someone moving behind her. She stopped running, swung around, and scanned the dark road behind her. Seeing nothing, she stood for awhile and listened. She thought of Mr. Monroe's Bigfoot story. She didn't know which would have frightened her more: a giant, red-eyed ape, or the sight of Pack coming at her with an axe.

He wouldn't hurt me, she told herself, as he resumed her jog. The forest seemed quieter than it had when she had started out, and she wondered if it was her imagination.

What would she do when she got back? Before she had seen the two people in the garage, Lindsey had been wondering if she should cancel the engagement immediately and just tell everyone she had decided that she and Pack were no longer compatible, that they had grown apart. She wouldn't have to tell anybody about the abduction. Her mother would blame her for the breakup, of course, but she was willing to endure that to keep from ruining Pack's life. He deserved another chance at love. He wasn't really dangerous, she had thought, just a bit possessive. The discovery in the garage had changed everything. She had no choice but to go to the police now.

Lindsey lost track of how long she'd been running through the darkness. It could have been twenty minutes or fifty. She thought, after a while, that she could hear the sound of rushing water somewhere in the distance. It was getting louder. Finally, she ascended one last hill, reached the top, and clearly heard the river in the darkness in front of her. Following the pale flashlight beam, she followed the road to the place where it ended.

Pack had not lied about the washed-out bridge. The asphalt on the road ended in a jagged tear. Lindsey probed the dark void beyond for any sign of the river. Finally, she saw it. Far away, almost beyond the reach of the light, she could make out its churning surface. The bluff was steep, and Lindsey could see no place to climb.

"Go ahead, Lindsey. Jump. If that's what you want to do."

Pack. Lindsey turned around and saw him standing on the hill behind her. He had followed her. Somehow, he had followed her without being seen or heard.

"Pack," Lindsey gasped. "You scared me."

"Where are you going?"

His voice sounded strange and hollow. She remembered an old movie she had seen as a junior high student. *Invasion of the Body Snatchers.* In the story, people were being killed and replaced by alien doubles, doubles with strange, droning voices...like Pack's.

"I have to c-call Neal," she said, her mouth suddenly dry. "I have to let everybody know we're okay." She couldn't keep her voice from shaking and silently cursed her own weakness.

Pack didn't respond.

"Look," she said. "They d-don't have to know you abducted me. I just want them to know we're okay. I'll—I'll tell them you were really upset and that you needed to talk."

Pack stood, as still and silent as a statue. After a long moment, Lindsey started to speak again.

"We can't go back, Lindsey. I think you've guessed that by now."

For a moment, Lindsey was too startled to speak.

"What? What do you...?"

"I know you were in the garage. I know you saw those people."

Lindsey thought about trying to deny it, but there was probably no point now. "Who were they?"

"The man was a friend of my dad's," Pack said. "He lives in Portland, so I didn't expect him to come back here."

"So you tied him up? And his daughter?" She struggled to hold her voice steady.

"He came up here unexpectedly and caught me in his house. I offered to pay him for using it, but he threatened to call the police. Things got a little crazy after that."

Lindsey didn't know what to say.

"What I really want to know, Lindsey, is how you found out about Chloe Davis."

Chloe Davis? The question took Lindsey completely by surprise. She searched her memory for the name but came up blank. "I don't know who that is," she finally admitted.

"Don't lie to me, Lindsey! Of course you know. How else could the little witch have known? How long were you going to play me?"

"Little witch?" She shook her head. "Shadow? Do you mean Shadow?"

He started down the hill toward her. Lindsey took a step backward and remembered the steep gulf at her back. Invisible needles pierced her skin.

"How did you find out? Who told you?"

"I don't know what you're talking about." She took a step sideways. The treeline was about fifteen feet away.

"It's not the way you think," he said. "I never meant for any of it to happen."

"Never meant for what to happen?" Pack was just a faceless shadow.

"You *know*."

"No, I don't know. If I knew, I wouldn't ask. What's going on, Pack? Help me understand."

He mumbled something and kept moving toward her. "She was crazy. She said she'd ruin my life. That's the truth, Lindsey."

"What happened?" Lindsey gasped. "What did you do?"

"Do you want to leave now, Lindsey?"

"I thought you said you wouldn't let me."

"I also told you earlier that I would. After two days. Remember? I'll make a deal with you, Lindsey. You can go right now, but, as I told you, the bridge has been washed out. If you want to go back, you're going to have to swim."

Lindsey stared down at the churning water and wondered about her chances of survival.

"It's fed by melting snow," Pack told her. "Have you ever tried to swim in ice water? Most people don't last long, but if you think you can beat the odds, it's up to you."

Lindsey bolted for the forest. Pack leaped after her. She screamed as he caught her. He spun her around. She hit him across the face with the flashlight. Howling and cursing, he twisted her arm behind her back, kicked her feet out from under her, and threw her to the floor of the forest. The air exploded from her lungs. Dried needles crunched beneath her as he shoved his knee into her back. She gasped for air. He had knocked the wind out of her.

"That was pretty stupid, Lindsey. If I wanted to hurt you, you know I could do it, but I don't. I'll let you up if you promise not to run away again."

Tears stung Lindsey's eyes. She tried to keep from sobbing.

"Do you promise?"

She gasped for breath.

"What's it going to be, Lindsey? Do you promise not to run away?"

"What if I don't, Pack?" she managed to whisper. "Are you going to sit on me forever?"

Or kill me? The thought sprang into her mind. *Kill me like you killed Chloe Davis.* Lindsey recoiled at the thought. Had he really killed that other girl? Somehow, she knew he had. She did not want to believe it, but somehow she knew it was true. Pack had killed someone, and if she provoked him, he might kill her, too.

No. He wouldn't hurt.... She found she could no longer complete the thought.

"Fine," he said. "I promise not to throw you into the river unless you try to run away." He stood up, pulled her to her feet, and held onto her upper arm. "We're going back to the house now."

Lindsey didn't respond, but she didn't fight him as they walked back to the house. She tried to work up the courage to pull free and run again, but the thought of being pinned down with Pack's knee in her back stopped her. He hadn't hit her so far, but she had no idea how far he would go if she really made him angry. She wondered how he had killed the other girl. Had he accidentally broken her neck? Strangled her? What had he done with her body? Had he thrown *her* into a river somewhere?

Lindsey would never forget the long, silent walk through the forest. When they finally made it back to the house, the sight of the rustic cabin was almost welcome. Pack dragged Lindsey onto the porch, opened the door, hauled her inside, and pulled the door shut behind them. Clinging tightly to her arm with one hand, Pack ascended the stairs. With his free hand, he pushed Lindsey ahead of him as he went. He opened the bedroom door and shoved Lindsey inside.

"Now," he told her, "get out of those clothes."

"What?" Lindsey's heart began to pound. "No."

"Take off your clothes, Lindsey. I won't tell you again."

She began to cry. She struggled for self-control as tears ran down her face. Pack walked over to the dresser and pulled open a drawer. Lindsey tensed to run but hesitated. She wondered if Pack had hidden a pistol in the drawer. Instead he pulled out a nightgown and tossed it onto the bed.

"Go into the bathroom," he said. "Change into this and throw your clothes out the door. I won't hurt you, but I can't have you running away again. You won't get far in just a nightgown." He shook his head. "I won't hurt you, Lindsey. As long as we've known each other, I just can't understand why you don't trust me."

You threatened to throw me into the river, she thought, but she said nothing. Her heart pounding, Lindsey went into the bathroom. With trembling hands, she undressed and pulled on the gown. She looked around the room for a weapon.

"What are you doing in there, Lindsey?"

"Nothing. Changing clothes."

"Open the door."

She pulled the door open. Pack was waiting. He was holding a chain. Did he intend to beat her with it? Or hang her?

"Now," he said, "come with me." He rolled the chain into a ball, shifted it to his left hand, and grabbed Lindsey by the arm. His fingers dug into her bare flesh. He led her out of the room, down the hall, and to a flight of stairs. A bulb burned at the top.

"Where are you taking me?"

"You shouldn't have tried to run out on me," he said. "I can't just let you get away with that."

"What are you going to do?"

He pushed her onto the stairs. There were walls on either side.

"Climb," he said. "All the way to the top and through the door."

Lindsey ascended the narrow stairs. There was a single door at the top. She twisted the knob and pushed the door open. A wedge of light slid across the plywood floor of an unfinished attic room. The floor was dusty, and the walls were made up of exposed studs and fiberglass insulation.

"This is your new room," Pack said. "After a few days in here, maybe you'll appreciate the old one."

"Pack," she pleaded, "you wouldn't do this to me. You couldn't."

"You shouldn't have tried to run away. Not now. Not this summer. I'm not going to let you run away from me again, Lindsey. Get in there."

Lindsey's legs were shaking. She felt the dusty wood beneath her bare feet. Pack took her by the arm and led her to a cross brace.

"Sit down."

"Pack," she said. "Don't..."

"Sit down!"

She sat. He wrapped the chain around the wooden brace, looped it around her shin, shoved a padlock through two of the links, and snapped it shut. Lindsey watched mutely as he walked to the attic door. He looked back at her.

"I'll see you tomorrow."
He slammed the door and left Lindsey in the dark.

Chapter 21: Exodus Dream

"Chloe Davis," Detective Montoya said as he placed the folder on his desk and opened it. Inside were printed copies of snapshots, police reports, and newspaper clippings. Photographs showed a smiling high-school senior, a girl in a red swimsuit with the word *lifeguard* across the chest, a girl in a white tennis dress posing with a racquet, the same girl surrounded by friends at a party—images, seemingly, of a vibrant young woman with a happy life. The newspaper clippings showed some of the same snapshots in a grimmer context. "Search for Missing Girl Continues." "No Clues in Search for Missing Girl." "Girl's Disappearance Remains a Mystery."

"She'd just graduated from high school and had a full scholarship at Cornell," Montoya said. "She was working as a lifeguard at an upscale country club when she vanished without a trace. But you already knew that."

"Is there any connection between this girl and Jason Packard?"

"He was working at the same club that summer. The police questioned him about it but never found anything to connect him to Chloe's disappearance. The detective in charge of the case said he had some lingering doubts about Jason Packard, but apparently his father has some political connections up there, too. Without any solid evidence, they had to drop the investigation."

"So, his parents knew about Chloe Davis?"

"Yeah."

"Anything else?"

"Odds and ends," Montoya said. "I had a report of a couple in a car matching Packard's out on Long Beach the night of the disappearance. They were apparently having a pretty heated argument. There may not be any connection, but we're looking into it. Packard also withdrew ten thousand dollars from the bank the day before the disappearance and bought about two hundred dollars worth of groceries. It looks like he was planning to go away for a while."

"No credit card use since then?"

"No. If he checked into a hotel, he must have used an alias. We haven't found anything under any of his known aliases so far."

"*Known* aliases?"

"Apparently, he was quite well known in his home county and some of the surrounding ones. Mostly for drinking and driving. Jason Pickard and Jason Packer were his two aliases of choice."

"Not very creative," Neal said.

"No," Montoya said, "but he could always claim the arresting officer misunderstood him. Especially if he wasn't carrying any ID."

"Anything else?"

"Ms. Holland hasn't used her credit cards either, and I'm not getting any cellphone use from either of them."

Neal nodded. "What else?"

"Well, it may be nothing, but Packard took the northern route to get here. He spent a couple of days in Alethea Falls. It's a little mountain town close to the Canadian border."

"What would he have been doing there?" Todd mused aloud.

"I don't know," Montoya said. "He may have friends there, somebody he's staying with. I put in a call to their sheriff's department earlier today, gave them a description of the last vehicle anybody saw Packard driving."

"You've been involved in cases like this before," Todd said. "How do you think this is going to end? Really?"

"I don't know," Montoya said. "It doesn't look good."

Neal and Todd were quiet as they walked back out to the parking lot.

"What do you think?" Todd asked as they climbed into Neal's car. "Do you think we'll ever see her again?"

Neal shook his head.

***

Lindsey awoke to the sound of someone fumbling with a lock. She thought, just for an instant, that someone was trying to break into her apartment. Then she remembered. She felt the plywood beneath her, smelled the stale air, and remembered.

The door opened. Fingers of light crept across the floor. Lindsey squinted into the glare. Pack's inky shape blocked the light. Lindsey couldn't see his face, but she recognized the familiar figure. For a silent eternity he stood and stared at her. The frozen shape didn't seem alive. It was as though Pack had propped a manikin in the doorway just to torment her. Lindsey swallowed hard. She was afraid to say anything, afraid she might provoke him. He probably stood there for a full minute before he stepped into the room and set a tray down on the floor. Scrambled eggs, toast, and juice.

"Pack, please..."

He turned away without a word, walked back to the door, and slammed it shut. Lindsey could hear him fumbling with the locks on the other side. For the hundredth time, she tested the chain around her ankle.

***

"What are we doing here?" Todd asked. It was almost nine o'clock, and the sun still blazed against the ocean's rippling skin. The Cutler Mansion was cloaked in shadow.

"Checking on Mrs. Cutler," Neal said. "She was really upset when I talked to her earlier today." They stepped up onto the porch, and Neal rang the doorbell.

The door sprang open, and Todd leaped back. He had not heard anyone coming. Cornelia stood framed in shadow.

"Come in," she said simply. "Mrs. Cutler has been waiting for you."

"I...." Neal began, obviously confused. "Okay." Cornelia turned her back. Neal and Todd fell in behind her. Todd pulled the door shut as they entered.

"Did you tell her we were coming?" Todd asked, his voice low.

"No," Neal said. "I guess I should have, but I didn't."

"Then how did she...?"

"This way, please."

They passed the sarcophagus, a tall painting, and a collection of spears. Cornelia led them into the sunroom. Mrs. Cutler's fan-backed wicker chair was turned toward them.

"Come in," she said. "Oh, do come in." Her voice sounded strained.

"I'm sorry I didn't call ahead," Neal said as they walked around the chair. "We just wanted to see how you were doing."

Mrs. Cutler looked frail. Her presence usually filled the chair as a queen's regal radiance fills a throne, but she seemed to have shrunk somehow. It was as though her body had become hollow and was starting to shrivel.

"Have you heard anything about Lindsey?"

"Nothing so far," Neal said. "The police think they may have a lead. Before he came here, Pack spent a couple of days at a place called Alethea Falls. Have you ever heard of it?"

"No, I'm afraid not."

"Detective Montoya says it's a small town near the Canadian border."

"Do you think he's taken her into Canada?"

"Maybe we'd better not jump to any conclusions."

"This is dreadful," Mrs. Cutler lamented. "Just dreadful." She covered her mouth as her eyes filled up with tears. She dabbed them with a handkerchief and took a deep breath. "There, now. We can't have that. We have to be strong for her. She would need us to be strong. You've been praying for her, haven't you?"

"Oh, yeah. Ever since the whole thing started."

"Good man. She'll need that. All of the prayers you can muster for her. She'll need them all. I may just sit here all night and pray for her."

"Are you sure you should?" Todd asked. "I mean, you can pray in bed, can't you?"

"No," she said. "I have to stay vigilant. I have to keep my concentration." She stared out the window at the ocean beyond. The old lighthouse, dark and brooding, clung to its craggy perch and kept its own silent vigil.

***

Lindsey heard the cry of seagulls, the rumbling of thunder, and the distant crashing of waves. The lamp flickered through the gloom around her, its shivering glare silently pulsing across the contours of the lantern room. The lumpy mattress beneath her smelled of sweat and mildew, and the band around her ankle was as tight as ever. She pushed herself upright and stood to stretch her cramping muscles.

How long have I been here? she wondered. *Is anybody even looking for me?*

She heard footsteps on the stairs. What was he going to do to her now? She locked down at her tattered gown. Those scraps of cloth were barely holding together. One sharp yank, and she would be naked before her captor, naked and undernourished. She had been strong once—fit and athletic—but weeks of captivity had drained the strength from her. Her arms and legs were skeletal, and her ribs were clearly visible beneath her colorless skin.

The door of the tower creaked open. A slender shape rose into the flickering light. The head turned.

"Sister! Oh, my darling, what has he done to you?"

Caitlyn? What was Caitlyn doing here? Was she dreaming or losing her mind? Hadn't she been in an attic room somewhere?

Lindsey began to cry. Caitlyn knelt beside her on the mattress. She saw the band on her ankle and the chain.

"He's been holding you captive all this time? Captive like a slave in a dungeon. How long have you been here?"

Lindsey tried to speak. Her voice was strange, unfamiliar. "I don't know," she managed to say.

"I have to get something to cut the chain." She stood to go.

"Wait," Lindsey said. "Don't leave me here."

"I'll be right back." She moved toward the door.

"Don't...."

"I'm coming right back, darling. I promise."

The hatch creaked open and gently closed as Caitlyn disappeared. She would never make it back. Lindsey was sure of that. Her captor would never allow it. He would probably kill her.

The hatch opened again a moment later. Lindsey half-expected to hear the wild laughter of her captor, to see Caitlyn's severed head tossed to the floor in front of her, but it didn't happen. When Caitlyn reappeared, she was clutching an odd-looking key.

"It's a skeleton key," she whispered. "Don't you love the sound of that?"

"Where did you get it?"

"Keep your voice down," Caitlyn said. "He's asleep down below. We have to get you out of here before we're discovered."

"If he catches us...."

"He'll kill you if you stay here, sister. There's not much time."

Caitlyn helped Lindsey to her feet. She picked up the dirty blanket Lindsey's captor had left for her.

"You'll need this. It's cold outside."

Her knees trembling, Lindsey made her way to the hatch. Caitlyn pulled it open, and the two of them started down the lighthouse stairs. They moved quietly, as quietly as they could, because every sound echoed. They made it to the bottom more quickly than Lindsey had believed possible. A lantern sat on the floor, its flame dancing inside the glass. She heard a rasping noise and saw her captor lying on a bench and snoring. Even asleep, the massive, bearded figure was terrifying. An empty bottle, its cork removed, lay on the floor. Caitlyn pointed to the heavy wooden door. Heart pounding, hands shaking on the latch, Lindsey turned the bolt and slid it aside. She twisted the glass knob, pushed the door open, and stepped out into the windy night. Caitlyn followed, silent as a shadow. Lindsey pulled the door closed behind them. It latched without a sound. The winding path that led to shore was barely visible above the waves. It looked like the bony spine of some ancient reptile.

"The tide's already coming in," Caitlyn said. "It's too late to get across, but there's a boat beside the dock."

"I can't make it," Lindsey said. "I can barely walk."

"Lean on me. I'll help you." A pair of rubber boots lay by the door. "Put those boots on. You'll need them to protect your feet."

Lindsey pulled the boots over her bare feet. The fit was sloppy, but they shielded her feet from the cold stone beneath. Pulling the blanket tight against her body, and leaning against Caitlyn, she started down the wet, winding path to the dock.

***

Lindsey awoke to the sound of rushing water. She was lying under open sky, wrapped in a blanket. Her head spun as she forced herself into a sitting position. She was in a fishing boat, floating down some dark, unfamiliar river. A blanket of fog hung above the water. It shrouded the inky tree-shapes on the distant shoreline. She thought for an instant that she saw an Indian village with pointed teepees, but when she tried to focus in on it, she realized it had not really been there.

There was nobody else in the boat with her, and she had no idea how she had gotten there. She had only the vague memory of a dream, a dream about a nineteenth- century lighthouse and Caitlyn. Caitlyn had helped her escape. Lindsey looked down at her ankle half-expecting to see a metal band there, and saw that she was wearing oversized rubber boots. The boots, she remembered, had been a part of the dream. Lindsey's head was aching the way it had that first morning, the morning after Pack had drugged her.

Apparently, he had drugged her again and somehow, even with her sense of reality completely warped by the drugs, she had still managed to escape. It was still too early to celebrate, though. Even though she'd managed to find her way out of Pack's clutches, she was lost on an unknown river and might still be miles from civilization. The blanket and the thin nightgown she was dressed in had probably saved her from hypothermia thus far, but her teeth were still chattering from the cold. The current beneath the boat, she thought, had picked up speed. If the river turned to rapids, her boat could be smashed against the rocks.

Sleep pulled at her consciousness. Pack's drugs were still in her system, and it was only a matter of time before she fell back into the inevitable clutches of sleep. She needed to find a place to rest before she continued. She looked at the shoreline around her. The bluffs were steep in some places and overgrown with brush in others. She picked up the paddle and tried to push herself closer to shore.

In the fog ahead of her, she thought she saw the glare of passing headlights and heard the sound of an engine. The gray arch of a bridge spanned the river ahead of her. She wondered for a moment if the bridge might fade as the Indian village had, but instead it grew clearer. The concrete and steel structure was about fifty feet above the river with high bluffs on either side. To make it to the road, she'd have to climb the rocky cliffs and claw her way through the brush.

The current really was picking up speed. She was sure this time that she wasn't imagining it. A waterfall? What if she was heading for falls? In these unknown mountains, the drop might be hundreds of feet.

Suddenly seized by panic, she fought to push the boat toward shore. Using all the strength she had, she managed to wrestle the boat to within a few feet of the high, tree-covered bluff at the edge of the river. She was searching for a path when a rock appeared in front of her. She dug in with her paddle and pushed for all she was worth. The bow of the boat struck the rock. Shrieking in metallic agony, the boat twisted and rolled over onto its side. Lindsey fought for balance and lost as the icy river seized her in its steely grip and dragged her to the muddy bottom.

Chapter 22: Post-Traumatic Life

When Lindsey opened her eyes, she wondered if she was still in a dream. Her vision was blurry, and she could hear voices reverberating through distant speakers. Her mouth felt as if it was packed with cotton.

"Pack?" she whispered. She thought she remembered falling into a river, clambering to the shore, and clawing her way through the brush. Had that been a dream or was she dreaming now? "Is anybody there?" She was so weak and her throat was so dry that she could barely push the words between her dry, saliva-crusted lips.

"I think she's awake," someone said. Lindsey wasn't sure if she had really heard the words or if it was part of a dream. "Can you hear me?"

Lindsey nodded. She tried to sit up.

"Don't try to get up too quickly. Give yourself time to wake up."

She could see a woman in scrubs standing beside her bed. A hospital?

"I'm thirsty."

"I'm going to raise your bed, and we'll get you some water. Do you understand?"

"Yes."

An electric motor whined, and the bed moved beneath Lindsey's shoulders. A moment later the nurse held out a glass and put a straw to Lindsey's lips. She sucked down a swallow of water. It was cold. She nearly choked on it. She cleared her throat.

"Where am I?"

"You're at the Alethea Falls Medical Center. This is the emergency room."

"How did I get here?"

"You stumbled into the road off Highway 35. Someone spotted you."

She gasped and started to sit up.

"You have to call the police," she said. "There's a man and a little girl chained up in a garage. I don't know what he'll do to them."

"Slow down," the nurse said. She placed her hands on Lindsey's shoulders and tried to push her back down to the mattress. Lindsey fought against her.

"My boyfriend took me to a house," she said. "I thought he had rented it, but he wasn't supposed to be there. The owner came back, and they got into a fight. The house is at the end of a long road. The bridge is washed out, but there must be another way in." She tried to organize the jumble of facts. "The owner is from Portland. My boyfriend's name is Jason Packard. My name is Lindsey Amanda Holland, and I think I'm going insane." She fell back to the mattress as tears filled her eyes. "I can't think. What did he do to me?"

"There were some powerful drugs in your system when you came in," the nurse said, "but you're going to be okay."

"I need to talk to the police," Lindsey said.

"I'll call them." The nurse started to leave.

"Thank you. Can you call my friends and tell them where I am?"

"I'd be glad to." She picked up a clipboard.

"Their names are Neal and Jolene Allen. I can't remember their number." She put her hands to her head. "I can't remember anything."

"Just give me names and a location," she said. "We'll find them."

Lindsey gave her the information, and the nurse excused herself. Lindsey looked down at her hospital gown and realized uneasily that someone had undressed her and bathed her while she was unconscious. It was a common practice with hospital patients, but after what had happened to her, it disturbed her more than it would have under other circumstances.

A moment later, a policeman came into the room. He was a short, muscular man with a shaved head and a cool, matter-of-fact manner. He started asking Lindsey questions. She was so groggy she could barely remember the answers. She drifted off to sleep during the interview. When she woke up, the man was gone.

***

A knock sounded at the door.

"Come in," Lindsey managed to say. The door creaked open.

"Lindsey." It was Jolene. Neal was behind her. Lindsey smiled when she saw them, but tears filled her eyes.

"Oh, honey," Jolene said. "I'm so sorry. Are you all right?"

Lindsey pulled them both to her. They released her a moment later.

"He didn't hurt me," Lindsey finally said. "He could have, but he didn't."

"The police found the house," Neal told her. "Your description led them right to it."

"The people in the garage…?"

"They're fine," he said. "Just a little shaken up."

"What about Pack?"

"He wasn't there. They've got a BOLO out on him. He's going to have to rent a car or steal one. It's just a matter of time."

"He mentioned somebody," Lindsey said. "A girl."

"Chloe Davis?"

"Yes. That was it. Do you have any idea who she is?"

"She was somebody he worked with one summer in Maryland."

"I think he might have killed her."

"She's a missing persons case," Neal said. "Pack was a suspect."

"He said she was crazy, that she would have ruined his life, and he said he didn't mean for it to happen. He didn't say what happened."

"Her death might have been an accident," Jolene said.

"Or maybe he lost his temper," Neal said.

"He said Shadow knew about it, and he thought the rest of us must know, too."

"Shadow knew the name," Neal said. "Don't ask me how."

"There are dark forces everywhere," Jolene said. "They're just as real as anything else we see. That's not something we like to think about."

"A world just as real," Neal intoned, "but not as brightly lit. A dark side."

Jolene looked at him.

"*Tales from the Dark Side*. Remember? Back in the eighties. Never mind."

Lindsey gazed out the window into a cool Washington morning. The grounds of the hospital were covered with Douglas firs. Across the street was a quaint mountain town with a spectacular backdrop of mountains towering on the horizon. A heavy layer of dew clothed the grass with its chilly wonder. The dark side, with its murders and demonic forces, seemed thankfully distant.

"It's pretty here."

"That's why you need to move up here," Neal said. "Pack's not holding you back anymore."

"Neal!"

Neal was right. It was all over. The wedding, the nice house in the town where they had grown up, the children.... It was over. All of her memories of Pack seemed like lies now, and Lindsey felt poised over a chasm of depression, a dark abyss that threatened to swallow her life. Tears came to her eyes. She brushed them away.

"Oh, honey." Jolene squeezed her hand.

"I've got to call my parents."

"I talked to them earlier," Neal said. "They know you're okay. They'll be glad to hear from you, though."

"I don't really want to talk to them," Lindsey said. "They'll ask for all the details, and I don't want to talk about it. Pack's parents have been their best friends since we were children. I don't want to tell them what happened."

"They already know," Neal said.

"Does Todd know?"

"He's been helping me look for you," Neal said. "I finally sent him home."

"I want to talk to my dad," Lindsey said, "not my mom."

"Why, Lindsey?" It was Jolene who had asked the question.

"Because she's not going to believe any of this. She's so crazy about Pack that I think she'd marry him herself if anything ever happened to Dad. She'll look for some way to defend Pack and make it my fault."

"Surely not."

"You don't know my mom. She'll say I put the wedding off for so long that Pack just got so frustrated he couldn't help himself. That's exactly what she'll say."

"I talked to her," Neal said. "Trust me, she's not going to say that."

***

It was about an hour before Lindsey worked up the nerve to call home. Neal and Jolene went out for lunch and let her make the call in private. Neal knocked on the door when they got back.

"Come in."

"How did it go?" Neal asked.

Lindsey's expression turned thoughtful. She seemed calmer now. She'd had a chance to release her emotions and deal with them, and she was starting to feel like herself again.

"I guess I didn't really know my mom as well as I thought," she said. "Mom cried and said it was all her fault for pushing Pack on me the way she had. And she asked me to forgive her. I wouldn't have believed it."

"A mother's love," Jolene said. "Sometimes parents aren't as hardcore as their children think they are."

"The doctor's releasing you to our care," Neal said. "Are you ready to get out of here?"

***

"Are you sure you feel like being here?" Jolene asked as she loaded Kona blend coffee into the coffee maker. There were no customers in the Dawn Treader Cafe at the moment.

"I'm fine," Lindsey said as she wiped down the countertop. "He didn't hurt me."

"Maybe not physically, but if you think you can just go back to your life like nothing...."

"Jolene!" Lindsey was surprised at the anger in her own voice. She stopped and composed herself. She held up her hand. "I'm sorry. I'm not fine. I'm not even close to being fine."

"Lindsey."

"I need to be here."

"I can handle it."

"I don't mean for you. I need to be here for me. I'd rather be here than anywhere else right now. I'd rather be here than just sitting at home thinking about how stupid I was to trust him."

"Nobody's saying that."

"I think I can function well enough to do my job here."

"I'm not worried about that," Jolene said. "I just thought you might need to at least take a day to rest up. You just got out of the hospital."

"If I rest today, I won't sleep tonight, and I really want to sleep tonight."

"I understand."

The bell rang as the door opened. Lindsey and Jolene looked up as Todd walked in.

"Hi, Todd."

"Hi, Lindsey. How are you?"

She put down the rag, brushed back her hair, and sighed.

"I...uh...guess that's what everybody's been asking you, huh?"

"Ever since I showed up at the hospital."

"I'm sorry I didn't make it to see you there," he said. "I'd already missed so much work while we were looking for you...."

"It's okay. I understand."

"You look great."

"Thanks."

"I'm glad to see you. Come here."

She stiffened as he hugged her but then surrendered to the embrace. When he finally released her, she sank into a chair. He sat across from her.

"Have the police found Pack yet?"

"Not so far. He hasn't used his phone or credit card."

"Have you thought about what you're going to do? Are you going back to Texas?"

"I don't know. My parents want me to come home, but I'd rather stay here and finish out the summer. That's what I told Neal I would do."

"After what's happened, I'm sure he would understand if you wanted to go back home," Jolene said from behind the counter.

"I know," Lindsey said, "but I don't want to go back. I don't know if I can face the memories. Not yet. It's funny. As relieved as I am not to be marrying Pack, I still feel such a sense of loss. We'd already booked the church. I'd bought my wedding gown. There was something comforting about knowing what my future would be. Now it's all gone."

"I understand."

"How's your project going?" she asked, changing the subject.

"Fine," he said. "I've mostly been filming reenactments. I've got an interview scheduled Friday with a guy at Mount Rainier, if you'd like to come along."

"I think I'd like that."

"What's this guy's story?"

"UFO abductee. At least, he claims to be."

"Sounds interesting."

"Great. You're my best assistant."

"I think you're forgetting about the séance. I can't believe I just fainted like that. I've never done that before."

"That was a strange night," Todd said. "There's something in those videos I've got to show you. I'm not sure how you'll take it."

"I'm almost afraid to ask."

"We'll talk about it later. It's nothing you should worry about. Just strange and interesting."

"Now you've got me curious."

He squeezed her hand as he rose to his feet.

"I'd probably better go," he said. "I'm on break from work, and they're expecting me back, but I had to try to see you."

"Thanks for coming by."

"I'll see you around."

The bell rang as he exited the shop.

"He's a good man," Jolene said.

"Everybody keeps telling me that."

"You don't agree?"

"I didn't say that."

The bell rang again as the mail carrier walked in with a package.

***

The rest of the day passed mostly without incident. Shadow dropped in because, according to her, she just happened to be passing by.

"It's cool that you're back okay," she told Lindsey.

Space came by and stood at the window for a while. Lindsey raised her hand to him, and he actually waved back. He had never done that before.

Neal came in around four o'clock.

"Where have you been all day?" Jolene asked.

"Hospital visits."

"All day?"

"One of the members did take me to lunch at the country club."

"You poor thing. I'm sure the food was terrible."

"I've got to spend time with my parishioners. What kind of pastor would I be if I didn't?"

"Hmmph."

"How's my Texan?" he asked, turning to Lindsey.

Lindsey was making a sandwich for a guest. "I'm okay."

"Are you ready to go home yet?"

"I guess."

"Have you talked to Mrs. Cutler yet?"

"I tried to call her," Lindsey said. "Cornelia says she's been sleeping all day."

"Worrying about you must have exhausted her," Neal said. "Todd and I went by there last night. She said she was going to stay up all night and pray for you."

"Don't make me cry," Lindsey said.

"I do have that effect on girls," Neal joked.

"Hmmph," Jolene said.

Chapter 23: A Night on the Town

"Where are you going, dear?" Mrs. Cutler stood at the door of the sunroom looking concerned. It had only been a week since Lindsey's, abduction, and her friends were still worried about her. Pack had failed to turn up, but Lindsey had convinced herself that he was somewhere far away. He had probably gone back to Texas to nurse his wounds.

"Out to the dock." Lindsey answered. She was standing in the hall with her sketchpad.

"Don't wander too far from the house."

"I'll be right out back," she said. "You can watch me from the sunroom."

"Do be careful."

"I will. Don't worry."

"Those stairs are steep."

"I know. I'll be careful."

Lindsey stepped out onto the lawn behind the house. The grass and plants were all perfectly manicured. She looked warily at he gazebo as she passed it, still disturbed by the memory of the bearded stranger who had stared at her when she was sunbathing. She didn't know if he had been offended by her swimwear or her presence. She clung to the handrail as she descended the steep set of stairs that led down the side of the hill to the dock below.

As Lindsey sat alone on the rough dock, a sketchbook across her knees, she felt every bit as timeless as the world around her. The beauty around her filled her spirit with life and light. Her problems with Pack seemed far away now, and she believed, for the first time in quite a while, that everything was going to be all right. The world seemed perfect, if only for a season. Waves crashed into the rocky shore as the sun's crimson disk burned its way through the clouds heaped along the horizon. The abandoned lighthouse, now an inky shadow, lay across a thousand feet of sun-dappled waves. The memory of her nightmares crept across her perfect calm with feet of ice. What was it about the beautiful old structure that stirred such dark visions?

A chilly evening breeze rumpled Lindsey's hair and whistled around the collar of her coat. She sat and sketched for hours with no sense of the passage of time. She did not realize the lateness of the hour until she realized she was having to strain to see her sketchpad. It was getting too dark to see, and she had not thought to bring along a flashlight.

The nightmares and the apparent spectral encounters that had plagued Lindsey during her first weeks in Oregon had not returned. Her abduction by Pack should have given her nightmares but, strangely, it seemed to have exorcized them. She was starting to wonder if they had been a subconscious manifestation of the misgivings she'd had about her upcoming wedding. Now that the wedding was off and Pack was, for all practical purposes, out of her life, the apparitions had accomplished their purpose and haunted her no more. That, at least, was what she told herself as she prepared to walk back to the house through the thickening shadows. As Lindsey packed away her sketchpad, she thought about the bearded, seaweed-tangled shape she had seen in her room that night and wondered if he might be waiting for her in the shadows of the gazebo.

"Well, good evening," someone said.

Lindsey whirled around. Caitlyn was standing on the dock.

"Caitlyn! You nearly gave me a heart attack."

"I'm sorry," Caitlyn said. "After what you've just been through. I didn't mean to sneak up on you."

"It's okay," Lindsey said. "I'm glad to see you. I've been wanting to see you since I got back, but you haven't been here."

"I know," she said. "The clinic has been working me overtime." She looked around. "Isn't it a beautiful evening? We should take a drive."

"Sure," Lindsey said. "That sounds great."

"Would you mind driving?" she asked.

Lindsey was taken aback by the request. She paused, then said, "Okay."

"The car keys are in the basket beside the front door," Caitlyn said.

They climbed the stairs together, then walked around the house and onto the front porch. Lindsey unlocked the front door and stepped inside. She found the keys easily enough.

"Let me tell them where I'm going."

"Okay."

Lindsey walked back to the sunroom and found Mrs. Cutler's chair empty. Not wanting to worry her host, Lindsey left a note on the kitchen table. Caitlyn was still waiting on the porch when Lindsey returned. The two of them walked around to the garage. Mrs. Cutler's Crown Victoria was waiting there. Lindsey wondered why they weren't taking Caitlyn's car. Then it occurred to her that Caitlyn might not have her own car, and since Mrs. Cutler hardly ever went anywhere, it only made sense for someone else to use it. She knew it was not good for a car to sit in the garage for months at a time.

Lindsey climbed into the car. It had a musty smell as if it had been closed up for a long time. Caitlyn climbed in beside her.

"It's musty in here," Lindsey said.

"Oh," Caitlyn said. "You're right. We'll have to buy some air freshener in town."

Lindsey turned the key. After some whining and protesting, the old car finally roared to life. It sounded like a grumpy old troll roused from a deep sleep. Lindsey backed out of the garage and, after fumbling around the dash for a moment, found the knob that turned on the headlights. As she rolled down the driveway, she saw Cornelia peering down at her from an upstairs window.

"Where do you want to go?" Lindsey asked.

"Downtown," Caitlyn said. "Beyond that, I don't really care. Where do you like to go when you're with your friends?"

"I mostly work at Cannon Beach," Lindsey said. "Todd and I spent an evening walking around Seaside once. That was fun."

"That's a nice area," Caitlyn said. "Let's go."

Lindsey navigated the steep roads and curving trails that led down the mountain to the main road. The forest, with its Douglas firs and ferns, was beautiful and a bit forbidding as the shadows of night began to fall. She kept thinking of the people she and Todd had interviewed and spectral visitors she had encountered—or imagined she'd encountered—and was glad to have Caitlyn there with her.

Lindsey found the main highway. The two girls rode in silence as they made their way to town.

"We must both be really tired," Lindsey said. "Have you ever known either of us to be at a loss for words?"

"No," Caitlyn said. She smiled sleepily.

They hardly encountered another car for several minutes. An eerie stillness seemed to hold the evening in its grip. It seemed, for a moment, as though there was not another living soul on the entire planet. Lindsey felt a sense of relief when they finally reached Seaside. As they rode past T-shirt shops, coffeehouses, and cozy, locally owned bookshops, Lindsey felt the strange hollowness subside. Men and women populated the shops, walked the sidewalks, and rode past in cars. Women in exercise clothes swung their arms rapidly as they power-walked along the sidewalks. Some of them held dogs on leashes.

Lindsey noticed the bars on the face of her cell phone and knew that she had service once again. She thought about calling Todd, Neal, and Jolene. Maybe she would call them later.

"Why don't we walk along the beach?" Lindsey suggested. "I'll pull in at the park."

"That would be lovely," Caitlyn said.

Lindsey parked the car, and the girls got out. There was a long, wooden pier leading out into the ocean. Sailboats were tied to the slips there.

"Good evening, ladies," a man's voice said. "Fancy meetin' you here." Lindsey looked up and saw a scarecrow figure standing against the darkening sky. He raised a cigarette to his wrinkled lips and took a deep drag.

"Space?" Lindsey said. She had not seen Space for several days and had wondered about him from time to time.

The vagrant nodded.

"How are you?" she asked.

"Cosmic," Space said. "In touch with the universe. Turned on to God."

"That's great," Lindsey said with forced brightness. She wondered, inwardly, if Space had really undergone any kind of religious epiphany. It seemed more likely that his pronouncements were the result of fried synapses in his brain or psychedelic drugs in his system.

"Space," Lindsey said, "this is Caitlyn."

"I'm very glad to meet you, Caitlyn," Space said. "Any friend of Leslie's is a friend of mine. If you ever need anything, just come down here and ask for Space. Everybody knows who I am."

Lindsey smiled when he called her by the wrong name.

"That's very generous of you, Mr. Space," Caitlyn said.

"Just Space, my dear." Space blew a smoke ring. "Just plain Space." He ambled away toward the end of the pier.

"Who is that?" Caitlyn whispered.

"He calls himself Space," Lindsey said. "I don't know his real name. He's always coming into the coffee shop asking Neal for money."

"He seems friendly."

"That's what's weird. That's the most I've ever heard him say. He usually just looks at me. Maybe he's getting better."

"You have to hope for that, don't you?" Caitlyn said. "When you work with people like him, you have to hope it does some good sometimes."

"I guess you see all kinds down at the hospital," Lindsey said.

"Oh, yes," Caitlyn said. "Yes, indeed."

"Which hospital do you work for?" Lindsey asked.

"Richards Clinic," Caitlyn said.

Lindsey saw Space standing at the end of the pier with his arms spread against the sky. She had intended to walk to the end herself, but she didn't really want to share the pier with Space while he was communing with the cosmos.

"Do you want to get some coffee?" Lindsey asked. "A latte or something?"

"Lovely," Caitlyn said.

They turned back toward town and walked to a well-lit shop near the beach. The walls were painted bright yellow and decorated with surfing memorabilia. A young man with a guitar sat on a stool in the front of the room and strummed. Lindsey and Caitlyn seated themselves. A short time later, a young woman with a menu approached the table.

"What can I get for you?" she asked.

"A caramel latte," Lindsey said.

"Will that be all?" the girl asked.

"What do you want, Caitlyn?" Lindsey asked.

"Nothing right now," Caitlyn said.

"Are you sure?"

"Yes. I'm fine, thank you."

"A caramel latte," Lindsey told the server. "Thank you."

The girl was looking at her strangely. Lindsey wondered if she had offended her without meaning to.

"Is everything all right?" she asked.

"Oh, yeah," the girl said. "Sure. Fine. I'll get your latte."

The girl turned around to leave.

"What was that about?" Lindsey said.

Caitlyn shrugged.

Lindsey finished her latte and dropped a few coins into the performer's tip jar before she and Caitlyn left.

"What do you want to do now?" Lindsey asked.

"Whatever you want." Caitlyn smiled.

"I really want to go home and go to bed," Lindsey admitted. "This was fun, though. I'm glad we got to spend some time together."

"I am, too."

They walked back to the car. Lindsey strapped in and started the engine.

"Don't forget to buckle up," she told Caitlyn.

"Oh, yes," Caitlyn said. She pulled the seatbelt around her body and fastened it. "I almost forgot."

They pulled out of the parking lot. In no great hurry to return to the mansion, Lindsey meandered through town. Seaside, with its hotels, shops, and tourists, was a cheerful place. It seemed a sharp contrast to the cold, austere beauty of the Cutler house. Lindsey realized she was a little bit reluctant to leave the lights of town for the dark highway beyond. Finally, after taking as many side streets as she could, she pulled out onto the highway and watched in her rearview mirror as the town was swallowed by darkness.

Lindsey and Caitlyn rode for a while without talking. Finally, Lindsey looked over and saw her friend slumped down in the seat.

"Are you all right?"

"I'm fine. To be honest, I'm positively exhausted."

"We should have stayed at the mansion," Lindsey said.

"Nonsense," Caitlyn said. "This evening was the most fun I've had in a while. I'm glad we went. Very glad we went." Her last words were little more than a whisper. Caitlyn sounded as though she was on the verge of falling asleep.

The wail of a police siren sliced through Lindsey like a bolt of electricity. She shot straight up in her seat. The shoulder harness forced her back down. She looked into the rearview mirror and saw a flashing blue light. Then she looked down at the speedometer. She had only been driving sixty miles per hour. The speed limit, she was sure, was sixty-five. What was going on here?

"What is it?" Caitlyn asked. "What's happening?"

"I'm not sure," Lindsey said.

Lindsey pulled over onto the shoulder of the road. The car pulled in behind her. Her mind clicked through a list of possibilities. Maybe Mrs. Cutler had let her inspection sticker expire. Maybe one of the taillights was out. Lindsey saw the car door open. A woman in a sheriff's deputy's uniform climbed out and strode toward her. Lindsey rolled down the window.

"May I see your driver's license?" the deputy asked as she scanned the interior of the car with a flashlight.

Lindsey fumbled through her purse. Her hands were shaking. Finally, she found the license and passed it to the woman.

"Wait here," she said.

"Yes, ma'am."

Lindsey waited. The woman returned a moment later.

"Step out of the vehicle, please," she said.

"Is everything all right?" Lindsey asked.

"Step out of the vehicle," the woman said again.

Lindsey pushed the door open and stepped out.

"Come with me, please."

"What's happening?" she asked. "What's going on?"

"Come back to the car."

Lindsey followed the officer back to the patrol car.

"Are you all right, Miss Holland?"

"I'm fine. What's going on?"

"You were recently abducted. Apparently, the people you were staying with thought something might have happened to you."

"No," Lindsey said. "It's a misunderstanding. I left them a note. They must not have seen it. I was taking a drive with Mrs. Cutler's niece."

"Are you saying there's someone else in the car with you?"

"Yes!"

"Where is she now?"

"She's in the car." What was wrong with this woman?

"Show me."

They walked back around to the car. Lindsey looked through the driver's side window. *The passenger seat was empty.*

"Caitlyn," she said. "Caitlyn!"

She pulled the door open and looked inside.

Chapter 24: The Lady Vanishes

A screaming guitar solo cut the darkness. Nimble fingers tortured writhing staircases of sound from strings of steel. Neal fumbled blindly around the nightstand as brilliantly executed arpeggios drilled through his skull. He could feel Jolene stirring on the mattress beside him. If he didn't find that cell phone in another two seconds, his sweet-natured wife was going to claw through everything in her path and silence his heavy metal ringtone herself.

His hand closed around the phone. He pulled it over into the bed, dropped it, picked it up, and punched the button on the screen.

"New Hope Fellowsh—Hello."

"Neal Allen, please."

It was a crisp, no-nonsense voice that he didn't recognize.

"This is he." What time is it, anyway?

"This is Detective Montoya from the sheriff's department."

"Yeah, listen. Thanks again for all the work you did to find Lindsey. What can I do for you?"

"I've got Lindsey here at the station."

"What's going on? Is she all right?"

"She's okay," he said. "But there's something strange going on. Can you come down here?"

"Yeah, sure. Be right there."

"Where are you going?" Jolene asked from the bedroom.

"The sheriff's station. Lindsey's down there for some reason."

***

It was after midnight when Neal and Jolene finally arrived at the sheriff's station. The deputy on duty called Montoya to the front desk.

"Come on back," he said.

"What's going on here?"

"She went for a ride in Mrs. Cutler's car. She didn't tell anyone she was leaving, and they thought Packard might have abducted her again. Naturally, they called us."

"Then why's she still here?"

"Well," Montoya said, "there's something strange going on, and I thought you should know about it."

"What is it?"

"She says she went out for a ride with Mrs. Cutler's niece, a girl named Caitlyn."

"She's talked about Caitlyn before," Jolene said. "They're friends."

"Not according to Mrs. Cutler's housekeeper. There's nobody named Caitlyn living there. She's never heard of a Caitlyn."

"What?" Neal rubbed his eyes. He was still half-asleep. "You've got to be kidding. Are you saying Lindsey imagined her?"

"I don't know," Montoya said. "But before I released her into your care, I thought you should know."

"Thank you," Jolene said. "We'll look into it. Where is she?"

Montoya led them down the hall to a meeting room. Lindsey was sitting by herself at the end of a long table. She stood as they entered. Neal and Jolene went to her.

"What's going on here, Lindsey?" Neal asked.

"It's like I told them," Lindsey said. "It was all a misunderstanding. I went for a ride with Mrs. Cutler's niece. I couldn't find Mrs. Cutler or Cornelia, so I left a note. They must not have seen it."

"She says the niece was in the car with her when our deputy pulled her over."

"She was right there," Lindsey said. "I walked back to the car with the deputy. She must have wanted to make sure Pack wasn't hiding in car somewhere. When I got back to the car, Caitlyn was gone."

"And the deputy didn't see anybody else in the car?"

"No," Montoya said. "She shined her light around and didn't see anybody."

"And I guess you called Mrs. Cutler?" Neal asked.

"I called her house," Lindsey explained, "and Cornelia answered the phone. When I tried to tell her what happened, she said she'd never heard of Caitlyn, that Mrs. Cutler doesn't have a niece named Caitlyn. That's crazy! She was right there in the kitchen when I met Caitlyn."

"That *is* weird," Neal said, "but it shouldn't be too hard to clear up. I'll just drive you back out here." He turned to Montoya. "Is it okay if we return the car?"

"Yes," he said. "But, if you don't mind, I'd like to follow you out there. There are a few questions I'd like to ask. I'll have someone call Mrs. Cutler and let her know we're coming."

Lindsey followed Jolene out to the minivan. Neal stood and waited while one of the policemen brought Mrs. Cutler's Crown Victoria around. Montoya followed in a squad car.

"I'll see you out there," Neal said. He kissed Jolene and climbed into the driver's seat of Mrs. Cutler's car.

Jolene and Lindsey climbed into the mission association's minivan and Jolene started the engine.

"I'm so glad you're okay," Jolene said. "We were worried sick."

"This whole thing is crazy," Lindsey said. "It doesn't make any sense. You've never met Caitlyn? Neither of you."

"No."

"She's a nurse," Lindsey said. "She works at the Richards Clinic."

"The *Richards* Clinic?"

"That's what she said."

"The Richards Clinic shut down twenty years ago."

"I'm sure that's what she said."

They followed Neal as he pulled off the highway. Montoya followed.

"You said this woman was Mrs. Cutler's niece?" Jolene said.

"Great-niece," Lindsey said. "She'd have to be. Mrs. Cutler is in her eighties, and Caitlyn is only twenty-four."

"I'm trying to figure out how they could be related. Didn't you say Mrs. Cutler only had one sister and that she had died in Japan?"

"Yes, but she could be related on Mr. Cutler's side of the family."

"Sure. That's got to be it."

The ride uphill and through the forest seemed even stranger than usual. Fog clung to the ground like a gray blanket. Jolene followed Neal across the spit of land that linked Mrs. Cutler's secluded hill to the rest of the world. The mansion's lights were on when they arrived. They threaded their way among the trees and pulled into the courtyard.

Detective Montoya followed as Neal and Jolene walked with Lindsey to the door. Lindsey felt her stomach tighten. Neal knocked. After a moment, the door opened. Cornelia stood in the doorway.

"Good evening, Cornelia," Neal said. "I just picked Lindsey up at the sheriff's station. We brought Mrs. Cutler's car back. Lindsey said there was a misunderstanding."

"Yes."

"She says she was riding with Mrs. Cutler's niece," Detective Montoya said. "A twenty-four-year-old nurse."

"Mrs. Cutler doesn't have a niece. I told her that."

"Her name is Caitlyn," Lindsey said. "She lives in the attic room. You stood and watched us eat breakfast the morning after I got here."

Cornelia stared at her for a moment, her expression unreadable. Then she looked back at Neal. "Mrs. Cutler does not have a niece. There is no one else living here."

"Why are you saying that?" Lindsey gasped. "She lives upstairs."

"Can anyone else confirm this?" Montoya asked.

"Ask Mrs. Cutler," Lindsey said. "She'll tell you the truth."

"She talks to herself," Cornelia said.

"Excuse me?"

"The morning after Miss Holland came here, I heard her talking to someone in the dining room. I thought she might be talking to someone with her telephone, but cellular telephones do not work here. She was doing the same thing earlier tonight. I saw her driving the car, and she was talking to someone, but the passenger seat was empty."

"I don't believe this!" Lindsey exclaimed. "Why are you doing this?"

"Just a minute...." Neal began.

"Caitlyn is as real as any of us," Lindsey said. "I'll take you to her room. I will show you where she stays."

"If you don't mind," Officer Montoya said, "I'd like to see that room myself."

Cornelia sighed and nodded.

"All right, Miss Holland," Montoya said. "Show us."

Lindsey led them up two flights of stairs to the attic room where she and Caitlyn had sat on the floor and put the jigsaw puzzle together. She twisted the knob and pushed the door open. The door creaked on its hinges.

An assembled jigsaw puzzle of a castle sat in the middle of the floor, just as Lindsey had remembered, but everything else had changed. The bed was gone, and the room filled with boxes. Sheets covered the furniture. There was a layer of dust on the floor and several sets of footprints making circles around the room. They had all been made by the same pair of shoes.

"Miss Holland," Montoya said, "could we see the tread on the bottom of your shoes?"

Needles of ice prickled Lindsey's skin. She raised one foot. Light fell on the treads. They were the same pattern.

"No," Lindsey said. "No. That's impossible." She wheeled around and pointed at Cornelia. "You! What have you done with her?"

The housekeeper stared at her without speaking.

"They've done something with her," Lindsey insisted. "She's real, I tell you. She's as real as any of us. This can't be happening."

Montoya frowned.

"I want to talk to Mrs. Cutler," Neal said.

"So do I," Montoya said.

"Mrs. Cutler wasn't feeling well this evening. She's sleeping."

"I'll talk to her later then," Montoya said. "The car's been returned, and the young lady is safe. Anything else can wait until tomorrow. Thank you."

"Neal," Lindsey said. "You believe me, don't you? About Caitlyn?"

"To tell the truth," Neal said, "it doesn't look good."

"But, I saw her," Lindsey said. "She's as real as any of us."

"I think we'd better take this slowly," Jolene said. "You've been through a lot these past few weeks."

"You think I'm crazy?"

"You were abducted," Jolene said, "and drugged. There may be some lingering effects."

"But, I saw Caitlyn *before* I was abducted."

"So, what do we do now?" Neal asked.

"You said she was a nurse?" Detective Montoya asked.

"She was a nursing student," Lindsey said, "but she was working at a hospital."

"An LPN studying to be an RN?"

"Maybe. That must have been it. I was sure she said she worked at the Richards Clinic, but Jolene tells me that the Richards Clinic closed down."

"I can call the local hospitals," Montoya said, "and the colleges. Do you have a last name for her?"

"No."

"Is it Caitlyn with a *C* or with a *K*?"

"I don't know."

"And no photographs?"

"No."

They left the room, returning to the spacious hallway. Cornelia closed the door behind them. Lindsey's mind was awhirl. The others were talking as they walked back downstairs, but their voices were just background noise to her.

What's happening to me? she kept wondering. It was as though she had stepped around the corner into some weird alternate universe where the people looked the same but reality was strangely twisted. Would she go home and find out she'd never had a younger brother or that her family's Boston Terrier had been replaced by a Rottweiler? They all walked outside and into the courtyard.

"Are you coming with us?"

"What?"

"Are you coming with us?" Neal asked again as they approached the minivan.

"What?"

"Do you want to stay with us tonight?" Jolene asked. "We can talk to Mrs. Cutler tomorrow."

"Yes," Lindsey said. She looked back at the mansion. "I think that would be best." She tried to sound more confident than she felt. At that moment, she had no idea what was best for anyone. "I need to pack some things."

"Do you need me to help you?" Jolene asked.

"Yes," she said. "I don't want to be alone."

Chapter 25: Threads

Lindsey lay awake for hours wondering what was happening. Even Neal and Jolene were looking at her strangely now. They wanted to believe her, but the sight of the empty room had stunned them. Who could blame them? Lindsey was still reeling from the experience herself. She thought about the experiences of the past few weeks, of the invisible figure that sat on her bed, and of the angry, bearded giant who had appeared in her room that night. She wanted to blame all of it on the trauma of being abducted by Pack, but most of the experiences had happened before the abduction. She had met Caitlyn before the abduction.

Joey Samson, one of her high-school friends, had been diagnosed with schizophrenia his freshman year of college. It had ruined his life. She had watched him change from a happy-go-lucky teenager to a sullen zombie who wandered the streets in dirty clothes and talked to himself in disjointed phrases that made no sense. His parents had spent thousands of dollars taking him to specialists, but nothing had worked for him. Medications that allowed most patients to live normal lives did nothing to relieve his symptoms. Poor Joey Samson. His mind was his prison, and only death would free him.

Lindsey thought of Space and wondered what he had been like before he had destroyed his mind. She wondered what the future held for her, if the nightmares she had encountered at the Cutler mansion would one day become her constant companions. She had heard rumors of patients whose hallucinations were so terrifying that their hands had to be restrained to keep them from clawing out their own eyes.

She didn't fall asleep until nearly four o'clock in the morning. In a disjointed dream, she saw herself pounding on the locked door of her room at the Cutler mansion until the bones in her hands broke into splinters and started slicing through the skin on her knuckles. With twisted, crippled hands, she pounded and scratched on the door for hours, but no one came.

Neal and Jolene got up at around seven o'clock to go to church.

"Do you feel like coming with us?" Jolene asked.

"Not really," Lindsey admitted, "but I don't want to be alone."

***

"I don't think my sermon had its usual energy," Neal said as they were leaving the retirement village.

"It was fine," Jolene said. "It's okay to slow down sometimes. How do you feel, Lindsey?"

"Better. Life almost seems normal again."

They rode to Astoria in near-silence. People were already crowding the theater's entrance by the time they arrived. Lindsey made her way through the lobby and spoke to everyone who spoke to her, but she didn't stand around and talk the way she might have on another day. She just walked into the auditorium, found an empty row, and sat down. Todd was practicing with the group onstage. He waved to her when he saw her. She forced a thin smile and lifted her hand.

The twenty minutes Lindsey waited for the service to start ground by at a torturously slow pace. Todd came by for a moment before the service started.

"I need to talk to you," he said as he hugged her. "I'll see you after church."

"Okay."

Neal took the stage, made the opening remarks, and led the group in prayer. The praise band played a few opening songs before Neal returned to the stage and called some of the college students up to talk about a mission trip from which they had just returned. Lindsey tried hard to pay attention, but her mind kept wandering. When the students had finished with their testimonies, the praise band returned. The more Lindsey tried to forget her problems and focus on God, the more impossible it became. Her eyes filled with tears. Lindsey got up, ran down the aisle, and shoved her way through the swinging doors in the back.

Starting to sob, Lindsey ran across the lobby to a carpeted stairway that led to the second-floor offices. She sank down on the first step, buried her face in her hands, and fought for control.

***

"I saw you leave," Todd told Lindsey as they sat on the stage after the service. "I was about to leave the stage and go after you when you came back. Jolene told me what happened last night. Are you all right?"

"I think I'm going insane, Todd."

"I doubt that," Todd reassured her. "There's definitely something weird going on, but I don't think it's just you."

"Then what do you think it is?"

"I don't know, but I don't think we need to jump to any conclusions yet."

"Maybe my parents are right. After all that's happened, maybe I should just go home."

"Yeah, but...."

"But what?"

"Aren't you the least bit curious? Don't you want to know what's really going on here?"

Lindsey paused, considering it.

"Jolene and I are about to leave," Neal said as he walked up to them. "Lindsey, do you want to ride with us or catch a ride with Todd?"

"Where are you going?" Todd asked.

"Back to the apartment," Jolene said. "Somebody else is covering the café, so we've got the afternoon off."

"So you can baby-sit your crazy friend?" Lindsey said wryly.

"We were actually going to run some errands," Jolene said. "But, if you need someone to stay with you...."

"I'll be okay."

***

Lindsey, Todd, Neal, and Jolene sat around a small kitchen table. The cream cheese and pesto pizza Jolene had prepared was based, she explained, on something she and Neal had eaten in a little pizzeria in Kohala, Hawaii. After a few minutes' small talk, Neal finally broached the subject that was on all of their minds.

"When did you first see Caitlyn?"

The room grew quiet.

"The first morning I was here," Lindsey said. "She walked into the dining room during breakfast and started talking."

"And there was nothing strange about any of it?"

"No," Lindsey said. "Not really."

"But...?"

"She spoke to Cornelia, but Cornelia just ignored her. I thought it was rude, but Caitlyn didn't seem offended by it. She just said Cornelia was...*taciturn*. I believe that's the word she used."

"And that's not a word you ordinarily use?"

"No."

"Okay. What else?"

Lindsey told about the Saturday she had spent at the mansion, about the afternoon she and Caitlyn had spent walking around the grounds together. Then she talked about seeing her on the night of the lock-in and how she had helped Lindsey find Shadow in the basement.

"And then there was last night," Lindsey said. "She wanted to go for a ride so we could talk and just see the town together."

"And those are the only times you've seen her?"

"There was one other time," Lindsey said, "but I wouldn't really count it. The night I escaped from Pack, I dreamed Caitlyn was there helping me, but my mind was so clouded by the drugs he'd used on me that I wasn't even sure where I was, when I was, or even who I was. For all I knew, I could have been in another time."

"But Caitlyn was there, and she helped you escape."

"Yes. There was a chain padlocked around my ankle. In my dream, it was an iron band. She used key to unlock it…a skeleton key. I remember her saying that."

"Wow."

For a moment they sat quietly around the table. The only sounds were the bubbling of the aquarium and the sibilant *whish* of a passing car.

"All right," Todd said. "What are our possibilities?" He had flipped open his laptop and was taking notes. "Lindsey thought Caitlyn was a real person. Let's start with that. Why would a real person just vanish?"

"Maybe Caitlyn's involved in something, and she had to disappear," Neal speculated.

"What are you saying, Neal? That she's a secret agent?" Jolene was incredulous.

"Maybe. Or a witness to a crime."

"And what about Cornelia?" Lindsey asked.

"Either she's helping cover for Caitlyn, or somebody threatened her, and she had to go along with it."

"But, why would they have invited Lindsey into the house and let her see Caitlyn if she was trying to hide?" This question was from Todd.

"You're right. They wouldn't have—unless Lindsey is part of the plan."

"Or maybe she discovered Caitlyn accidentally," Todd suggested.

"Hold it," Jolene said. "I think you guys have watched too many spy movies. It doesn't hold together."

"That's just one possibility," Todd said. "There's also the psychological angle."

"That I'm losing my mind?" Lindsey said. "That's what you really think, isn't it?"

"No," Todd said. "Not exactly losing your mind. But, it could be some kind of stress reaction."

"What kind of stress reaction?"

"I think you knew Pack had a dark side," Todd said, "maybe a lot darker than you wanted to admit to yourself, but you were afraid to face it. Maybe all of that manifested itself as these things you were seeing."

"But, why did it start when I moved into Ms. Cutler's house? Why didn't it happen back in Texas?"

"The house was a trigger. It was big, old, and scary-looking. As long as you were home, you were surrounded by familiar things that gave you comfort. When you came out here, you lost your coping mechanisms."

"That makes sense. Caitlyn showed up when I really needed her."

"Right," Todd said. "She's like an alter ego that helps you find the courage to do things you need to do but don't have the confidence to do on your own."

"That's called an encourager," Jolene said.

"She *is* an encourager," Lindsey said. "But, I've got plenty of encouragers in my life. Why would my subconscious need to create another one?"

"Good question."

"And why am I still seeing her? Pack's out of my life now."

"You may not be engaged to him anymore, but you dated this guy for years. If you think you can get over the break-up, the abduction, and all of that in a little over a week, I'm afraid you're kidding yourself. You're still dealing with it, Lindsey. They'll catch him eventually, and there will be a trial. You'll have to face him there. Maybe you've shoved it all into your subconscious, but it's still there, and it will be there for a while."

"What do you want me to do?" Lindsey asked. "Would everybody feel better if I started crying and breaking things?"

"You need to talk to a counselor," Jolene said. "Neal and I have a friend in Astoria we've sent people to. You'd love her."

"Thanks," Lindsey said, "but I'm a little afraid to talk to a counselor. What if she decides I'm really crazy?"

"Things aren't like they used to be," Todd said. "A lot of mental conditions can be treated these days."

"They'll probably put me in a straitjacket and give me shock treatments."

"No, they won't," Neal said. "They'll just turn you loose on the street and let you go around talking to yourself."

"Like Space," Lindsey said. "Thanks. I feel better now."

"He could use somebody to hang out with."

"Neal," Jolene said.,"this is serious, honey. Lindsey's really worried."

"I know that," Neal said. "I wouldn't joke about it if I really thought it could happen. You know that. Right?"

"There's still another possibility," Todd said.

"What other possibility?"

"That this is some kind of paranormal event."

"A paranormal event?" Neal repeated. "Are you saying Lindsey saw a ghost?"

"Or an angel," Jolene said.

"A guardian angel?"

"She helped Lindsey escape and helped her find Shadow."

"But, why would a guardian angel want to put a puzzle together or go on a joyride?"

Todd swung his laptop around so the others could see the screen. It showed Lindsey holding a camera. Dark wood and mirrors surrounded her.

"Look at this," he said. "What do you see?"

"What is this?" Neal asked.

"It's a frame from a video clip I shot during a séance. Drew, the guy who shares my studio, found it when he loaded the video into the computer. Look behind Lindsey. What do you see?"

"It looks like somebody reflected in the mirror."

"But, you can see through her," Todd said. "And look at the hands on Lindsey's shoulders."

"Are you sure those are hands?" Neal squinted. "They do look like hands."

"Let me see," Lindsey said.

Todd rotated the laptop slightly to give Lindsey a better angle. She focused in on it, rocked back in her chair, and brushed back her hair.

"There was something about that room," she said. "The whole time we were there, I had the strangest feeling that somebody was watching me."

"Wait," Neal said. "Don't tell me you're buying this. Do you know how easy this would be to fake?"

"A still picture would be easy to fake," Todd said. "A moving picture isn't so easy."

"But, you could fake it. You know you could."

"Yeah," he said. "I could fake it. Separate Lindsey from the background with a garbage matte, drop a transparent layer of the ghost in behind her, drop a transparent layer with the hands on top of her."

"Exactly."

"I don't know. Drew sounded pretty freaked out when he called me."

"Of course he did. That's part of the gag."

"Were there any more pictures of the figure?" Lindsey asked.

"Not this clear," Todd admitted. "There were some bright spots and distortions in the image, but this frame is the clearest. My camera caught it right before you fainted."

"I still think your friend faked it," Neal said.

"My sketchbook," Lindsey said suddenly.

"What about it?"

"I drew Caitlyn's portrait. Do you think it would help to know what she looks like?"

"Maybe," Neal said. "Where is it?"

"In the van," Lindsey said. She and Jolene left the apartment and returned a moment later. Lindsey already had the spiral-bound tablet open to the smiling portrait of a young woman with curly blonde hair and freckles.

"You've captured a whole personality here," Jolene said. "You can see the joy of life in her eyes, but there's sadness, too. Something in her eyebrows and the corners of her mouth."

"Shadow says I made her look sad, too," Lindsey said. "Maybe everybody I draw looks sad."

"Shadow *is* sad," Neal said. "The Goth look may be for show, but the darkness isn't all a put-on."

"Could I have a copy of this?" Todd asked.

"Sure," Lindsey said.

"I want one, too," Neal said. "It could come in handy."

Jolene went to the corner of the living room to use the copier.

"Jolene and I are about to run some errands," Neal said as the copier hummed. "You're welcome to stay here."

"Will you stay with her?" Jolene asked Todd. "Ordinarily, I wouldn't leave a young man and woman alone together like this, but after what happened...."

"No problem," Todd said. "I think I can control myself for a few minutes, anyway. I do need to run to the studio for something, but Lindsey can come with me."

"That's okay," Lindsey said. "I didn't sleep much last night. I really was hoping I could take a nap."

"As long as you don't let anybody in," Jolene said. Lindsey locked and chained the door behind them when they left.

Chapter 26: The Portrait

"Did you notice Cornelia wasn't in church today?" Jolene asked. "She hasn't missed in months."

"She may be mad at us after last night," Neal said as he drove. "I hope we can get to the bottom of what's going on."

They reached the gate to the winding drive that led to Mrs. Cutler's mansion. Neal rolled down the window and punched the number into the keypad. The gate opened as it had done before, and Neal coaxed the minivan up the shady path.

"Do you think we'll learn anything new?" Jolene asked.

"I don't know," Neal said. "But I'm not giving up without talking to Mrs. Cutler."

They made the final curve, and the mansion appeared before them. A golden summer sun hung in a deep blue sky. As they rode along the bridge of land that connected the forest road to the hill on which the mansion sat, they could see the brilliant blues and greens of the ocean below. In the distance, they could see people walking along the beach. Sailboats glided across the waves. It was, for most people, a flawlessly beautiful day.

Neal and Jolene climbed out of the minivan and walked across the courtyard to Mrs. Cutler's porch. Neal rang the bell. For a moment, they didn't hear anything. Finally, a moment later, the door opened, and Cornelia appeared.

"Hi, Cornelia," Neal said. "We missed you in church today."

Cornelia didn't answer at first.

"You're here to see Mrs. Cutler?"

"Yeah," Neal said. "And you. How are you, Cornelia?"

"I'm fine. Thank you. Mrs. Cutler is in the sunroom. I'll take you to her."

"Okay."

They followed her down the hallway to the large room in the back of the house where they had met Mrs. Cutler on that first night. She was sitting in her fan-backed chair by the window, sipping tea.

"Oh," she said when she saw them. "Please, come in. Sit down, both of you."

Neal and Jolene sat down across from her.

"Cornelia," she said. "Bring them some tea, please."

"Yes, Mrs. Cutler."

When the German woman left, Mrs. Cutler focused her attention on Neal and Jolene.

"I suppose you're here about Lindsey," she said. "How is she?"

"Confused," Jolene added.

"Yes," Mrs. Cutler said. "Yes, I imagine she would be."

"We didn't see you last night when we brought the car back," Neal said. "I wanted to talk to you."

"I had already gone to bed," she said. "It was not until today that I found out what happened. That detective—Mr. Montoya, I believe—came by earlier. I told him it was all a simple misunderstanding. We overreacted, I'm afraid. We were just so concerned about Lindsey."

"I don't think you overreacted," Neal said. "Not after what happened. It's the other part that doesn't make sense. Lindsey said she met your niece, a girl named Caitlyn. Cornelia says there's no such person, that this Caitlyn doesn't really exist."

"Caitlyn," Mrs. Cutler said. "That's such a lovely name. I don't always like the new names the young people are naming their children these days, but I do like Caitlyn. Very much."

"Yes," Neal said. "It is a pretty name, but we were talking about your niece. Do you have a niece or a great-niece named Caitlyn?"

She sighed, looked down, and shook her head. "No," she said. "No, I don't. I'm sorry."

"And there's no one by that name who lives here?" Neal asked.

"No," she said. "I'm afraid not. Did she say what the girl looked like?"

"Like this," Neal said. He held out the inkjet print of Lindsey's sketch.

"Oh, dear." The expression in her eyes was haunted.

"Do you know this girl?"

She hesitated, put her hand over her mouth for a moment, and then pulled it away.

"No," she said. "That is—no. No, I don't."

"What do you think is going on?" Neal asked as he put away the portrait. "Do you think Lindsey's lying about seeing your niece?"

"Oh, no," Mrs. Cutler said firmly. "Not at all."

"So, she's crazy then?"

"No," Mrs. Cutler said. "I never said that."

"But, you're saying she saw somebody that doesn't exist," Neal said. "We're running short on options here."

Mrs. Cutler looked down at her teacup. The cup, Neal and Jolene noticed, was clinking against the saucer as her hands shook.

"This house," she said as she looked out the window at the glistening ocean beyond. "This house...." Her voice trailed off.

"What about the house?" Neal asked.

"It can...." She struggled for words. "It can get to you. There are...powerful forces here."

"Are you saying the house is haunted?" Neal asked.

"Yes," she whispered. "I suppose that word is as appropriate as any."

"And this girl Lindsey saw," Neal prodded. "You're saying she was a ghost?"

"A ghost," Mrs. Cutler said. "This house is filled with them."

Cornelia entered with a tray. Neal and Jolene drank tea, ate ladyfinger cookies. They talked with Mrs. Cutler for a while longer but didn't get anything else out of her. Finally, they got up to leave.

"Thanks for talking to us," Neal said.

"Thank you for coming," Mrs. Cutler replied. "When you see Lindsey, please tell her I'm sorry about everything that happened."

"We'll tell her," Jolene said.

"Will she be back tonight?"

"Her clothes are still here," Neal said. "I guess she'll have to come back soon."

"I'm glad. Tell her we don't even have to talk about it, if she doesn't want to."

"We'll tell her."

"I would be very grateful if you would do that."

"Have a good day, Mrs. Cutler."

"Goodbye, Neal. Goodbye, Joanne."

Neal winked at Jolene.

"That was strange," he said as they stepped out into daylight.

"Do you think there's something she's not telling us?"

"Oh, yeah," he said. "You saw the look on her face when she saw the sketch. She nearly fell out of her chair. Did you see her hands shaking?"

"She was afraid," Jolene said. "What do you think she was afraid of?"

"I don't know," Neal said, "but it could be the key to everything."

"Where are we going now?" Jolene asked.

"Astoria," Neal said. "I've got a hunch about something "

***

"No, man. I swear. That video is exactly the way it came out of the camera." Drew was sitting in front of a bank of video monitors, chasing cold pizza down with an energy drink.

"Look," Todd said, "I'm not mad. I admit, you had me convinced. It was a good trick, but Lindsey's really gone through a lot, and I need you to tell me the truth."

"I am telling the truth. That was the original file. It's what the camera saw. Check the time code, man."

"You could have reset the clock on the camera."

"Yeah, I could have. But I didn't. Do you know how long it would take to set up a prank like that? Compositing is meticulous work, bro. Why would I put that much effort into something that wouldn't make me a dime?"

"You could sell it if you convinced enough people it was real."

"All right. You got me there. But, I still didn't do it. I slept late that morning and just barely had time to look at the files before I called you."

"How do I know that?"

"What? You don't believe anything I say now?" Drew bit off a mouthful of pizza and chewed it.

"I'm not saying that. Lindsey might be in trouble. There's something strange going on, and I need you to help me figure out what it is."

"Sure, man," he said through a mouthful of pizza. "What do you need me to do?"

***

Neal stepped through the double doors into the lobby of the Astoria Police Department.

"Is Detective Montoya in?"

"He took the rest of the day off," the woman at the desk said. "He'll be back tomorrow. Can I leave him a message?"

"Yes," Neal said. "There's something I'd like to leave for him."

"That will be fine."

"Great," Neal said. He reached into a folder and pulled out the print he had made of Lindsey's sketch of Caitlyn. There was a note attached.

"I'll see that he gets it."

"Thanks." Neal started to leave.

"Wait," the woman said. "Does this have anything to do with the Cutler house?"

"Yes."

"Wait right here."

***

Lindsey sat in Neal's recliner with her feet propped up and a Bible open on her lap. The apartment was dimly lit and almost silent. The only sounds Lindsey had noted were the bubbling hum of Jolene's aquarium, the sigh of the air conditioner, and the rising and falling of vehicle noises. Lindsey was just starting to nod off when a knock sounded at the door. Lindsey set her Bible aside and rolled out of the recliner. The knock sounded again. Lindsey felt the tight weave of the carpet beneath her bare feet as she went to the door.

"Who is it?"

"Caitlyn."

Lindsey gasped. Her heart began to pound. She tried to speak, but the words froze in her throat.

"Lindsey, please. You have to help me."

Lindsey looked through the peephole in the door. Caitlyn stood pacing on the front porch.

Don't let anybody in, Jolene had warned her.

But, I have to know the truth, Lindsey argued against her friend's remembered warning. With unsteady hands, she unlocked the door and fumbled with the safety chain. Finally, sliding the chain out of its slot, she tugged open the door and stood staring at the young woman before her. There was no aura of the supernatural about her. She looked reassuringly solid.

"Where have you been?" Lindsey demanded. "Do you have any idea what I've been through?"

"I'm sorry I left you," she said. "I couldn't let the police see me."

"Who are you?" Lindsey demanded. "Mrs. Cutler says she's never heard of you."

"She said what she had to say to protect herself," Caitlyn said. "There's more going on here than you can imagine. You have to come with me. You have to help me."

"I can't," Lindsey said. "Don't you see what's happened? Everybody thinks I'm crazy because of you."

"I'm sorry about that," Caitlyn said. "I never meant for any of that to happen. You have to believe me. You have to trust me. You're the only one who can help me now."

"Are you real?" Lindsey said, her voice breaking. "Are you even here at all?"

"Touch my hand," Caitlyn said.

Lindsey reached out and squeezed the long-fingered hand. The flesh was warm, and she could feel the bone structure underneath.

"You see," she said, "I'm as real as you are."

"It doesn't prove anything," Lindsey said. "It could be part of the dream."

"Please," Caitlyn said. "You have to trust me this one last time. Come with me, and you'll understand everything."

"Where are we going?"

"Home."

Lindsey hesitated.

"Lindsey, please. I need you. There's no one else."

"All right," Lindsey said. "I'll go with you. I have to know what this is about." Lindsey pulled on her shoes and a light jacket.

"Thank you," Caitlyn said as they left the apartment together. Lindsey locked the door and slammed it behind her. The sun's fiery orb burned through the tops of hemlock trees. The evening air was cool and crisp and fragrant with the scent of Oregon's thriving ecosystem.

"How are we going to get there?"

"We could rent a scooter," Caitlyn said. Across the street was a shop that rented scooters to tourists.

"Okay," Lindsey said. "Wait here."

A bell rang as she stepped into the shop. The girl behind the desk was renting a scooter to another customer. Lindsey looked over her shoulder. Caitlyn was out of sight around a corner. She pulled out her cell phone and punched Todd's number on the speed dial setting.

"The Dawnstar customer you are trying to reach is not available," an automated voice informed her. "To leave a message, press one or wait on the line. To leave a call-back number, press three."

Lindsey punched one and heard the tone.

"Todd," she said. "This is Lindsey. Caitlyn just showed up at the apartment. I'm going back to the Cutler house with her. Call me when you get this message." She hung up.

Moments later, Lindsey emerged from the side door of the office into a storage area. She had a biking helmet on her head and a key in her hand. The girl who owned the shop pulled out a ring of keys and unchained a hot-pink scooter from a metal rack.

"It's full now," she said. "Be sure to fill it with gas before you bring it back."

"Sure," Lindsey said. "Thanks."

"No problem."

Caitlyn stepped into sight just as Lindsey stepped through the open garage door at the side of the shop.

"You do know how to drive one of these, don't you?"

"Do you want to drive it?" Lindsey asked.

"That's okay," she said. "I trust you."

Lindsey peered into the polished glass window of an art gallery and saw Caitlyn's reflection there beside her own. She looked as real as any of the other people passing on the sidewalk or driving by in cars.

Lindsey climbed on the scooter and started the engine. Caitlyn climbed on behind her. The engine let out a high-pitched whine as Lindsey twisted the throttle and sent the lightweight vehicle shooting down the narrow street like a fiberglass rocket. Space stood smoking a cigarette on the corner, his lanky frame propped against a lamppost. Lindsey raised her hand in greeting, but he showed no sign of having seen her. Whatever parallel universe he dwelled in for most of his waking life, he was apparently living there now. Lindsey wondered if she would be joining him there soon.

Chapter 27: Cold Case

"Come in," Montoya said as he answered the door. His house was on a hillside overlooking the town of Astoria. From his porch he could see the roofs of other houses, the buildings of the town, and the Columbia River. Neal and Jolene followed him inside.

"You have a nice place."

"Thanks. The deputy at the station said you have something to show me."

"Yes," Neal said. He held out the inkjet print. "This is Lindsey's portrait of Caitlyn."

Montoya frowned as he saw the picture. Then he slowly began to nod.

"I think you'd better come with me."

He led them back to the dining room. There was a yellowed manila envelope sitting in the middle of the table.

"What's going on?" Neal asked.

"Have a seat," he said. "I'll tell you."

They seated themselves around the table. Montoya picked up the envelope and pulled a file folder out of it. It was filled with sheets of typed paper, scrawled notes, yellowed newspaper clippings, and some photographs.

"I've been at the police station for thirty years," he said. "I got this file from a guy who was there before me. I was just a rookie, and he was about to retire. He was kind of a mentor to me."

"What's the file about?"

"Katherine Cutler."

"Are you telling me that little old lady has a criminal record?"

"She was never convicted," he said, "but she was under suspicion once. Nobody would have blamed her if she had killed her husband, but she was cleared. Danforth, the guy who gave me this file, was the detective in charge of the investigation." He slid one of the articles across the table to Neal. It was from the *Astoria Examiner*:

SHIPPING MAGNATE FOUND DEAD
January 26, 1947
Police are still investigating the circumstances surrounding the death of shipping magnate Niles Cutler, 52, of Meriwether Cove, Oregon. Cutler's body was pulled from the ocean late Friday afternoon near the abandoned lighthouse at Meriwether Point. Cutler's death was the result of head trauma caused by a gunshot wound. The weapon was found outside the lighthouse. Cutler's widow, Katherine, 24, was found chained inside the structure. She has claimed responsibility for her husband's death. Cutler's household servants insist Mrs. Cutler was not responsible.

"'Claimed responsibility?'" Jolene quoted. "She confessed to killing her own husband?"

"She confessed," Montoya said, "but the team that conducted the investigation concluded that she couldn't have done it. She was locked inside the lighthouse at the time. The poor woman had been chained up in there for nearly a month."

"Could she have chained herself up in there?" Neal asked.

"To give herself an alibi?"

"Right."

"Not without help. The trapdoor leading into the tower was padlocked from the outside. From what Danforth said, she was half-starved. He said it nearly broke his heart to see her. He almost didn't get to her in time, and he blamed himself for that."

"Why?"

"Mrs. Cutler's German housekeeper had come to the police station a couple of months earlier, claiming that Cutler had been locking his wife in her bedroom for weeks on end. Danforth and some of the others went out to investigate, but the bedroom was empty. There was no sign of Mrs. Cutler at all. Her husband claimed she was out of town visiting cousins. Danforth was suspicious but didn't really have enough evidence to charge Cutler with anything. It wasn't until they found Cutler's body floating near the lighthouse that they thought to look for his wife there." He slid a second clipping across the table to them.

WIDOW CLEARED IN HUSBAND'S DEATH
January 30, 1947

Katherine Cutler, 24, has been cleared of all charges surrounding the death of her husband, Niles Cutler, on January 25. Cutler's body was found floating in the ocean a few hundred yards from the isolated lighthouse near the Cutler mansion where he apparently took his own life. Cutler was believed to have been drinking at the time.

Katherine Cutler surrendered herself to the police when they found her, weeping and hysterical, locked in the lighthouse. Further questioning of the Cutler household staff and investigation of the Cutler home led to Mrs. Cutler's exoneration and to the arrest of two household servants on charges of abuse. Mrs. Cutler, according to sources in the Cutler household, could not have been responsible for her husband's death because she had been imprisoned in the lighthouse at the time of Cutler's apparent suicide. Distrustful of his young wife, Cutler had apparently kept the young woman a prisoner in the Cutler mansion and, later, in the lighthouse. Attempts to escape were met with harsh disciplinary measures.

"She must have felt so guilty for wanting him dead that she confessed to the crime," Police Detective Ronald Daniels told reporters, "but there's just no way she could have done it."

"I've got two other things to show you," Montoya said. He pulled a snapshot out of the folder and passed it across the table. "Does this look familiar?"

"It's her!" Neal said. "That's Caitlyn, the girl in Lindsey's drawing. Why didn't you tell me you'd managed to find her? This proves Lindsey was telling the truth."

Montoya shook his head. "You don't know who this is, do you? This picture is over fifty years old. That's Katherine Cutler."

"Wait. What?"

"That's what Mrs. Cutler looked like at the time her husband died."

"But, how would Lindsey have known that?"

"Maybe she saw a picture."

"I guess that's possible. Or maybe her sister has a granddaughter."

He passed them another picture.

"I think you'd better look at this."

Neal picked it up and studied it. Then he passed it to Jolene.

"Do you know what this means?" Jolene frowned.

"It means this situation's even weirder than we thought," Neal said. "We've got to show this to Lindsey."

"Be careful if you go back to that mansion," Montoya said. "It's a pretty weird place. Danforth kept a file on it for the rest of the time he was with the department. Did you know Mrs. Cutler never leaves the place? She sends her housekeeper to run all of her errands."

"I knew she was reclusive. I thought it was something that had happened as she got older."

"She's been reclusive since she was in her twenties," he said. "She used to venture out occasionally, but now she stays there full-time. She thinks there's some kind of curse on her, that she's not allowed to leave."

"You're kidding."

"Did you know she's brought exorcists out to the mansion to try to lift the curse? Apparently, the exorcisms didn't take.

She's had three different guys out there that we know about. There may have been more."

"This is bizarre," Neal said.

"And we sent Lindsey right into the middle of it," Jolene said.

"At least she's nowhere near there now."

***

Todd was coming out of the coffee shop, two steaming caramel lattes in his hands, when he heard the chime from his cell phone. After balancing the lattes as carefully as he could manage on the sloping roof of his car, Todd picked up his phone and saw the envelope icon. He had a voicemail message.

"Todd, this is Lindsey. Caitlyn just showed up at the apartment."

His mental world exploded around him.

"I'm going back to the Cutler house with her. Call me when you get this message."

Todd found Lindsey's name on his contact list and punched her number.

"We're sorry. The customer you are trying to reach is not available. Please try again later or leave a message at the sound of the beep."

"Lindsey," Todd said. "I'm coming!"

He slapped his phone back into the holster on his belt, and spilled one of the lattes as he was trying to get the car door open. It ran down the windshield as he dropped into the driver's seat and slid the surviving latte into the cup holder. He started to call Neal but decided to wait. If he hurried now, he might catch Lindsey before she got too far from the apartment.

He kept his eyes out for her as he wound his way through the crowded streets of Cannon Beach. Finally, he pulled up at the apartment complex, ran up the stairs to the door of Neal and Jolene's apartment, and pounded on it. There was no answer.

"Lindsey!" he called out as he pounded on the door again.

More silence. Lindsey had already gone.

Todd walked back down the stairs to his car and unlocked the door with the remote. Just as he was about to get in, he heard the scrape of a boot against the sidewalk behind him, turned, and saw Space ambling past.

"Hi, Space."

"Good evening, sir. Good evening."

He was in a talking mood for a change. Todd tried to remember if Space had ever spoken to him before and decided he had not.

"I was just looking for Lindsey. Have you seen her?"

"Yessiree. She left here on a motor scooter about five minutes ago."

"A motor scooter?"

"Yep. Rented it from that shop over there acrost the street, she did."

"I see," Todd said. Clearly, this guy was on one of his mental spacewalks. "Thanks."

"Caitlyn was with her," Space said.

Todd's hand stopped halfway to the door handle.

"Did you say you saw Caitlyn?"

"Yeah, she was ridin' on the back of the scooter."

Todd stood frozen for a moment while his brain processed what he had just heard.

"What did she look like?"

"You know," Space said. "That's her."

Todd turned, his pulse quickening, but saw no sign of anyone. Following Space's gaze, he saw the inkjet print of Lindsey's sketch lying in the clutter of books, videotapes, and camera equipment on his backseat. Concealing his excitement, he opened the door and pulled out the picture.

"I've never met her," he said. "Does she really look like this?"

"Yep," Space said. "That's her all right. Tall. Skinny. Reddish-blonde hair."

"How long have they been gone?"

"I don't know. Maybe five minutes."

"Not long then."

"Could have been an hour. The space-time continuum is a mysterious thing. It's all perception, you know."

"Oh, I see. Well, thanks, Space. I'd better go looking for them."

Space nodded.

Todd sank into the driver's seat and slid the key into the ignition. *Lindsey wasn't hallucinating. Caitlyn is real.* He started the car and took off for the Cutler mansion. Maybe he would finally find some answers.

***

Caitlyn held tightly to Lindsey's waist as the scooter buzzed down the highway like an angry hornet. Larger vehicles passed them even though Lindsey was pushing the little vehicle for all it was worth. Finally, she reached the entrance to Mrs. Cutler's drive. Dread knotted her stomach as she squeezed on the brake and turned into the shady side road. Caitlyn said nothing as she glided up to the keypad and punched in the access code. The gate opened, as it always did, as though it were being pushed open by invisible hands. Lindsey twisted the throttle and coaxed the scooter between brick pillars and deeper into eerie territory. The gate creaked shut behind them. A lump formed in Lindsey's throat.

"I'm not sure this bike can take these hills with both of us riding," she said.

"I think it will do fine," Caitlyn said, "I really do."

Lindsey drove the bike up the hill, around a curve in the road, and deeper into the dark path before them. Tree canopies shrouded the road in shadow. The sun really was getting low. As the path twisted and turned, Lindsey could, at odd intervals, see the ocean through the trees. She squeezed the brake to reduce her speed. What was she getting herself into?

"Are you all right?" Caitlyn asked. "It's not much farther now."

***

Todd had the accelerator punched nearly to the floor and a death grip on the steering wheel. The tires screeched around a curve. The side of the car almost raked the guardrail. On the other side was a sixty-foot plunge into a dark gulf. Todd forced himself to let up on the accelerator.

"Help her, Lord," he prayed under his breath. "You know what she means to me. Don't let anything happen to her."

Trees appeared on both sides of the road as the road sloped upward into a steep grade. Todd dropped down into a lower gear as the car began to hesitate.

Todd looked into the rearview mirror. Panic jarred him. There was another face staring back at him from the backseat. It was a dead man's face. The filmy white eyes were narrowed in rage.

Todd slammed on the brakes. The car skidded on the asphalt. He whirled around in the seat as fast as the safety harnesses would allow. The backseat was empty. There was no one there.

Gasping for breath, Todd looked back into the rearview mirror and saw only his own face and an empty back seat. He adjusted the mirror, moved it to the left and to the right. The face was no longer there. Perhaps it had never been there at all.

Todd saw another car coming up behind him. He punched down on the accelerator. The car jerked back into motion.

I'm losing my mind, Todd thought. *I've gone completely....*

The wheel jerked beneath Todd's fingers. He fought to pull it back, but the wheel wouldn't budge. Todd looked back into the rearview mirror. The pale, bearded pirate's face had returned. It was laughing silently, hysterically.

An air horn wailed. Todd looked up and saw a pair of headlights bearing down upon him.

"Lord, help me."

Todd jerked the wheel. The wheels screamed against the pavement as the car spun out of control. The airbag inflated as the windshield imploded. Shards of glass rained through the air like a stinging hailstorm. Tree limbs clawed at Todd's face and hands. A tree trunk slammed against the side of the car. Todd's head went through the glass, and the lights went out.

Chapter 28: A Slippery Path

The Cutler mansion sat imperiously on its rocky throne and glared out through the trees at the small scooter as it emerged from the forest road. Lindsey felt the mansion's surly gaze as she turned from the driveway and drove down the hill toward the trail she and Caitlyn had walked on that rainy afternoon. Waist-high grass blew past her, slapping her knees as she went. She braked as she neared the entrance to the shady trail that would lead her to the lighthouse. The scooter's headlamp lit the path before her. She saw the gnarled roots and the slabs of rock and knew she and Caitlyn would have to go the rest of the way on foot. She turned off the scooter's engine, pulled off her helmet, and laid it in the basket in front of the handlebars.

"Well," she told Caitlyn. "We're here. What now?"

"I'll show you," Caitlyn said. "Thank you for coming with me, Lindsey. I hated to put this burden on you, but there was no one else to turn to."

They both climbed off the scooter. Lindsey shoved the vehicle into the shadows of the path and put down the kickstand. Lindsey wondered if she was walking into some kind of trap. She looked into Caitlyn's pleading, hopeful eyes and wondered if her friend was really what she appeared to be or if some dark and cunning presence was leading her into something deadly. *I don't have to go any farther,* she told herself. *I could get back on that scooter and drive back to Neal and Jolene's apartment. I could get on a plane for Texas, go back to my old life, and forget this place ever existed.*

She looked down at the scooter and at the dark path ahead. Pale slats of evening light cut their angled paths through twisting trunks and leafy canopies. They swept across heaps of ferns that looked like they could have been plucked from some Jurassic rainforest and knotted roots from a fairytale land of elves and wizards. Where, in the beauty of Eden, was the serpent hiding this time?

"Two roads converged in a yellow wood," Lindsey whispered as the words from the Robert Frost poem sprang into her mind. In the poem, a traveler stood in a place where the path before him split, and he was forced to make a choice. One road was well worn and often used while the other, the "road less traveled," was overgrown and not as well-kept. *I chose the road less traveled,* the poet had proclaimed, *and that has made all the difference.*

"Are you all right?" Caitlyn said. "Lindsey?"

"In for a penny," Lindsey whispered, "in for a pound."

They didn't say much as they made their way down the path, stepping over roots and fallen trees. Openings in the canopy gave them glimpses of the churning ocean beneath them. The sighing and crashing of waves mesmerized them with the calming music of the ancient deep. Even when they couldn't see the waves, they could still hear them. Moments later, they emerged into the open as the trail twisted to the left and cut its snaking path down the side of the hill. Lindsey followed Caitlyn, as she had before, clinging to rough tree roots and outcroppings of rock to steady herself as they clambered down. They reached the rocky bottom moments later.

"Where are we going now?" Lindsey asked. "The cave?"

"The lighthouse."

Lindsey squinted into the setting sun at the gray shape that loomed across the waves. The tide had not come in yet, and the wave-scoured path that led to the lighthouse was still visible above the waves.

"All right," Lindsey said. "Let's go, then." She had seen the lighthouse repeatedly in dreams, but never in reality. She wondered if the dark interior of the crumbling structure before her would bear any resemblance to what she had seen in her dreams. The path along the rocks was slippery. The waves had smoothed the rocks and coated them with slime.

A wave crashed into the rocky path, swept over it, and drenched Lindsey halfway to the knees. The tide was coming in, and the waves were growing larger and more violent.

I'll be trapped here, Lindsey thought. *Once the tide comes in, I'll be stuck here until tomorrow.* She thought about turning back, but curiosity drove her on.

Another wave crashed against the path. This time it soaked her to the knees. She cried out as the cold water bit into her legs, and she struggled to maintain her footing.

"Are you all right?" Caitlyn asked.

"I'm wet." Lindsey growled. The lighthouse was about three hundred yards from shore, and the sun was lying right on the horizon. How long would it take her, struggling down this slippery path, to reach the rocky island? If it took too long, she and Caitlyn would both be swimming.

"We're going to be stuck out there all night," Lindsey told Caitlyn. "We could have at least brought camping supplies."

"There's no time," Caitlyn insisted. She kept saying that. What was so urgent about their errand? Lindsey was a planner, and this whole evening was going against her nature. She wanted to help Caitlyn, to be a true friend to her in her hour of greatest need, but this whole situation was getting ridiculous. Another wave slammed into the ridge and sprayed Lindsey with water.

"All of this must seem outrageous to you," Caitlyn said.

"All of what?" Lindsey snapped. "I don't even know what 'all of this' is! You haven't told me anything."

"I know," Caitlyn said, a sad smile forming on her lips. "But you'll know soon enough."

"Why did you pick me for this?" Lindsey said as she pushed against the ocean. "Why not somebody else? I'm not brave or heroic. I'm a homebody."

"Loving your home doesn't make you weak," Caitlyn said. "It can be a source of strength."

"That still doesn't answer my question."

"I know. I'm sorry."

***

"That's it," Jolene said.

Neal hit the brakes when he saw the flashing lights. There were two police cars and an ambulance. He drove carefully past the scene of the accident and pulled over onto the shoulder before stopping. Neal and Jolene got out of the car, closing the doors behind them, and started toward the ambulance. Neal surveyed the scene. Skid marks had left their dark imprint on the surface of the road and turned to deep gashes where the car had left the road. The front of the car had punched a jagged tunnel through the roadside vegetation. It had plowed through the blanket of needles that carpeted the hillside, ripped bark from the sides of trees, snipped off several smaller trees, and finally collided with the trunk of a century-old hemlock tree. The car was almost completely shrouded in shadows and debris. Neal felt Jolene take his hand. Her narrowed eyes reflected his own dark thoughts.

The spinning lights on the roofs of the police cars and ambulance shot needle-leafed shadows through the underbrush. Muffled radio voices cut through the mountain air.

The doors of the ambulance were open. Todd was sitting in the ambulance with a bandage on his head. The front of his shirt was soaked with blood.

"You say something distracted you?" one of the officers said as he summarized Todd's story on a notepad. "What was it?"

"I thought I saw someone in the backseat," Todd admitted. "It was just a flash, but it scared the living daylights out of me."

"And that's when you jerked back on the steering wheel and lost control?"

"Right."

Todd smiled sheepishly and lifted his hand in greeting when he saw Neal and Jolene standing behind the officer.

"Are you friends of his?" the officer asked.

"Yeah," Neal said. "He called us."

"We're almost finished with him," the policeman said. "Mr. Wilkes, I'm afraid I'm going to have to charge you with failure to maintain control. I don't know why you're so jumpy, but it nearly cost two people their lives. If you had hit that truck, you and the driver might both be lying under blankets now."

"Yes, sir. I'm…sorry about that."

"Take your ticket by the courthouse. They'll tell you how much you owe and act as a cashier to receive your payment. In the meantime, drive carefully."

"I will. Thanks."

He sighed as the officer walked away.

"You need to go to the emergency room for stitches," a paramedic told him. "That's a serious gash. We can take you there, or you can ride with your friends now that they're here."

"I think I'll ride with them," Todd said. "Thanks for taking care of me."

"No problem."

Todd climbed out of the ambulance. Jolene hugged him and nearly burst into tears.

"What happened?"

"I'll tell you when we get to the car," he said, his voice low. "This is crazy."

"What are they going to do about your car?" Neal asked.

"They've called a wrecker," Todd said. "He has an electric winch with a very long cable."

They climbed into the car.

"We have to get to the Cutler house," he said. "Lindsey's out there."

"Lindsey's at the apartment."

"No, she's not. I just came from there."

"I'm taking you to the hospital first," Neal said as he started the engine. "Jolene and I will get Lindsey."

"We have to go now," Todd said. "She may be in trouble. This is a whole lot weirder than we had any idea."

"You're telling me," Neal said. "Wait till you hear what we discovered."

"Lindsey's with Caitlyn," Todd said. "Space saw them leave. Both of them."

"Space saw Caitlyn?" Jolene gasped.

"Space sees a lot of things that aren't there," Neal said.

"He saw Lindsey's sketch on the backseat and recognized her."

"Show him the picture," Neal said.

Jolene picked up a yellow clasp envelope and slid out a stack of photocopied pages. One of them was a photocopy of the snapshot Montoya had shown them. She passed it to Todd.

"That's her," Todd said. "Who is she?"

"Katherine Cutler," Neal said. "The way she looked in 1947."

"That's a strong family resemblance," Todd said. "She *has* to be Mrs. Cutler's niece."

"Great niece, in this case," Jolene said. "That was sixty-eight years ago."

"Mrs. Cutler's sister died," Neal said.

"She could have had a child before she died," Todd said.

"Show him the rest of the folder," Neal told Jolene.

***

The waves were churning violently, and the land bridge that connected the lighthouse's stony base to the mainland was almost underwater. The lighthouse was only about twenty feet away. There was a weathered dock, Lindsey noticed, at the edge of the island. She had not noticed it before, but it had been in her dream.

A blast of water hit the path, and Lindsey's feet flew out from under her. She slammed her head against a rock, and the world went dark.

A moment later, she woke up choking on cold water and thrashing against the waves. Her shoes felt like concrete bricks, and her sodden clothes felt as heavy as a suit of armor.

"Caitlyn!" she cried. "Cait...!" She swallowed a mouthful of water and strangled on it. She coughed violently, gulped air, and beat against the water with all the strength she could muster. She sank beneath the surface, kicked herself back up. She had drifted away from the land bridge, and the current was dragging her further away still.

"Caitlyn!" she screamed again, her voice high and hysterical. The path was empty. Caitlyn was nowhere to be seen.

***

"Neal!" Jolene cried. "Slow down!"

Neal hit the brakes. Gravel shot out over the edge of the driveway, peppered the fence, and tumbled out into space. Neal made his way around the last winding curve and rolled up onto the brick courtyard in front of the mansion.

"What did you say she was driving?" Neal asked.

"Space said he saw her leave on a scooter. He said she rented it from that place across the street from your apartment."

"They rent them to tourists," Neal said. "It's a good way to get around town. I don't see it. Are you sure she's here?"

"She left a message on my cell phone. She said she was coming here."

"Did you try to call her back?"

"I tried. She didn't answer."

They climbed the stairs onto the porch, and Neal rang the bell. When no one came, he rang again.

"It may be broken," he said. He pounded on the door with his fist.

The door flew open. Cornelia glared at him.

"Where's Lindsey?" Neal asked.

"She's not here."

"She said she was coming here. I need to see Mrs. Cutler."

"She's not feeling well."

"This is important. It could be an emergency."

They stared at each other for a moment.

"Come with me."

Neal, Todd, and Jolene followed her through the parlor, down the long corridor that ran through the center of the house, and to the sunroom in the back. Mrs. Cutler was sitting in her fan-backed chair, her face a mask of pain.

"What's wrong with her?" Todd asked.

"Headaches," Mrs. Cutler said. "Terrible, monstrous headaches." Her voice sounded weak and distant as though it were coming from somewhere far away.

"We're sorry to disturb you," Neal said as he knelt by the arm of her chair. "We're looking for Lindsey. Have you seen her?"

"She hasn't been here," Mrs. Cutler said.

"She said she was coming here with your niece."

"Oh, dear."

"You know who she is, don't you? You recognized the girl in her sketch?"

"Of course I recognized her," she said, her voice bleak. "It's my Katie."

"Katie?"

"Kathleen. My sister."

"She looks just like you," Jolene said. "The way you used to look."

"Oh, no, dear."

"But weren't you identical twins?"

"Not exactly identical," she said. "We were mirror-image twins. That mole is on her left cheek. I have the same mole on my right. She's right-handed, you see, and I'm a lefty."

"Tell us about Kathleen. What happened to her?"

"She starved to death in that horrible prison camp," Mrs. Cutler said. "Those Japanese soldiers... I'll never forgive myself."

"Why? Because you left her behind in China? Because she begged you not to go, but you went , anyway?"

"Oh, no, no, no," she said. "No, it wasn't like that at all. I never would have gone with Niles, but she insisted. She said it was my one chance to live a happy life."

"How did it work out?" Neal asked her. "Were you happy?"

"For a while," she said. "Niles and I traveled the world together. Such adventures we had. I never even thought of Father or Katie back there in China. I never even wrote back to say goodbye. When the news of their deaths came, it nearly destroyed me. Niles was so good to me then. So kind."

"Do you know anything about Blackbeard?" Todd suddenly asked.

"Where did that come from?" Neal squinted at him as if he was losing his mind. "That's pretty random, man."

"My sister and I loved to read about pirates," Mrs. Cutler said, her face brightening. "We adored *Treasure Island*. Mr. Kipling wrote such wonderful novels. And then there was Captain Hook in *Peter Pan*. But Blackbeard was a *real* pirate, and that fascinated us all the more. "

"Do you remember Blackbeard's real name?"

"Of course," she said. "It's…oh, my, memory fails me at the most inopportune time these days. What was it? Oh, yes. Edward Teach."

"Teach?" Jolene said. "Like the man Lindsey saw."

Neal looked out the window, squinting against the gloom. Lightning flashed across the sky. The lighthouse flashed white and fell into darkness. Thunder shook the windows.

"Is there somebody at the lighthouse?" Neal asked.

"There's not supposed to be."

"I thought I saw something move over there. Do you have a telescope? Some field glasses, maybe?"

"Yes," she said, her hand against her forehead. "Cornelia, could you get the telescope for Neal?"

Cornelia returned a moment later with an old-style spyglass. Neal took it, slid open the door, and stepped out onto the balcony. A cool wind tousled his hair. Neal held the glass to his right eye and peered into the wind. In the fading light of a rust-red sunset, the rocky island was covered with shadows. Neal squinted and swept it across the barren landscape.

"There," he said. "By the dock. It's her."

"Which one?"

"Lindsey. She's in the water."

"We have to get out there," Todd said. "Do you have a boat?"

"There's an old one by the dock," Mrs. Cutler said. "It belonged to my husband."

"There's nothing there now," Neal said. "Where can we get a boat?"

"Leo has a boat," Jolene said. "He lives at the bottom of the mountain."

Mrs. Cutler cried out.

Chapter 29: The Scene of the Crime

Fighting the waves and the numbing cold, praying every inch of the way, Lindsey made her way to the dock and grabbed the ladder. She barely had the strength to climb it. Water poured from her clothes as she forced herself up. She cried out as one of the rotten rungs ripped free and nearly spilled her back into the ocean. When her head reached the level of the dock's flooring, she saw Caitlyn sitting on the dock. She was soaking wet and trembling.

"Where did you go?" Lindsey cried. "Why didn't you help me?"

"I couldn't," she said. "I tried, but...." She shook her head and covered her face with her hands.

Lindsey fought her way up onto the dock and collapsed there for a moment. The muscles in her arms and hands burned. There was no strength left in her legs. A wave of nausea struck her. She thought for a moment that she might throw up, but the feeling subsided. An icy wind burned through her sodden clothes. She was really cold now, and night was coming. Hypothermia, she knew, was a serious matter. If she and Caitlyn didn't get inside that lighthouse and find some shelter there, they would freeze to death.

"Caitlyn," she called. "Caitlyn?"

"Can you forgive me, Lindsey?"

"Yes," she said. "I forgive you, but we have to get inside."

"Yes," Caitlyn said. "We have to get inside. There's something we have to do."

***

Neal's minivan shot down the beach road like a rocket. Jolene bit her lips and clung to the seat. Neal cut hard, sending them skidding sideways into Leo's yard. Jolene screamed, and gravel flew. Neal slammed the gearshift into park, leaped out of the car, ran to his friend's front door, and pounded on it.

Todd and Jolene climbed out just as the lights came on in the house. Leo appeared behind the screen door, wrapped in a towel.

"Oh, my gosh," Jolene groaned. "He's always doing this to me."

"Leo!" Neal cried. "I gotta borrow your boat."

"In this storm? That's crazy."

"It's an emergency. There's a girl on the island."

"The lighthouse island? That's a dangerous place. Let me get you the key, man."

"Thanks, Leo. You're the best."

***

The island was strewn with rocks, seaweed, and debris that had washed in from the ocean. It smelled like dead fish. Lindsey picked her way carefully along the path that ran from the dock to the tower. A gust of wind nearly knocked her off her feet.

"He's coming," Caitlyn said suddenly. "We have to hurry."

"Who's coming?" Lindsey said. "What's happening?"

"Hurry!"

A gunshot split the air. Lindsey screamed and dove for the ground. The wind howled, and a huge wave struck the island. Lindsey looked wildly around but saw no one. The lighthouse was only twelve feet away. Bending low and covering her head, Lindsey scrambled for the metal door. A second shot grazed the wall over her head. Chunks of plaster rained down. Caitlyn was huddled just outside the door. Lindsey dove past her, almost tripping over her, pulled the door open, and rolled into darkness.

The inside of the lighthouse was almost silent. The only source of light was a small window over the stairs.

"Bolt the door!" Caitlyn cried as she burst in.

"Why don't you do it?" Lindsey cried, exasperated, as she stumbled to the door and slammed the bolt into place.

***

Waves hammered the boat's fiberglass stern. Jolene clung to Neal's arm as he drove, her teeth clenched. Both of them wore lifejackets.

"I hate water," she said.

"I told you to stay behind," he said.

Lightning flashed across the heavens.

"The dock's on the leeward side of the island," Todd yelled loudly enough to be heard over the wind and the straining engine.

"Where do you think I'm trying to go?" Neal yelled back.

Todd held the glass to his right eye and scanned the tiny island for any sign of Lindsey. He could see a boat tied to the dock, and the battered metal door of the lighthouse was shivering with every blast of wind. The boat rolled hard to the right. A fire extinguisher tumbled out onto the deck. Neal pulled hard on the throttle. The boat leaped forward and pitched sideways. Jolene and Todd screamed.

***

"We have to hurry," Caitlyn said.

"You keep saying that!"

"You've come this far," Caitlyn said. "Just a little farther now. Come on! We have to climb to the top."

Lindsey's legs were still shaky from fighting the current, but she didn't argue. Gripping the metal handrail, she willed herself upward. Her wet shoes beat out an echoing cadence on the concrete stairs. The inside of the tower looked exactly as it had in the dream. Nothing had changed. That seemed wrong somehow.

What am I doing here? she thought to herself. *Maybe I really am losing my mind.*

Fear swelled inside her as she heard someone pounding on the door beneath them.

Help me, God. This is insane. Please, help me. She closed her eyes, set her teeth against the pain in her thighs, and willed herself to climb faster…faster…faster. The pounding on the door continued. Who was out there? Who had been shooting at them, and what did he want? Faster…faster.

Caitlyn drove herself upward into darkness as the light from the window subsided. Then, slowly, the stairwell ahead of her grew brighter. She passed another narrow window and kept climbing. The tower had not looked so tall from the shore, but it seemed to go on forever now. Faster…faster. Burning pain pinched down on her legs. She felt as though her muscles might, at any moment, tear free from her bones and send her flying, face-first, into the steps. She drove herself on and on, panting as she went and pulling herself along the handrail. The stairway ahead of her grew brighter. The spiral staircase ended as she stepped through an open hatch and into a circular chamber. Light poured in from the outside and glared against a curved wall of mirrors at the back of an extinct beacon.

Lying on a stained mattress was a girl in a ragged nightgown. A metal band encircled her ankle and a plate of half-eaten food lay on the floor beside her. She turned and looked at Lindsey. The face was Caitlyn's.

"Caitlyn?" Lindsey gasped. "How did you…?"

A second Caitlyn stood in the hatch behind her.

"This is Katherine," Caitlyn explained, "my sister." She knelt on the mattress beside the other girl. "This is Lindsey. She's come to help us."

The other girl began to cry.

"She can't help us," she sobbed. "No one can help us."

Lindsey heard an explosion at the base of the stairs. There was a cry of animal rage, followed by the reverberating thunder of heavy boots on concrete stairs.

"He's coming," Caitlyn said.

"Who is it?" Lindsey demanded, her voice shaking. "Who's coming?"

"Captain Teach."

"What do we do?"

Lindsey searched the chamber for weapons. On a shelf, well out of the reach of the chained girl, was a wrench. It was covered with dust and cobwebs, but there wasn't much rust. Lindsey ran to the wrench, picked it up, and held it with both hands just as the hatch slammed open.

"Wretched meddlers! Ye'll pay with yuir lives!"

The massive figure burst into the room and raised himself to his full, ponderous height and fixed his pale, filmy eyes on Lindsey.

"Ye was warned, missy. Ye was warned over and over. Now it's time to join them in their fate."

Chapter 30: Puppet Show

Todd and Jolene tumbled through the hatch, wind and water howling at their backs. Todd wrestled the metal door shut behind them and slammed the bolt into place. Neal had stayed with the boat.

"This is insane," Jolene gasped. "There wasn't a cloud in the sky."

Todd scanned the room with his flashlight. The walls were painted concrete, and the floor was littered with debris. There was a lantern hanging on the wall. Todd wondered if the tower had ever had electricity. Maybe there had been a generator.

Someone screamed in the darkness above them.

"Lindsey!" Jolene yelled.

Todd leaped onto the stairs, Jolene hard on his heels. Muffled echoes tumbled through the darkness: shouting voices, breaking glass, crashing metal.

"Lindsey!" They both cried out her name as they bounded, breathless, up the narrow stairs, their flashlight beams lighting the way before them.

"Todd!" Lindsey cried. "Look out! Don't come in here!"

The hatch above them was open. Todd and Jolene looked at each other.

"Stay down here," Todd whispered. "I've got to see what's going on."

Todd raised his hands above his head and stepped slowly through the hatch.

***

"Todd, no!"

"Well," the pirate-thing rasped. "More lambs to the slaughter."

Todd stared at him, his eyes wide with disbelief. Teach gestured with his pistol.

"Get over there with the lot of them."

Todd hesitated.

"Do what he says," Lindsey said as she sat huddled beside the sisters on the mattress.

"It's no use," Katherine said. "Oh, Katie, we should never have brought her into this."

"What is this?" Todd asked as he joined Lindsey on the edge of the mattress. "What's going on here?"

"I'll be askin' the questions, laddie," the gigantic figure roared.

"Why are you doing this to them?" Lindsey demanded of him.

"Did ye not hear me, wench? I'll be askin' the questions."

"What do you want to know?"

"What're ye doin' here?"

"I'm here for them."

"Here for who?" Todd whispered.

"What business is it o' yourn? What are they to you?"

"Who is he talking about?"

The sisters huddled together.

"Them," Lindsey said, turning to the twins. "These girls."

Todd shook his head.

"You don't see them?"

"There's nobody there, Lindsey."

"Then it isn't real? This isn't real?"

"I don't think so."

Lindsey rose to her feet. The pirate glared at her, his pale eyes burning beneath the ridge of his craggy brow.

"You're not real," she said. "You can't hurt me."

"Lindsey," Todd said suddenly. "What are you doing?"

Lindsey started toward the shambling figure. "I come against you in the name of Christ."

"Lindsey, no!" Todd leaped and grabbed Lindsey. The pistol exploded as they tumbled to the floor. The pirate howled in rage.

Lindsey untangled herself from Todd. The room around her had changed.

Rain pelted the windows around them and painted the dust-caked glass with ripples of distortion. A rotting mattress lay in the floor, feathers pouring from a rip in the side. Katherine and Caitlyn were nowhere to be seen, but the giant figure in the long coat and three-cornered hat remained. He stood in the dim light, howling in pain and clutching his powder-stained hand as blood poured between his ravaged fingers. His ancient pistol had misfired. It lay in splintered ruins at his feet. Something was different about him now. His long beard had shrunk to about a weeks' scraggly growth. The color had returned to his flesh. The light from the window brushed across his features. The sight of his face jarred Lindsey to the core.

"Pack? Pack, is that you?"

He turned, still moaning in pain, and fixed his gaze on Lindsey. His eyes widened in confusion. "Lindsey? Baby, is that you?" His tone was soft, vulnerable. He looked lost.

"Yes, Pack. It's me." She started toward him.

"Lindsey," Todd said. "Be…."

Pack shrieked. Wild-eyed, he burst forward. Todd hurled Lindsey to one side and leaped into the path of the larger man. He scooped up a wrench and threw every bit of his strength into one bone-jarring blow. Lindsey watched as the wrench slammed into the side of Pack's skull, threw back his head, and brought the big man crashing down on top of him. Todd's head hit the floor.

They both lay still for a moment, Todd on the floor beneath Pack's larger form. Lindsey thought for an instant that the impact had knocked him unconscious. She noticed for the first time that his head was torn open, but the wound was already taped. Todd opened his eyes and pulled himself free of Pack's dead weight. Lindsey helped him to his feet.

Jolene, flashlight in hand, pushed herself up through the hatch. Thunder rolled outside.

"Is everybody all right?" she asked. Her flashlight brushed across Pack's fallen body. "What happened here?"

"I don't know," Todd said. "This is really weird." He bent down to check on Pack. He reached for the larger man's wrist with his right hand, then switched to his left, fumbling for his pulse.

"Is he alive?"

Pack snorted in his sleep.

"Yeah," Todd said. "He's alive. Crazy, but alive. What's going on here, Lindsey?"

"I don't know," she said. "I was following Caitlyn. She brought me here to help her sister."

"Her sister?"

"Katherine. She was chained here like somebody in a dungeon."

Todd walked over to the mattress. "Jolene, could you shine the light over there?" Jolene complied. Todd reached down, and picked up a piece of chain with a metal band in the end. Another section lay coiled on the floor. The chain had been cut, possibly by bolt cutters.

"She was here," Lindsey said.

"Yes," Todd said. "She was. Sixty years ago, Katherine Cutler's husband imprisoned her in this tower. Montoya told Neal and Jolene about it."

"Sixty years?" Lindsey gasped. "So, that was Mrs. Cutler? And Caitlyn is her sister? The one who died in China?"

"We've got to go," Todd said. "Neal's waiting."

Pack groaned softly.

"What do we do with him?" Jolene asked.

"We can send the police for him," Todd said. "I don't think I can manhandle him down the stairs."

"Why was he talking with that strange accent?" Jolene asked.

"I think he was possessed," Lindsey said.

"Possessed?"

"By the ghost of a pirate. I know it sounds crazy, but when I first saw him, it didn't look like Pack. Caitlyn called him Teach."

"Edward Teach," Todd said. "That was Blackbeard's real name."

"He *does* look like Blackbeard," Lindsey said. "But, why would Blackbeard's ghost be haunting Mrs. Cutler?"

"We have to get out of here," Jolene said.

"But, I have to help them," Lindsey said. "They brought me here to help them."

"There's nobody here to help," Jolene said. "We're the only ones here. We've got to go."

Lightning lit up the tower. A cannon burst of thunder cracked the sky.

"What's happening to me?" Lindsey asked.

"I don't know," Todd said. He looked at Pack's fallen form. "But you're not the only one it's happening to."

They descended into darkness, thunder rumbling through the concrete walls around them.

***

Emotionally spent, Lindsey stumbled out of the lighthouse toward the waiting dock. As she stepped out into the rain, she turned around and ran her hand along the rain slick wall.

"What is it?" Todd asked.

"Pack was shooting at us," she said. "I was looking for a bullet hole."

Todd scanned the wall with his flashlight.

"There!" she said. The plaster had been blown away just above the door.

"That happened a long time ago," Todd said. "See how the paint is peeling."

"I give up," she said. "It doesn't make any sense."

Todd clung to her, and did his best to shield her from the storm. It was a sweet gesture, she thought, a sad smile forming on her lips, but he couldn't protect her. He couldn't save her.

Todd shined his light ahead of them as they walked to the end of the rain-spattered dock. There was no sign of a boat there, only churning waves.

"Where is he?" Jolene cried against the wind. "Neal! Neal!"

A cluster of lights appeared in the gloom. One of them was flashing across the surface of the water. The rumble of an engine cut through the sounds of wind and rain as the dark shape of a boat resolved itself against the gray of the ocean. Neal wrestled with the steering wheel. The boat spun around. He reversed the engine and backed smoothly up to stop beside the dock. Todd dropped to his knees and grabbed the rail that ran along the front of the boat.

"Get in," he yelled to the girls. "Hurry."

Lindsey stepped around Todd and plunged into the rocking boat. Jolene leaped in behind her and helped her into a seat. Todd swung over the rail into the boat and pushed against the dock. Neal pushed down on the throttle and the boat roared away from the island.

"Did you see the way I backed into the dock?" Neal said as Todd dropped into the seat beside him. "That was so smooth. I'll never be able to do that again." He looked around at the others. "What's wrong with all of you? What happened back there?"

Lindsey watched the island shrink away behind them. Her teeth were chattering, but she wasn't sure if it was from the cold or the stress. Waves lashed the ocean around them. She thought about Pack lying on the floor of the tower, and a lump formed in her throat. As badly as he had treated her, she still felt sadness for him.

Take care of him, Lord, she silently prayed. *And help me to know what to do now. It doesn't make any sense, but Caitlyn came to me for help. How can I possibly help her if she's already dead?*

The boat rumbled, bouncing across the waves. The light on the bow flashed, weirdly freezing the rain in silver and black snapshots. The pulse was almost hypnotic.

Lindsey peered through the rain and fog at the distant lights of houses and hotels that lined the rocky coast. The silvery tips of the churning waves were strangely beautiful.

Caitlyn said Katherine was her sister, Lindsey thought. *Mrs. Cutler said she had a twin sister, but it wasn't Caitlyn. It was Kathleen. She called her Katie. Not quite the same name, but almost. Caitlyn said I had to help them, but they're not really here. Katie's dead, and Katherine is....*

She looked up and saw the Cutler mansion clinging to the rocks above them. In one of the windows, she could see the dark shape of a human figure.

"We have to go to the Cutler Mansion," she said, sitting up suddenly.

"What?" Jolene turned.

"We have to go back to the Cutler Mansion," she said. "We have to set her free."

"Set who free?"

"Mrs. Cutler. She's still in the lighthouse. She never escaped."

"Lindsey, sweetie, you're not making sense."

"In her mind," Lindsey said. "She's still...." An icy hand seized her face, and spun her head around. Captain Teach glared at her through the glazed eyes of a dead man. His hair and beard were tangled with seaweed.

"Meddler!" he cried, water spewing from him mouth. "Meddling intruder!" He seized her shoulders and dragged her over the side of the boat. Jolene screamed and wrapped herself around Lindsey's legs. Lindsey cried out in pain as her spine bent backward against the metal rail.

"Help me!" Jolene cried as Todd leaped to his feet and ran to the front of the boat. Teach's arm was wrapped around Lindsey's throat, and he was pulling her down. Lindsey felt her buttocks sliding over the rail as Jolene clung to her ankles. Todd seized her right arm and pulled for all he was worth.

"Something's pulling her down!" she heard Todd yell. "There's something else here!"

"Oh, God," Jolene cried. "Dear God, whatever it is, make it let go. In the power of the Father, Son, and Spirit, we stand against the forces of evil and the strongholds of Satan." Prayer flowed out of her as she fought down the panic that threatened to paralyze her. "We fight not against flesh and blood but against the powers of darkness in the heavenly places. In Your power, we come against it, Lord. In Your strength alone, we fight back against it. Ancient and powerful...."

Teach let her go and plunged into darkness just as Neal cut the engine. Clawing for handholds, gripping sodden cloth and wet skin, Todd and Jolene dragged Lindsey back into the boat. Todd pulled her hard into his arms.

"Thank you," she gasped. "Thank you."

"We have to get you away from here," Jolene said. "There's something evil here, something powerful. We have to get you as far from it as we can."

"No," Lindsey said. "I can't run away from this. I have to face it."

"Face what?" Neal said. "An invisible ghost? A legion of demons? We don't even know what we're talking about."

"None of us can see what you see," Todd said. "Not more than a glimpse, anyway. I did see one of them in a mirror just before I drove off the road."

"Your head," Lindsey said suddenly. "Is that what happened to your head?"

"He needs stitches," Jolene said. "That's one more reason to get out of here."

"It might not let us go," Todd said. "It sent me into the ditch. It might wreck all of us."

"Or it might leave us alone," Jolene said, "as long as we're going away from it."

"But, we have to help Mrs. Cutler," Lindsey said. "We can't just let it have her."

"She never leaves the house," Todd said. "Isn't that what you said?"

"Montoya said she thinks she's under some kind of curse," Neal said. "That she can't leave."

"Maybe this thing, this Captain Teach, won't let her leave," Lindsey said. "Maybe he's held her captive here for over sixty years."

Lightning flashed. Thunder cracked.

"That was too close," Neal said. "We've got to make a decision now. Do we head for Leo's place as fast as we can go and get the heck out of Dodge, or do we head up to the Cutlers'?"

"There's a dock right behind the mansion," Lindsey said. "You can let me out there. I can't ask any of you to take anymore risks because of me."

"We're not leaving you alone!" Jolene protested.

"Don't you see?" Todd said. "You're the most vulnerable of all of us. They're invisible to us, but they're completely solid to you. Whatever wavelength they operate on, you're closer to it than we are. It may work both ways. What would pass right through us might kill you."

"I'm going back to that house," Lindsey said. "I don't know what will happen to me there, but I have to go back. Caitlyn practically begged me to help her. I don't know why she thought I could help her, but I'm not turning my back on her."

"We could come back and help her tomorrow," Neal suggested. "It's like Sinbad the comedian says: in the horror movies, they always wait until the sun is about to go down to start hunting Dracula. Nobody ever goes at ten in the morning."

"Neal," Jolene said, "this is serious."

"I *am* serious."

They all looked at him.

"Fine," he said as he pulled back on the throttle. "It's after midnight, and we're going to kill Dracula." He aimed the boat for the dock behind the mansion. "If we live through this, it's going to make one heck of a sermon illustration."

Chapter 31: Into the Storm

Neal pulled Leo's boat into a slip at the end of the dock. Todd climbed out and tied it securely into place. Frightened but resolute, Lindsey climbed out onto the dock. Neal and Jolene followed.

"Do you see anything?" Jolene asked.

"No," Lindsey said as she scanned the gloom around them.

"Let's go, then," Neal said.

They hurried along the dock, flashlight beams cutting the darkness ahead of them. Lindsey silently communed with God as waves hammered at the pilings beneath them. Where the dock met the hillside, a set of steep concrete stairs meandered their way up the side of a cliff into darkness. They were cracked in places where the ground beneath them had eroded away and fallen into the sea.

"Did Mrs. Cutler ever tell you how her sister died?" Neal asked suddenly.

"She starved to death in a Japanese prison camp," Lindsey said. "I don't think Mrs. Cutler ever really forgave herself for leaving her behind."

Neal and Jolene looked at each other.

"Neal and I did some digging around for information about Mrs. Cutler's father. There was a lot more on the Internet about him than you might expect. He really was a well-respected missionary. But, the story Mrs. Cutler told you isn't exactly…."

Thunder shook the steps beneath them, and a wall of dirt and rock tumbled past. Shouts erupted from the dock. Lindsey turned and saw a squad of uniformed Japanese soldiers racing toward them with bayonets drawn. The conning tower of a submarine sliced though the waves like the head of a prehistoric sea monster. Fire flashed from the deck cannon.

"Run!" Lindsey cried.

The others followed as she drove herself up the gritty, rain-soaked stairs.

"What are we running from?" Neal yelled up to her.

"Japanese soldiers," she said. She felt foolish as she said it. "And a submarine."

A deck cannon fired, and more of the cliff fell away.

"They're fighting us," Todd said. "They know why we're here."

"We're completely unprepared for this," Jolene said. "We should have had people praying and fasting for us."

"I told you," Neal said. "We should have come back tomorrow."

The deck gun fired again.

"Something about this whole scenario feels weird," Todd called out as he ran.

Neal's eyes widened. "Ya think?"

"Why would you have ghosts of Japanese soldiers haunting this place when no Japanese soldiers ever died here?"

"A Japanese sub did attack the west coast," Neal said. "Right near here. They sank a ship."

"Are you kidding?"

A stone gate lay about twelve feet above them. Beyond it was level ground and the back of the house. Brooding hemlock trees cloaked the path in darkness.

"But why haunt this place? Why here?"

"That's…actually a good question," Neal said as he drove himself up the stairs and nearly ran into Lindsey. "Shake a leg, chick!"

"Sorry."

"How old is Caitlyn?" Jolene asked.

"She said she was twenty-four," Lindsey said as she stepped through a gate and onto level ground. She scanned the shadows around them. Then, suddenly, her eyes were drawn to the gazebo, to a shape inside. Captain Teach was standing there like a dark monument. He was shrouded in shadows, but his glare sliced through the gloom like a beacon from a lighthouse.

"Look out!" she cried. "He's here!"

"Who's here?"

"Teach!"

She looked back at the gazebo. The figure had vanished.

"I think we should stop and pray," Jolene said.

"Don't you think we should wait until we're inside?" Neal asked.

"I don't think it makes any difference where we are," she said.

"I was thinking about the rain."

"GET OUT!" Teach's voice roared.

A blast of wind hurled Lindsey through the air like a doll. She collided with her friends, rolled over them, and landed in a flowerbed.

"What was that?" Neal yelled as he got to his knees.

"Are you all right?" Todd yelled as he ran to Lindsey.

"Did you hear him?" Lindsey gasped as she rolled onto her side and tried to sit up. Chunks of mulch clung to her hands and clothes.

"I felt something go through me," Todd said. He dusted her off as he pulled her to her feet.

"It was like a wall of force," Jolene said. "We really need to pray."

"All right," Neal said. "I'm all for that. Prayer chain." He grabbed his wife's hand. Jolene reached out with her free hand and caught Lindsey's hand. Todd placed his hand on both of theirs.

"Pray," Jolene said.

"All right!" Neal said. "Let's pray. Dear God, we don't know what we're up against here, and we don't have any power against it. All of our hope is in You. You've told us to shine Your light into the dark places of the world, and that's what we're here to do. We pray that You'd free Mrs. Cutler from whatever is holding her here. Give us courage where we have only fear. Perfect Your strength in our weakness. In the name of Your Son, our bridge between earth and heaven, we pray."

Still holding hands, they advanced toward the house. Wind tore at their clothes as they went. Rain hammered the sidewalk. The rear entrance to the house was on a lower level than the front. The sunroom, with its railed porch, was on the level above them. A dim light burned inside.

The door burst open. Cornelia leaped out, her hand on her heart. Lindsey half-expected to see a butcher knife clenched in her fist.

"You have to leave!" the housekeeper cried. "She can't hold them back. They'll kill you all!"

"Wait a minute," Neal said. "You knew about this, didn't you? You knew about it the whole time!"

"We've had the house blessed by a priest, cleansed by a psychic, prayed over by a minister," she said, "but they keep coming back. They always come back."

"Who keeps coming back?" Todd pressed her. "Who are they?"

"The dead," Cornelia said, her expression bleak. "The restless dead."

"I want to see Mrs. Cutler," Lindsey said, the wind blowing around her. "I want to talk to her."

"It's no use," Cornelia said. "There's nothing you can do. You have to leave."

"Works for me," Neal said.

"Neal!"

"We can come back tomorrow."

"I want to see her!" Lindsey said again.

"GET OUT!"

A lightning bolt splintered an overhead limb. Neal leaped onto the back porch, the others piling on behind him.

"Let us in, Cornelia!"

"Follow me!" she said. "Hurry!

They crowded through the door, their wet bodies slapping against each other. Todd pushed Lindsey through ahead of himself and slammed the door shut behind them. They huddled, gasping, in the hallway, water dripping from their sodden bodies.

"Where's Mrs. Cutler?" Neal demanded.

"She's upstairs," Cornelia said. "In the sunroom."

"How long has this been going on?" Todd asked.

"The angel in the bedroom has been with Mrs. Cutler since she was a small child," Cornelia said.

"The angel in the bedroom?"

"An invisible presence. She tucks people into bed and sings to them as they sleep. Others showed up after she came to live here. The Egyptian girl. The Japanese submarine. The little boy."

"And Caitlyn?"

"Mrs. Cutler has never mentioned her."

"What about Captain Teach?"

"He first appeared about a month after Mrs. Cutler's husband died."

"And he's the reason she never leaves…?"

"Look out!"

A chandelier ripped out of the ceiling and crashed to the floor. Upstairs, Mrs. Cutler screamed.

"Mrs. Cutler!" Lindsey yelled. She leaped for the stairs, the others running behind her. The stairs tilted weirdly beneath them. The handrails writhed in their grip as they clung to them.

"We come against you in the name of Christ!" Neal yelled. "Upon this rock I will build my church, and the gates of hell will not stand against it!"

They tumbled off the stairs and into the second-floor hallway.

"Mrs. Cutler!" Lindsey yelled. In the sunroom at the end of the hall she could see the shape of Mrs. Cutler's high-backed chair silhouetted against the storm.

"Come on," Neal said. "Form a circle around her."

Lightning flashed outside the window. Neal, Jolene, and Lindsey ran, hand in hand, into the room. Todd and Cornelia followed. Mrs. Cutler sat slumped in her chair.

"Mrs. Cutler!" Lindsey said, taking her by the hands. "Mrs. Cutler, can you hear me?"

"GET OUT!"

The roar shook the windowpanes.

"Mrs. Cutler," Todd said, kneeling beside Lindsey. "Mrs. Cutler, you have to stop this. You have to stop him."

"I can't!" she cried, her voice heavy with despair.

"Why does she have to stop him?" Jolene asked. "Todd, what are you thinking?"

"You told me about Niles," Neal said, "how good he was to you when your father and sister died. What happened after that?"

"He changed," she said. "It was gradual at first. He started suffering from bouts of depression. He would sit in the gazebo for hours, staring out at the ocean. He didn't want to see anyone. He began to drink heavily, accused me of seeing other men when he was away on his purchasing trips."

The house groaned. The floor shivered slightly.

"It was ridiculous, of course. I never would have done anything to hurt him. Not after all he had given me. But, I couldn't convince him. It reached such a state that he started locking me in my room. He made me a prisoner in my own home. Cornelia tried to help me, and he threw her—physically threw her—out of the house. Then he took me to the lighthouse on the island and chained me to a rail in the tower. That's where the police found me. They told me Niles was dead, that they had found his body floating in the ocean. He had...there was...."

She stopped, and took a breath.

"He had been shot, shot in the head. Somehow, I already knew. Even before they told me, I knew how he had died. I knew exactly where they would find the gun he had used."

"And that's when you started seeing Teach?"

"Yes," she said. "Almost a month later."

"He's Niles, isn't he? Some distorted expression of Niles."

"I'm afraid he is," she said. "I'd hoped that in heaven he would return to the man he was before the illness."

"It may not really be him," Todd said.

"But, you never saw Katie?" Neal continued. "You never encountered your sister as a ghost?"

"No."

Thunder rumbled through the house. The lights flashed and went out. Light from outside painted the room in a gray wash.

"It's okay," Todd said. "I've still got my flashlight." He switched it on and placed it on the floor. A cone of light lit the darkness around them.

"I have to tell you something, Mrs. Cutler," Neal said. "This is important. I found records of your dad's ministry. Katie didn't die in a Japanese prison camp, Mrs. Cutler."

"What? Don't be ridiculous!"

"What are you saying, Neal?" Lindsey was stunned. "Katie's still alive?"

"No," he said. "I've got pictures of her gravestone out in my car. Kathleen and your mother both died the day you were born, Mrs. Cutler. You were the only one to survive."

She gasped.

"Is that really true?" Lindsey stammered.

"No," Mrs. Cutler said. "It's not true. It couldn't be. Katie and I…we were inseparable."

"Katie died," Todd said. "You never really knew her, except in your own imagination. She was your alter ego, your other self. Your mind created her because you needed her. Just like it created the illusion of your mother as an angel, singing to you and tucking you in at night."

"They were real," Mrs. Cutler said, tears forming in her eyes. "As real as anyone I've ever known."

"You made them real," Todd said, "and somehow your mind even found a way to manifest them physically. They're not ghosts or angels. They're a part of you."

"And that creature?" she said. "The Niles-Teach thing?"

"He's a part of you, too."

"But, why is he keeping me here?"

"I think he's a prison guard," Todd said. "He's not the one who sentenced you. He's just the one carrying out the punishment."

"What are you saying?"

"You left your father back in China," he said. "He died before you could say goodbye or make amends. From what you've said, he probably wasn't the easiest man to live with, but you still loved him."

"Yes," she said as she wiped away tears. "He was a wonderful man. So courageous and dedicated to his work. So good to the Chinese people. My mother's death nearly broke him, but he wouldn't give up and go home. He never forgave me for leaving him."

"Surely he understood," Jolene said. "I think he would have wanted you to be happy."

"After he died," Mrs. Cutler said, "his missionary agency found me and sent me his personal effects—what was left of them, anyway. It was mostly some worn old books he had used. I found his diary there."

She stopped, took a breath, and fought for the strength to continue.

"The day I left with Niles, he wrote, 'Katherine has left me today. She has chosen the things of the world over the things of God. May the Almighty have mercy on her soul.'" She wiped her eyes. "That was the last time he ever mentioned me."

Rain slapped against the windowpanes, and wind whistled around the edges of the house.

"I'm sorry," Lindsey said. "Maybe he just couldn't face what he was really feeling. He had already lost so much. Maybe…." Her voice trailed off.

"Why were there bullet holes in the wall of the lighthouse?" Todd asked.

Mrs. Cutler flinched visibly and put her hands to her face.

"Because Niles had returned to the lighthouse to kill me," she whispered. "He was mad, intoxicated, and angry beyond all reason. He was going to kill me."

"And you fought back, didn't you?" Todd said. "You used your abilities to protect yourself. Which ghost was it? The mother protecting her daughter, or the sister acting out your subconscious desires?"

"I don't know," she said. "I only remember bits and pieces of what they see. I never saw Katie after I came to America, but I think she was there that day. I think… maybe…he saw her and thought I had escaped. He shot her, thought he had shot me, and took his own life."

"In remorse."

"Yes," she said. "He killed himself because of me."

"Because he loved you. Sick as he was, he still loved you."

"He may have been bipolar," Todd said, "what they used to call manic-depressive. Sometimes they become alcoholics in an attempt to self-medicate. Either way, it wasn't your fault."

"Caitlyn came to me for help," Lindsey said. "She showed me her twin sister chained in the room at the top of the lighthouse. I think she wanted me to help her set that girl free."

"Cornelia said you brought priests and ministers out here to try to cast out the spirit that's keeping you captive here," Neal said. "It didn't work. You know why I think it didn't work?"

"It didn't work because exorcisms only work on evil spirits," Mrs. Cutler said, her voice just above a whisper. "Not on guilty consciences."

The house shivered around them. The beams in the wall shrieked in protest.

"Lindsey!" a voice said suddenly.

Lindsey turned and saw Caitlyn standing in the door. She gasped and started to speak. Caitlyn raised her hand to silence her.

"Listen to me, Lindsey. You have to get them out of here now! Hurry!"

"We have to get out of this room," Lindsey said suddenly.

"And go where?" Jolene asked.

"An inner room," Caitlyn said.

"The bathroom," Lindsey said. "Hurry!"

Todd and Lindsey helped Mrs. Cutler to her feet. Wind and rain beat against the windowpane behind them. They moved Mrs. Cutler toward the bathroom as fast as her shaking legs would carry her. Neal ran ahead, throwing open the door while Todd followed with the flashlight. The room was large enough for all of them. The walls were paneled with oak; the floor and tub were hewn of marble; and there was a vanity with a mirror and an ornately carved chair. The room would have been at home in the luxury suite of a Hollywood resort. Mrs. Cutler sank into the chair in front of the vanity. Her weary reflection stared back at her.

"Oh, my," she said. "I do look repulsive." She picked up a brush.

"It's okay," Lindsey said. "Don't worry about it."

An explosive thud struck the house like a battering ram. Shattering glass rained in the hall and skidded across the floor. The beams in the walls shrieked in agony. Neal ran to the door and looked back at the sunroom.

"A tree just came through roof of the sunroom," he cried over the roar of the storm. Wind howled through the hall. Neal pulled the door shut behind him. Wind roared through the hallway beyond the door like the passing of a train. The house shook and rumbled. Bottles of cologne rolled off the table and shattered on the floor. Todd's flashlight bounced across the floor.

"Get in the bathtub!" Mrs. Cutler told Lindsey. "Do as I say!"

"Look out!"

Stars flashed through Lindsey's skull, and the world went dark.

Chapter 32: Showdown

"Help me," Katherine sobbed as she lay huddled on the mattress. "Oh, please help me." Caitlyn, her mirror image, lay beside her, weeping.

Thunder echoed through the gloom, thunder and the pounding of fists on wood.

"Open this door, ye miserable wenches!"

The lighthouse. Lindsey was back in the lighthouse.

"Go away!" Lindsey cried. "Leave her alone!"

"Ye had yuir chance to get away, Lindsey Holland. Now ye'll be a'payin' with the lot of 'em."

Lindsey Holland? Teach knew her name now.

The trap door shattered. Snarling with rage, Teach forced his lumbering bulk through the opening. His filmed-over eyes burned with madness, and spittle ran between his clenched teeth. He looked like a hungry bear.

"That's not Niles," Lindsey said, her voice shaking. "That's not the way he would want you to remember him." She dropped to the mattress beside Katherine and pulled at the chain that bound her ankle. An inch-thick stainless steel bracket held it to the floor.

"I'll make ye pay fer yuir sins, ye wretched harlot."

"He was sick." Lindsey glared into the raging giant's face. "He wasn't himself. He wasn't really like this."

His expression changed. Just for an instant, Lindsey saw a flash of something she couldn't recognize. Not rage but…was it fear? Remorse? Suddenly, another thought struck her with the force of revelation.

"God isn't like this, either."

The giant flinched. Then he rose to his full height, his bristling mane fairly brushing the rafters, his dark form towering over Lindsey like a tree.

"'The God that holds you over the pit of hell, much as one holds a spider, or some loathsome insect over the fire, abhors you, and is dreadfully provoked: His wrath towards you burns like fire; He looks upon you as worthy of nothing else, but to be cast into the fire, He is of purer eyes than to bear to have you in His sight; you are ten thousand times more abominable in His eyes, than the most hateful venomous serpent is in ours. You have offended Him infinitely more than ever a stubborn rebel did his prince, and yet it is nothing but His hand that holds you from falling into the fire every moment.'"

Sinners in the Hands of an Angry God? Why was Blackbeard the pirate quoting a Puritan sermon?

"John 3:16 and 17," Lindsey shot back. "For God so loved the world that He gave His only begotten Son that whosoever believes in Him should not perish but have everlasting life. For God did not send His Son to condemn the world, but that the world might be saved through Him."

The giant backed up a step and took a breath.

"'The same shall drink of the wine of the wrath of God,'" he snarled, "'Which is poured out, without mixture into the cup of His indignation; and He shall be tormented with fire and brimstone in the presence of the holy angels, and in the presence of the lamb. And the smoke of their torment ascendeth up forever and ever.' It's in the Word of the Lord, dearie. Do ye deny it? Do ye deny that He struck down the firstborn of Egypt? Do ye deny that He drowned the people of the ancient world like rats, that He burned Sodom and Gomorrah to ashes and killed every livin' soul who touched the holy Ark? Do ye deny that He smote Ananias and Sapphira? Do ye deny the Word o' God?"

"God has a face of wrath," Lindsey said, "I don't deny that. There's a wild, inhuman part of him that's like an angry hurricane. Anything touched by sin burns up in His presence, but He doesn't want to hurt *us*. That's not His heart. That's not the face He wants to show us." She turned her back to the giant and turned to Katherine. "He can't keep you here anymore. Not if God sets you free."

"She's payin' for her sins," the giant growled. "This is what she deserves."

"Don't listen to him," Lindsey said. "He doesn't speak for God. He doesn't know anything about God. All he knows is rage and bitterness and fear. I don't care what your father told you. This isn't God!" She leaped to her feet and turned on the hulking figure.

"His anger is but for a moment, but His love is for a lifetime. The thief comes to steal, kill, and destroy, but I have come that they might have life and have it more abundantly. Delight yourself in the Lord and He will give you the desires of your heart. As far as the east is from the west, He has removed our sins from us. As a father pities His children, He knows that we are but dust. It is not God's will that any should perish, but that all should come to repentance. So great is His love for us that while we were yet sinners, He sent His Son to die for us."

She paused and took a breath. The figure stepped forward

"The Lord is my shepherd. I shall want for nothing. He leads me to green pastures. He leads me beside still waters. He sets a table before me in the presence of my enemies. Even when I walk through the valley of the shadow of death, You are with me. Your rod and Your staff, they comfort me. Surely goodness and mercy shall follow me all the days of my life, and I shall dwell in the house of the Lord forever."

The figure stood and scowled at her.

"Seek ye first the kingdom of God, and all these things shall be added unto you. I came not to save the righteous, but sinners. Blessed are the poor in spirit, for they shall be comforted. If we confess our sins, He is faithful and just to forgive our sins and cleanse us from all unrighteousness. I have written these things that you may not sin, but if you do sin, we have an advocate, Jesus Christ, the righteous. For we do not have a high priest who is unable to sympathize with our sins, but He was tempted in every way we are and yet without sin.

What shall separate us from the love of God? Shall sword or famine or nakedness? I tell you, nothing can separate us from the love of God, His son not sparing who…sent His son…?"

She tried to remember the verse, to think of more verses, but nothing would come. The giant started forward.

"There once was a man who had two sons. The youngest took his inheritance and wasted it on riotous living. Finally, one day, he found himself in a pigpen eating the husks that were given to swine to eat. He came to his senses and said, 'Even the hired servants in my father's house have it better than this. I'll go home and see if my father will have me back as a slave.' But when his father saw him coming down the road, he ran to him and threw his arms around him. He put a robe on his body and a ring on his finger and told his servants to kill the fatted calf, because his son had returned home to him. But, when the older brother heard about it, he was angry. He said, 'In all my years of living here, you haven't given me so much as a goat to have a party with my friends, but when my stupid younger brother comes home, after wasting his money on harlots, you kill the fatted calf and throw a party for him.' The father said, 'Please don't be angry. You have always been with me, and everything I have is yours. But I had to rejoice. Don't you understand? Your brother was dead, and now he is alive.'"

She stood for hours, pouring out every verse about God's love and forgiveness that she had memorized as a child and in the church youth program. She told the parable of the lost coin, and of the lost sheep, told the story of the woman at the well, and of the sinful woman who had fallen down before Jesus and washed his feet with her tears and dried them with her hair. As long as she was speaking, the grim figure just stood and listened, but every time she stopped, he started to come forward. The storm howled outside of the lighthouse as she dredged her memory for stories, verses, and songs. Finally, her throat raw and her voice nearly exhausted, she rasped out all four stanzas of "Amazing Grace."

Teach had stood and glared at her throughout the entire recitation. Finally, as Lindsey choked out the last note, the pirate snarled, turned his back, and disappeared down the trap door. Lindsey dropped to the floor in exhaustion and lay there, gasping.

"Thank you," she heard Katherine say. No longer sobbing, no longer chained, she knelt down beside Lindsey and embraced her.

***

"Lindsey? Darling, can you hear me?"

"Lindsey," Todd said. They hovered, ghostlike, in the yellow beam of the flashlight.

"I'm okay," Lindsey said. "What happened?"

"You got hit in the head by a falling mirror," Neal said.

She sat up. A wave of dizziness hit her for an instant, then subsided.

"How long was I asleep?"

"About a minute."

"A minute? That's all? What did I miss?"

"A lot of howling and shaking," Neal said, "but that was mostly Jolene."

"You're too funny for words."

"Is that like, 'So funny I forgot to laugh?'"

Neal opened the bathroom door. It rasped against the facing. Gray light fell across him.

"Let me have the flashlight," he said.

Todd picked up the flashlight, stood, and took it to him. Neal flashed it around the hallway beyond as the others pressed in behind him. Jolene clung to his shoulder. Todd helped Lindsey to her feet. Stepping over broken glass, they moved out into the hall while Mrs. Cutler and Cornelia held back. The floor was littered with broken glass and plaster. A chair lay on its side. Wet needles stuck to the walls and floor. Neal shined the light back toward the sunroom. Slimy, twisted tree branches reflected the beam. He turned the light in the other direction. The front door lay open in the distance. It looked as if it had been blown off the hinges. The floor in between was covered with broken furniture, pictures that had been ripped from the walls, overturned shelves, and wadded-up rugs.

"Come on out," Neal said. "But be careful."

"Oh, my." Mrs. Cutler gasped when she saw the house. "What a horrible mess!"

"We'll help you clean up," Neal told her. "It may take a while."

Stepping around debris, they reached the stairs just inside the front entrance.

"Wait here," Neal said. "I'm going to check upstairs."

They waited in the gloom as the flashlight beam swept its way along the stairs. Neal stopped at the top, probing around him with the beam.

"Can you see this?" he asked.

"See what?"

Todd followed him up the stairs. Lindsey wanted to follow, but Mrs. Cutler was clinging to her hand.

"What is it?" Lindsey asked when Todd returned a moment later.

"The roof's been torn off," Todd said. "The whole third floor is open to the sky."

"You can't stay here," Neal said as he came down the stairs. "This house isn't habitable, and it's going to take a while to put it back together."

"How did you know what was about to happen?" Jolene asked Lindsey.

"Caitlyn," Lindsey said, her voice trembling. "She told me to get everybody out."

"Well," Neal said. "I guess it's a good thing we didn't decide to come back tomorrow."

"What are we going to do, Mrs. Cutler?" Cornelia sobbed.

"Anything we want to, dear," Mrs. Cutler said, a note of fire returning to her voice. "We're free."

Chapter 33: New Day

Todd and Lindsey spent most of the next week digging through the ruins of Mrs. Cutler's mansion, salvaging everything they could. Neal and Jolene were there much of the time, and they managed to mobilize quite a few volunteers from Neal's churches as well. Shadow, Nefertiti, and the rest of the youth worked alongside seniors from the retirement village. Mrs. Cutler sat in her fan-backed wicker chair beneath a canopy roof and supervised the operation. Neal, Todd, and some of the others grilled hamburgers and hotdogs for the volunteers from the church. Others brought food from home and turned the operation into a weeklong picnic. Neal managed to secure a vacant condo in the retirement village as temporary quarters for Mrs. Cutler and Cornelia while the mansion was undergoing repairs.

Men with chainsaws had cut the fallen tree out of the sunroom and patched the hole with plywood and transparent sheeting. Most of the furniture on the upper floor had been scattered along the hillside, but everything of value that remained had been hauled away and placed in storage. A shroud of blue tarps covered the top of the house. New trusses would have to be custom-built, shipped in, and lifted into place with a crane.

The house, as Todd had remarked, had been like a museum, and Todd, Lindsey, and the other volunteers had lost no time moving the paintings, the hand-carved furniture, and the rest of Mrs. Cutler's Old World treasures into climate-controlled storage units. Some of the artifacts were damaged or missing, but a remarkable number had survived. The mummy had been torn from her coffin and had suffered some damage, but she was receiving gentle treatment at the hands of a local artist who repaired museum artifacts.

"The poor thing," Mrs. Cutler had said. "I want her to receive the best of care. I insist upon it."

"She'll be good as new," Neal had reassured her. "Well, as new as 3,000-year-old mummies get, anyway."

***

On the last night of the clean-up effort, Neal stood beside the grill with a spatula and flipped the sizzling burgers. An evening breeze carried the scent across the hilltop, and the volunteers started to gather around the makeshift pavilion. Mrs. Cutler sat in her chair, sipped her tea, and spoke with her neighbors.

"You're in pretty good spirits for a lady who just had her house blown away," someone said. Mrs. Cutler turned and saw Detective Montoya walking toward her.

"You know," she said, "you're right. I haven't seen so many people in years, and they're all so generous and wonderful. What can I do for you, Detective?"

"I'm just tying up loose ends," Montoya said. "Frankly, your case has haunted me—pardon the expression—for years. I don't know how I thought it would end, but all of this is pretty unexpected. I think it's safe to say that one young lady made all of the difference."

"Lindsey?" Mrs. Cutler said. "Oh, yes. She's an angel sent from heaven."

"I think that's most of it," Todd said as he approached them. "Everything we didn't move is wrapped in tarps. It should keep until the new roof is in place."

"Wonderful," she said as she squeezed his hand. "I don't know what I would have done without all of you."

"What are you going to do now?" Montoya asked. "You've been in this house for a long time. There's a whole world to see."

"I was thinking I'd like to go back to China," she said. "One last visit before I'm too old to travel."

Montoya nodded.

"I know what you're thinking, detective."

"You're only as old as you feel."

"Poppycock. I'm a relic. A fairly sturdy one at the moment, though."

"Did anybody see where Lindsey went?" Todd asked.

"I think she went looking for Nicole," Mrs. Cutler told her.

"Nicole?"

"You know. Shadow."

"Could you take me to them?" Montoya said. "I've got a few last questions for them before I close the book on this case."

***

Dressed in old clothes and wearing leather gloves, Shadow worked alongside the others. Without electricity, the house was dark inside, dark and strange. Shadow carried a lantern with her but always carried an extra flashlight clipped to her belt as a spare. The house no longer seemed as supernaturally haunted as it had before, but the memories of her previous experiences there followed her just the same.

"Neal's got hamburgers ready," Lindsey said as she came down the stairs. "Everybody else has already eaten."

"Lindsey."

"What is it, Shadow?"

"Could you come with me to the cellar?"

"Okay. Why?"

"There's something I need to do." She picked up a hammer.

"Hey," Todd said. "Where are you two going?" Detective Montoya was with him.

"We're on our way to the cellar," Lindsey said, "if you'd like to join us."

"Sure," Montoya said. "Frankly, I'd like to have a look at it. Everything about this house fascinates me."

"What's the word on Pack?" Lindsey asked as they walked down the corridor.

"They've set his bail at over a million dollars. I don't think he'll be getting out before the trial."

"You don't know his family," Lindsey said. "Did he ever confess to anything?"

"In a way," Montoya said, "but he's not admitting any of it was his fault. He claims Chloe Davis's death was accidental and that he dumped her body in the ocean. That doesn't make sense to me. If he had nothing to hide, why dump the body?"

Lindsey opened the door to the stairs. All of them walked down the wooden steps into the earthy darkness.

"What are you going to do?" Lindsey asked Shadow as they entered the sub-basement that had served as Cutler's wine cellar.

"Fix the door," Shadow said. "Fix it so it doesn't lock people inside."

"Somebody should have done that a long time ago," Lindsey said. "I don't know why they didn't."

"Shadow," Montoya said, "or should I call you Nicole?"

"Whatever."

"I'm curious. Lindsey's told me about the night all of you were staying here, how you went missing and everybody was looking for you."

"That's when I got locked into the secret room."

"Right. What were you doing down here in the first place?"

Shadow studied him warily.

"It's okay," Lindsey said. "You can tell him."

Shadow waited a moment longer. "Okay," she finally said. "I don't care if you believe me or not."

"I'm just listening," Montoya said.

"Okay. We had all gone to bed. The girls were in the big room with the fireplace. I woke up, and everybody else was asleep, but I thought I heard somebody crying. I went downstairs and saw a lady standing at the window. I said something to her, and she turned around and looked at me. I knew, the second I saw her, that I'd seen her face before. Then I realized where. It was the same face that was on the mummy case upstairs." Montoya, Todd, and Lindsey stood and listened as Shadow told the rest of her tale.

***

"Are you okay?" Shadow asked.

The woman turned. Shadow froze. Her face was the face from the sarcophagus upstairs. The mummy's ghost was standing right there before her. The woman smiled slightly, even through her tears, and touched Shadow lightly on the cheek.

"I'm sorry I woke you," she said. Her voice was soft and kind. She had an accent.

"Why were you crying?" Shadow asked her.

"Because I miss my home and my family."

"Where are they?"

"My home is far away," she said. "My family is dead."

She rippled like the rain on the glass, then vanished. Shadow gasped and took a step back. She turned around and saw the woman again. She was standing behind her this time.

"Don't be afraid," she said. "Come with us."

As Shadow squinted into the gloom, she could see the others. They hung, half- materialized, as though they had been watercolor-painted directly onto the air itself. There was a little Chinese boy, a young woman in medical scrubs, and a woman in an old-fashioned dress that had a high, ruffled collar. A cameo hung at her throat. The other shapes were less distinct, but there were enough of them to fill the entire hallway.

Shadow heard someone moving in the hallway behind her.

"Come," the Egyptian girl told her. "Quickly." The others beckoned to her as well.

***

"They seemed frantic," Shadow told Lindsey. "They led me down here and showed me how to open the secret room. They told me to go inside, shut the door, and wait. After a while, when nobody came, I tried to open the door and realized I was trapped. I thought they had tricked me. Maybe they wanted me to die and join them in the house. Like the Haunted Mansion at Disneyland. 'Nine hundred ninety-nine haunts, and they're always looking for one more.' Then Lindsey came and got me out."

"Caitlyn told me where to find you," Lindsey said. "She's probably the girl you saw wearing medical scrubs. Why were you so afraid of Pack?"

"I saw him, too. He opened the secret door and walked in. I thought he had come to find me, but then he walked right through me, and I realized he wasn't really there. He was a ghost, too. That didn't make sense to me, you know, because he was still alive. There was something wrong about him, something hungry and crazy and evil. I started toward the door, and everything went dark again. That's when I started screaming and pounding on the door, and you came and let me out."

"Why would you see Pack in this room? Why would you see something that never happened?"

"I don't know."

Shadow reached up and rocked the lion statue forward. The door swung open on rusty hinges. She lifted her lantern and shined it on the latch. Lindsey gasped.

"What happened here?"

The room was in chaos. The table had been turned over and the books scattered. Clothes, men's clothes, were strewn around the room.

"I take it the room didn't always look like this?" Montoya stepped into the room behind Shadow and Lindsey.

"No," Lindsey said. "Somebody's vandalized it. I wonder...."

Lindsey picked the shirt up and held it in the light.

"This looks like a shirt I bought for Pack," she said. She grabbed the pants, reached into one of the pockets, and pulled out a wallet. She flipped it open and saw the driver's license inside:

Jason Winston Packard.

"So, Packard was here," Montoya said. "He was inside the house."

"It makes sense that he would come for Lindsey," Todd said, "but what was he doing down here?"

"And what kept him from getting to Lindsey?" Montoya asked.

**

"Quite a story," Montoya said as he started to get into his car. "Almost beyond belief." The sun hung low on the horizon. Even after the storm damage, there were still enough trees to shroud the courtyard in shadow.

Lindsey, Todd, and Shadow stood around Montoya as he was leaving. Neal and Jolene had joined them.

"What do you think?" Neal asked. "Do you believe any of it?"

"Actually, I do," Montoya said. "Every word. I must be getting superstitious in my old age. Strange as it may seem, this is like the fulfillment of a goal I've had for most of my career. I always wondered if I'd live to see the mystery of Niles Cutler's death explained. I figured the explanation would be strange, and your story certainly fits the bill on that. Who would have thought one little lady could generate so much energy?"

"Not when you know the lady," Neal said.

"Good point," Montoya said. "What's next for you, Lindsey? Back to Texas?"

"Eventually," she said. "Todd and I still have a documentary to finish. Now that we've got a story of our own to add, it may take a while."

"Let me know if you need a detective's perspective for your movie," Montoya said. "I've been on the news a few times. Some people say I've got presence."

"We'll be in touch," Todd said.

They watched as Montoya drove out of the courtyard and around the bend, then vanished into the wooded path that led down the mountain.

"Has anybody seen Mrs. Cutler?" Jolene asked. "I told her I'd drive her back to the village."

They found her sitting in the gazebo behind the house. Her sunroom was closed for repair, but she had already replaced her fan-backed wicker chair, and some of the crew had carried it to the gazebo for her. Someone had even prepared a cup of tea for her. She had been sipping it just before she had fallen asleep, but it had grown cold.

"Is she okay?" Shadow asked.

"Mrs. Cutler?" Jolene said gently. "Mrs. Cutler?"

She woke with a start. "Oh, my. Is that you, Jo Ellen?"

"It's me." Jolene smiled. Maybe one day Mrs. Cutler would get her name right. "Are you ready to go home now?"

"I was just there," she said.

"You were where?"

"Home," she said. "Back in China, in a lovely house by the sea. There was a big, enclosed porch, and rooms for guests. You were all there with me, and I was introducing you to my father. It was all so perfect. So perfect."

"It sounds wonderful," Lindsey said. "I'm sorry we woke you."

"It's all right, darling." She patted Lindsey's hand. "Help me to my feet, dear. Cornelia's probably wondering what happened to me. She's such a worrier."

As they were getting into the car, Lindsey took a long look back at the lighthouse. Silhouetted against a blazing summer sky, the old structure no longer looked haunted or menacing. It seemed like a noble old sentinel from another time. Lindsey could almost imagine that she saw a young woman, tall and slender with strawberry blonde hair, standing on its shores.

Goodbye, Caitlyn, she thought. *Thanks for everything.*

Notes from the Author:

The inspiration for this project, like all of my others, came from a variety of sources. As a college student, I did summer ministry work for the Baptist Student Union in both Washington D.C. and Hawaii. Those ten-week assignments took me out of my native culture and comfort zone and introduced me to some fascinating people. Neal, Jolene, and their entrepreneurial approach to ministry are products of those experiences. The coastal Oregon setting was inspired by later events. About ten years ago, my brother, a life-long Southerner, moved out to the West Coast, married, and started a new life. When I went out there and saw the rainforests, rocky coasts, tourist towns, and lighthouses, I knew I had found the setting for a story.

(Spoiler alert here, if you're reading this before reading the book!) The plot device for the story was inspired by movies like *A Beautiful Mind* and *Identity* and books like Ted Dekker's *Three* and Dean Koontz's *Cold Fire*. I wanted to take the "illusion people" concept a step further by allowing someone else to see them. Some Christian readers may be troubled about whether I'm advocating New Age ideas like astral projection and psychic powers. I am not trying to make any assertions about the nature or reality of supernatural powers. That element of the story is fantasy like the super powers in the X-Men films. The idea was to take a character's internal conflict and make it externally visible. It was a plot device used for storytelling purposes. Nothing more.

As always, I have a number of people to thank. Dr. Dennis Hensley proofed this manuscript and offered suggestions for its improvement. Mr Jan Duke, formerly a police chief in Kelso, Washington, helped me in writing about police procedure. Shirley Wise proofed the manuscript for continuity errors. Other friends and relatives asked about the story often enough to keep me going back to work on it.

My students and collegues at Southern Arkansas University are always a source of inspiration and encouragement, and I'm thankful for the time I've spent with them. I'll also remain eternally grateful to my friends and mentors at the Louisiana Tech University Baptist Student Union (Baptist Collegiate Ministry now) for setting me on good path.

www.ingramcontent.com/pod-product-compliance
Lightning Source LLC
Chambersburg PA
CBHW020230180626
46810CB00006B/2123